THE
WHITE
BOOK

ISBN-13: 979-8732942125

THE WHITE BOOK

A NOVEL BY

GEORGE SHADOW

PEOPLE ARE TALKING ABOUT
THE WHITE BOOK!

"Fantasy at its best. Coming from Nigeria, this is beautiful."
   - Okechukwu Ibe

"Impressive. Crafting such a story from scratch is no mean feat."
   - Jessica

"Yes, I've read the first book. I thought that was the end. This second book was a welcome surprise."
   - Chidimma

"Action-packed from page one. I am eagerly waiting for the third book."
   - Stephen

"This should be a movie. Period."
   - Dawson

"Riveting, spellbinding and fascinating."
   - Helen Uduji

ISBN-13:
979-8732942125

Cover Art by
José del Nido.
www.josedelnido.com

Story by
George Shadow, a.k.a. **Ukachukwu Chidube Ononuju George**, from Imo State, Nigeria.
www.georgeshadow.com

This book was printed in the United States of America.

To order additional copies of this book, contact:

mailgeorgeshadow@yahoo.com

or call 07030815856 if you are in Nigeria.

For
My Beloved Mother
Lady Chinwendu Pearl Ukachukwu
1947 - 2016

ON THE SUBJECT OF
SHIFTING SHADOWS, THE
PAST & THE FUTURE...

NOW, the story was finished, the boy thought as he turned and gaily hopped back to the house, unaware of the invisible forms staring impassively at his receding figure while hovering some distance above him.

One of these hellish entities, the largest amongst them, turned its hollow face upwards and gazed blankly into the future. Those it had sent after the girl would be late for the rendezvous. It just hoped they could retrieve the second book from this human being before setting off for the gathering, because without this other volume, they would never succeed.

And if they failed, heaven and hell would continue to exist. All their efforts would have been in vain, and the one unearthly being standing in their way from the very beginning would proclaim this defeat to the four corners of the universe.

That must never come to pass, the spirit declared, drawing strength from the fact that everything appeared to be turning out perfectly well for its group. The angels-turned-demons now had a schedule to keep...with Yahweh, Himself, and this was an achievement the infernal creature could never have envisaged when they set out on the mission to retrieve the scrolls from Man.

What now remained was to pick up the other manuscript, and the stage would be set for the next step in their onward journey to victory.

The ritual.

The final chapter in the destruction of their most-hated enemy. The culmination of all their efforts. The crowning event in their determined

i

march to freedom and justice. Their sole objective from the very beginning.

Yes, victory was still some way off, but they were this close to achieving it, because those the fallen angel had sent after the girl were more than capable of retrieving the second manuscript from her.

The one its maker called the White Scroll.

Chapter 1
THE HOMELESS GIRL

PORTWOOD Police Sergeant Kimberley Reyna stopped her Cherokee and stared at the young person lying on the frosty road in the full glare of her headlights. She got out of her car and ran over to the shivering little blond-haired girl, who held on to a book with both hands and wore a dirty blue dress.

Officer Reyna pulled off her thick squad jacket and wrapped it around the young girl. She carried the kid to the Jeep, wondering how this youngster had ended up lying on that frigid road.

The girl must have been out in the chilly open for a long time. Kimberley guessed her to be eleven or twelve years old. Of course, the cold had eaten deep into her body and the police officer hoped to get to Portwood Hospital before any ominous signs popped up.

Swinging open the front passenger door, Kimberley placed the girl on the seat and adjusted the interior heat. She closed the door and ran over to the driver's side to slide in behind the steering wheel. She had left the engine running, so she stepped on the gas and picked up her radio.

"HQ, are you receiving?"

"HQ here. How can I help you, Raccoon 5?"

"Little girl got lost, Kate. Found her out in the cold. On my way to the hospital, but I need EMS to meet me halfway ASAP. I repeat; EMS halfway ASAP."

"On the double, Kim…. Hope she's okay?"

"She's shivering and muttering to herself."

"EMS called up. What's your location, Raccoon 5?"

"Driving past David's shop right now. I think I'll meet them around Aaron's Avenue."

1

"Okay, Raccoon 5. Message delivered."

As the patrol Jeep hurtled down the street en route to the hospital, Kimberley's attention kept going back to the book her young companion held on to. She could only make out an ash-colored leather cover and decided to inspect the volume later since its owner needed saving first.

The snow made driving difficult at the speed Kimberley maintained, but she knew she had to get to the hospital before things got worse for her young friend. At present, the kid was going through bouts of shaking while staring blankly at the windshield.

"They…are…coming…."

"What did you say?"

"They…are…coming…," the little girl whispered again, coughing afterwards. "They…will…never…stop…until…until…"

"Until what?" Kimberley had her eyes on the road. "Take it easy, dear; they'll never get you now…whoever 'they' are…. We just need to get you to the hospital."

"No…." The shivering kid sounded alarmed. "T–They won't stop…ever…."

"And why won't they stop?" Kimberley asked. "Why are they coming for you?"

No reply.

"Why are you so scared of them?"

No reply, except coughing.

"Where are you from?"

The shivering girl said nothing.

"Did you run away from home? Did they make you run away?"

More coughing.

"And what's with the book? Why are you holding on to it like that?"

The little girl said nothing.

"Okay. I guess you don't want to talk then."

The blond-haired girl coughed again and Kimberley sighed. She wondered what to do in order to get her young, jittery friend to talk.

"Jehovah…God…protect us…," the girl whispered.

"You're safe with me," Kimberley said. "Nothing will harm you as long as I'm here to protect you." No reply. "By the way, what's your – OH, SHIT!!"

A lone figure stood in the middle of the road.

Kimberley turned the wheel and felt the skid as the Cherokee swerved wildly, blowing up snow dust and missing the stranger by inches. They veered off the road, and for a moment, it looked as if the SUV would hit a lamppost, but then it flipped over before sliding noisily on its roof, missing the structure by a foot.

The little girl was shouting...
Kimberley blacked out...
The Cherokee hit a tree.

*   *   *

Kimberley woke up amidst bright lights. Officers and patrol cars surrounded the vicinity. The Portwood police sergeant lay on a stretcher some paramedics had brought up to the double doors of an ambulance. She hoped her colleagues had also rescued the little girl she had tried to save.

An EMS team pushed her stretcher into the warm ambulance. Her boyfriend blocked her view as someone closed the heavy van's doors. "You all right, Kim?" he asked her.

"Yeah, Jim. I'm fine."

"Boy, was I worried about you!" Portwood Police Lieutenant Jim Abrachinsky sounded relieved. "Waited for you at Aaron's after you called in. Came out here when you didn't show up and your radio wasn't responding. What happened?"

"Dunno.... Someone was standing on the road..."

"Who?" Jim began. "A man, woman, boy or girl?"

"Don't know really...we sped off the road...and I-I can't remember what happened next." Kimberley's left hand shot up to her head when she felt a dull ache there. "Where's the girl, Jim?"

"She wasn't here when we got here," he told her. "Must have wandered off before we arrived."

"We need to find her." Kimberley gingerly sat up.

"Don't worry about that, honey," Jim said, gently pushing her back down. "We're looking for her, and we'll definitely find her. Right now, you need to rest."

Kimberley frowned. "I'm fine," she said aloud for everyone's benefit, including the two paramedics hovering around. Her head ached painfully. "Trust me, really. I am fine. I just need medicine for this damn headache."

"Headache?" Jim looked worried. "You say you don't remember what happened after you left the road?"

"Yes, I don't. What happened?"

"You probably blacked out, Kim," Officer Abrachinsky said. "You will have to see Dr. Stone."

"Okay," Kimberley said. She turned to one of the paramedics. "I don't have bruises or fractures, right, Bruce?"

"None that I know of, sergeant," the man replied. "But..."

"And I feel no pain apart from my headache."

"Which could mean something far worse, Kim," Jim said. "You know we need to be careful here."

"Yes, we need to," Kimberley agreed, looking around. "I need to get to my car."

Jim smiled. "You'll need to go to the hospital and do a CT scan first?"

"Okay." Kimberley turned to him. "What happened to my car, Jim?"

"Your car didn't just veer off the road," Jim said.

"It flipped over and hit a tree, sergeant," Bruce said with a smile. "This means you could have blacked out from the collision and your headache might be due to something we need to investigate."

"Yeah, sure," Kimberley said. "But can I get some items from my car before we leave?"

Lieutenant Abrachinsky sighed and turned to the paramedics. "Okay, boys," he said. "Let's get her what she wants."

"I'll get your things before we leave, sergeant," Bruce said. "Don't worry, I'm the driver."

Kimberley started. "I want to see the car, Jim."

This didn't go down well with the outspoken Bruce. "But…"

"I'll be responsible for whatever happens to Sergeant Reyna from here on out, Bruce," Lieutenant Abrachinsky said.

EMS Officer Bruce Riddle nodded. "As long as she's not dizzy and has no blurred vision…"

"I have none of that," Kimberley said.

"Alright." Bruce turned away. "I'll need to call Dr. Stone."

"Okay," Jim said. "Guess that's the right thing to do."

"We need to find that girl, Jim," Kimberley began.

"Already sent out word," the Portwood police lieutenant said. "Unless she's pulled some disappearing trick, we'll find her pretty soon, promise."

"She–She was saying something about some people coming for her and…and then she was shouting some funny word when we lost control."

"Really?"

"Where's my car?"

"Outside, of course," Jim said. "Wait, you don't have your jacket, Kim. You'll need it to go out there. Where is it?"

"I gave it to the little girl, Jim." Kimberley stood up, glad that the paramedics did not restrain her.

"You feel okay, sergeant?" Bruce had concern on his handsome face.

"Give her a minute, Bruce," Lieutenant Abrachinsky said. "I'm right behind her."

Kimberley opened the ambulance doors and peered into the cold wilderness outside. The bright headlights and rotating police lightbars did not deter her. "Where is the Jeep, Jim?"

"Over there," Jim pointed out. "Think we can fix it?"

The Cherokee was a mess.

"How did you come out of such a wreck without any fractures or bruises?" Jim asked.

"Question is what happened before the collision?"

"Yeah, of course," Jim began. "And how did that little girl get away from this scene without leaving a trace of blood or any footprints in the snow?" He frowned.

"Mysterious," Kimberley said. She got out of the ambulance and walked over to the Jeep, her boyfriend right behind her.

A team was trying to turn the squad car the right way up, but had so far made little progress. The front bumper was bashed in, and its front wheels faced peculiar angles. The roof appeared beyond repair and the windshield was completely shattered.

"I must have lost consciousness before this crash, Jim," Kimberley said, staring at the unfortunate tree blocking the upturned Cherokee. "That means something else must have caused my blackout."

"There's no way to know that, Kim. Let's stick to what could have..."

"No," Kimberley said. "I think something mysterious caused it."

"Wow. Are you suggesting UFOs?"

"I'm serious, Jim."

"Okay," Jim said. "Any idea what actually happened to you and the girl before this accident?"

"Nope. Still can't remember what happened." Kimberley sighed and turned to her man. "How did I come out of this with just a headache, Jim?" He could only shrug.

"You tell me, Kim. Beats me."

As soon as her car's rescuers had failed in another attempt to turn it over, Kimberley bent down and yanked her driver's door open. The Cherokee's deployed airbags created some difficulty for her as she reached out into the Jeep. Rummaging through a dashboard compartment, she collected her personal items and shut the door before the salvage team could decide to try again.

Why was that idiot standing in the middle of the road?

"Have sent out word for that fellow as well," Jim said behind her as she stared at the motorway. Skid marks were on the ground before them.

"Can remember the Cherokee's warm interior getting cold pretty fast after we swerved away from him," Kimberley said, shivering. "Gave me the chills."

"So you think it was a man."

"Well, I..."

"You just need to relax, Kim. Let me handle this." Jim drew close to her just as she looked up. She was feeling better already. Trust him to take charge, she thought with a smile. "We need to go back inside, Kim. You need some warmth, and you need to visit the hospital."

"Thanks, dear...just worried about the girl, that's all."

"Tell me you will go to the hospital right now?"

"I promise," she said, the smile still playing on her lips. Her head ached. "And I promise to take my pills now..."

"But you need to go to the hospital afterwards, Kim," Jim emphasized, placing one hand on her forehead. "I don't want you to forget that, not when you're in the middle of an impromptu inquiry despite the fact that you just had a bizarre experience."

"Of course, but I..."

"Officer Reyna," Bruce called out from the open ambulance. "Dr. Stone is insisting that you come to the hospital for a CT scan immediately."

"We're done here," Lieutenant Abrachinsky returned.

"Yes, we are done here," Kimberley said. "I just need to..."

Something caught her eye in the snow.

It was a book.

The leather-bound volume the little girl had been guarding.

Chapter 2
THE PACKAGE

AIDEN tapped his right foot to the rhythm of an unseen drum on the subway floor, occasionally glancing at the flight of steps to his right and left, as well as the four dark subway passages beside these steps. He'd been waiting for an hour now and felt so lonely and insecure in that cold, abandoned place that he started having second thoughts about waiting for the man.

The man.

The mere thought of this person made him shiver uncomfortably and he wondered why he had agreed to take the job in the first place.

The dude must have killed many times in his life and Aiden shook with fear at the thought of seeing this man again. Maybe the fellow was even killing someone at that very moment, hence the delay.

The distant gunshot convinced the boy to scamper up the nearest flight of steps. He would have to call the man later and claim an accident as an excuse. The meeting would have to be rescheduled.

Of course, the area had many criminal gangs locked in territorial battles for business space. Sporadic gunshot wasn't unusual in this part of town during such an ungodly hour.

Aiden only feared for his life. Walking away sounded better than that gunshot. He suddenly found himself wondering what his contact would do to him if he could not deliver a proper excuse for rescheduling the meeting. The man might even conclude that he was trying to play a fast one and start looking for him in order to gun him down!

No, the boy thought, stopping cold in his tracks. He did not want to die that way. He would have to deliver the parcel as planned. He turned and walked back down the steps.

He heard footsteps in one of the dark subway passages and braced himself, his heart beating loudly in his ears. The girl's sudden appearance from the darkness startled as well as baffled him, and he kept staring at her until she stopped a few feet from him. Now his thumping heart slowed down.

She had on an oversized police jacket atop a mucky blue dress, and like Aiden, her face was very dirty.

Aiden looked her over and, with his free left hand, felt his own dirty clothes in realization. She must be as homeless as he was.

"I am Aiden," he introduced. "Who are you?"

No reply. She'd been looking around her all this time, fidgeting and coughing now and then. Now she hugged her bosom in a nervous manner. Aiden wondered who she was and why she was there at that point in time.

"Who are you?" he repeated, still puzzled. Why was she feeling so cold despite the thick jacket with inner fur lining? He wished he were the one wearing it in that terribly cold subway.

"I...need...you...to take me to the...station..."

"What?"

"I...need...you...to take me to the...police station...right now, please?"

This bold appeal startled Aiden. It was as if she was scared of someone.

Something.

"Look," he began, "you shouldn't even be here right now, really – trust me. Now, go away quickly before he..."

"Before he does what?" a new voice demanded and the boy turned to see the man he'd been waiting for standing at the foot of the steps opposite him.

"Carl Bain," Aiden let out before realizing his mistake. "Sorry...sir," he quickly added, looking around like a caged animal.

"You don't know protocol," Carl Bain said. "I'll make sure you pay for that mistake."

The sweaty shabbily dressed fellow had a stoic appearance complete with deep brows and a cold stare. Indeed, he looked the part of a very bad man through and through. His overbearing presence was quite intimidating and Aiden took a few steps backward.

The boy's heart rate jumped when he noticed the smoking gun in the man's right hand and remembered the gunshot. This guy must have killed someone before coming down for the parcel!

"So where is it?" Carl Bain demanded. "Let me have it."

"Hey! What are you doing?" The girl had suddenly snatched the small package from Aiden and was quickly bounding up the steps behind him. Aiden hesitated for just three seconds, turning to say something to his emotionless contact and thinking better of this before scampering after the young thief.

"Hey, stop! Come back here, boy!" the man with the gun shouted. "Where's my stuff?" He went after the kids.

Out on the roadside, a police officer standing near his patrol car had stopped the girl. Aiden hesitated initially, but upon seeing his criminal contact's head pop out of the subway, he joined the duo a few feet away.

Alarmed, the criminal, Carl Bain, stopped to observe what was happening halfway up the subway steps. He saw the policeman pat the boy on the head when the latter came up to the squad car. Now it looked like the girl was giving something to the cop. Was it the package? Better not be, he thought, else he would smother both kids with his bare hands when this was over.

The little girl pointed his way! He saw the cop heading towards the subway before ducking and going back down the steps. He raised his gun and disappeared into the darkness, just as the law enforcement officer started down the steps.

Aiden glared at the girl now and then as they both stood near the squad car. His visible anger stemmed from the obviously awkward turn of events. Now, he could never disappear for fear of being caught by this new nemesis currently hiding in the subway, and he couldn't steal the parcel in the patrol vehicle and take it back either, because the cops would start looking for him. He could only remain where he stood since the police would protect him from the Gang just as they had done the last time. If they took him back to the station, the least they could do would be to label him a homeless antisocial child and take him back to social services or, worse still, put him in juvenile prison as a juvenile delinquent for some juvenile number of years.

"Why did you do that?" he burst out, glaring at the empty road to his left. "You could have gotten us both killed, you know?" The girl must not have heard him, because she kept staring at the squad car as if it was the solution to all her problems. "Hey," he snapped, grabbing her right arm as well as her attention. "Why do you act so strange, huh?"

"C-Can you drive?"

"What?"

Gunshot preceded a shout of pain and both kids turned to the subway in consternation. Who fired and who got shot?

Another gunshot caused them to visibly jerk in fright, and then...silence.

Nothing.

The man stepping out of the subway wore ordinary clothes.

"Get in the car!" Aiden shouted, running over to the driver's side. The girl was already doing this. Car doors were thankfully unlocked. The rear windshield shattered.

"He's shooting at us!"

Aiden stepped on the gas and the cop car sped off.

Carl Bain let off three more rounds before breaking his run. Luckily, the eerily quiet park was still empty. No crazy bystander gawked at the man with a gun. Cursing, he went back to the subway and emerged in a police uniform with two bullet holes on its back. He walked over to his car parked a few feet away and slid in behind the wheels.

* * *

Sergeant Kimberley Reyna looked at her handiwork spread out on her office desk. She had mistakenly separated the book leaves when she tried to pull off a single thread she noticed jutting out of the book's spine. She never knew that this thread held all the leaves and the cover together, so she was genuinely surprised when the leather-bound volume fell apart.

Dr. Stone had given her a clean bill of health after she underwent a computed tomography scan at the hospital. The good doctor had prescribed headache medication and bed rest for her, but she had gone directly to the police station after taking the pills for her headache. Ever since then, she'd been engrossed in finding out whatever she could about the strange book after taking it apart, but so far she hadn't made any progress.

Again, she picked up some of the book's leaves and scrutinized these using the fluorescent light flooding her office from the ceiling. The papers had blank pages save for some names repeatedly written in different languages through two or three sheets. One of these names was written more times than the other names.

Rachel.

The English version of the name was clear enough.

Whose name was that? And who was he or she to the girl the sergeant had tried to save earlier that night? Rather, was it the girl's name? Was her name Rachel?

Kimberley had grown impatient with the lack of answers to the many questions she'd raised about that night's incident ever since she picked up that girl from that snow-choked road. Nothing seemed to be working out for her in this difficult inquiry.

For instance, no one was looking for a girl that fitted her new friend's description, not even the mental home down at Bright Street, according to Jim. In addition to this negative news, the stranger who had caused the accident hadn't been found and brought in...yet. A discouraging development for a very strange evening.

Sighing, she placed the book leaves back on her desk, their wet surfaces glistening in the bright light flooding her office from above her. She still wondered how the book's pages remained permanently wet despite the fan she had left on in the room. She had spent the bulk of her time in the office pondering over this creepy phenomenon.

A sudden blast of cold air startled her. It definitely wasn't the fan.

"We need to see her!" someone said in the main hall and Kimberley looked up to see the girl she'd tried to rescue that evening talking to Patrol Officer Lyndon Bates amidst a very busy night staff. Where did they find her?

Kimberley moved to her office door. The familiar boy with the little girl she'd tried to save earlier that night was also trying to get a message across, but the girl was more persistent. "Please we need to see her! She's with something of mine!"

Lyndon tried to herd both kids back to the reception hall as Kimberley stepped out of her office. "This is no place for kids," he told the children. "Get in there and I'll go get her for you."

"Wait!" Kimberley called out to him and the little girl instantly recognized her when their eyes met.

"I want my book back, miss," she told Kimberley, stepping forward only to be stopped by the tall male officer.

Kimberley couldn't believe her eyes and ears. Whatever happened to the little girl's coughing and stammering? "Where have you been?" she asked the strange girl, moving towards the trio in the middle of the quiet hall. "Why did you run away? What's with this book of yours? Who did you say was coming after you back in the car?"

"You won't believe me if I told you," the girl replied in a tense voice.

"What are you two going on about?" Officer Bates wanted to know.

Kimberley grabbed the little girl and started towards her office, the other two following closely behind. "Where did you find her, Aiden?" she asked the girl's companion.

"I didn't find her," Aiden replied with a frown. "She found me."

"Okay, how did she do that? Sure you didn't find her?"

"Of course, not," Aiden said. "Why are you all focusing on her alone?"

"Not true, Aiden," Kimberley said. "I haven't forgotten you ran away from your foster home some days back, if that's what you mean. We'll discuss that later."

Aiden gulped. Was that bad news?

"What have you done?" the girl exploded on sighting the scattered book leaves on Kimberley's table when they got to the sergeant's open office door. She rushed over to the desk and started collecting the scattered leaves of the book. "You have destroyed it!" she accused.

"What's going on, Kim?" Lyndon asked his superior as he closed the door behind him. Kimberley looked at him and shrugged, shaking her head. Now she turned back to the strange girl.

"And what, exactly, have I destroyed?"

"What will stop them from killing us all?" the girl returned, glaring at the police officer. "And for everyone's sake, I hope I'm wrong!" She turned back to the desk and started organizing the book's leaves together.

Cold air swept across the room a second time.

"A bad man is after us, Kim," Aiden said in the quiet room. "And he has a gun."

"And why is he after you?" Kimberley seemed only slightly distracted by this news. "What have you done this time?"

"He...He wants this...." Aiden revealed what he had in his hand. A package wrapped in polythene.

"And why are you bringing this up now?" Kimberley asked him absent-mindedly.

"Well, I thought this was the right moment to bring it up if I was ever going to get your attention, since none of you guys have taken any interest in me ever since I came in here with the girl. Maybe parking the squad car a few blocks away has been a mistake, since its shattered rear windshield would have done a better job of getting your attention."

Kimberley stared at the boy. "What?" The strange girl moved to pick up the book leaves arranged on the desk and the police woman stopped her by holding an arm. "Lyndon?"

The patrol officer took the package from Aiden and untied it. He studied the white powder in it and looked at his senior colleague. "Coke?"

"What?" Kimberley frowned. "Aiden, where did you get that?"

The girl's scream interrupted the boy's babbling reply. Everyone's attention shifted back to her. Visibly on edge, her hands were trembling as she glared at Kimberley. "They're coming!" she snapped. "You've got to let me go! They will kill everyone here if you don't!"

"Who are 'they'?" Kimberley had gotten pretty furious, herself. "Just tell me what I want to know and I'll let you go!"

"Calm down, Kim," Lyndon cautioned. "She's just a kid." He turned to another officer drawn into the room by the girl's scream. "It's okay, Jack. We can handle this." Some officers had also been distracted outside and most of them were staring at the office. "Back to work, people!"

Lyndon admonished and they hesitantly obeyed him.

"Who are 'they'?" his senior colleague softly asked the girl. "Why would they kill everyone if I don't let you go?"

"It's a long story," the little girl snapped. "And I have no time! You have to listen to me! Please, I beg you!" She tried to shake herself free and Kimberley let go of her arm.

"Look, young lady," Officer Bates began, wagging a finger at the strange girl. "We cannot let you go if you don't tell Miss Reyna what she wants to know…lives could be at stake, you know." He was beginning to lose his cool like his superior.

"Already told you," the girl cried, exasperated. "It's a long story."

"Which you should be halfway through by now if you have started already," Kimberley said, rolling her eyes upwards and raising her hands in frustration.

"It's getting cold in here," Aiden observed, hugging himself, but nobody even glanced at him. Again, they must have forgotten why he was there despite everything he'd just revealed, he thought.

His strange new acquaintance in this equally strange scenario went for the separated sheets again, but Kimberley stopped her and handed her to Lyndon.

The girl looked long and hard at the stacked book leaves on the table, everyone closely watching her facial expression. "Please, don't do this!" she begged for the umpteenth time, turning to Kimberley with pleading eyes. "Y-You have to listen to me. Just…Just let me go before they come! I really don't have any time!"

In reply, the female sergeant shook her head and walked over to her desk. The little girl wasn't getting it, she thought in dismay. "What's your name?" she demanded from her young headache.

"Rachel."

"Figured as much." The two males in the room turned confusedly towards Kimberley with raised brows. "Her name's written all over some pages in this…this mystery book of hers," the female sergeant tried to explain, searching for the word that best described the sheets of extraordinary paper lying before her. "And please, please, please, can someone tell me why the pages of this damn book are always very wet?"

"Uh…because it fell into snow? Outside?" Aiden suggested timidly.

"Nope…I mean…the freaking thing seems to be oozing out water without getting soggy and…and torn, see?" Kimberley picked up the stack of leaves and water trickled onto her desk in a steady stream. She dropped the stack and the bizarre occurrence ceased. Only the girl lacked any sign of surprise amongst the other three, but the senior cop cared less about that now. "I need answers, Rachel," she emphasized. "And I need them now."

"I-I can't…"

"Why not?"

Rachel began to say something and then swallowed hard, her eyes wandering across the room and resting on Kimberley's fixed gaze. She had tears in her eyes. "It – It is too late now," she whispered, blinking back stinging tears. "They're already here and we're all doomed."

Cold air swept through the room again.

"Getting cold in here," Officer Bates warned, beginning to take his hands to his chest. A mistake he instantly regretted, because Rachel shook free from him and grabbed the mysterious collection of book leaves on the desk.

Kimberley moved to stop the little girl, but only pulled her up after she had lifted the item away from the table, while Lyndon drew one of her hands towards him, knocking Aiden out of the way in the process.

The lights went out as the room's temperature fell fast.

Rachel was shouting….

*   *   *

Aiden woke up first, searching the darkness all around him and feeling a slight headache. He must have hit his head somewhere. He discovered that someone's lower limbs lay across his and realized it was the male cop, Lyndon, whose legs were sprawled over his own.

"What–What happened?" someone demanded to his right. Kimberley. Lyndon stirred and got up.

The lights came back on.

"Where's the girl?" Aiden asked, flinching from the glare.

"She–She must have disappeared, again," Kimberley said, getting up to look around at the chaos now her office. Her things from the desk were all strewn across the floor and the table was lying on one side. The mysterious book was also missing. "We must find her," she said in a shaky voice, feeling another headache coming right up. "She's the key to unraveling all this."

"I'm still here," someone called out from outside Kimberley's office.

Rachel sounded so defeated. The three inside the room stepped out into the main hall of the police station only to discover why the strange little girl's voice had turned into a sad one. The scenario was as if a hurricane had swept through the hall, throwing down chairs, upturning tables and smashing television screens.

And the lifeless lay everywhere.

"Jesus bleeping Christ!" Officer Bates exploded, scampering over to turn one of his colleagues and feel the officer's pulse. Nothing. The man was visibly and obviously dead.

Kimberley's knees buckled as she looked around dazedly. She was still trying to take it all in. Aiden's hands remained on his head.

Lyndon moved over to another fellow lying a few feet away. Dead. He saw something like ash on the ground near an officer's desk.

"T-They take their dead with them," Rachel pointed out.

Her voice was like a ghost's, wafting into Lyndon's consciousness like the implausible scene they'd just been surrounded with.

"It's quite unbelievable, but true," the little girl continued in a shaky voice. "We're still alive! It still works!"

"What the hell do you mean by that?" the policeman demanded from her, visibly surprised by her present utterances.

"It – It still works," Rachel repeated in a small voice, looking around her with unease. "But we've got to leave now before they come back for it!"

"What the hell do you mean by that?" Lyndon repeated with a frown. "What the hell have you been saying all this while?"

"There's no one here to save!" Kimberley interrupted, cutting the conversation. "Everyone's dead!" She crept up to Kate, the female dispatcher she'd radioed earlier that evening.

This officer sat on her chair staring into oblivion amidst the chaos surrounding her.

Feeling the woman's pulse, Kimberley dropped the hand and shook her head in bewilderment. They were all dead. What had happened that very instant the lights went out? Who had come into the station and smothered all her colleagues in the twinkle of an eye?

Aiden's immobile figure stood near Kimberley's office door. He closed his eyes and opened them to stare again at the chaotic situation around him.

Lyndon stepped into the chief's office and froze when he saw the man lying near a water purifier. He stepped up to the body and bent down to close the eyes as a mark of respect. Dazed, he closed the office door behind him as he stepped out of the room.

"No! Please, God, no!" Kimberley screamed on spotting someone's body lying a few feet from the hall's entrance. "No! Oh, please…no! No! No!" She ran over and fell beside the body, realizing it was really Jim. Her tears poured out like a fountain as she shook all over. The others could only watch in despair as she cried her heart out.

Rachel had tears in her eyes as well. "I-I tried to…to warn you this would happen…," she croaked, and the female sergeant turned to her, their eyes locking across that lifeless hall.

Slowly, Kimberley got up, reaching for her side arm. "It's time to talk!" she hissed. "Who the hell did this? I know you know."

"Jesus, no, Kim!" Lyndon warned, getting to his superior as she started towards the cowering girl. The police woman's eyes were red with rage as Lyndon blocked her path, physically halting her steps.

"I swear to God I'll kill you if you don't start yapping!" Kimberley kept saying to herself, struggling to wriggle out of her subordinate's strong grip. She started swinging the gun around in blunt anger, while Rachel kept drawing further backward. Aiden had also drawn back in alarm. "I swear to God I'll kill you if you don't start talking right now! Who did this?"

"She's just a kid, Kim...contain yourself!" Lyndon snapped at his superior and she turned from him and the girl. "Okay," he began, easing his hold on her, "you have to hand over the gun...right now!"

Kimberley bowed her head in indecision.

"Sergeant?"

The gun exchanged hands.

"You know I have to put you under arrest for this?"

Kimberley nodded, looking away. Aiden and Rachel appeared confused by this new twist. "But she's done nothing wrong!" the boy protested. "She didn't shoot anyone, did she?"

"No, boy, she didn't, but she just got way out of line. I just need to read her rights to her and handcuff her, and then we can find out what's happening here."

"W-We've got to leave this place before they come back," Rachel warned. "Can't this wait?"

Lyndon ignored her, trying to appear calm and in control as he turned back to his superior officer and brought out the cuffs. Despite what had happened – the tragedy all around them – he knew he must do what he was about to do. That was called protocol. "Sergeant Kimberley Reyna, I'm putting you under arrest for..."

The shot was deafening, its aftermath devastating. Officer Bates let out a loud cry and dropped like a sack of sand as Kimberley swooped down on the gun she'd handed him. Another shot rang out but the kids were already scampering into her office as she scurried in behind them.

"Who's the new guy now?" she breathed, peering out from around her door. Another shot whizzed past and she ducked, hitting her head on the leg of her upturned desk. "Damn it!"

"Don't think he's new," a wide-eyed Aiden began. "Bet he's the guy I've been trying to tell you about! I think he has found us!"

Kimberley peered out again, searching the vast hall for signs of movement. She saw the man hiding behind a shattered window. The boy could be right.

Rachel swallowed hard and turned to the sergeant. "We've gotta leave right now?" she croaked. "M-My book?"

"I'm not done with you, yet, honey," the police woman hissed. "I'll get those answers if it's the last thing I do." She swerved out and let off some shots at the window. The fellow outside responded with a sustained volley. Kimberley drew back and shook her head. "This is not working!"

"Didn't you hear what I just said?" Rachel wondered aloud, looking at the officer long and hard. "I said we could leave this place with my book."

Aiden stifled laughter and rather scoffed. "And how is that possible, Miss Magic? How are we gonna do that?"

In reply, the girl brought out the separated book leaves from underneath her arms and the other two started. "So, you took it?!" Kimberley accused. "You took it and caused all this mayhem! Y-You killed him! You killed Jim and the others!"

"No," Rachel stressed. "I didn't kill anyone!"

Another shot whistled into the room and all three shifted further away from the door. Kimberley stretched out her right arm and fired thrice into the hall. "Wait till we get out of here!" she whispered as she drew back from the doorway, but Rachel was just busy shuffling through the book's pages. The little girl was barely listening.

"We can't...can't go back into the past," she said.

"What?"

"We can't go back into the past...we–we have to keep going forward if we are to stand any chance of defeating them."

"What are you saying?" Aiden began, staring at the weird girl. "Who are these people you keep mentioning? Were they the ones who attacked us?"

The trio heard a soft thump outside. Their assailant must have jumped into the hall through the broken window.

"What do we do now?" Aiden whispered, turning to Kimberley with wild fear in his eyes.

"I...I need a pen," Rachel said and the other two glared at her.

"Yeah, you think this is a joke?" Kimberley snapped, checking the rounds in her clip. She was almost out. More shots were fired at them from outside. "This is crazy!" she whispered and pulled out her pen. "Here! Wonder why I'm doing this! What the hell are you gonna do with a pen right now, huh? Write us out of here?"

Aiden stared at Kimberley. "Do you really believe her?" He was unconvinced. "She's insane!"

"Hey!" the man outside shouted. "I know you're in there, Aiden! I just want my package, okay? Seems your cop friends are no use to you right now! Look around you! Wonder who did my job for me?" He started laughing.

"It's him!" Aiden whispered, cringing back with heightened fear. "He'll kill us if we don't give him what he wants!"

"Not doing that," Kimberley said, shaking her head and picking up the package from where Lyndon had dropped it in the confusion that had earlier ensued. "That's against the law."

"Like....Like when you wanted to kill Rachel?"

"Very funny....Who said I wanted to do that?" the police sergeant asked him, and when no answer was forthcoming: "What's the story with this guy, anyway?"

"N-Nothing, really...," Aiden began, fidgeting with his hands as he spoke. "I-I was just going to give him the coke and he shot a cop and we had to escape in the cop's car...and..."

"What?" Kimberley turned sharply. "You drove down here?"

"But I've already told you I did," Aiden said.

"I obviously didn't hear you then," Kimberley said. "You drove down here? Who taught you how to drive at fourteen years?" Another bullet flew past. This one was too close for comfort. "Okay, we gotta leave right now."

Rachel nodded in agreement. "Here, hold my hands, both of you." She was quite serious and the others hesitated before obeying. "Not the jacket," she corrected them. "Touch my skin."

Her two companions were really not listening.

"I want you to tell the cop with you to throw out her gun, Aiden!" Carl Bain bellowed from outside. "She's a broad and I don't like killing broads! I will count to three and if she doesn't do this before three, all hell will break lose here!"

"You heard him," an alarmed Aiden told Kimberley. "He means it, Kim!"

Rachel grabbed Kimberley's free hand and turned to Aiden. "Hold me," she commanded him.

"What?"

"Hold my hand if you want to leave with us!"

He obeyed her without hesitation, and once the girl made sure that they were all connected via their hands, she scribbled her name on a sheet of the book in her possession.

"You can write on its pages?" Aiden wondered aloud, and when the strange girl failed to catch on: "They're wet?"

"Yeah...they're wet, but I-I can write on...the pages if-if some conditions are met."

"Seriously? Is that not…"

"One!" Mr. Bain shouted outside. "Two!" He peered out from behind the metal cabinet he was protecting himself with and stared at the empty space before the door ahead. There was no gun on the floor. "Three!"

He got up pumping bullets into the office before him as he walked towards the door with his right arm stretched out. His shots were calculated ones leveled at the open door as well as the walls surrounding it. He was equally ready to spring away from the line of fire should his opponent suddenly emerge before him and start shooting.

But nothing happened.

He got to the door and backed one of its walls, breathing hard.

Still, nothing happened.

Scanning the room from his vantage position, he suddenly bolted into it, swerving to both sides of the door in a quick, responsive manner, but there was no one behind the door.

Carl Bain was perplexed. He dropped his outstretched arms.

The room was empty.

Then he saw some clothes on both sides of the door, and a single sheet of paper lying near a police jacket. He stooped to pick it up. It had only one name on it.

Rachel.

Chapter 3
RACHEL'S BOOK

AIDEN freaked out as he got up, clinging to a horizontal pipe for dear life. He began to look around in wild confusion, his hands shaking in fear.

"Wh-Where are we? What the hell happened just now?!" Kimberley cried to his right. She wore a military uniform beneath a bulletproof vest, and an M16A4 rifle with a mounted ACOG sight hung lazily from her right shoulder as she tried to maintain her balance in the knee-deep water they were all trying to make sense of. On seeing her, Aiden started screaming. "Will you just shut the hell up?" she demanded in a troubled voice, glaring at him, and he clamped up, but not for long.

"Our....Our clothes?" he tried to point out to the female sergeant and she looked at him quizzically.

Then she realized what he was saying. "HOLY SHIT!" she mouthed, feeling her clothes and the gun. "HOLY SHIT!" she shouted. "What the hell's going on?"

"No time to explain," Rachel began; wading forward to Aiden's left. She sounded very anxious. "First, we need to move on."

"What?" Kimberley cried, still touching her clothes for some sign of familiarity.

"We need to move on," the little girl repeated. "We've got to move very far away from the point of entry, and then think of what next to do. The Gray Ones take a longer route, so we've got some time. The book brought us here, but we cannot stop here."

"The...Gray Ones? The....The book?" a confused Kimberley stammered. "Either you're mad or I'm mad! How did a book bring us here? I give you my pen and–and...and you write down something and…and what the hell just happened? Are you nuts?"

"No, I'm not nuts," the little girl said, offended by the question as she furtively looked around her like a caged animal. "What does it mean to be nuts?"

The other two gaped at her.

"Crazy?" Aiden explained. "Insane?"

"No, I am not crazy," she told him.

Kimberley shook her head in confusion. "Then are you an alien or something?"

"What does it mean to be alien?" Rachel asked Aiden.

Again, they gawked at her.

"Not of this world?" Aiden began. "From another planet?"

"No, I am not alien," the little girl told him, and turned to Kimberley, who was still bewildered by it all. "Look, it's…it's the book they want," she blurted out, visibly on edge as she kept the odd volume to her bosom.

"The…b-book?" Kimberley stammered. "What about it?"

"They've been chasing me after Father gave it to me down at the…at the Mine," the strange girl continued, her eyes wandering off to the tunnel's mouth some distance away, through which light spilled in from outside. "The book brought us here, but we need…we need to move on, because they are surely coming for it."

"Are you saying the book is a sought of…transporter?" Aiden asked, wide-eyed.

"Yes," Rachel said.

Kimberley held her forehead. "Okay, you said you'll take us out of the station," she began. "Thank God for that, though…we can now figure out what happened and find out which part of town we've landed in." She made to move forward.

"We're no longer in your town." Rachel sounded confident despite her current state of mind. "W-We're no longer wearing the clothes we wore at the station, so the book must have…must have moved us."

"Wait…you mean we are no longer in Portwood?" Kimberley stared at the weird girl. "You must be joking, right?" She looked around her with a puzzled expression. "Can't recall a tunnel as big as this in Portwood, though," she admitted.

"The sewage system?" Aiden suggested, and Kimberley shook her head.

"Been down there once," she revealed. "Looked nothing like this."

"Maybe it's some place you haven't been to?"

"Not possible," the sergeant said. "I've got the town map in my office. There's no place as big as this."

As if in reply to her unanswered questions, muddy water gushed out from a side compartment and splashed through the three of them on its way out of the tunnel's mouth. Kimberley found herself protecting her automatic rifle the best way she could as the stream went through. And then it dawned on her. She'd been protecting the weapon as if she had undergone training for that kind of situation in the past. She couldn't find any other plausible reason.

"When did I join the Marine Corps?" she asked herself, bewildered. "Look," she said, shaking her head while pointing at Rachel and the tunnel's dark interior with her hands. "I don't know who you are, where you came from or what you did, but we need to go back this very minute! You just undo whatever you did, okay? Who knows what is happening back there right now? Jesus Christ!"

"We–We have left your time, miss," the little girl revealed a bit awkwardly. "We–We have gone into the future."

"Are you now saying the book is a sought of…of time machine?" an astonished Aiden asked. Rachel stared at him. "Umm…something that helps you travel through time?"

"Yes," the little girl said.

"Dammit!" Kimberley yelled, shaking her head in disbelief. "Give me that!" She stretched out her hand for the book, but the girl drew back and she almost slipped in her frustration. A second attempt also proved futile, but she snatched the leather-bound volume at the third effort.

"You're not a Bookbearer!" Rachel cried as she moved to retrieve her book. "I'm the only one who can use it!"

"A Book– what?" Kimberley frustrated her opponent's efforts with an outstretched arm, but before she could do more, the little girl started jumping up in the muddy water, unfortunately landing on her left boot and causing her to cry out in pain. She lost her guard and, in the ensuing confusion, lost the book as well. She fruitlessly tried to get it back. The girl stumbled into a tiny compartment on the tunnel's wall and drew away from reach. Mouth agape, Aiden could only stand and watch.

"We cannot go back," an alarmed Rachel said when the sergeant started reaching back for her gun. "The book only takes one forward. It cannot take one back, and besides, those things must have left your town – they only want the book."

"Best we listen to her, Kim," Aiden interrupted, fearful of where all this was heading. "Seems she knows her way around this…"

"Or she's the only crazy creature around for miles," the police officer sniggered, trying to regain her composure. Well, she still agreed with the boy, though. 'Better not screw things up,' she thought. If there was a balance, this little girl with the strange book might be the answer to the entire saga. If there was a balance, that is, because she still could not believe what had happened – how the police station had suddenly become a murky tunnel at the blink of an eye. "So, where the hell are we?"

"No time to know that," Rachel said, her eyes glued to Kimberley's M16A4 rifle. "Look, we are hopeless if we continue staying here. Father said to keep moving until I can find someone who can defeat them."

"Them?" the female officer asked an umpteenth time, and stretched out a hand in order to help Rachel out of the small cubicle, but the girl hesitated. "I won't hurt you or try to take the book," she declared. "I promise."

"Just step away and hand the gun to your friend," Rachel told her. "I don't trust you."

Surprisingly, Kimberley obeyed, eyeing the rifle in Aiden's hands as she stepped away. There appeared to be no point in trying to do things her way now. Until she could comprehend what was happening, that is.

Rachel got out of the compartment and marched towards the tunnel's mouth ahead of the others, the book underneath her right arm. She walked like she had a deadline to keep. "Who are they?" Kimberley asked her, beginning to struggle forward like the other two. "Who are these people you keep mentioning?"

"The Gray Ones."

"The Gray what?"

"Those things that killed your people back at…at your station? I've been running from them ever since they killed my father down at the Mine…. They're also called the Booklords…"

Aiden frowned. "The Book what?"

"The Booklords," Rachel repeated. "You see, they've always been after the book, so…"

"And where was that?" Kimberley cut in. "The killing of your father, I mean…"

"My father died in Rome. The Booklords killed him before the Romans found the Mine."

"The Italians, you mean."

"No. The Romans." The little girl failed to notice that her companions had stopped dead in their tracks. "I escaped with the book before they could get me. Father had already told me what to do some days before the attack."

"And what do you mean by Romans, Rachel?" Kimberley asked some distance behind her.

"Romans," she repeated. "The Emperor's soldiers?"

"No freaking way!" Aiden exploded. This was going too far, but judging from what Rachel had already done with the book, believing this new claim shouldn't be difficult for them to do, right? The girl stopped and turned. "Are you saying you came from the ancient world?" he asked her. "Are you a Roman citizen?"

"No," she replied, frowning. "I'm a Jew. The Romans enslaved my people and my father said the books will eventually free us if we can defeat the Booklords and perform the ritual with the other book."

"The other book?" Kimberley frowned. "You mean there are two of these things?"

"Uhuh."

"But–But how come it's a book?" Aiden wanted to know, trudging forward again. "I mean, you say you come from ancient Rome, but did they have books in those days? I mean, they weren't called books back then, right?"

"Aiden, don't encourage her," Kimberley rebuked him, eyeing the young girl. "For all we know, she could be a magician's daughter."

"Codex?" Rachel clarified, ignoring the police officer. "It used to be a tough, new type of codex, but it's now a book. It's been changing form since I left Rome…"

"Right, whatever!" Kimberley moved forward again. She'd heard enough and the sooner they left that freaking tunnel and established a location, the better for them. Whatever tricks the weird girl had up her sleeves would surely be revealed for the phony hoax they were once a location was established.

Of course, the idea of a girl from the past coming into the present was quite unbelievable, but even more so was the suggestion that a mysterious book or time portal made it possible for her. Such things could only be read in fiction. This was why the police sergeant had decided not to take back the book after her struggle with the girl in the tunnel until she was sure of where they were. Rachel could well be a loony who escaped from the mental home down at Bright Street. Jim could have been wrong.

Still, Kimberley found herself wondering why the book's pages were always wet, and how on earth did they manage to leave the police station?

A seemingly hot and hazy environment spread out beyond the tunnel's mouth. "Are we in Saudi Arabia?" a puzzled Aiden asked the other two.

"That's unlikely," Kimberley said, curiously peering forward. "But this sure looks like…"

"Iraq?"

"That's ridiculous," the female military personnel snorted.

"But possible," Rachel said calmly.

Kimberley shivered reluctantly. The strange girl's countenance always gave her the chills.

They heard gunshots.

"It's a semiautomatic," Kimberley noted, squatting at the edge of the tunnel's mouth and demanding for her M16A4 with an outstretched right arm. Aiden returned the rifle and moved away from the open with Rachel.

The staccato burst had come from their left, below a semi-arid terrain tapering down and away into the dusty distance, beyond which Kimberley could not see a thing. The area before her was also unfamiliar, more of a hilly landscape culminating in a high plateau some distance from the tunnel. She could see that this flat area was walled and had guard towers on all four corners of the rectangular wall. Like a military outpost.

Return fire came from one of the guard towers, and Kimberley spotted a deep trench running towards the plateau some feet from the tunnel's right. The water gushing from the latter was pouring into this ditch and she pointed it out for the others. "We'll make for that gutter," she told them as an exchange of fire ensued between the two parties fighting far away. "It's our only chance." Then she realized the two kids were scared out of their wits from the deafening noise of machine gun fire coming from the guard towers and drew back to them. "See, I'm right here," she assured them, expertly readying the M16A4. "No one will get hurt. Besides, they don't know we're here, yet."

"How did you know that?" Aiden asked her in a scared voice.

"Because no one's shooting at us, Dumbo. Now haul ass while I cover. Quietly, though." Kimberley moved back towards the tunnel's mouth. Two successive explosions rattled them and the machine guns fell silent. A third one started chattering. "Move it, will you?"

Aiden edged forward, feeling his heart thumping in his ears. Rachel followed behind him, and they stopped behind Kimberley. The noise was so loud that Aiden covered his ears with his hands. "Now what?" he asked their protector.

"Into the trench."

The boy crawled on all fours out into the open, and quickly fell into the gutter. Rachel followed suit, and jumped in behind him just as a bullet whizzed by!

"They've spotted us!" Kimberley said. She let off some rounds as she crashed into the dugout. More bullets flew past. "Keep your heads down and run!" she bellowed, and as the other two sped away, she followed them in a crouching stance, occasionally lifting her arm above the trench to shoot at their aggressors.

A metal door snapped open before Aiden. Rachel almost tumbled into him when he broke his run. A bearded soldier beckoned to him at the door and the girl pushed him forward.

Aiden realized that the man wore Kimberley's uniform and willingly ran up to this soldier.

"Where's the sergeant?" the fellow asked.

"Right behind us!" Aiden puffed, going through the door like a bullet.

The new guy revealed an M16 and moved out into the trench. He opened fire on their attackers' positions as Kimberley appeared in the distance.

"Thanks, Mike!" Kimberley shouted as she quickly sped past the other soldier into the safety zone. How did she know his name?

This marine had drawn enemy fire away from her and now withdrew to slam the armored door behind him. "Whatever happened back there?" he asked the three breathing hard before him.

"You tell me!" Kimberley retorted, hands placed on knees as she tried to catch her breath. "What the hell's going on here?"

"We're under attack, Lin," Mike told her, moving away towards a metal ladder.

"I know but…wait, what did you just call me?" a surprised Kimberley demanded, looking up sharply.

"Lin," the new man repeated, halting his climb as he spun round to return her stare. "Does this sound like a joke to you?"

No reply, save for the deafening sound of gunfire outside.

"Where are we?" Aiden asked the soldier. The one question on everyone's mind.

"Whatever happened to you guys back there, Lin?" the man rather demanded in consternation, peering into Kimberley's face from where he hung. "The sergeant wants to see you ASAP. I hope you have some good news for him." And he vanished above their heads.

"Good news?" Kimberley scoffed as she reached for the ladder, which was attached to the side of the bunker-like compartment they were presently in. Aiden and Rachel made to follow, but she shook her head. "You two better stay here till I know where we are and what we're dealing with," and she disappeared upwards.

She soon came back with a white face.

"We're in Afghanistan!"

*   *   *

He started when he realized he was no longer holding a pistol, but an AK-47 semiautomatic, then his gaze rested on his clothes. He wore a

26

grayish-white attire, and…and his feet? A pair of slippers had replaced his shoes!

"What the hell?" he exploded, and looked up when he heard gunshots. "What the hell?" he repeated, snapping around when an open pickup truck rumbled past him.

"Daud, the attack has begun!" a skinny fellow holding up a rocket-propelled grenade launcher behind the vehicle's driver shouted. "Quick, join the others near the outpost!"

"What the hell?" Carl Bain repeated, still trying to figure out what was actually happening amidst the deafening sound of deadly fire now coming from behind a distant hill. How did he get there from the police station, and which attack had just begun? Where the hell was this place? He trudged up towards the hill, behind which the truck had disappeared. Perhaps a clearer picture would materialize after he got a better view of where he was, he thought.

Perhaps he was dreaming. Who knows? Maybe he was asleep or unconscious. Maybe he'd been knocked out by that female cop and now lay in a cell, out cold. Worse still, maybe he was…dead? Maybe the cop had shot him in the head and he was now dead. Was he in hell? Heaven? He was a bit unsure of this. No, he should be dreaming. What kind of a dream was he dreaming then? What kind of a hellish dream was he dreaming? He realized he was now very close to the little hill's summit, and as he scaled it, a clearer picture did emerge.

The pickup truck was already approaching the scene before him, but that was not what instantly caught his attention. A US flag fluttered in the wind above a fenced enclave from which he could hear the unmistakable sound of machine gun fire. Men dressed like him lay flat on their stomachs below a slope falling off before this facility. These men were shooting in the outpost's direction from this position. Suddenly, he saw one of these fellows cry out and throw his hands in the air before collapsing on the dusty ground. Then the guy with the rocket launcher collapsed beside this man as soon as he jumped out of the truck. The launcher was picked up by another fellow who equally collapsed on his dead comrade, and nobody picked the weapon again.

Was he in Iraq? That was a military outpost those guys were attacking, no mistake about that. But.…But how did he get to Iraq without boarding an airplane and hopping over? "What the hell?" he grumbled for the fourth time, feeling flustered and angry. And why did that dude call him Daud? Was this some kind of joke? How did he become a militant attacking a US outpost all of a sudden? How did they expect him to fight his country in Iraq, whoever 'they' were? He was never going to do that – he was a very patriotic US citizen, despite his criminal background, and even if he could kill his fellow citizens owing to the need for cash inside his country, he was never going to do anything to…

Then he saw her.

It was her alright. The female cop back at the police station. She was the US soldier working the machine gun from within the military outpost.

The picture sharpened in his head.

The paper he'd found in that office with a single name on it.

Rachel.

He had tried to straighten the paper with his thumbs, and then…

This.

Carl Bain cocked his Kalashnikov.

Chapter 4
AFGHANISTAN

"WE'RE all gonna die!"

"No, we're not."

"We're all gonna die!"

"No, we're not!" Kimberley snapped, jerking her head in Aiden's direction. "Now shut the hell up, will you?" The exchange of gunfire above their heads had dramatically increased in the past few minutes, but she envied Rachel's calm demeanor. The little girl had an accusing 'I told you' look and was hugging her cursed book some feet from the shaking Aiden. "Okay, we've gotta hold ourselves together and – and climb up that ladder, you hear me?"

"We're all gonna die!" Aiden repeated and Kimberley glared at him. Was that pee on his pants?

"We have to leave now," Rachel said. "The Gray Ones won't be far behind us – they always take a longer route, but we've gotta get going. We have to leave this place and…and time due to the situation here."

"And what do you mean by that?" Kimberley demanded.

"We have to use the book again."

"Oh, so you now want to use the book again?" Kimberley asked; arms akimbo. "For a moment back there I thought you could handle the situation without using the book again…and who knows where that your bloody book will drop us now, eh? Okay, let me guess…another hell?"

Rachel flinched from the outburst, but remained adamant. "Look, things don't look good in this place," she argued. "If you haven't noticed, they're fighting a war out there and…and we need a better environment to think. We could end up somewhere more peaceful this time."

"Or worse.... No. We're going up that ladder." The Portwood police sergeant had a resolute expression. "I'd as well face this reality right now than any other fantasy that magical crap of yours will come up with."

"Are you forgetting something?" Aiden began.

"What?" Kimberley asked him.

"We're kids? They're fighting up there?"

"I'm not convinced," Kimberley said. "Could be a rehearsal for a movie, and..."

"You think we're part of this rehearsal?" Aiden had a puzzled look.

"Maybe?" Kimberley hated the way Rachel glared at her.

"Are you for real right now?" Aiden began. "Do you believe what you just said, Kim?"

"Well, I...." Kimberley glanced at Rachel.

"Suit yourself," the strange girl said, flipping open the book.

"No, you don't." Kimberley had her right finger on her rifle's trigger and her left hand outstretched towards the girl. "Just hand it over before I do something we'll all regret."

"Can we all please calm down?" Aiden pleaded with alarm. Rachel handed Kimberley the book and he stared at it. How...when did its pages get sewn back together?

Kimberley still had her semiautomatic pointed at Rachel. Aiden couldn't find his voice. The sergeant pushed the book into a large pocket on her left thigh.

Above them, there seemed to be a lull in the fighting and Aiden thought that could be a good sign, but then the compartment shuddered as an explosion rocked the outpost above their heads and the fighting resumed. He lost his nerves all over again. "I don't think that's a rehearsal, Kim," he finally said.

"We'll just have to go up there and find out," Kimberley said.

"Don't do this," Rachel pleaded. "We can still leave now without those above knowing. We could be sent to...to somewhere safer this time." Fear had started edging back into her voice, but Kimberley's gun remained pointed at her as the cop soldier turned to the boy standing beside her.

"Aiden, up the ladder with you two," she ordered him, and a dejected-looking Rachel walked over to the structure and started climbing its rungs before the boy could obey the command.

Kimberley went up after Aiden as the guns outside continued their insistent chatter.

"They're actually fighting, Kim!" Aiden cried when he peeped out of the armored trapdoor in the bunker's ceiling. "Go back down! It's not safe out there!"

"Let me see for myself," Kimberley said, pushing him all the way out through the trapdoor.

She saw chaos when she peeped out of the bunker. Bullets whizzed past now and then, but this did not stop her from coming out and crawling up to Aiden and Rachel.

Aiden tried to inch backwards into the bunker and mistakenly kicked the armored trapdoor covering its entrance. The heavy barrier fell back into place with a click. "The door's shut!" he wailed, sliding sideways until his hands reached the door's handle and pulled on it. "I don't know how to reopen it!"

"And it's your fault, Miss Kim!" Rachel snapped, sliding sideways in order to help Aiden.

Kimberley stared. She'd been wrong about the situation here. Everyone had a gun and lay behind sandbags, directing fire at the group attacking the camp. These fighting men kept calling out to one another as bullet magazines flew about, yet the Portwood police officer remained where she lay on her stomach. She could not move.

A grenade successfully thrown into the base had wrecked havoc in the middle of the fenced area. Three bloody bodies lay sprawled at varying angles around this mini ground zero, but someone had dragged a far greater number of the dead into a military truck parked very close to the opposite fence.

Another soldier snatched Kimberley's gun and crashed behind a sandbag as he opened fire. A fortyish-looking man glared at the transfixed military sergeant from behind his rifle's butt. "Why you lying there doing nothing, girl?" he exploded. "Grab a gun!"

"Sir, yes sir!" This as she quickly crawled to a mounted machine gun her comrades were apparently ignoring, while Rachel and Aiden crept behind sandbags. The quick response had been involuntary, as if it'd been mechanically bored into her brain many years back. How she skillfully swerved the hot weapon towards the sound of distant shots before opening fire was also beyond her.

Kimberley downed four militants and a skinny fellow brandishing a grenade launcher before realizing that her hands were covered in blood. Not hers. The marine initially manning the weapon she now operated lay dead beside her.

A bullet whizzed past her.

She just had time to dodge another closer shot before realizing that there were no sandbags protecting the machine gun's shooter! She was a sitting duck! This was why the men had overlooked the gun despite its deadly force.

Kimberley crouched low and tried to unhinge the weapon from its stand, but it wouldn't budge. She used a small rock to hit the tripod repeatedly, but it remained staunchly embedded in the metal bars sunk into concrete before her. Several bullets whizzed past her and she quickly fell flat on the ground. Who the hell locked down a machine gun in concrete and with no sandbag protection? Who the hell would do such a dumb thing?

"Forget it, Lin!" someone shouted on her left. It was Mike from the bunker and she frowned questioningly. More bullets came her way. "Cassidy does some crazy things around here – I couldn't remove it, too. Just find cover before you get yourself killed."

"No, there has to be some way," Kimberley refused.

"We need to go right now before it's too late," Rachel shouted from behind a heap of sandbags. "I can sense them near!"

"We better listen to her, Kim," Aiden persuaded in a shaky voice, peeping out from the other side of the sandbags.

The military sergeant ignored him. "What happened to the gunners up at the guard towers?" she asked Mike.

"Grenade attack." Mike unleashed lead on the enemy. "Those guys didn't stand a chance. The Taliban got them before we took out their launchers."

"They still have one left," Kimberley told herself. "We need the machine gun, Mike."

"I know, but what can we do with that thing stuck there?" He downed another fellow crawling up to where the rebels had left their rocket-propelled grenade launcher and turned back to her. "What the hell are you doing?"

"If I can just…." Kimberley pushed Cassidy's body away and pulled a sandbag lying nearby towards her position. She started pushing it up to the machine gun's concrete base while maintaining her horizontal position.

"Think that would work?" Mike wondered, firing away.

"Maybe," Kimberley muttered. The sand bag got wedged between the gun's stands and concrete support. "Fair enough," she concluded. Still lying flat on the ground, she brought up a second sandbag beside the first one. Now the bullets weren't whizzing past her position that much.

She engaged the enemy again; riddling the rocket launcher with bullets and watching it fizzle with satisfaction.

"And it worked!" Mike cheered. "Surprise…."

"Sir, message from HQ!"

"And what're they saying, huh? When're they sending me my attack copters, huh?"

"They say there's a slight delay…the choppers will be late…"

"The choppers will be what?"

"The choppers will be..."

"Dammit!" the US commander pumped off more bullets at the insurgents trying to overrun his base. "Dammit! Give 'em all you've got, boys, or it's toast for all of us!"

The men surrounding him knew without being told. Their automatic rifles chattered continuously, spewing empty shells all over the place. Since both guard towers were presently unoccupied, Kimberley's machine gun was the only one in operation at the moment.

"Look, Kim, we gotta leave right now!" Aiden cried in the din surrounding them. His voice was almost missing, and he was afraid to show more of his head from behind the heap of sandbags.

"We gotta go before it's too late, miss!" Rachel assisted from the other end of the heap. "This is not your war! It's one ahead of your time and you'll never be in it."

"Very funny...we're already in it," Kimberley countered, crouching to direct her fire towards a distant cave some militants were trying to stage a comeback from.

"Hey, Lin...you gotta move those kids back to the bunker...it's not safe here," Mike advised.

"No time for that now, Mike, and I can't tell them to leave cover. They're safe where they...damn!" she cried, clutching her left shoulder as she crashed to the floor. "I'm hit!" The panic-stricken kids behind her stared at her with visible dread. If only she had remained on her stomach. "Just got hit!"

"I know." Mike had dropped his rifle. He quickly took over the machine gun, swinging it towards the shot's direction. "The guy's got good aim."

"Seen him?" Kimberley asked as she lay on her back while clutching her wounded shoulder.

"Yeah," Mike said, watching with satisfaction as the fellow scampered to safety once bullets from the blazing machine gun started raining down on the rebels below. "He looks kinda weird for an Arab insurgent, though," the marine continued. "No beard or moustache?" A bullet swished by his helmet and he withdrew from the furious weapon lest a second one did him in. "Why?"

"Why what?" Kimberley asked, flinching in pain.

"The dude down there...he looks like an American to me. He moves like a pro, too. There. Behind the pickup truck?"

"Yeah...seen him." Kimberley peered again at the man. "Is that..."

"It's him, Kim," Aiden shouted from behind her. "How did he find us?"

"I must have dropped the page we used to get here in your office and...and he must have come across this paper!" Rachel shouted from the other end of the sand mound. "He must have figured it all out!"

"Says Miss Careful." Kimberley was furious. "Thanks!"

"Figured what all out?" Mike wondered aloud, trying to get the elusive fellow returning fire from behind the pickup truck. "What're you guys on about? Do you know this guy?"

"Yes, he's an old friend." Kimberley smiled at her dry humor. The others looked on with concern as she reached into a pocket on her combat pants and surprisingly brought out the parcel their tenacious aggressor was after. "This guy's not just after cocaine."

"Okay...when did you meet him? During your mission?" Mike asked her, turning his attention back to the man trying to kill them from across the dry terrain.

"Yes," Aiden stammered. "He was sent to kill my father." He realized he had an accent.

"Well...aren't you bright for your age?" the male marine commended. "I bet your father sent you to a private school there in Kandahar." He couldn't help seeing his female superior hold up a strange-looking metallic object covered in a white powder-like substance. "What the hell is that?"

"I don't know," Kimberley said. It was a solid silver-plated cube the size of a matchbox, and she'd gotten it out of the package Carl Bain was after. "He wasn't after the cocaine," she told herself again.

"Is that what he's after?" Aiden asked.

"Is that white powder cocaine?" Mike wondered aloud.

"Probably not," Kimberley lied, studying the object in her hand. "What the hell is this?"

"Maybe a new kind of bomb or something?" the other soldier suggested, letting off some more rounds at the enemy. "Look, you gotta get it back to Intelligence when all this is over."

"Aim for the gas tank."

"What?"

"The truck's gas tank," Kimberley repeated. "Shoot it. That'll smoke him out."

"I'll miss from this..."

Kimberley grabbed the M16A4 rifle and placed the pickup truck's tank in her sights. The man down below scrambled to get away before the vehicle exploded, flinging him farther from where he'd been trying to run to. "Bull's eye!" she snapped and flinched from her shoulder wound.

The explosion had shaken the insurgents and it looked like they were beginning to lose ground. Many had lost their lives and it was pointless to press on.

A loud shout went up from the defenders hunkered down the length of the sandbag mound when a few civilian trucks appeared in the horizon and the fighting rebels started what was obviously a tactical retreat.

"Yeah!" a soldier pumping his fist in the air some distance from Mike shouted. "That's the way to fight!" His comrades voiced their agreement in various ways, and then all eyes turned to the female sergeant who'd made the victory possible.

"Lin, you know you're a hero, right? You got the pickup truck despite your being wounded! That deserves a Purple Heart if you ask me!" Mike smiled as he tore off a part of his shirt and placed it on Kimberley's wound, although she'd stopped losing blood. "Here, apply pressure on it. Where's the medic?" The fellow was already coming over with a first aid kit.

"It's a shoulder wound?" the military doctor asked as he knelt before Kimberley. "You'll survive...looks like a flesh one. We just need to find the bullet right away, clean the wound and stitch it up..." He opened his medical box and brought out a bottle of spirit and some tools. "Hold steady – this will hurt," and he tore open her uniform at the shoulder...

Moments later, the bullet had been pulled out and the wound cleaned and stitched up. 'Good," the doctor began. "You need to rest down at the..."

"No...," Kimberley cut in, glancing at Rachel before continuing. "We don't have much time...we've got to go."

"Go where?" the medic asked her.

"Em...never mind, but I don't think I'm still top priority. You must have others far worse than me, don't you?" The doctor was confused, but nodded in agreement. "Now, go...my friends can help me down the ladder when I'm ready." Mike was staring at Kimberley and she didn't like that. "What?" she asked him.

"You even sacrifice yourself for others," he whispered. "How did you know we got just one medic? That others need him now that you're stitched up?"

"Well...he's the only one I've seen," she replied. "So I figured...you know...and like you said, I'm already stitched up." Was he thinking of personally recommending the Purple Heart?

"Good job, sergeant," the outpost's middle-aged commander began as he trudged up to where Kimberley lay. "When they told me you were in town, I knew something big was up. Whose kids? His?"

"Em...yes, sir," Kimberley replied. Strangely, she knew what the man was talking about. "I couldn't get him to come with me, but he wants his kids to be safe."

"And where is he right now?"

"Probably dead, sir. Our enemies think he's a traitor."

"Oh well, poor kids," the commander bemoaned, arms akimbo. "Get them down to the mess hall for some chow and...come to my bunker after you've rested yourself, sergeant. You need to hook on to Intelligence ASAP."

"No," Rachel refused, frowning.

"What?" The commander was visibly astonished.

Kimberley glared at the little girl. Her stare meant 'shut up,' but Rachel had other ideas.

"They're coming, miss. I can feel it," she said.

"Will you stop calling me 'miss'? My name is..."

"What does she mean, sergeant?" the outpost commander demanded. "Who's coming?" Many soldiers had turned towards the group. The little girl was good at drawing attention.

"She's still scared, that's all, sir," Kimberley lied, frowning compassionately at her feminine headache. "Console your sister, Rahim," she told Aiden.

At first, the boy thought he didn't hear his female companion correctly, and then he felt a funny familiarity with the name she'd just given him and quickly moved over to Rachel, who wouldn't let him touch her.

"Oh well, it's a war, kid," the commander explained to the little girl and turned away. "Carry on, people." He was off to something better than a whining child, and his men followed his lead. The little girl was just excited and anxious like everyone else.

"I need water," Kimberley croaked and Mike stood up.

"Stay with her, boy," he ordered Aiden and headed for the ladder. "We'll move you as soon as I come back."

"When're you going to listen to her, Kim?" Aiden whispered as soon as the marine had left.

"When I feel like it," the female cop said coldly.

"It's getting cold you know," the boy tried again.

"It's getting late. We're in the middle of winter."

Rachel was longingly staring at Kimberley's camouflage pocket in which rested the book. She looked away. "You still don't believe me, because you're scared," she accused.

"The hell I'm not," Kimberley whispered. "I just don't believe anything you've told us."

"Huh?" Aiden was dumbfounded. "We're in Afghanistan, Kim," he cried. "Which other proof do you need?" He drew back in anger, pointing at Rachel. "You know, I think she's right, Kim. You're scared stiff! You're not in control, 'cause this whole thing just got bigger than Portwood and…and you can't handle it! You just can't put a finger on it, can you?"

"Shut the hell up," Kimberley whispered. "Just shut it for a sec, will you? For all I know, we could be in one of those new reality shows down at Portwood Studios! This could be a damn set."

"But…"

"Not another word," she snapped. "We're gonna find out what's going on my way. Period."

"But…" Rachel began.

"Don't try me," Kimberley warned her. Mike was coming back to where she lay.

"Tell him or I'll sing," Aiden whispered and Kimberley simply scoffed.

"Says the lily-livered boy," she jeered.

Aiden's blood boiled. He made to say something loud enough for Mike to hear, but Rachel stopped him and turned to the injured military woman. "So, when're you gonna believe me?" she asked the sergeant. "When more people die?" She sounded so exasperated. "God, you still don't get it, do you?"

Kimberley was staring at her. At least her cooler head was prevailing. "I can't promise any…"

"You'll be safe, dear," Mike assured the little girl. "That's what Linda can promise you."

He knelt and offered Kimberley a bottle of water, which she quickly opened and drank from. A welcome distraction from the heated environment and Rachel's reproachful eyes.

"That will give you some strength," Mike assessed, standing up and leaning towards Kimberley. "Now, we need to…"

"Hey…that dude's shooting at us."

"Which one?"

"The one behind the burnt-out truck…there, see him?"

"Yeah."

A soldier cried out and crashed to the ground, and everyone scampered up to the sandbag defense they'd earlier vacated.

Mike turned to Kimberley and the kids. "Wait here," he told them and rushed up to where his comrades were trying to counter the new treat. M16A4 fire resounded as they all directed their fury at the pickup truck's junk down below. Another soldier yelped and sprawled. "I thought he was killed in the explosion?" Mike wondered aloud when he spotted the insurgent refusing to give up.

"It must be our man," Kimberley told Aiden some distance from the action, struggling to sit up. "How did he manage it? I saw him get hit."

"Don't let him run for the cave!" came to their ears from one of the men trying to nail the remaining militant. "He'll disappear if he gets there!"

"Miss Reyna, this is our chance to leave this place," Rachel urged Kimberley and Aiden agreed vigorously.

"No," Kimberley repeated, staring at the little girl. At least, the weirdo now knew her surname. "No way we're doing that...."

"They won't know, Kim," Aiden pleaded. "They're preoccupied right now."

"Not happening," the injured officer refused grudgingly. "My word is final."

"Very well then."

Aiden sighed as he stood up before Kimberley. She wondered what he was up to.

"Like you said," he began, "we're already in this war...right?"

"What?"

He suddenly embraced her.

"No, you don't," the startled woman said, realizing she was helplessly weak. The weapon she spotted lying next to the first aid kit was out of reach, since the struggling Aiden had been able to keep her arms incarcerated beside her.

They both fell backward in his death hug.

"Hey, what's going on?" Mike shouted from the defense post.

Rachel hesitated.

"Get the book, you!" Aiden shouted at her.

Kimberley started kicking her legs in the air to dissuade the girl from doing this, but Rachel managed to clasp both hands around one of her thighs in the heat of the scuffle, bouncing around with the rhythm of the leg.

Some other soldiers had turned around with Mike and were now hurrying towards the struggling trio. The little girl had pulled out the book from Kimberley's thigh pocket, but the army sergeant was holding on to her leg, preventing her from completely getting away.

No one realized it was getting very cold pretty fast.

"Stop it, will you?" Mike ordered when he got to Aiden and grabbed the boy's arms. Kimberley swerved towards Rachel as soon as she was free, but the little girl succeeded in keeping the book out of her reach while being pulled up. "What's the meaning of this?"

Someone screamed. It was like everything had suddenly gone into slow motion. Lance Corporal Mike let go of Aiden, a.k.a. Rahim, as he turned towards the scream, and the boy went for Kimberley's waist while she tried to grab the book from Rachel, a.k.a. Rahim's sister.

Before his very eyes, an amazed Mike saw blurry gray shapes blazing through what looked like several of his comrades suspended in mid-air. One of these bizarre entities knocked his body into the air and he felt like he was dying from the inside. His head bounced on the ground when he hit it and, through bloodshot eyes, he saw Rahim's sister screaming as these horrible things grappled with her for a...a book? The creature attacking him filled his view with its horrendous face and snarled in a gurgled voice, abruptly fading into ash.

Another scream. It was Kimberley, a.k.a. Linda. Something held on to her wound and caused her pain, but it wasn't Rahim. The boy had been flung away by one of their attackers and lay in a heap near the hole going down the bunker.

It was all over before anyone could blink.

"WHAT JUST HAPPENED?" Mike exploded, trying to sit up as his vision cleared. "WHAT ATTACKED US?" Apart from him, the female sergeant and the two kids, every other person in view lay motionless on the hard ground. "OH, MY GOD!" Mike ran up to a comrade and checked the soldier's pulse. The man was dead. "What the hell's going on?" he wondered aloud, quickly picking up a rifle lying near the first aid kit. "What the hell's going on?" A whimpering Sergeant Linda had let go of the little girl, holding her painful shoulder and scanning the mayhem caused by their uninvited guests with an incredulous stare. Rahim lay near the bunker's door rubbing his eyes as well as his bloody left leg.

"This is your fault!" the little girl shouted at Mike's female comrade, raising more unanswered questions. "I wish I never met you!"

"Wh-What do you mean?" the soldier found himself stammering as he stared around. "Is everyone dead?" He stepped up to the ladder going into the bunker and disappeared down it.

"You caused this," Rachel said, eyeing Kimberley through slits. "We could have left when we had the chance."

"Yes," Aiden grumbled, glaring at Kimberley. "We could have prevented this from happening."

"How?" Mike asked, emerging from the bunker with a white face. "What is going on, Lin?" he asked Kimberley, who just sat there looking defeated and broken. "Can't believe everyone's dead."

"Everyone's dead," the female sergeant repeated in a choked voice. "Everyone's dead, and it's my fault."

"We need to leave this place," Mike snapped, waking from his trance. "Those things could come back, you know, and..." He caught sight of the book with the little girl and remembered a very puzzling scene in the terror that had quickly unraveled around him a few seconds ago. "What's with the book?" he asked her. "Why were those things after it?" The kid couldn't say a word.

"It's nothing, Mike," Kimberley lied, but her marine comrade was no fool.

"Strange as it sounds, did you get that book from them, little one?" Mike demanded. "Did you know they will attack us?"

"We all knew about them," the boy, Rahim, revealed, standing up.

"What?" Lance Corporal Mike couldn't believe his ears. He turned to his comrade for confirmation, but she simply looked away. "Okay…what was your mission, Lin?"

There was no reply.

"What the hell was your mission, Lin?" Mike repeated, suddenly choking up as he tried to blink back blinding tears. He reloaded his M16. "What did you uncover during this mission, Lin?" He pointed the gun at her.

Rahim and his sister rushed behind the female sergeant on seeing this and she looked up. "Go ahead and shoot me, Mike," she replied dejectedly. "I–I don't deserve to live anymore."

"Wh…What was your mission, soldier?" Mike shouted, trying to control his rage. "Tell me before I put a bullet through your…"

The Lance Corporal threw his arms into the air and Kimberley went for his falling rifle. She spun it round and opened fire in one quick motion, forgetting her pain as she crashed to the ground on her side. Carl Bain dodged her shots by going behind a stationary truck, and she ceaselessly pumped more bullets into the vehicle's body, keeping him where he was.

"Get to the bunker!" she ordered Aiden, and the boy dragged Rachel's cowering figure from where they'd been taking cover. Kimberley had their enemy pinned down, so it was a matter of scampering down the ladder without looking up. The wounded officer followed them, spewing venom at the army truck as she got to the ladder and started down it. The next instant, she was slamming the armored trapdoor and bolting it shut.

Carl Bain stepped out once she stopped shooting and unleashed his rage on the cursed door, shouting at the top of his voice. His bullets soon ran out and he spat at the structure preventing him from getting his enemies. "I'll keep coming after you until you give me what is mine, damn it!" he growled.

But down below, nobody heard him, because Rachel had already performed a simple ritual with her mysterious time portal.

Chapter 5
SIERRA LEONE

THEY walked as fast as their legs could carry them.

"Where're we going?" Aiden asked.

"Can we just stop?" Rachel cried. "We don't even know where we are."

Kimberley said nothing. She wore a white overall, like a doctor's coat, and she wasn't with an M16A4 rifle anymore, which was a bigger headache at the moment. "Still got the book?" she asked Rachel and the girl nodded, trying to keep up with her long strides. The boy struggled as well.

"Can we just stop?" Rachel repeated, trying to catch her breath. "Where are we?"

"Africa," Kimberley said.

"How did you know?" Aiden began. "This could be Haiti or...or Jamaica."

Kimberley shrugged. She'd forgotten he was a brilliant student. How he left school was another story. "That old sign by the road," she simply said, pointing at a signpost beside their path.

They were really in Africa. Apart from the guidepost, some dark-skinned children were playing nearby as the sun mercilessly beat down on them. Oddly, Kimberley thought the kids were risking their lives by playing together. Whatever made her think that?

"Freetown, Sierra Leone, fifteen miles?" Aiden read out.

"That helps, really," Rachel groaned as she trudged on.

"Why don't they attack us now?" Kimberley wondered aloud.

"What?" Rachel asked her.

"Why don't they attack us now?" Kimberley repeated, turning to the little girl as she walked.

"They take a longer route?" Aiden began.

"I don't believe that," Kimberley said, glaring at Rachel.

"The–The book is still cold," the younger female replied. "But it won't be for long, so we have to…"

"Figured as much," the sergeant muttered. She'd known about the bizarre occurrence for some time now. Everything going chilly before going crazy. It happened at the station back home…and at the outpost in Afghanistan. And it came from the book? "This–This cold actually wards them off?" she asked Rachel.

"Yes," the girl said. "Since I've been traveling with the book, I have…I've always known that the cold air it emanates when the Gray Ones are near protects me. Looks like it only defends the…Bookbearer and his or her fellow travelers against the Gray Ones when…they attack. Every other living thing around at the time always…dies."

"Interesting," Aiden said.

"Very funny," Kimberley said.

"We must hurry," Rachel said. "They will definitely appear anytime soon." She quickened her pace, looking around furtively.

"You wanted us to stop moments ago, now you're pushing us to move faster?" Aiden grumbled.

"We have no choice now if we want to live," Rachel said. "The Gray Ones…"

"They haven't killed us yet, have they?" Aiden quipped.

"Yes, but…"

"If they want to attack us, the right time is now," Kimberley said. "We're sitting ducks here." She pushed her hands into her laboratory coat's side pockets and felt something hard and cold in the left one. Carl Baine's cuboidal property. "That's weird," she muttered.

"What's weird?" Aiden demanded.

Before she could respond, Kimberley heard a car coming up behind them, on a bend down the dusty road. Looking the other way, she saw the minivan. "Let's ask for directions, shall we?" she told the kids.

Aiden sighed. "If only we knew what we should be doing here," he said.

"We will meet Ezra here," Rachel revealed.

"Who?" Kimberley demanded.

"Ezra. My father's friend back at the Mine."

"How did you know that?"

"I wrote down his name and touched it to bring us here," Rachel said. "We'll just have to find him before…"

"And that's how you've been going around?" Aiden interrupted her.

"By writing down and touching people's names?"

"People I know," the little girl clarified.

"So you mean to tell us that you write down these names and you touch anyone and you go to the place in time this person currently resides?" Kimberley was holding her forehead.

"Well, yes," Rachel said.

"But you'll move these people further into the future when you write down their names, right?" Aiden wondered aloud.

"I guess so," Rachel said, frowning.

"Still you'll meet them when you touch their names, wherever you've moved them to, wherever they eventually find themselves in space and time," Kimberley concluded for the strange girl. "Just brilliant," she added sarcastically. "Will you know this Ezra fellow when you see him?"

"Who wouldn't?" Rachel began. "He's short, fat and always happy. Who wouldn't recognize him a mile away?"

"And where do you think we'll find him, smart girl?" Aiden put in.

"In a school or some university," the little girl revealed. "I usually find the people I am looking for in such places."

"So we'll find him in a university here," Kimberley started.

"Or a hospital," Rachel added. "Anywhere there is professional work going on."

For once, Kimberley admired the girl's attentive evaluation of the bizarre situation they'd all found themselves in, wondering whether this same strange individual was saying the truth, or comfortably stammering.

The old Toyota Sienna drew nearer. It had three African occupants. A man and a woman sat at the front, while a young boy took up the last seat behind the man, who drove the car.

"Good evening, Dr. Katie," the driver said through his open window once he pulled up. "I hope all is well?"

"How do you mean?" Kimberley blurted out. She had no idea where the conversation was headed.

"I mean, you're on foot, doctor," the man explained. "What happened to your car?"

"It broke down a few minutes ago," Kimberley said. She didn't know what she was saying. Then she realized she had briefly held the man's hand moments ago. Did that contribute in anyway to the words she'd been uttering? Strangely, she felt so.

"Is it the red Cherokee back there?"

"Yes," Kimberley replied.

"Can it be fixed now?" the man asked her. "Luckily, I have my tool kit with me."

"Don't worry," Kimberley said. "A team is coming for it, and us, just that they're really taking time." She still felt strange. "Where are you going with your family, Sankoh?" That one came from nowhere.

"I'm taking my son to the capital," Sankoh said. "He's not feeling well and I think a doctor needs to look at him."

"What's wrong with him?" Rachel wanted to know, looking around as if she was expecting an unearthly intrusion anytime soon.

"Nothing serious, young lady," Sankoh replied. "Nothing a hospital visit cannot take care of." The woman seated beside Sankoh nodded. Kimberley knew this lady to be the man's wife.

The sergeant-turned-doctor looked at the boy sitting far behind the man driving the Sienna. Her new doctor's knowledge of Ebola told her that the emergency was being handled as well as the present situation would allow. Besides, the boy's father seemed quite sure of his assessment of his son's condition and she saw nothing unusual to doubt his evaluation when she looked his child over.

Now, she turned back to the car's driver. Speaking about the virus could rattle the man's confidence in deciding what was best for his son. And besides, the boy would get the best available treatment in the capital. "We need to get to Freetown as well," Kimberley said. "Can we hitch a ride with you?"

"Of course," Sankoh said. "You must be itching to get back to your work on the virus. That is very important work, right?" His wife nodded again.

"Exactly," Kimberley said with ironic satisfaction. The man just brought up the one thing she'd tried to keep from him. "I am not just a doctor; I'm also a scientist investigating the Ebola virus."

"Well, yes, that…that is correct," Sankoh stammered, staring at the lady in a laboratory coat. "At least, you told us that much when you came to our town meeting yesterday, remember?" He opened the car door to the passenger space behind him and looked on as the little girl with the American scientist refused to enter his car.

"I'm not going with you," Rachel told him.

"Why not?" a frustrated Kimberley asked.

"You know why," Rachel burst out, turning to the female-sergeant-turned-scientist. "We're putting them in danger! The Gray Ones will get them if we travel with them since the book cannot protect many people at once."

"What do you mean, my dear?" Sankoh asked her.

"She is talking of a movie she saw yesterday, sir," Aiden said as quickly as he could. "Please ignore her."

"We don't have all day, Stacey," Kimberley told Rachel. "Besides, the Gray Ones will catch up with us if we don't get to Freetown and meet Ezra before they get here, right?"

"Maybe," Rachel said, uncertainty written all over her face.

"Are we still thinking about this?" Kimberley grumbled, and both kids climbed into the Sienna before she followed suit. She helped them fasten their seatbelts before locking herself down.

"So we'll find this…Ezra in Freetown?" Aiden whispered to Rachel and Kimberley frowned at him.

"Maybe," Rachel said.

"It doesn't matter if we catch the virus, Mum," Aiden whispered to Kimberley and Sankoh's wife turned around in consternation. "We'll leave this place and time once we meet Ezra and he succeeds in stopping those things, right?" This question went to Rachel.

"Maybe," the little girl repeated.

"What things?" the woman in the front passenger seat asked Aiden.

"Don't mind him," Kimberley told her. "Harvey likes making things up. Too much time on his PlayStation."

"Are these your children, doctor?" Sankoh wanted to know.

"Yes, they're leaving the country," Kimberley said, glancing furtively at Aiden and Rachel. "They–They're off to a holiday back home." She knew better. The Ebola situation was getting out of hand and, having lived for sometime in the country with her kids, she'd thought it best to send them back before things got worse. Where did all that memory come from?

"You mean it's not about the pandemic?" Sankoh asked, starting his car's engine.

"Yes."

"So, you don't travel with luggage?"

"Their father took their things to Freetown yesterday," the police-sergeant-turned-Ebola-scientist lied.

Sankoh's wife turned to her husband. She looked worried.

"We've been very careful with David," Sankoh told Kimberley as the Toyota slowly picked up speed. "We've made sure since this whole thing started that he's home-schooled. So, I really don't think his condition is anything other than a simple cold."

"The hospital will find out what the matter is," Kimberley told the man's wife in a bid to allay her fears. "Hope you took his temperature?"

"36.5 degrees," Sankoh said. "That's why I don't think it is anything worse than a cold."

"I pray you're right," his wife said.

Kimberley noted the frown on the woman's beautiful face. She also caught Aiden glancing at the boy in the car's back seat from time to time. She nudged him, but couldn't help looking, herself.

David could be Aiden's junior by a year. He just sat there respectfully and quietly. He smiled at the American scientist, whose attention appeared drawn to his face for reasons best known to her.

Kimberley's gaze remained on the boy's face, because her voice had failed her when she saw what she saw.

Was that blood on his nose?

The Sienna bounced once and flipped over as if upturned by a gigantic hand. Glass shattered on both sides of the vehicle as Sankoh's wife started screaming. Everything slowed down as long shimmering hands plunged into the vehicle's cabin through the broken windows. Kimberley realized she was shouting like the others. She saw the hands before her scarily pass through Sankoh's head in a ghostlike manner. His wife didn't escape the same fate.

The slow motion stopped and the old Toyota slid off the dusty road on its roof, halting a few feet away.

*   *   *

Carl Bain looked around and sighed. He wore white like the other four men. White with a surgical cap, goggles for his eyes, respirator for his lungs, and yellow rubber gloves and boots for his hands and feet respectively. The piece of paper with the girl's name had brought him here once he touched the name like he did the first time. At least, he thought, his Caucasian targets would stand out if they were in the vicinity since all he could see were black faces.

"Hey," he called out to one of the men with him. "Where are we?"

The man appeared puzzled by the question. "Excuse me, sir?"

"Where are we, I mean, which part of town are we in?" Carl Bain tried to reframe.

"We're miles from Freetown, sir," another man said, quizzically looking at the foreigner.

"Okay," Carl Bain said. "Thanks." Freetown meant Sierra Leone, so he'd been brought to West Africa by the mysterious paper. "Have you seen any other foreigner here?"

"That should be in Freetown," the first man said.

"Right, so I need to get to Freetown now," Carl Bain said. He moved to remove his gloves.

"No, sir, please don't," a third man warned him. "We're already in an Ebola-infected house. You know you can only do that when you go outside."

"So, where the hell is the exit door?" the American snapped.

"Our instructions are to bury the occupant of this house, disinfect the rooms before going back to Freetown, sir," the first man said angrily. "If you go back to Freetown now, your action will cause us our jobs."

"Watch me," Carl Bain said. He turned to leave the passageway in which they all presently occupied and two of the men blocked his path. They were both tall and hefty looking men. "Out of my way, will you?" he ordered them, eyeing a frying pan hanging from a nail on the wall to his left.

"We'll soon go back to Freetown, sir," the fourth man, who carried a spray tank, said. "This is just a burial procedure, and it will not take time."

"Don't think that because you're a white man, you can do anything you want to do here, sir," the first man threatened respectfully. "You have a job to do like the rest of us. You're behaving like this, because you're in Africa."

"And remember you're here to witness this and report back to the center in Freetown, sir," one of the men blocking his way added. "Which car do you even want to go to Freetown with? Just know that I'll never hand you the keys to our SUV. Freetown is very far from here, if you must know." His fellow Sierra Leoneans joined his short laughter.

Carl Bain studied the situation. They would all join hands to pummel him if it came down to a fight, and even if he could finally dash to safety, he couldn't walk to Freetown if it was miles away like they just told him. He still needed to get the car keys from one of the hefty men now blocking his path. The fellow would never hand over that possession without breaking his neck first. He wished he still had that Kalashnikov. "Okay," he said as the Africans looked on. "Let's be quick, then."

He slammed his right fist into the face closest to him, dodged an incoming blow from his right and kicked the man with the spray tank in the groin. Grabbing the frying pan on his left, Carl Bain avoided a second blow from the hunk with the car keys and slammed the cooking utensil into his first attacker's left flank.

Mr. Keys got an uppercut from the pan and sprawled on the floor.

The remaining Africans tried to avoid being hit by the mad American holding the instrument that had knocked out their colleague. They hoped for a chance to charge this offensive white man again as they drew nearer.

But Carl Bain had other ideas. He attacked first, swinging the aluminum pan in an arch, which connected with a head and blacked someone out.

The last man turned and fled just as the foreigner stopped before Mr.

Keys, who lay motionless on the cold floor.

The American bent down and felt the knocked-out hunk's sides for signs of a key. "Your friends underestimated me," he told the fellow carrying the tank, who lay groaning some feet away. "Now I'll be on my way."

Looking around, he found a pair of scissors on a table in the passageway and used it to slit the hefty man's protective suit to free the car keys.

"You're a mad man," the African carrying the spray tank said. "Now, he'll be infected with Ebola!"

"He won't be worried about that if he's dead," Carl Bain pointed out.

"But he's still breathing."

"Then he'll be worried when he wakes up. You can use that thing you're carrying on him, then. This is an emergency, right?"

Stepping outside with the frying pan in hand, Carl Bain noticed the angry villagers chanting a few feet from the compound. They didn't pose any threat since they couldn't attack him for fear of the virus. He pulled off his goggles, respirator, gloves and boots, and discarded the protective suit. Nobody approached him when he left the compound. They just made a pathway for the mad foreigner with a frying pan as he walked to the Toyota RAV4 parked beside a mango tree. Who knew where he would find the trio holding his property now? Who even knew whether these targets of his were still in that African country?

The last thing Carl Bain saw as he drove away were his friends in the brawl trying to resuscitate Mr. Keys in front of the Ebola victim's house. Of course, they must have notified the authorities about the incident, but being chased by the local cops and army did not bother the American behind the RAV4's wheel as much as knowing that he must have exposed himself to a deadly virus he'd never heard of before then.

All this would go away once he killed that police sergeant and retrieved his property. The virus, the authorities now probably chasing him, and this cursed country. He would find a way to go back to his time and place with the paper, which must have come from that white book the little girl with his prey had with her. Maybe he would confiscate that book as well. Maybe it would help him get back to Portwood faster.

Chapter 6
DAVID'S INFECTION & THE SIENNA OFFENSIVES

KIMBERLEY started and searing pain shot through the back of her head. She looked around her and realized the car's ceiling hung beneath her. She still had her safety belt on, meaning that they still sat in the Sienna. Upside down, that is.

The vehicle started rocking from side to side.

"They're getting bolder. We must hurry now!" a fearful Rachel said beside Aiden, who turned his head slightly, feeling the car's ceiling with his hands.

"Let's get out," Kimberley told the boy and struggled to free herself from her seat. Using her left hand, she blocked her fall onto the car's ceiling before slowly lowering her body once she was free from the seat.

She forced a door open before unfastening Aiden and helping him to crawl out of the car. The boy gasped at seeing Sankoh and his wife still strapped to the front seats and rocking from side to side with the car's rhythm. Kimberley didn't know how to deal with that tragedy at the moment, although she knew that Aiden and Rachel must have figured out what happened to their hosts on their own. What of the man's son?

Turning back into the vehicle, she picked out the boy, David, at the back row of seats. He looked terrified. "Hang on in there," she told him, and proceeded to unfasten Rachel's seatbelt, gently lowering the little girl afterwards.

As Rachel crawled out with her precious book firmly underneath her right arm, Kimberley adjusted the seats so that she could get to the boy at the back, whose nose wasn't bleeding.

What had she seen before the accident?

"Daddy…," he began.

"I'll look him up," Kimberley told the boy. "Let's get you out first." She could be wrong about his having the virus. After all, his father found his temperature to be fairly normal.

An explosion jolted her as Sankoh's son screamed from the back seat. Looking back, Kimberley saw that the Toyota's rear windshield had shattered. The car's mysterious rocking increased to become vibrations shaking her soul. Destabilizing fatigue gripped her in slow motion, and she thought she saw long eerie hands grope into the vehicle a second time. Amidst screams coming from Rachel, Aiden and David, who was still with her in the car, Kimberley blacked out when an unearthly hand reached for her face as a fading image of a small gust twirling round Rachel's book in the distance persisted before her.

She woke up sprawled on the upturned car's ceiling.

"Daddy," David groaned and Kimberley recollected what just happened. The dragging fatigue had gone, so she knelt upright, reached out and released the boy's seatbelt. He craned his neck to see what sat in the car's driver's seat, but Kimberley prevented a good view by turning him towards the open door and guiding him out with some force. She silently thanked Aiden for instinctively pulling the boy to the Toyota's rear as soon as he got out of the car. "I want to see my parents!" the boy said as the sergeant-turned-scientist crept out of the upturned vehicle.

A worn-out Rachel sat before the Sienna's open door amidst heaps of ash Kimberley could not fit into the picture before her. Aiden still held the boy, David, to her left. "That was a second attack," Kimberley said.

"And we–we survived it," Rachel breathed, scratching her hair.

"There was no warning," Kimberley realized. "The weather didn't turn cold like before the previous attacks."

"It didn't warn us in the car as well," Rachel pointed out.

"Maybe they've found a way to go round the book's warning system?" Aiden suggested with a frown. "What good has the warning done for us, anyway? None at all."

"I want to see my daddy!" David began again.

"You've got to calm down first, okay?" Aiden cajoled the younger boy, resisting his efforts to break free. "Just calm down first, okay? Then you'll see him."

"No."

"What are those?" Kimberley asked Rachel, pointing at the ash-like mounds littered around the place.

"What's left of them," Rachel said. "What's left of the ones that froze out and were left behind."

"You mean the book did this to them?"

"Yes," the little girl said. "They used to go with their dead, but they don't do that anymore."

"Wonder why," Aiden said as he held David, who had stopped struggling.

"They almost took the book this time, Kim," Rachel began.

Kimberley noted the fear in the strange girl's voice. Rachel had also called her by name for the first time. The Portwood police sergeant felt protective.

"I want to see my parents!" David cried, again.

"They'll soon be back," Aiden replied. "They left us a short while ago."

"I don't believe you," David said. "They're in our car. Let me see them."

"They're dead," Rachel said. "They have really left us."

Stunned by Rachel's insensitivity, Aiden released David, who ran up to the front windshield and gaped at the black forms strapped to the Sienna's front seats. He started crying.

"Now, see what you've done," Kimberley accused Rachel, glaring at the little girl while walking past.

"Yeah, see what you've done," an angry Aiden directed at Rachel as he followed the police sergeant. "I hope you'll go console him now."

"He would have found out sooner or later," Rachel said, frowning all of a sudden. "How did he survive the first and...and second attack?"

"No time for that now," Kimberley said, stepping away from the Toyota Sienna. "We need to get to Freetown as quickly as possible and find Ezra." Actually, she had thought of that same question moments ago.

"What about him?" Aiden wondered aloud, pointing at Sankoh's son.

"David, come with us," Kimberley urged, and the boy rejected the idea by shaking his head. "I hate to say this," the sergeant-turned-scientist said, "but he's not our priority now."

"Maybe his people will come looking for him, or someone would definitely drive by soon," Aiden added, deep in thought. "Nobody should go through this."

"Remember I warned that this would happen, Kim," Rachel reminded the sergeant. "I could have stood my ground if not for you two."

"And if you had done that, we wouldn't have made it this far by now," Aiden said.

"Yeah, maybe, but David's parents would still be alive by now," Rachel shot back.

Kimberley sighed as she watched David crying near the Sienna's front end. She reached into her pant's side pocket and brought out something she had always felt was lying right there in the pocket. A mobile phone. "Maybe he won't come with us," she said, "but we can still call for help."

The phone at the other end rang twice before someone picked up the call. "Emergency, may I help you?"

"Yes, I came across an accident on my way to Freetown from Hastings," Kimberley lied. "I think the only living victim is suffering from Ebola, hence I cannot help him since I'm not protected."

"Name, please?"

"Dr. Katie Halverson, *Médecins Sans Frontières.*"

"Okay, doctor, we'll take it from here," the operator at the other end said and hung up.

"Thanks," Kimberley said, putting back her cellphone. She looked at David one last time, smiled at him and turned away. Starting up the dusty road, with Aiden and Rachel closely behind her, Kimberley sighed. The boy was not bleeding from the nose. That meant he might just have the common cold, but calling for help using Ebola as an excuse was necessary since she wasn't sure about his condition, and they had exposed themselves to him for no fault of theirs. If David was infected, her only hope now lay on their having several days to a few weeks on their hands before manifesting symptoms of the disease and putting people they come in contact with at risk.

"Must we walk?" Aiden complained.

"We need to keep walking until we're picked up," Rachel said. "We can't wait around for a third attack. It will take them time to regroup since they just lost many, but we need to be on the move. We can't just wait or hang around for them."

"If only we had a car," Aiden groaned, trudging on alongside Kimberley. "We can't outpace or outrun these guys, you know, but we can quickly get to Freetown and find Mr. Ezra if we had a car."

"You have a point," Rachel said.

"There could be a fatal accident if we're in a car next time they attack us," Kimberley reasoned. "The open could be our best chance of survival now." Unnatural cold permeated the atmosphere as soon as she finished uttering these words, and she turned to a frightened Rachel, eyes questioning.

"They're coming back, aren't they?" Aiden asked. "What do we…."

Everything became a blur as the rushing wind swept Aiden off his feet and pushed Kimberley back towards the Sienna. The boy from Portwood crashed to the ground as Rachel shrieked away.

"What's going on?" Aiden cried, trying to grab and hold on to some small shrubs for dear life. Kimberley struggled to maintain her balance to his left. Rachel he couldn't spot in the confusion surrounding him, but he knew he just heard her voice.

"Stay together!" she kept shouting despite the din made by the howling wind. "Stay together! They want to separate us!"

From the corner of his eyes, Aiden noticed that David had left the Toyota's side. The African boy could be shielding himself behind the vehicle, he thought. A better situation than the scenario he'd found himself in at the moment as he tried to maintain his grip on the little shrubs keeping him from going backward.

Just then, someone pulled him up from the ground. Kimberley knelt before him, her knees going behind the small deep-rooted shrubs for support. The Portwood police officer struggled to maintain her grip on Rachel's right hand as well. Aiden followed her lead and hooked his shoes behind the little plants nearest to him, immediately appreciating the additional stability this action gave him and the woman before him, who'd been pulling him in order to prevent the unearthly wind from pushing him back to the car.

"Can't...Can't hold you two anymore!" Kimberley cried, feeling her grip on the two kids loosen. "I'm feeling tired!"

Aiden also felt drowsy. Like it was bed time. "I'm sleepy!" he warned.

"Noooo!" Rachel said. "Don't let them separate us! They're trying to weaken you two before they...."

Kimberley screamed and let go of the two before her. She saw Aiden fighting with the wind to remain where he knelt before she blacked out.

Aiden quickly caught Rachel's free hand before the wind uprooted him from his good foundation. Both kids fell and slid back dangerously with Kimberley's body. The Toyota's front end blocked their path, sticking them underneath the car's front windshield and hood, while Kimberley's body went round the car's windshield and disappeared from view.

The wind swept round the heavy automobile's streamlined shape, allowing the vehicle to remain where it lay on its roof.

Aiden felt helpless and worn out. He peered round the Sienna's windshield and gaped at Kimberley's body wrapped round a sturdy shrub a few feet away, He turned to Rachel, who shook with despair. "They're coming, right?" he asked her.

"Yes," the girl said, tightly clutching her precious book to her chest.

"Is that not cold?" Aiden asked her drowsily, nodding sluggishly towards the book.

"Yes....Yes, it is," Rachel agreed, her teeth beginning to chatter.

"I can help you...keep warm," Aiden offered, beginning to draw her close to himself.

"But...But you're not a...Bookbearer," Rachel shouted, halting him. "You–You could both...die this time!" she added. "Aiden, I'm so...so sorry!"

"Kim's not dead," Aiden said. "I–I don't believe it."

"She...She could be dead," Rachel said. "I've seen this before...." Tears streamed down her cheeks. "They–They attacked her from behind."

"Not true!" Aiden cried, starting forward a bit shakily. "Kimberley!" he shouted. "Please, get up!" He felt heavy, and couldn't move another inch. Suddenly dazed, he blinked twice before falling on his face.

Rachel screamed. Long hands got to her book from before her, their owners whining horrendously. She tightened her arms around the book as the weaker demons froze off with the wind. Despite the cold power emanating from the ancient scroll and surrounding the little girl like a force shield, more infernal hands got to her arms after brazenly penetrating the spherical region surrounding her. These unearthly appendages struggled to unclasp the girl's hands from the white book. A second set of spirits reached out and started pulling the book out of her grip, hoping to succeed as soon as her arms failed her. "Father, save me!" Rachel shouted in despair, feeling her will to fight giving way with the strength in her arms. "Father, help me!"

She had repeated every defensive word he ever taught her that fateful day just as she had faithfully done ever since she fled the Mine. Why were things no longer working as they should? Her arms felt weak, as if they were infused with a drowsy spell.

Since the demons could not get into her mind, Rachel realized that they had gone after her physical members instead, especially her upper limbs. Try as much as she could, her arms refused to obey her mind anymore. Her prayers were failing her. Her world was crashing down. The hope of getting back to the Mine was fast fading. Nothing was working anymore. Her will, and arms in extension, had lost the battle for her.

The Gray Ones had won.

Suddenly, the torment her arms were going through ceased. She tried to maintain her grip on the revered book, but her fingers felt numb. The white book slipped from underneath her arms and she thought the end had come.

It turned into ice and Rachel stared at the savior her father had sent to rescue her. Aiden held the book with her, his teeth chattering as some of the Gray Ones, weakened by their lengthy stay near the unearthly powers emanating from the book, burst into ash all around the children. Seeing failure staring them in the face for the umpteenth time, the stronger demons retreated as the howling wind slowly faded away.

"How did you do that?" an amazed Rachel asked Aiden, trying to resist the cold surrounding her.

"No idea," Aiden said, looking around. "Guess it worked, though."

"Yeah, for now. Are…Are you really from your town?"

"Yes," Aiden replied with surprise. "Why do you ask?"

"I–I really don't know."

Rachel had a quizzical look on her face as she sat there staring at Aiden, who appeared uncomfortable with that level of attention. "Kimberley!" he remembered, dashing out of their partial enclave with renewed vigor. The Portwood police sergeant raised her head and uncoiled from the shrub. Aiden stopped before her, delighted to see her alive.

"Look…. Look for David," Kimberley told the boy, sitting up. "I blacked out again, didn't I?"

"Yeah, but you're still alive, that's what's important, Kim," Aiden said, turning away to look for Sankoh's son.

David had hidden behind the Sienna all through the third attack the Gray Ones orchestrated. He stepped out when the foreign boy approached him.

"You okay?" Aiden asked the West African boy.

"Yes," David said. "I thought it would rain."

"Me, too."

"Your sister was so scared of the wind that she could not stop crying."

"Yes," Aiden agreed, looking the other boy over. "Sure you don't want to come with us?"

"No, I will wait here. Someone will come for me."

"Okay, Aiden, let's go," Kimberley called out to her younger companion from the Sienna's front end. She hoped someone would stop for the African boy and take him to a hospital. She just wished she could do more than leave him out in the open without any help for his sickness save for a call to the Ebola health center in Kerry town. With Aiden following her, she turned and walked towards Rachel.

Wait.

"Disease!"

"And what about that?" Aiden asked.

"I know this is far-fetched, but infection could be exactly why David can't be killed by the Gray Ones," Kimberley said.

"Is that possible?"Aiden wondered aloud. "I mean, he's not infected, right?"

"He could have a cold like his father said," Kimberley aired grudgingly. "For one, he's not showing any visible symptoms of Ebola if he has it, so I don't know for sure if he is infected with the virus or just having a common cold, and I don't know whether this protection from the Gray Ones comes before the symptoms show or afterwards in the case of Ebola."

"Wow," Aiden said. "I can't understand all that, you know?"

"Yeah, I'm sorry," Kimberley apologized. "Forgot you were a kid."

After awhile, Aiden turned to the officer. "David's nose was bleeding when I met him behind the car," he began.

"Oh no!" Kimberley exclaimed. "I was right after all."

"Is that important?" Aiden asked.

"He must have cleaned it with his T-shirt in the car," Kimberley told him. "A hemorrhaging nose indicates a more deadly strain of the Ebola virus, and we've ignorantly exposed ourselves to this boy."

"At least, we now know what might have protected him from the Gray Ones, right?" Aiden summarized.

"Of course," the sergeant agreed, trying to appear calm. "Any infection like the common cold, or Ebola if I was wrong about the common cold, could be the reason for that. Whatever it is, he's being protected by the very same thing he's suffering from."

"Okay," Rachel said, a puzzled look on her face. She'd kept to herself for a good reason. Aiden's help near the Sienna still baffled her.

"But all this will not matter if we find this Ezra guy in time and leave this place as soon as possible," Kimberley concluded. "Though we have to mind how we relate with people now since we're potential carriers of this crazy disease I still don't know how I got to know so much about."

Aiden was quizzically staring at her.

"These people will remain here long after we've gone, so we need to be careful from now on," Kimberley broke down for him.

"Right," Rachel grumbled.

"That's confusing," Aiden said. "You're implying there are millions of alternate times and worlds out there?"

"That's comforting to know," Rachel chuckled. "The book is mysterious. I don't think that's what she's implying."

"Shouldn't we just worry about the mystery we're witnessing right now?" Aiden began. "And if there are millions of alternate times and worlds out there, we really need to leave before the infection spreads through us?"

"No need to worry," Kimberley told him. "We still have several days to a few weeks before we start showing symptoms of the infection if we have the virus, and there is no transmission if those symptoms don't show, so we should be long gone before then. Am I saying too much?"

"Yes?" Rachel seemed frustrated. "We've got to focus on defeating the Gray Ones?"

"Of course," Kimberley agreed.

They trudged on for a few more minutes.

"I helped Rachel fight off the Gray Ones this last time, Kim," Aiden announced and Rachel glared at him.

"How?" Kimberley appeared lost.

"You know, I helped her hold the book and it felt cold, but they couldn't fight her anymore."

"That's great," Kimberley said dryly, frowning. "Yeah, maybe the three of us should hold it next time. Maybe that would end all our problems and take us back to Portwood."

"You don't believe me." Aiden felt bad.

"You talk too much," Rachel told him. "Thanks, though."

"And I do believe you," Kimberley added. "Thanks for saving all our lives." Of course, the boy would front signs of bravery to cover his inadequacies in the face of the daunting situation they'd all found themselves in. A normal mammalian reaction to scenarios eliciting stark fear. She doubted the story.

"Did you notice that the small shrubs and grass all around us have dried up?" Aiden asked her.

"Yes, I did," Kimberley replied, taking Rachel's hand. "They leave nothing alive, right, Rachel?"

"Right," the little girl said.

Moments later, the time-travelers set out towards Freetown, grateful to be alive amidst the madness all around them. A signpost they walked past announced to the world that the state capital was two miles away.

Overhead, a brewing storm darkened the sky.

*   *   *

The raging winds persisted, twirling up to the higher levels of the atmosphere with the fury unleashed on the local weather by the invisible entities exhibiting pitiless frustration in defeat. Howling with demonic annoyance at the four corners of the Earth and beyond, they duly ascertained their spiritual territory, expressing their sorrowful disappointment in an unearthly manner reminiscent of their former glory as Yahweh's Angels of Perseverance.

They'd been beaten back again. No thanks to the powerful endowment granted the Bookmakers by their biggest enemy of the current mission. And as a result of this, the white book remained beyond their reach, in the hands of a little girl whose father had bestowed the greatest responsibility he would ever know, even as he lay dying on a cave floor.

The indescribable shapes of the Gray Ones shimmered, wafted and shifted about in the stormy atmosphere their anger had created way above any human settlement. Searching for answers to their faceless existence in the swishing silence of the physical logic all around them, they continued their grumbling in hell's own language despite the fact that one of their worst enemies at the moment resided in that gloomy abode of unquenchable fire and brimstones. Of course, they knew that no concrete conclusion could ever be drawn from this pointless endeavor of questioning every aspect of their destiny while under punishment for disobeying Yahweh, yet they could not resist this boring habit honed over thousands of years of fruitless wandering.

Embarrassingly, the Black Ones had succeeded in retrieving the other book from the boy, and were patiently waiting for success on their part. One that now seemed quite elusive owing to the losses they were incurring in the course of this physical expedition.

Amidst the gloom pervading their tortuous beings, their leader, a tough veteran of the Beginning, meandered about with a message of hope and eventual success. This gave the weaker ones some form of consolation for their kind already lost to the white book's defensive mechanism, which was a hellish protection that had exhibited its raw power time and time again.

The grotesque demon leading the group came to a halt above the land mass down below and identified their target leaving the upturned vehicle with her two companions and the mysterious book. The book's unearthly protection was weaker when they had only her to contend with, but now that there were three travelers, things had become a bit more complicated. The said spiritual defense appeared to have been strengthened by the coming of the other two individuals, who, it seemed, were yet to understand what was going on. The problem these two naïve humans posed for the demons was clearly highlighted by the events that had occurred near the damaged car moments ago, when the demons had pressed home three attacks to no avail.

Angrily, the faceless demon leader unleashed multiple thunder strikes on the surrounding countryside. The number of fallen angels already destroyed by Lucifer's breath was staggering and the mission could not afford to continue on this wasteful path.

A new plan was needed, and quickly, too.

*   *   *

He'd been riding the motor bike for almost three hours now despite the developing storm, tensing up whenever a police or military truck sped past. The authorities would still be searching for a stolen Toyota RAV4, he thought with a wry smile, increasing the motorcycle's speed.

Of course, the RAV4 had been a big mistake. Replacing it with a Honda bike near a gas station was the best decision he could come up with, and he did this after he saw himself on a TV newsflash walking out of a deceased woman's house with a frying pan in one hand.

He had taken the helmet with a tinted visor, gloves and scarf from the bike's dead owner. These items were doing a good job of hiding his identity from the soldiers and policemen he had been coming across these past few hours. He just hoped the signposts along the way were accurate about the distance he still had to cover to get to Freetown.

Three kilometers outside Freetown, Carl Bain came across an accident few feet from the dusty road he'd been traveling on. A Toyota Sienna rested on its roof facing a direction perpendicular to the road. The ploughed soil markings behind the minivan gave one the impression that it had flipped over and then slid off the road when the accident occurred. The boy crying while kneeling beside the upturned car's front end had blood on the front of his T-shirt, and this only increased the American hitman's curiosity. Why were cars just swishing past without stopping to offer assistance to the victim of such a calamitous accident?

Carl Bain stopped the bike and alighted from it. Without a word, he stepped over to the Toyota and peered into it, missing nothing. The vehicle had a shattered rear windshield, and the explosive force that did this could be assessed by observing the numerous tiny glass fragments scattered all over the car's ceiling.

Walking past the tearful boy without saying a word, Mr. Bain frowned at what he saw next. Two burnt figures still sat upside-down, strapped to the car's front seats. He wondered what relationship these two had with the kid. Were they his parents? Probably.

Slowly, the foreigner looked his present companion over. The kid's bleeding nose could have been due to the accident, he thought, or something else. Ebola? That could explain why no driver wanted to stop and help. How he knew about symptoms of the disease he could not tell. "Hey, boy," he began, "what's your name?"

"David."

"What happened here, David?"

No reply. Just tearful sobbing and sniffling. Carl Bain sighed and scanned the area. He noticed the scorched grass and small dried-up shrubs surrounding the car. He squatted to look into the Toyota through its right open passenger door. Nothing to see inside. Just more sand and ash.

Ash?

Looked like ash, really. The area surrounding the upturned Sienna had heaps of the thing littered about, as if dumped around chaotically. And what of the caked brown sand inside the car and on its ceiling? The American felt the dirt was more than enough for a boy traveling with his parents.

"Did you have any other passengers with you, kid?"

"Yes, sir," David replied.

"What happened to them, then?"

"They went that way," the boy said, pointing towards the direction Carl Bain was headed. "They did not wait for me."

"Why not?" the American asked. "Why did they leave you behind?"

"I do not know them, sir," the boy replied. "They are not my people, so I refused to go with them."

"What do you mean they're not your people, kid?"

"They have white skin, sir. They are your people."

"Interesting," Carl Bain said slowly. "How many are they?"

"Three, sir. A female doctor, a boy and a girl."

"Thank you, son," the American said, striding back to the bike with a renewed sense of purpose. As he distanced the area, he saw an ambulance appear on the road behind the upturned Sienna.

It started raining heavily.

Chapter 7
EZRA

THE downpour continued to pelt the vehicle's roof and reduce the visibility of its side windows. The truck's windshield wipers were at full speed, repeatedly swishing to and fro in the merciless rain as the Toyota Hilux sped through the deserted streets of Freetown, evading portholes and bumping around whenever it couldn't dodge these road traps. Presently, Kimberley noted the many police and military checkpoints they had passed along the way. President Ernest Bai Koroma was clearly leaving nothing to chance, and how she got to know his name she couldn't tell.

"The streets are empty," Aiden quipped.

"Can't you see it's raining?" Kimberley asked him.

"What of the outbreak?" Aiden began. "It's raining now, but..."

"Yes, the government ordered a lockdown due to the outbreak," the police driver who had picked up the three time-travelers on the outskirts of the state capital said. "We know it's a desperate move as well as a face-saving measure."

"Why do you call it a face-saving measure?" Kimberley asked him.

"Our leaders have lost the fight to contain the epidemic without outside help, doctor," the man said. "Some families are anonymously leaving dead bodies in the streets of various towns and cities around the country for fear of being quarantined by the authorities if they properly deposed of these bodies."

"Wow," Kimberley said.

"They are also aware of the accompanying castigation if the news of death gets to neighbors," the police officer added.

"So they follow a more contagious line of action," Kimberley concluded for him.

"Yes, exactly, doctor."

A gray dress pegged to a line and fluttering in the heavy downpour reminded Kimberley of the Gray Ones as the pickup truck sped past. The Portwood police sergeant marveled at the persistence of Rachel's infernal pursuers, wondering how long they could withstand these ferocious attackers with the strange girl before something tragic happened. The bizarre shifting entities were yet to attack Kimberley and her co-travelers again after their third offensive that day. Risking the ride into town became necessary due to the urgent need to shelter from the rain and find Rachel's link as soon as possible. So far, no unfortunate event had unfolded as a result of that decision.

Ironically, Kimberley thought, their second threat and very agile human nemesis, who'd followed them all the way from Portwood with the aim of retrieving his small metal cube, had remained markedly absent ever since they appeared in the small West African country of Sierra Leone.

Kimberley hoped that this mad man had lost his way in the labyrinth of time and space, maybe showing up in Jupiter or one of those Godforsaken planets seven hundred years after the present date. That would be comforting to know, really, since she feared dying in another time and place through the activities of this unwavering fellow, who appeared bent on snuffing out their lives at all cost.

The ominous possibility of facing a similar fate in the hands of the Gray Ones equally horrified the sergeant-turned-doctor. She hated this madness Rachel's book had unleashed on her life, as well as Aiden's. How were they going to revisit Michael in Afghanistan, and Jim, her boyfriend, and all those now dead in their wake, and possibly bring these individuals back to life, if at all such a miraculous phenomenon existed? Impossible. Could the book do that? Could the book reverse time?

"The rain is slowing down," Aiden said. "The vehicle's wipers are doing less work."

"Sure," Kimberley said, deep in thought. Had Rachel been telling them the truth when she said that the book could only make one go forward in time? Was there some way these horrendous events could be erased and things returned to the way they used to be? If there was such a way, Kimberley thought, then shouldn't she force it out of Rachel if she had to? Shouldn't she do this now that she thought they were running out of time?

The Toyota Hilux slowed down and stopped. Their guide had brought them to one of the city's two Ebola treatment centers, and as they jumped down from his police truck in the drizzling rain, Kimberley felt relieved that they had made some progress in their journey despite the odds against them. "Thank you," she told the police officer as she took in the surrounding countryside.

"The man you're looking for is the new head of the laboratory here, doctor," the driver said. "Your description fits him exactly."

Silently, Kimberley thanked Rachel for earlier describing the man they had all come to know as Ezra. She had only relayed to the police officer what the little girl had told her about the man's features: short, fat and always happy. "I never knew he had..."

"Yes, this Israeli arrived a few days ago," the driver interrupted, grateful to be of help. "I got the information from one of the men working here with the burial teams."

"And what of the boy?"

"He was picked up by an ambulance a few minutes ago. They'll bring him here very soon and run some tests to know if he has the virus."

"Okay, good job then," Kimberley said, glad that David would get the care he deserved after the tragedy his family had gone through while helping strangers.

"Good luck, doctor," the officer said, starting his car and putting it into reverse, "and thank you for all the work you're doing for my country."

"Thank you, too," Kimberley whispered as the vehicle zoomed off. Hopefully, they would find Ezra in time for him to help them defeat the Gray Ones before their viral symptoms showed up. It didn't matter where they went after this, as long as they left that place and time with the book's help, thereby ridding themselves of the scourge called Ebola.

"What now?" Aiden asked, staring at the EBOLA CENTER sign before the health facility's heavily guarded gates. "I hope they've got food. My tummy's rumbling."

Kimberley looked him over. Though danger still loomed, the tension had dissipated enough for her to notice what her fellow travelers had on. Aiden looked good in his gray T-shirt and blue denims despite the muddy smears on him, while Rachel's pink sweater and purple pants reminded Kimberley of her younger days. "Yes, let's go in," she finally said. "I hope they'll have some food, too."

A military guard at the gate gave them a cursory nod before flinging open a small side gate for them to pass through, his fellow soldiers looking on. "Welcome, doctor," he said, nodding a second time towards Kimberley, who nodded back.

"How do they...how did he?" Kimberley whispered as soon as they were out of earshot.

"You have an ID card on your coat pocket," Rachel pointed out, eyes straight.

"Oh, right," her senior companion said, noticing the small tag for the first time. No wonder the police driver identified her correctly. He'd left her wondering about that little thing, really.

White makeshift tents surrounded by more traditional structures filled their view. Medical personnel, health workers and some soldiers completed the busy picture. Four men in personal protective equipment stepped out of a building carrying a body bag and headed towards a parked ambulance near the gate as the trio crossed a busy road before this building. Burial team, Kimberley thought.

She steered the children towards a central structure she felt was the command post. "If he's in charge of the laboratory, I think we'll get Ezra's location from staff working here," she explained to Rachel's puzzled stare. "No need to start looking for the research lab on our own, right?"

"Yeah," Aiden supported. "My hunger won't allow for such a waste of time."

"Maybe, we should find a place to eat first," Kimberley proposed, eyeing her younger male companion.

"No," Rachel objected. "We must find Ezra first."

"And die of hunger in the process?" Aiden asked her. He grinned when she couldn't reply him despite his discomfort. He could hear his stomach groaning as he stepped into the building and his smile turned into a scowl.

The building had air-conditioning. Its structure consisted of a locally sourced wooden frame, which bore the weight of its hurriedly attached plywood wall panels well enough. Several tables lined one end of the vast room into which the entrance door introduced any visitor, and behind these set of identical furniture sat a squad of young men and women attending to telephones on the tables.

"Excuse me, but can you direct us to the research laboratory in this facility, please?" Kimberley asked the first person she came across.

"Sorry, doctor," the young African lady said with a smile. "I joined the center yesterday and I'm not yet familiar with its management arms. You can ask someone else, or maybe you'll meet who you're looking for here."

"Okay, thanks," Kimberley said and looked around her.

"Let's look around," Rachel proposed. "Maybe we'll find him faster that way."

"Okay," Kimberley agreed. She searched for a foreign face in the sea of humanity sweating away despite the air condition humming in the background, but found none. "Remember, don't touch anything or anyone," she told her kids, watching Stacey look around for their target as if her life depended on it. "We're not in the clear, yet." She doubted if they heard her since they seemed to have gone out of earshot. Well then, she must...

A face she knew too well had come up on a flat screen mounted on a corner of the large room's wooden wall support. A newscaster was warning the public to be on the lookout for the foreigner on the display, who had killed a motorcyclist that day. Disturbed by this new twist to their unfolding situation, Kimberley watched their human nemesis climb into a Toyota RAV4 and zoom off, wondering how he had been able to remain on their trail ever since he started chasing them. A piece of torn paper from Rachel's book, perhaps? The fellow must have come into the country behind them, and should be looking for them at that very moment. How she wished they would be able to find this Ezra in time and...

"Can I help you, doctor?"

"Yes, sure," Kimberley said, turning to the voice she thought had a tinge of Middle Eastern flare. "I guess I've found you," she added, smiling. Of course, he was short, fat and looked very pleased with himself. "You must be..."

"Dr. Isaacs, borrowed by the UK government from the Israeli Center for Disease Research," the fellow wearing a pair of thin-rimmed glasses chuckled. "And you must be Dr. Katie from your pocket tag."

"Yes, of course," Kimberley said, gratefully taking his outstretched hand. "I'm Dr. Katie Halverson from *Médecins Sans Frontières*, or Doctors without Borders in English."

"So, can I help you, doctor?" Dr. Isaacs, who Rachel also called Ezra, asked the Portwood sergeant, smiling contagiously.

"Well, sure, I'm...I'm bringing in a boy I met on my way here. He appears to be showing symptoms of the disease."

"No problem," the man said, still smiling. "Our laboratory is now fully functional and we'll get a result as soon as possible when he arrives."

"Okay."

"As you know, the British government is putting together a huge response unit for this crises and the RFA *Argus* will dock here in Freetown a few days from today. We have supplies coming in on that ship and I must excuse myself now, doctor," the Israeli said, stepping backward.

"Great," Kimberley began, realizing what she must do. "We equally have heavy machinery on that ship and I hope you don't mind if I can run through some specifics with you in your office?"

65

"Fine by me, doctor." The man's smile remained unwavering.

And Kimberley sighed in relief. She saw Rachel and Aiden coming back, their faces unabashedly expressing their excitement.

"And these must be your kids, doctor," the short jovial man before her said.

"Yeah," Kimberley replied, seizing Rachel's right hand as the little girl walked up to the man with determined steps. "They are leaving for the airport a few minutes from now."

"Okay, this is the right time to leave, right?" Ezra said, shaking Aiden's right hand. He laughed heartily. "Just a joke, doctor, just a joke. Come, let us all go to my office."

As the disease researcher led the way towards his office, Kimberley dropped Rachel's hand by her side. "Not yet," she whispered to the impatient girl.

"But we have to hurry!" Rachel shot back, tucking the white book underneath her left armpit. "There's no time!"

"I know," Kimberley said softly. "Have some patience, okay?" The sergeant-turned-doctor knew that only the strange girl could change Dr. Isaacs to his ancient self. Neither she nor Aiden could do that magic, perhaps since they were both from Portwood and their present target never resided there in the past.

There were so many people in the emergency response room, though, and Kimberley knew they couldn't risk any mistake at that point. If Dr. Isaacs was to become his old self with Rachel's help, then it must be done in a secluded area, like his office.

"Do you know that Freetown was first settled in 1787 by four hundred formerly enslaved blacks sent from the UK?" Dr. Isaacs told them as they passed a sparsely occupied passageway.

"No, sir," Aiden replied.

"These blacks were African-Americans, Afro-Caribbeans, Africans, Southeast Asians, and blacks born in Britain," their host continued warmly. "They established the 'Province of Freedom' and the settlement of Granville Town on land purchased from local Koya Temne sub-chief, King Tom, and Regent Naimbana."

"You seem to know a lot about this town," Kimberley commended, watching the passageway traffic. Not yet, she silently told a restless Rachel by shaking her head from side to side. There were still people in the passageway.

"Yes," Ezra said to Kimberley's assumption. "History is a hubby I pride myself in, Dr. Katie. Right, here we are." A paneled door stood flush with the passageway wall after which the long corridor veered off into another corridor to their left. The short doctor used his key to unlock this door, which led into his office.

Rachel touched the man's hand as they all trooped into the room furnished with a small desk and four locally made chairs. Kimberley noticed his pupils disappear for awhile before reappearing with a different shade of brown as its hue. She couldn't be more grateful for his next question, meant for the strange little girl from the Mine.

"Rachel, is…is that really you?" Dr. Isaacs wondered aloud, staring at the little girl he knew to be his friend's daughter. His countenance had changed, but his smile remained on his face, though a bit more subtle.

"Yes, dear uncle," Rachel began, stepping forward. "Shalom."

"Shalom. You survived! Praise the Lord," Ezra said with relief, and then his smile faded. "You brought me here from France? You fled with the white book, or a piece of it, right? Is that…it?"

Rachel nodded, showing her uncle the book. "I came with my father's blessing," she said. "He said I should move forward in time until I find someone who can help me defeat our enemies." The little girl was closely watching the man's reaction with Aiden and Kimberley. "I escaped before father could give me the names of those he said would help me, and I've been looking for those I know ever since. I need to go back to Rome after defeating the Gray Ones."

"And they are after you?"

"Yes, uncle. They give me no rest."

"Then you must…"

Aiden cleared his throat and the other three individuals turned to him. "Sorry," he began, "but do you have anything to eat in this place?" he asked the man called Ezra. "My stomach's quite empty."

*   *   *

At first, the ambulance driver refused to come out of the vehicle, cursing the man urging him to do this in the local Creole dialect. When he finally stepped out, he didn't shake the motorcyclist's outstretched hand, nor did he want to hear the man's confusing explanation afterwards. He didn't even notice anything unusual in the fact that the bike rider gesticulated more often than was necessary and communicated in an awkward voice whenever the need to say something arose. The Sierra Leonean ambulance driver with a wife and two kids in Waterloo only felt that this fellow standing before him covered from head to toe in fashionable motorcycle garb was delaying his lunch break back at the health center by going on and on about a sick woman presently lying in the forest flanking the road.

Of course, the ambulance driver was also covered from head to toe in gear necessary for his work. What he didn't know was that the motorcyclist disturbing him had already decided that this personal protective equipment, or PPE, which the African wore, would be a nice fit, since they were of the same height and size.

"So, where is she?" the Sierra Leonean wanted to know, impatiently heading towards the thick undergrowth beside the road.

"Very close by," Carl Bain muttered softly behind the man, pointing further into the forest. "She is vomiting."

The driver quickened his pace on hearing this. He didn't see his guide bring out motorcycle rope and twist the ends around both hands. He only wanted to help a fellow Sierra Leonean and get back to the hospital and his lunch before his break ended. He stopped after pushing through the thick undergrowth for some time and scanned the area. "Where is she?" he asked the man behind him without looking back.

Tough synthetic cord dug into his windpipe and he struggled to catch his breath. Unable to loosen the braided baggage rope, he groped for the hands behind their strength, falling on both knees when he realized the futility of this attempt. Now he punched away at the human trunk behind him with both elbows in a bid to distract the person snuffing out his life, and when this did not work, he tried to scream, producing only hoarse sound. All this effort at breaking free from his attacker forced him to gasp for air that failed to reach his lungs, and now short of breath, he noticed his vision deeming quickly and pulled on the biker's jacket and helmet with his failing strength, knowing that death stared at him in the face. He stopped doing this when he couldn't muster enough strength to continue doing so, and towards the end, he could only swing his arms around. Pointlessly.

Carl Bain knelt down behind the African and waited for the flailing hands before him to go limp. His victim's head slumped forward in death, and he waited some more to be sure of the man's current status before loosening the weapon he had used to murder the careless man.

Few minutes later, he emerged from the forest in the dead man's protective gear, hopped into the ambulance, made sure that the sick boy was still sitting in the emergency compartment behind him and started the engine.

"Where is the other man?" his only passenger called out to him.

No reply. Carl Bain started the engine and put the gear control in drive.

"We are going to be late," the boy complained.

The new driver looked straight ahead. "Don't worry, boy," he sneered in that same awkward voice. "I'll get you to the hospital in no time." And the boy said nothing, having hopefully noticed nothing out of place.

The ambulance started moving.

*   *   *

For the first time since they left Portwood, Kimberley's mind went back to all that had happened after she came across Rachel's freezing body on that snow-covered road near David's grocery store. Jim's death she was yet to accept, often telling herself it was a bad dream that would unravel once morning arrived. But then, she would put food in her mouth, feeling the table's hard wood before her with her left hand as she ate, and the realization that this was really happening would dawn on her in a brutal manner. And her heart would start bleeding all over again for her dead boyfriend.

'Why did he have to die?' she kept wondering, throwing angry stares at the little girl eating across the table. If not for Rachel's appearance that snowy day, none of this would have happened. None of her colleagues at the station would have died. No, not Patrol Officer Bates, or the others.

Or Jim.

Jim would still be alive.

Feeling embarrassed, Aiden stopped eating when Kimberley turned her intense gaze on him. "What?" he gestured with his free hand.

"Been wondering why you left school," she mouthed. "You're very brilliant, you know."

Aiden's countenance changed and he dropped his head to concentrate on his plate. Obviously, he didn't like the subject.

"I've always wanted to ask you a question," Kimberley began, turning to Rachel as she changed the subject.

"Okay?" The little girl stopped eating and looked up.

"Why is your name all over the book's pages? I mean, if you've been going places with the names of your father's friends, where did you go to when you write down your name all that time?"

"I use my name to escape from the Gray Ones when I can't defend myself anymore," Rachel replied. "I appear somewhere and then write down the next name I had in mind, so that I can get to him or her."

Kimberley frowned. That sounded sensible.

"You haven't done that ever since we met," Aiden pointed out.

"I-I haven't been in a desperate position ever since I met you guys," Rachel stammered.

"Really?" Kimberley asked her. "We all know that's not true, Rachel."

The little girl did not look up from her food. "Okay, let's just say I haven't used it ever since I met you guys."

Ezra cleared his throat to get the attention of the three at table in his office. He tried to say something but the words wouldn't come out. An anticipatory Rachel had stopped eating; looking at him like her life depended on his next words. He swallowed hard and looked straight at her, summoning the courage to finally say it like he should. "You must go back."

"What?" Rachel began.

"What?" Kimberley cried, turning to the little girl. "I mean, what's he saying?"

Aiden had an expressionless face. His thoughts had gone wild all of a sudden.

"Rachel, what does he mean by what he just told us?" Kimberley demanded.

"I...He...," Rachel stuttered.

"What's the matter?" Dr. Isaacs finally asked. "Did I say something wrong?"

"No, doctor," Kimberley said, shaking her head from side to side. "Just that your niece here, or whatever, told us something entirely different about being able to go back to our time with the book?"

"And what did she tell you?"

Kimberley glared at Rachel. "I mean, you said that's impossible, right?"

"Yes," Rachel replied, trying to avoid all the eyes in the small office.

"And why would you say that?" her uncle asked her.

"To think that we trusted you," Aiden snapped. "You've been lying to us this whole time!"

"No...I–I didn't want to be alone anymore!" Rachel cried, turning back to face the others. "I–I was afraid!"

"And so you lied to us," Kimberley concluded for her. "You made us go through what we've gone through, because you were afraid of losing us as friends? We couldn't go back to our own homes, because you didn't want to lose us as friends? Who does that to a friend, huh?"

Rachel kept quiet. There was nothing more to say.

"How do you go back with the book, Ezra?" Kimberley asked the little girl's uncle.

"Well, you write your name behind the leaf on which you've earlier written your name when you wanted to be brought forward in time."

"Wow," Kimberley said. "That simple, huh?"

"But that's not all that I wanted to tell you," the Israeli doctor said, turning back to Rachel. "Rachel, you must find a way to give the book back to the Gray Ones."

"No!" Rachel cried, standing up and walking away from the group.

"Okay, I didn't get that," Aiden said, confused.

"What do you mean?" Kimberley asked Ezra, her hands spread out. "I mean, why should that be a priority now?"

"That's the only way," the short man said, his permanent smile having since disappeared. "That's the only way to stop all this…madness."

"Father said to go forward until I find someone who can help me," Rachel said with conviction, tightly embracing the leather-bound book with both arms. "There is no other way."

Ezra seemed desperate. "Look," he said, going round the table in the office to get to his dead friend's daughter. "Your father will be proud of you, Rachel. You've done your best. This is the only way to have rest."

"You're telling me to give up."

"No, I'm just saying you deserve to be free of all this," her uncle urged her. "You need not be the Bookbearer if you don't want to."

"And what happens if she gives the book back to those…things?" Kimberley wanted to know.

"That must be after you're returned to your time, doctor."

"Actually, I'm a police officer in my time," Kimberley pointed out.

"Well, officer…"

"Sergeant Kimberley Reyna."

"Well, sergeant, the Booklords will stop at nothing until they take back that book."

"The Booklords?" Aiden began. "They're also called the Gray Ones, right?"

"You know them as the Gray Ones, but actually, they are not the only group of Booklords. The second group is the Black Ones," Ezra told him. "This second set of Booklords went after the black book."

"The black book?" Kimberley asked him. "Is that the other book's name?"

"Eh, yes, my dear," Ezra said. "Fitting names, eh? Black and white. Hot and cold."

"The black book gets hot?" Aiden asked. "What's it…"

"Made of?" Ezra brightened. "Well, it's…"

"What's the story behind the Booklords?" Kimberley interrupted. "What must we know now?"

"Can't go into details," the Israeli said, looking worried. "Just know that it's in your best interest to return the book to them."

"Why?" Aiden wanted to know, and Rachel's uncle sighed.

"Look," he began, "these things have been after me ever since I fled the Mine. They've been tormenting me in order to get information about the book from me."

"Okay," Kimberley said, frowning.

"Truth is that they desperately want that book back, and they can't get it unless the Bookbearer with it gives it back willingly. At least, it's a lot easier getting it that way than the way they've been going about it."

Aiden sighed. "And how did you know all this, sir?"

"They communicated with me in my sleep," the man said, studying the boy.

"Uncle Ezra, how could you?" Rachel cried. "How could you make such a mistake?"

"It wasn't a choice I made," her uncle said. "They controlled my mind. They can control anyone they want to."

"They cannot control me," Rachel snapped.

"Believe me, child," her uncle said. "They can do any…"

"You've failed your people, uncle," his little niece interrupted, turning to Aiden and Kimberley. "Let's go."

"Go where?" Kimberley asked the little girl. "We still have unanswered questions."

"Please, don't listen to him anymore, Kim," the strange girl begged her. "He's lying to you."

"Like you lied to us?" Aiden asked.

"What more do you want to know, sergeant?" Ezra asked Kimberley.

"Why do you keep talking about returning the book to them?" she asked him. "Do these…these Booklords own the book?"

"Actually, there are two books," Ezra began.

"Yep, we already know that," Aiden quipped.

"And these two books were crafted with the help of these…things. These…demons."

"So, it's not really their property?" Kimberley asked the man.

"It's…It's partly owned by them," Ezra tried to explain. "They put in more work than the Bookmakers."

"Another new one," Aiden noted.

"Not true," Rachel denied. "The Bookmakers are my people who made the physical books from a special papyrus before the Booklords imparted spells into them."

Aiden kept staring at her.

Kimberley slowly let out breath. "Okay."

"God gave us the two books," Rachel said, "and after He fell out with the messengers He assigned to us, these angels-turned-demons wanted to seize the power in the books and God gave us the Fire and Ice of Masada to protect the books with."

"Fire and Ice of what?" Kimberley began.

"That was folklore cooked up to encourage us, my dear," Ezra told his niece. "Even your father knew the truth."

"No!" Rachel cried. "You lie!"

"I think so, too," Kimberley said, having made up her mind. "You've been lying to us, doctor."

"No, you have to believe me, sergeant," Rachel's uncle said. "Everything I just told you is true."

"You're working with those things for whatever selfish reason," Kimberley pointed out, "and I can see that now." She turned to Aiden. "Let's go."

"Hello, she lied to us?" Aiden began, pointing at Rachel. "Can we trust her again?"

"Please.... Please don't go," Ezra pleaded with them. "Please take my advice and return that evil book."

Kimberley noticed the unease in his voice. "And why should we go back to those things you called demons?" she wanted to know. "Demons aren't good news, you know?"

The doctor drew nearer. "They–They just want the book and nothing more," he said. "They have the other volume in their possession now. They need this one as well."

"They don't have the black book, uncle. They cannot face the Fire of Masada," Rachel said. "We need to go now, Kim."

"Wow," Aiden said, holding his head. Every statement in this journey kept throwing up more unanswered questions. He joined the other two as they headed for the office door.

Ezra looked like he could choke. "Anyway," he began. "They–They promised to fix things in your time if the book is returned to them."

Kimberley's heart skipped. "Did they promise that?" she asked.

"Yes," the man said. "They promised to bring things back to normal. To bring back the dead."

Kimberley froze in her tracks.

"Will they bring back Father?" Rachel asked her uncle. His face told her all she needed to know. "He's lying, Kim," she urged her fellow time-traveler, who seemed to be having second thoughts.

"Aiden, let's go back," Kimberley said, Ezra's last statement the reason for the change in her decision. She turned to Rachel. "Your uncle is right, Rachel," she said. "You need to move on. Come live with me in Portwood if you don't want to go back to your place and time."

The little girl stared at her, aghast. "Can't you see what he has done to you, Kim?" she demanded. "He's lying to you. We need to leave now before the Booklords show up." She turned to Aiden for support.

"I'm tired of running, Rachel," the boy said, looking down at his feet. "We need to stop running."

"Listen to your friends, Rachel," Ezra persuaded his dead friend's daughter, stepping forward, and the little girl ran to the door.

"No!" she cried, shaking the door's handle. "Stop talking!" Tears welled up from within her. She wanted to obey her father so badly, because she knew he had told her the truth. He would never lie to her. Of course, she could leave alone with the book if she wanted to, but she would then have to start looking for new friends again. She would then face the prospect of being lonely and afraid again. "I thought you were my friends," she cried, sobbing softly.

"Friends don't lie to one another," Aiden said. "We can't trust you anymore, Rachel."

People started shouting outside the office.

"What's happening?" Kimberley asked no one in particular.

Dr. Isaacs stepped forward and Rachel drew away from him. He unlocked his door and opened it. The confusion grew louder. The medical doctor looked outside his office. "Can't see anything around here," he said. "It must be in the phone room."

"The book is growing colder, Kim," Rachel announced in a trembling voice, drawing everybody's attention, especially her uncle's, back to herself.

"No, not here," the short man said, becoming panicky all of a sudden as he closed the door. "You must leave now!"

"What?" Kimberley couldn't believe her ears. "I thought you said we should return the book to the Gray Ones?"

"Yes, but–but not here," Rachel's uncle said, going over to the single window in his office to close it. "They told me they'll kill me if I couldn't convince the Bookbearer to give up the book."

"Then convince her," Aiden said. "She's right here."

"Unless you don't trust them," Kimberley told the Jew, keenly watching his dramatic behavior. She'd been fooled again. "Rachel, let's go."

The little girl brought out the book, but before she could open it, someone banged loudly on the door.

"What is it?" Ezra called out.

"We need to see your guests, sir!" the person replied. "It's a matter of utmost importance to the state!"

Before the Israeli doctor could respond, a vicious kick broke the door's lock, pushing the wooden structure back on its hinges and smashing it into the paneled wall of the small room. Five soldiers and two of the health center's personnel stood outside the small office. They all wore personal protective equipment and the soldiers had their firearms trained at the people in the office. Kimberley, Aiden and Rachel looked at one another in surprise.

"Step out of the office, please," a soldier ordered them, and they all obeyed him.

"What is the meaning of this?" Dr. Isaacs demanded from a fellow doctor, who he noticed among the health workers with the soldiers.

"An emergency, Dr. Isaacs," the man replied. "A driver with the Kerry Town facility says the suspected case he picked up from the road and brought here this afternoon described coming in contact with your guests, and now this suspected case has tested positive to a deadly form of the virus."

Kimberley sighed.

David.

Chapter 8
A DEADLY ALLIANCE

"BUT–But that can't be true," Dr. Isaacs said, stepping forward to stand beside Kimberley. "This is Dr. Katie Halverson of *Médecins Sans Frontières*, and I know she is an Ebola research specialist with expertise and experience in dealing with Ebola victims."

Kimberley rolled her eyes. Was she really all that?

"Well, sir," the doctor in the seven-man quarantine party began, "the driver of the ambulance that just came in says Dr. Halverson and the two kids with her had contact with the Ebola case he brought in, prior to an accident this same Ebola victim confirms they were all involved in."

"And due to this, Dr. Isaacs, they are to be quarantined immediately," a soldier directed, his AK-47 unwavering.

"That's okay," Kimberley said for want of something to say.

"I think that is the right thing to do," Dr. Isaacs agreed. "There's no need for us to get all worked up about it."

"And you too, doctor," his colleague told him. "You'll be quarantined with them."

"What?" Ezra couldn't hide his surprise. "If that's the case, then every staff in that communications room should be quarantined as well, including the soldiers at the gate," he said. "This is ridiculous."

Kimberley noted the cold weather and glanced at Rachel, who stood beside her. The little girl could not open the book and attempt escape without being noticed, though leaving at that moment was their best option if they didn't want to wait around for the Gray Ones. Who knew what would happen to any of them in a fight with those things this time around?

"Well then, Dr. Isaacs, I think you have no choice in this matter since you have been with these contacts longer than any staff who walked past them in the phone room. You know how this works," the doctor speaking for the quarantine task force concluded.

Dr. Isaacs felt he could convince the man. "But," he began.

"Please, sir," the doctor spokesman interrupted, "all your comforts will be taken care of during your quarantine, so there's no need to delay this any longer."

Again, Kimberley glanced at her two fellow time-travelers. Aiden held the book for Rachel while watching the ongoing scenario in order not to attract attention. The Jewish girl slowly opened the leather-bound volume, reaching out to Kimberley with her right hand.

"Watch them with that book!" someone in the seven-man party muttered and Kimberley started.

He was there.

She kicked the soldier standing next to her in the groin and grabbed the man's weapon as he doubled over. Covering Dr. Isaacs with the gun, Kimberley glared around menacingly. "Nobody moves or he dies!" she warned the startled Africans and personnel looking on. The man she had kicked lay on the floor groaning in pain. "Harvey, get your sister behind me," she told Aiden.

"I hope you know what you're doing!" Ezra told her, raising his hands in mock submission as Aiden pulled Rachel behind Kimberley.

"Now, we're going to go and if anybody does anything funny, the doctor dies," Kimberley announced, beginning to step backward with the kids behind her and her human shield in front.

"You must drop the weapon, doctor," the commanding officer leading the quarantine task force told Kimberley. His hands were trembling despite the deadly weapon they held. "You don't want the trouble you are bringing upon yourself and your family."

"I'll kill him if you test me," Kimberley returned. "And I mean it."

"No, she doesn't mean it," Carl Bain said in the same voice he'd been faking throughout that day, turning to the officer-in-charge. "Shoot her before she escapes with her children and spreads the virus."

"That man killed a motorcyclist today, captain," Kimberley told the Sierra Leonean commanding officer while maintaining her backward pace with the other three with her. "You might as well tell him to remove his PPE right now, because he's the man your army and police have been looking for, and he must have murdered the driver of that ambulance in order to get here."

Carl Bain raised his hands frustratingly and this deceit convinced the soldiers and health workers with him.

"He's a driver for the Kerry Town Ebola Treatment Center," the soldier leading the party said, looking at the suited Carl Bain with confidence. "You're wrong, doctor."

"Did you verify his ID, doctor?" Kimberley directed at the physician who earlier spoke for the group. "I bet he's been wearing that full suit ever since he came in here."

The soldiers now hesitated for a moment. Two of them faced the purported treatment center driver while the rest maintained their initial stance. The doctor with the group scratched his head. Of course, they had all assumed that the driver was genuine.

"Can we see your identification, please?" one of the officers pointing a gun at Carl Bain asked him.

"She's lying, dammit," Carl Bain snapped in his fake deep voice. He couldn't bear to see his three targets slip through his fingers again. "Shoot them, dammit!"

Still, the African soldiers hesitated. The female doctor could be telling the truth now that they'd paid more attention to the so-called driver's voice. However, this man standing in their midst and speaking in a weird manner seemed to be more interested in the trio holding the Israeli doctor hostage. He made no attempt to get his ID like he'd been told to do by one of the officers surrounding him, rather, he watched detachedly as the female doctor and her two companions approached the corner with their precious human deterrent.

Once they reached the end of the passageway, Carl Bain lost it.

He elbowed one of the corporals and started struggling with the man for his Kalashnikov. Before anyone could grasp what was happening, the American picked off the other soldiers with the gun while the Sierra Leonean private still held the weapon. Now he wrested away the rifle from its owner and turned it on the soldier as well as the whimperer who got kicked in the groin.

The Ebola suspects had since disappeared round the corner at the end of the passage. Carl Bain shot the doctor acting as spokesman for the task force before going after them and his precious package.

A corridor linked a large room to the corner Kimberley and her group had fled across. Bursting into the busy room filled with health workers, Kimberley turned and opened fire on the American hustler once he showed up after his killing spree.

Carl Bain had to dock back into the passageway he came from and fall on his knees in order to avoid bullets flying through the wooden wall panels. He released his own hell with a free hand bent round the corner.

And bodies dropped like bags of sand around the fleeing contact suspects and Dr. Isaacs, who ran ahead of Rachel and Aiden.

"When are you gonna use the book, Rachel?!" Aiden yelled as he ran.

"Once we stop running!" Rachel returned in flight.

"That must be very soon!" Ezra stressed. "The Booklords are definitely on their way!"

The group stopped behind a fallen metal cabinet, struggling to catch their breaths as Carl Bain's rifle rained death on the room's confused occupants. Rachel brought out the white book and turned to Kimberley in alarm. "I don't have any pen!" she cried.

"But you don't need any," her uncle reminded her. "You're going back in time, Rachel."

"No, I must finish what Father started," his friend's daughter said.

"Ezra, you're a doctor," Kimberley interrupted. "Give her your pen."

Aiden frowned, though he said nothing.

"Yes," Kimberley told him. "I have made up my mind to move forward. From what Ezra here have told us, the Gray Ones are not to be trusted."

"That is not true, doctor," Ezra began. "I…"

"Rachel lied to us, Kim," Aiden said. "Should we trust her?"

"Time will tell if she lied to us," Kimberley replied. The Portwood sergeant still felt she could find more truth in a young girl than in an adult like Ezra. She noticed the Bookmaker dejectedly hand Rachel a pen before she peered out from the side of the metal cabinet.

Pandemonium ruled the place, with people running around in confusion. Kimberley couldn't return fire for fear of hitting innocents, but her opponent cared less.

His right finger keeping his weapon's trigger depressed, Carl Bain emerged from the corner and walked towards the large room, pumping bullets into people's bodies. "Dammit!" he cried suddenly, his shoulder jerking backward from the direct hit. Falling to the ground, he felt his blood soak his Ebola suit at the left shoulder. More bullet holes appeared on the soft panels walling the corridor and he studied the situation from his position on the floor. The remaining center's guards must have opened fire in his direction from the compound outside the room and its connecting corridor.

Kimberley saw her opponent crash to the ground and gladly witnessed the gunfire directed at his position from outside. "What's keeping you, Rachel?" she asked the little girl beside her, turning to see what her young acquaintance was doing with the book. "Anytime now?"

"She can't write on it!" Aiden whispered fearfully.

"What do you mean she can't write on it?" Kimberley snapped.

"Its pages are frozen solid!" Ezra told her. "A massive attack is coming! May God help us all!"

"We–We can't go until they…they finish with us!" Rachel stammered.

Kimberley stooped beside the little girl to see what they were saying. The book's open two pages were like sheets of solid ice. "This time, we'll hold the book together," she told Aiden and Rachel.

"We could go backward, you know?" Aiden pointed out and Rachel glared at him.

"We can't trust what Ezra told us," Kimberley said. "He's in league with the Gray Ones. No, we have to press forward."

Ezra said nothing.

Crawling back to the corner before the long passageway, Carl Bain started shooting sporadically at the paneled walls of the structure's short corridor without seeing his targets stationed outside the building. The American heard satisfying yelps and screams from outside, though the present episode was a distraction. He needed to quickly enter the room his main targets were hunkered down in.

When more bullet holes appeared very close to his new position, Carl Bain moved further back into the passageway while maintaining his rapid fire with one hand. Noting that more soldiers could come at him through the passageway, he picked up the rifle of a dead soldier with his left hand and pointed it into the long passageway, perpendicular to his present direction of engagement. The bullets zinging around him were still too close for comfort.

"It's no use this time," Aiden said when Rachel tried to write on the white book again. The thin film of ice on the mysterious book's pages were very slippery. "What if we go back?" he suggested again.

"No," Rachel cried, angrily turning to him.

"It could buy us some time," Kimberley said after some thought. "Why is that happening?" she asked Rachel.

"What?"

"The names on the book's pages," Kimberley pointed out. "Why are they glowing blue?"

"I don't know," Rachel replied. "They do that all the time."

"The book must be trying to tell us how we could get out of this perilous situation," Ezra suggested.

"By touching any of the glowing names?" Aiden deduced.

"Of course," Kimberley said, turning to the stubborn girl beside her. "We could still press forward after this if we want to, Rachel," she said. "It really doesn't matter where we go, as long as we get out of here."

"We must move forward," Rachel insisted.

"We'll still do that afterwards," Aiden tried to make her see.

"Just put your finger on your name, already," Kimberley told Rachel.

"I won't!" Rachel said, closing the book. Kimberley took it from her and she became livid, reaching out for the book with both hands. "Give it back to me!"

"And why should I?" the sergeant snapped, taking the book beyond the strange girl's reach with her left hand. "Your father should never have trusted you with it in the first place, you know?"

"Only a Bookbearer can control the book's defense against the Booklords, sergeant," Ezra warned the police officer.

"This one doesn't deserve to," Kimberley returned. "She's a stubborn little..."

Icy pickles shot out from the book in-between her fingers and drove into a visible dome that emerged from nowhere, enveloping the four behind the metal cabinet. Several screeching demons appeared on this phenomenon's exterior like large black strokes of paint and remained plastered to it as if they could not enter or leave it. As if gravitational pull kept them there.

"Oh God!" Ezra whispered.

"They're here!" Aiden cried.

Kimberley's body froze as the icy extensions from the book she held in her left hand grew in size. She couldn't move at all, because cold unlike any she had ever witnessed in her life had crept into her being and soul. "Help me!" she whispered, fearing the worst. "Help me!"

Rachel responded by pushing her left hand in-between the long spiky strands sprouting from the white book in order to touch the volume.

Immediate warmth swept through Kimberley when the little girl touched the book. She realized she could move her right hand a little, cursing herself for not heeding Ezra's warning. The spikes from the book started giving off a bluish light that illuminated the dome's interior and supplemented the sharp rays of sunlight filtering in-between the opaque, ghost-like shapes now surrounding the book's defense.

Outside the room, Carl Bain saw the swirling storm around him. Some of the gray shapes swishing past him collided with him where he lay sprawled on the floor and his screaming knew no bounds as they tore through his body.

The Gray Ones converged around the book's unearthly dome in numbers never before witnessed. Droves of gray shimmered from the bottomless hell they called home, piling up around their colleagues surrounding the icy figment of the book's imagination. The weak ones quickly froze away as others took their place from hell. The ones strong enough to penetrate the dome without getting fried did so, reaching as far as its occupants and the book before freezing off. More reinforcements replaced their fellow demons around the book's defense and those it protected.

"Rachel, we need to get out of here!" Kimberley whispered with all her strength.

"I can't open the book," Rachel complained. "It's clasped shut!"

"Here, lemme help!" Aiden cried, going underneath Kimberley's left arm before reaching out for the book. He tried to force it open to no avail. "It won't budge!"

"I think they're trying to destroy the book's protection by confronting it with their infinite number and collapsing it on us in the process!" Ezra cried. "We must leave now!"

Aiden's fingers quickly became numb from their rubbing the book's frozen cover, but he refused to give up. "Something dramatic should be happening right now, Kim!" he cried.

Kimberley dropped the Kalashnikov she held in her right hand and assisted Aiden when she realized she could move her right arm about. Of course, she knew what the boy meant by 'something dramatic.' If he could join hands with Rachel to chase away the Gray Ones near Sankoh's car, then the three of them should be able to do, at least, something dramatic in the present situation.

Kimberley used to doubt the story.

Now, she badly wanted to believe anything.

The police sergeant pulled harder at the white book's cover. Harder than she had ever done. And the book's stiff cover rewarded her persistence by parting a bit.

"It's opening!" Aiden cried. "We only need to try harder!"

"Where is Ezra?" Kimberley asked.

Rachel turned to see that her uncle had left their spherical protection. "Uncle, no!" she shouted. He stood in the middle of the room, his hands raised high in the air.

"He slipped out just like that?" Aiden asked, putting a finger through the dome's shiny surface. Perhaps one could easily leave its protection, he thought. Would coming back in be just as easy?

Ezra, also known as Dr. Isaacs in the present dispensation, felt elated outside the white book's visible protection. "You cannot kill me now!" he shouted at the gray entities swarming past him as if they couldn't see him. "I am now invincible, you hear? YOU CANNOT KILL ME, YOU HEAR? I AM NO LONGER AFRAID OF YOU!"

"What're you doing?" Kimberley asked him, having regained her voice. "You will die, you fool!"

"No, I won't," the man said, marveling at the sight all around him. "I injected an attenuated strain of the Ebola virus into my cells this morning before your visit. Looks like they won't attack me because of this. I have defeated them with science at long last, my dear! Now, they'll leave me alone."

Kimberley gaped at the Israeli. So, they were right about David's infection saving his life from the Gray Ones? she thought. Which other ailment could do the same thing?

High above the area on which the massive battle for the book had commenced, the demon leading the Gray Ones focused its attention on the loud-mouthed fool praising himself down below. This weak human being, who could not convince the Bookbearer to part with the book, must be dealt with as quickly as possible.

Screeching horribly, the former angel shimmered in Ezra's face, intending to turn the man's will against himself or penetrate his flesh, all to no avail.

Ezra laughed at the grotesque thing before him instead, beating his chest. "I am invincible, you hear!" he shouted at the demon lord.

The fallen angel could only float impassively before him.

Stupefied, the three within the protective dome watched with horror as some of the demons fighting to penetrate the book's defense peeled off and descended on Dr. Isaacs instead.

"No, please don't kill him!" Rachel shouted, meaning to go out to help her uncle, but Kimberley held her back.

"Ha, ha, ha, ha, ha!" Ezra laughed as the unidentifiable shapes swarmed around him innocuously. He seemed to have forgotten about the man with the gun who'd been firing at them moments ago, because all the guns had stopped chattering, and what now remained was the imposing presence of the gray forms floating and twirling about, as well as the damp atmosphere of death these unearthly forces had brought with them.

Looking beyond the dead bodies strewn around the large room and adjoining corridor, the leading Gray One saw that the one man who had dared to struggle with its colleagues still lived.

Carl Bain twisted and turned as horrendous shapes of all sizes darted through his body, suspending him in the air many seconds at a time. It looked like something was keeping him alive, because all his opponents and the people working in the health facility lay dead within and around the center's buildings. Several howling evil things had appeared from nowhere to rip their bodies apart. Evil entities many now dead had assumed to be Ebola spirits since the virus had killed a lot of people in the treatment center.

Only the Ebola suspects near the steel cabinet, Ebola patients lying in the health facility's wards, and the man trashing about in the corridor, remained alive. While a magical dome protected the four behind the metallic file cabinet, the Ebola patients in the wards and the man in the corridor still lived for no known reason.

The volume of spirit-like beings zooming through Carl Bain's body could have destroyed any other person a long time ago, yet the American hitman still lived, shouting in pain as wave after wave of these things smashed into him to visibly emerge from the opposite part of his body.

His would-be killers prepared to attack him en mass by gathering at the door leading to the corridor.

"Where are they going?" Kimberley wondered aloud as most of the Gray Ones surrounding their dome defense and Rachel's uncle pulled off and wafted towards the corridor in which lay their human headache. "That guy is still alive?" she asked, wide-eyed.

For all their efforts, the book had refused to open a bit more. Even Rachel's little finger could not slip through the space the time-travelers had achieved between the white book's front cover and pages. Few demons atop the dome meant a reduced offensive against the white book, yet the unearthly protective force surrounding the mythical volume held over the three inside. Only Rachel's uncle stood outside this defense, smiling like he now had the upper hand and knew the secret to life as a result of this.

Instinctively, Ezra stepped back and touched the magical hemispherical phenomenon surrounding his friend's daughter and her acquaintances. His fingers could not penetrate it and he tried again, frowning. When he repeatedly got the same result, he tried to push his palms into the dome to no avail. A kind of magical force field held back his limbs from sliding into the infernal dome. Realizing what this meant, he started looking around fearfully.

"You have locked yourself out," Kimberley said, reading the man's thoughts correctly. "You think they will use the man in the corridor as a weapon."

"What?" Aiden's eyes were huge.

"Not really," Ezra denied, his facial expression telling a different story. "Give me the gun; I need to defend myself if it comes to that."

And Kimberley slid the rifle out of their dome-like protection without a second thought.

"Now, you must find a way to give me the book!" Ezra snapped, surprising even his dead friend's daughter.

"Uncle, how could you?" she shouted. "How could you lie to us?"

"I have no choice, my dear, if I must survive this," her uncle said.

"You fool!" Kimberley said coldly. "You think you can get away with this?"

"Do as I say or I'll kill you," Ezra ordered, pointing the Kalashnikov at her forehead.

"You forget nothing can pass through the dome," Aiden reminded the man, peering out from underneath Kimberley's hand.

Ezra tried to push the gun's muzzle through the book's defense and met a brick wall. He moved back and fired at the visible manifestation without warning, jolting Rachel into hugging Kimberley with all her might. The bullets simply ricocheted off the icy cage protecting the book.

"Not a good plan, right?" Aiden quipped.

"Dammit!" Ezra muttered, turning the gun and hitting the dome repeatedly. Nothing happened. "Give me the book, Rachel," he snapped in frustration. "Give it to me right now!"

"No way," Kimberley said. "I hope those things get you out there."

A huge swarm of gray persisted at the door leading to the short passage where Carl Bain struggled for his life. The demons seemed to be waiting for a signal, something to launch them towards the American lying before them. The ones around this man howled as they went in opposite directions, caressing their victim's hands while actually pulling him up and apart, arms spread out. Soon, the hitman dangled in the air in-between them, repeatedly registering his agony by screaming whenever the pain he bore became unbearable.

"What are they doing?" Rachel asked, peering out beside Kimberley.

"I don't know."

Again, the demon leader shimmered before Carl Bain, its hollow face an empty gloom. It screeched in hellish language and slowly merged with its victim.

"YEEEEEEEEAAAAAAAAAAAGGGGHHHH!" the American hustler let out, feeling submerged in gruesome pain. The screaming and merging continued for some time, with every physical ounce of the man rejecting the demon's interference, until the Booklord emerged from behind him and he slumped forward, sweating profusely and breathing hard.

Ezra gulped and moved backward.

"Wondering what you'll soon face?" Kimberley asked him, smiling wickedly. Aiden had resumed the herculean task of trying to open the book and she joined him alongside Rachel. Their lives could depend on whether they would succeed in doing this in time, she thought.

Now, the Gray Ones hanging at the door swished over to Carl Bain's suspended body and fused with him. Mouth wide open, he simply shook and gasped as this action took place. His eyes turned grayish and more furrows appeared on his forehead. His muscles toughened and his clothes and personal protective suit tightened around his body. He felt renewed and energized by his will to live with sharper and keener senses tuned to his environment.

"God help me!" Ezra whispered, gaping at this unearthly

transformation. The gun in his hand had become uselsss all of a sudden.

The Booklords now emerged from their new tool, having finally engorged him with power no living human being could contain. Carl Bain floated to the ground and picked his rifle as if a superior being controlled him. As if he must obey this superior being.

Subsequently, the demons wafted back to the dome in droves.

"Let me in, please!" Ezra begged those inside the book's mysteriously defensive entity, his eyes darting about for alternate escape routes.

"You brought this on yourself," Aiden told him.

"Uncle, run!" Rachel cried when the man now made new in the image of the Booklords headed their way.

Dr. Isaacs dashed out of the room's other door, firing sporadically at the human demon walking towards him. When he realized that the projectiles he had launched simply went through the monster after him, he threw away the gun and fled into the Ebola center's compound.

Carl Bain lifted his AK-47 and took aim at the short man running towards a fleet of parked cars near the center's gate. The sound of a single shot rang out far beyond the compound and its collection of dead bodies.

As Ezra's body crashed to the ground, the American hitman turned and walked back into the building from which he had emerged, ignoring some scared Sierra Leonean Ebola patients peering out from the windows of their quarantine wards. Since these were infected by the virus, the Booklords had avoided them while destroying every other living thing in the health facility.

"He's coming back!" Aiden cried, struggling to pull the white book open. Kimberley and Rachel joined him, ignoring the screeching Gray Ones plastering their infernal bodies on the dome every other second.

Carl Bain entered the room and opened fire on the spherical structure protecting the book. He turned the gun and tried to smash the impediment before him using the gun's butt and powerful swings. Discarding the useless weapon after this, he repeatedly slammed his fists into the icy contraption, ignoring his demonic masters fluttering about him as well as those plastered to the dome.

"We're safe in here as long as he can't break it!" Aiden cried, his fingers losing sensation again as he kept up his effort to open the cold book.

"We shouldn't wait to see if he can, should we?" Kimberley asked him. "I think it's opening!"

The white book parted some more, revealing more space in between its front cover and frozen pages. Rachel tried to slip in her little finger and shook her head. "I still can't," she said, dodging a ghostly arm from outside as the fearsome human figure confronting them landed another fist on the shell protecting them all.

The grayish shapes around the trio kept reaching out into the book's protection, simmering in flames as they tried to get at the precious scroll. The dome's human occupants tried to avoid these extended infernal limbs, but when they couldn't, the searing heat burned into their clothes and painfully scotched their skin, causing them to lose focus for a few precious seconds before the attacking limb freezes and wafts out of the magical cage.

"Yeow!" Kimberley screamed again when a thin hand pushed its way down her right leg and froze off as quickly.

Carl Bain looked around for furniture and found a table with which he attacked the dome once more, shattering the wooden construction atop the structure.

Aiden looked down to avoid a burning hand and discovered something interesting. "Here, try using this," he told Kimberley, wincing from a fresh burn on his shoulder as he handed the Portwood sergeant a piece of splintered wood.

"Where did you get that?" Kimberley demanded as the megalomaniac outside landed another blow on the stoic dome surrounding them.

"The wooden floor," Aiden replied. "The magic shield must have broken it up when it appeared around us!"

Nodding, the Portwood sergeant prodded the white book's cover with the wooden tool Aiden had given her. "It's working!" she told the others. "Quick, help me push it in!" The book opened a bit more with Aiden's help. Kimberley used the wooden fragment to prevent the space they'd created in between the pages from collapsing.

Rachel forced her little finger into this space.

"How would she see her name?" Aiden asked Kimberley.

"The names were glowing a while back," Kimberley returned.

"They're still glowing," Rachel said.

"So you just need to move towards a glow," Kimberley advised.

Carl Bain stopped hitting the dome with his fists, which were now bloodied and painful. He heard a faint crack when he kicked the icy contraption before him with his right foot. He repeated the action and got a satisfactory response from the book's mysterious cage.

Those in the unearthly structure heard this as well and fearfully looked at one another.

"Anytime now, Rachel!" Kimberley hastened the little girl.

"The wood is hindering my movements!" Rachel told her and the sergeant tried to shift the wedge a bit.

Again, Carl Bain landed his left foot on the dome and heard that same sound from the structure. Smiling, he walked over to his gun and picked it up.

Gunfire erupted in the large room, masking the pitiable screeches the horrendous Booklords were making. Some of these ghostly forms started pushing themselves into the once-invincible manifestation protecting the book, while Carl Bain's Kalashnikov rifle chattered away at its surface. Moments later, this hollow entity shattered into smithereens to reveal an empty space within.

Carl Bain vanished as well.

Chapter 9
ALEXANDRIA

"I'VE changed clothes," Aiden announced, patting himself all over. "That means we must have left Africa, and..."

"No time for that now," Kimberley interrupted, getting up from a chair and looking around her. She wondered why many people were shouting outside the large hall in which they'd found themselves in. She could hear clashing swords. Was that a large crowd fighting outside? "Are you with the book?" she asked Rachel.

The question jolted Rachel for a second. She looked lost and frightened. "No, I–I'm not."

"What?" Kimberley cried, the implications of the little girl's admission sinking in.

"But how?" Aiden asked.

Rachel turned to the wide ceiling-to-roof windows opening up to a balcony that ran round the hall, directing her companions' gaze to the rooftops of other buildings dotting the area outside. "I've been here before," she said. "Last time around, I found the book in a building across the yard from this place, but I almost got killed outside."

Kimberley thought the Jewish girl looked more learned for her age. More noble.

"They're fighting outside," Aiden said. "I think we've left Africa, though."

"Don't be so sure," Kimberley told him, looking around her. "We must have gone to another part of the continent, because I think I've seen those wall decorations in a history book before." She realized she'd been sitting on a throne-like chair and felt her attire for the first time. She wore a free-flowing gown with bracelets decorating her arms and sandals shoeing her feet.

"Yes," Rachel said. "We're still in Africa."

"Okay," Kimberley said, picking up a sheathed sword with fine decorations on its hilt, which lay beside the chair she previously occupied. Did Rachel have a new accent? Her attention went back to the markings and designs on the walls of the hall surrounding them. "We're in Egypt. Ancient Egypt."

"How did you know?" Aiden asked her, looking her over. "Come to think of it, you look like a queen, Kim."

"And you two look like my relations or something close to that," Kimberley added. "Come on, the Gray Ones and that mad man should be on their way and we must leave with that book before they show up."

She made for the huge double doors at the end of the lengthy hall with the others closely behind her. It appeared shut for a reason, which became apparent once the time-travelers reached it.

"They're fighting behind the door," Aiden said.

"Intruders must be trying to get in," Kimberley realized. "The guards must be outside these doors trying to fend them off."

"What do we do?" Aiden asked her.

"What did you do when you showed up here the first time, Rachel?" Kimberley asked the little girl.

"I didn't show up in this hall."

"Great," Aiden said in defeat.

"There must be an escape passage or something," Kimberley thought, turning from the door. "Come on; let's feel the walls for cracks, slits and stuff."

"That will take ages," Aiden complained.

"So we better start now," Kimberley told him. "Spread out."

People started banging on the door from outside as the trio fanned out inside the huge hall, feeling with their hands and searching with their eyes for any sign of a hidden contraption or a secret door.

"Found it!" Rachel announced near the golden throne at the hall's other end, and the others hurried to where she stood. An adult-sized gaping square opened into blackness beside her.

"And you also opened it," Aiden applauded. "Looks scary, though."

A swishing sound drew everyone's attention to the middle of the hall. A lone figure emerged from smoke swirling around him and drew two daggers from his sides. This character wore a toga and a sleeveless shirt-like top. Red bands wound round his bulging arm muscles and his bald head shone whenever evening sunlight filtered into the hall from the long windows. Kimberley cursed softly.

Carl Bain.

"It's him," she said. "Aiden, take Rachel down that passage. Be careful in there for there could be some traps. I just hope you will find your way out of this building." She took a burning reed torch from the wall above the secret exit and handed it to the boy. "Find the book and move on without me if I don't show up."

Aiden looked depressed. "But..."

"Go now," Kimberley urged him. "I must defend you two here. There's no other way."

Aiden nodded and took Rachel's right hand.

"We'll see you again, Kim," the little girl said as her older mate guided her through the secret door while holding up the torch.

"I hope so," Kimberley muttered, turning to face the present danger as she unsheathed the sword she still held.

"Your reign is over, false queen!" her old foe said as he approached her. "Egypt will forever be grateful to me for killing you!"

Kimberley laughed. The troubleshooter did not know who he was, thanks to the white book and the time shift. He must have even forgotten his cube.

The cube.

She wondered whether she still had it.

"And you must return what you took from me before I kill you!" the man continued. "My new friends relish the thought of killing you now that the white book is not in sight!"

He remembered.

Kimberley drew back when flames sprang from the two daggers Carl Bain wielded. Six black forms appeared behind him and drifted towards her. She thought of Aiden and Rachel in the dark escape passage.

"They will not go far, my love," the man she knew to be Carl Bain chuckled. "My new friends have already gone after them, and the white codex."

"They will never submit to you," Kimberley said, taking a defensive stance with her sword. When did she learn to do that? And what's with her accent, and language? That didn't sound like English, did it?

Her assailant came at her, his long flaming daggers expertly thrusting forward in-between her swings and jabs, which he skillfully avoided. His six infernal companions formed a circle around the fighting duo, and Kimberley wondered what they were up to as she fought off wave after wave of fiery attacks from her opponent.

*   *   *

Aiden led Rachel down some stony steps, the flaming reed torch showing the way. Egyptian hieroglyphs dotted the illuminated walls as both kids descended lower and lower into the tunnel. This suddenly opened up into a sizeable room filled with all kinds of artifacts, and coffin-like structures.

"I hate coffins," Rachel said.

"Me, too," Aiden said. The shapes on the walls didn't help the situation either, and he had to turn away from some very grotesque drawings. Rachel, on her part, didn't look away like him despite all her talk about being scared of coffins, and he felt embarrassed by his behavior, though he still couldn't stomach the sight of the images on the walls.

"That door could be our only way out." Rachel's voice brought Aiden back from the world of coffins and bizarre images. The door she indicated had Egyptian symbols etched on its wooden surface.

"Remember, Kim said we should be wary of booby traps," Aiden said.

"So far we've seen none," Rachel pointed out, taking another step towards the door.

"Rachel, no," Aiden warned her. "I think that door is booby-trapped." But his companion ignored him and took another step. Again, he thought she was showing bravery where he was exhibiting cowardly caution. "Well, maybe not," he added, trying to save face.

"We'll have to find out by ourselves, won't we?" Rachel said, walking up to the door. "Besides, I don't think it's..."

The swishing sound interrupted her mid-sentence. She could only turn towards the thumps on the wall beside her. Fifteen arrows had just missed her en route to this wall, digging into the wooden block specifically placed on the wall to receive them should they miss their target.

"Don't move!" Aiden yelled, stopping in his tracks. "There could be more traps!"

Rachel's mouth remained open as she stared at the arrows embedded beside her. She could have been killed.

"There're markings on the ground."

"What?"

"There're symbols on the ground," Aiden repeated. "And I can read these symbols, wow."

"What do they say?" Rachel asked him. She couldn't look down for fear of setting off another trap.

"It says we should...be afraid? That we are...are, that we're...are now intruders...into...Cleopatra's tomb? Ok, that's not good." Aiden had lost the little composure he thought he had left. He started looking around, fearing what could be lurking in the shadows created by the burning reed. Things like unknown booby traps and weirdities ready to spring out into the open once they took another step. "Cleopatra is not happy with us right now, Rachel," he told his companion.

"I know," Rachel said. "What do we do now?"

"I really don't know. Why should she even set traps for people who never met her?"

Light from the reed torch danced about, brilliantly creating more weird shapes on the surrounding walls. These bizarre silhouettes attacked the children's imagination as they helplessly stood in the middle of the dead Egyptian queen's tomb wondering what to do next.

Aiden thought the black shapes all around might turn into the frightening unearthly demons after the white book and his pulse quickened. "We must get out now, Rachel," he said.

"How?" the little girl asked, rooted to the spot she presently occupied.

"I honestly don't know," Aiden whispered. His attention had shifted to one of the images on the wall beside him and he just stood there transfixed as he stared at it. Did it just move or was it the dancing flames of the reed torch that were playing games with his relevant faculties?

It wasn't the reed torch.

The black shape before him moved again.

"Oh, no!" he cried, drawing back. Sharp spikes sprang out behind his feet and he stopped cold.

"Aiden!" Rachel cried when she saw the black apparition floating towards them. "They're here!" She made to move forward, but more ancient spikes sprang up from the ground before her. "And we don't have the book to protect us anymore!" she said in a shaky voice.

Aiden took her hand with his free hand. Funny how she'd become scared all of a sudden, meaning that the situation they'd just stumbled into was a very dangerous one.

Rachel drew closer to her companion as more Booklords emerged from the walls of the cavernous tomb and floated towards them. The dark emptiness these ominous spirits possessed as faces seemed to be drawing her mental essence farther into the oblivion within their bottomless souls, so she closed her eyes and prayed to Yahweh. From the darkness now surrounding her, voices whispering in various languages and dialects wafted to her ears, and she realized she could understand every single word.

"Bookbearer!"

"Spare yourself this torture!"

"Disown the book!"

"It is useless to you."

"You will die now if you refuse!"

"No, I will not!" the Jewish girl screamed, jolting Aiden into holding her more tightly with his left hand.

"Rachel, what's going on?" he whispered, beginning to sweat. The reed torch picked out more dark forms emerging from the darkness beyond. The Gray Ones were closing in from all sides and it looked like something sinister was about to happen. "Who're you talking to?"Aiden asked the Jewish girl. He shook her when she did not respond. "What's going on?"

Rachel did not hear him. She'd been thrown into a world of voices trying to drive home one particular message. Disown the book and be saved from the calamity about to befall. She could not shut out the voices in her head, so she started praying over the cacophony they were making in order to suppress the growing urge to give in to their demand.

Aiden started as the black forms around them lurched forward, and formed a tighter circle. He had almost let go of Rachel before realizing that he was feeling tired all of a sudden. His hand refused to obey him, though, and Rachel had to hold him as she recited a prayer in the tongue of her people. The reed torch slipped and fell on the rocky floor of the cave before his knees buckled and he slumped to the ground, Rachel still holding him.

"Aiden!" Rachel cried, breaking her recitation to fall beside her co-traveler in consternation. He wasn't breathing and several scary thoughts ran through the girl's mind. Was he dead? Defiantly, she stood up and faced her aggressors.

"Give us the book!"

"You will die now if you refuse!" the voices kept up in Rachel's head.

"I will not fail!" she screamed, feeling weak. She stumbled and fell atop Aiden's crumpled body, her eyes staring at the reed torch still burning on the tomb's floor. A scarab beetle scurried past on the ground before her and she blinked back the tears forming at the corners of her eyes. She had failed her people.

"Give us the book!"

"Give us the book or you die!"

"Give us the book!"

"Give us the book!"

"Disown the book!"

The reed torch went out.

"Give us the book!"

"Disown the book!"

"Give us the book!"

"Disown the book!"

"Disown the book!"

"Disown the book!"

"NOOOOOOO!" the little girl whispered, her eyes beginning to droop. She saw long black hands reach out for her arms and pull her up to her feet. Aiden lay at her feet, but they ignored him. Obviously, he was out of the picture if they had killed him, but if he still lived, he was useless to her as long as she did not have in her possession the only tool she could protect her life, and the lives of her newfound friends, with.

Searing pain shot down her spine through the unearthly limbs holding her upright. Unimaginable forces forced her eyes open to stare into the blackest hollow she'd ever seen in her life.

"Rachel, disown the book and live," it whispered into her ears.

"I won't," Rachel repeated, glaring at her instigator.

"Listen to your uncle, Ezra," the thing before her continued, Dr. Isaac's face briefly appearing before her bordered by the bleakest gloom. "If you do not, you will still die and we will still take the book by force."

"We will blind you."

"And tear you limb from limb."

"And deliver your soul, as well as your friends', to the Otherworld."

"No!" Rachel screamed.

"Then you must die!" the demon leader before her whispered in Ezra's voice.

"Yahweh," Rachel whimpered, "please help me!"

Yet her eyes tore inwards and black death sipped into her soul. The Booklords lifted her above their heads so that she hung in mid-air overlooking their vast number packed into Queen Cleopatra's huge tomb.

Bright light tore into the infernal bodies of the congregated demons, peeling them away from the cave in one large swipe. The demon leader before Rachel disappeared before this unique light got to it, and the Jewish girl collapsed onto Aiden's stiff body before slowly opening her eyes.

A figure holding a shimmering reed torch stood before the door of carved Egyptian symbols. This man bent down towards her as she finally lost consciousness.

*   *   *

The glaring fire surrounding the long daggers hid their positions, its brightness occasionally burning into her eyes, but she kept up her swings until a lucky one caught her attacker in the arm.

Carl Bain swore, but did not stop his thrusts, rather increasing the tempo. Kimberley remembered he now had the blessing of the Gray

Ones as she started defending herself with her sword, blocking his powerful moves with calculated countermoves.

"What's the matter, man?" Kimberley mocked as she worked. "I thought Osiris gave you some strength in your previous life? Now, you cannot defeat a woman?"

And Carl Bain smiled. "I wanted you to understand the meaning of defeat by experiencing how powerful you could be before losing everything!" With a wave of his hand, an unknown force pulled his opponent's sword out of her hand and flung it as far away from her as possible. The weapon clattered to the temple's stone floor near the hall's main doors.

Kimberley backed away from the man with the flaming daggers, feeling lethargic all of a sudden. "What have you done to me?"

"Nothing, my former queen," Carl Bain said, smiling as he drew nearer his opponent. "You look surprised by my magic. Yet you know from whence it came."

Kimberley looked up. The Gray Ones had made Aiden feel drowsy once. They had her surrounded at the moment. She fell on all fours and her opponent stood before her. Powerful hands grabbed her neck and forced her head to look up.

"Where is it?" the American hustler growled.

"Where is what?"

"The package, you fool! Speak before I kill you."

"I–I don't know what you're talking about," Kimberley said. "Perhaps you mistake me for another from the afterlife." She grinned and Carl Bain swore under his breath.

Holding the Portwood police sergeant by the neck, he lifted her up into the air, smiling as her feet left the ground. "Enough of this Egyptian bullshit, my dear. You know exactly what I'm talking about. Now, where is the parcel the boy gave you at the police station back in Portwood?"

"May Osiris forgive you," Kimberley said with a straight face.

She crashed into a wall and crumbled to the ground, cursing painfully as she spat out blood. "You claim to be one of them, Khabawsokar, yet you still use your old magic," she accused her foe, frowning when she realized she just used a foreign language fluently. What was she even saying?

"Yes, the Christians have allowed me to keep my magic, my dear," Carl Bain agreed. "They know what it could do for them in the war against the old order."

"The order and cults protect the ways of our forefathers."

"The ways of the past are meant for epic tales and history!" Khabawsokar snapped, levitating the princess a second time with his magic.

"Small wonder you cringe from their cross, which they willingly stole from us!" Kimberley choked, feeling unseen hands tightening their grip round her neck.

"I don't deal in petty symbols!" Carl Bain said with bloodshot eyes. "Now, for the last time, where is my package?"

"I–I must have left it in Sierra Leone," Kimberley stammered, drifting back into her old self. "It's–It's not in my possession right now."

"You lie!" Khabawsokar snarled. "You know where they kept the white codex!"

"The white what?" Kimberley was puzzled. "Wh–What has befallen us?" It looked like a set of alternate realities were playing out at the same time for them. Carl Bain was Khabawsokar and vice versa, and she was a princess whose name she was yet to find out. The Portwood police sergeant hoped that this was not a bad sign.

"I must return to Sierra Leone with you and retrieve my parcel," Carl Bain said.

"I'd rather die than...follow you," Kimberley said and her opponent shook her in anger and drew her close before shaking her again with his magic.

"I can do all things now, you know," the American hustler snapped. "My gray masters have given me power beyond all knowledge and we are..." He spotted something on Kimberley's chest through an opening in the transparent dress she wore and reacted as he should by peeling away until he disappeared into thin air.

Kimberley crashed to the ancient hall's hard floor and looked around her in amazement as the Gray Ones surrounding their fight arena, the 'masters' Carl Bain had just finished praising, vanished with their protégé. She felt round her neck and touched a necklace she quickly brought up to her gaze.

An ankh amulet was attached to the gold chain hanging round her neck.

She'd been saved by a petty symbol.

Chapter 10
AMENHOTEP & THE SONS OF OSIRIS

THE image shimmered before her and grew twelve times its size to surpass whatever she'd earlier imagined. It drew nearer before stretching out a hand towards her face, and the little girl screamed at the top of her voice.

"Princess, you are awake," someone said in a foreign language before her and she opened her eyes, blinking twice. A young man holding a reed torch and wearing native Egyptian attire came into focus. He had a curious expression on his face.

"Aiden," Rachel remembered, beginning to sit up.

"Ramses is fine, Princess Anippe," the man said in the same language he had earlier introduced, placing a hand on her chest. "You need to rest now."

"But–But where is he?" Rachel demanded in English. "Who are you? What did you do to him, and...and what did you just say right now?"

The young man peered into her face instead. "The scroll spirits must have affected your memory, my princess, like the first time you came," he said in his tongue. "And you now speak a language only the gods can understand. Here, let me help you."

Before Rachel could respond to this, the man touched her right hand with his left hand, and a wave of change swept through the little girl's mind. Strangely, her pupils lost color before taking up sharper hues and coming to bear on the initiator of this peculiar biological occurrence. "Amenhotep," she began in the man's foreign language, curiously staring at him. "Where are the others?"

"The daughters of Isis are in hiding, my princess," Amenhotep said in the same language. "The sons of Osiris are here with me."

Rachel saw that the young man was not alone. A dozen other men wielding swords, spears and spiked wooden clubs appeared from the darkness surrounding her into the illumination created by the reed torch Amenhotep held in his right hand. Sitting up, she spotted some boys in the crowd as well.

"Ramses, or Aiden as you divinely called him, now sleeps in a coffin, my princess," Amenhotep continued, pointing to a wooden box behind Rachel.

"A coffin?" Rachel, or Princess Anippe, frowned. "What for?"

"So that he can rest after your encounter with the scroll spirits, my princess," the surprised Egyptian replied. "Why is that..."

"The Gray Ones," Rachel correctly identified as the scroll spirits. She wasn't surprised she'd retained her alternate memory, which had happened before. "How did you stop them?"

"They fear the ankh, my princess," a man standing beside Amenhotep said. He held up a wooden carving of a sign that looked like a cross with a curved handle replacing one of its four arms. "They fear life, itself."

"The scroll spirits attacked you, my princess," Amenhotep said. "This should not be so."

"They want the codex for themselves," Rachel told him. "They do not want to guard the codex and its Earthbearer any longer."

"The white codex?" the young man asked her in awe. "You mean the white codex is back here in Alexandria?" His kinsmen drew nearer to hear Princess Anippe's answer.

"It is in the Library of Scrolls as we speak," Rachel revealed, trying to appreciate the situation she had just found herself in. "I–I could not defeat the Christian Emperor and save Egypt just like I promised you the first time, Amenhotep. The scroll spirits betrayed my trust and assisted our enemies since they want the white codex for their selfish rebellion against Osiris."

"Now I see," Amenhotep said, nodding. "The scroll spirits must have turned against us if they want the white codex."

Rachel nodded in agreement. She had created the back story to the present happenings the first time she appeared in Egypt, which was immediately after she escaped death in the hands of Emperor Constantine's soldiers in Rome. Of course, she never thought she would have to return to Egypt and face the sons of Osiris and daughters of Isis again.

"And if they cannot do this alone for fear of the ankh," Amenhotep continued, "then I believe they must have brought in the Christians to do this work for them."

"The Christians?" Princess Anippe frowned a second time.

"The Purge has begun, Princess Anippe," Amenhotep said uneasily.

"The Purge?" Rachel understood what the man meant. The first time she appeared in this city, the locals had talked about the looming annihilation of remnant cults of the traditional deities by the Christians.

"The rumors are true," a boy on Rachel's left said. Much older than the little girl his kinsmen now surrounded, he looked and sounded very learned. "They now call us 'pagans.'"

"And they want to kill us all if we do not turn from the ways of our fathers and follow the Hebrew deities," one man wielding a club said.

"We hid ourselves and our families due to this rumor," Amenhotep added. "Now our worst fears are upon us. The Purge has started in earnest."

"They are trying to enter the Temple of Isis as we speak," the boy near Amenhotep said.

"Who?" Princess Anippe asked him.

"Christians, my princess," another man said. "The scroll spirits will return with the Christians after they realize that these haters of Osiris will prevent us from using the ankh if they join forces."

"Then we must hurry," Rachel said. "They must not lay hands on the white codex."

"Of course, my princess," this Egyptian agreed. "We must go to the Library of Scrolls at once and retrieve the white codex, but we must know that this will not be an easy task anymore. The first time you met us, princess, we were not hiding for our lives."

"Perhaps you will not abandon us this time," Amenhotep added. "Perhaps this time, you will help us by using the white codex just like you promised us. At least, we can now defeat the scroll spirits and force them to assist us with your help and the ankh."

"Yes," Rachel began in English, biting her lips, "about that..."

"Rachel," Aiden called out to her from his coffin bed. "What's going on? Why am I in a coffin? Who're these people?"

"Aiden, eh...Ramses," Rachel cried in correction, standing up and looking around her. "You are alive!"

"He is over there," Amenhotep directed the little girl, pointing the way. His fellow Egyptians made way for their divine princess child to leave the circle and go to her brother.

Aiden climbed out of the coffin. "Why am I in a coffin? Who put me in there?" he complained. "Creepy. I hate coffins."

"I know," Rachel said, hugging him, "but I'm glad you're back."

Aiden seemed taken aback by the hug.

"You discuss with Ramses in the tongue of the gods, my princess," Amenhotep observed from afar. "May we know what you are telling him?"

"Only the Chosen can understand what we are discussing, my dear Amenhotep," Rachel replied.

"What did he say?" Aiden asked her. His fellow time-traveler seemed quite flustered and edgy.

"Look," she told him. "We are in grave danger."

"How?" Aiden straightened.

Rachel cleared her throat. "The first time I was here after escaping from the Mine," she began, "I lied to the scroll spirits that I will give them the white codex if they allow me to get to the Library of Scrolls and retrieve the codex without harassment."

"The scroll spirits?" Aiden looked confused. "You mean the Booklords?"

"Yes," Rachel said.

"The white codex is the white book?"

"Yes."

"And why did you think that the Gray Ones would allow you to take the white book just like that?"

"Because they know it is easier to get the book from me if I give it to them willingly." Rachel paused. "By the way, I pulled it off back then. I don't know if I can do so again."

"It is time, my princess," Amenhotep interrupted, strutting forward.

"Yes, of course," Princess Anippe said. "We must leave now."

"Rachel, what's going on?" Aiden asked, throwing furtive glances at the Egyptians. "Who are these people?"

The sons of Osiris came to surround the two children they apparently revered and Amenhotep cleared his throat. "Welcome, the divine Prince Ramses, brother of Princess Anippe, divine daughter of Isis. We have heard so much about you and we hope your divine powers will help us to defeat our enemies just as your sister had foretold many weeks ago in her first coming." He wanted to take Aiden's hands but Rachel offered him her hands instead.

"What did he just say, Rachel?" Aiden asked the Jewish girl.

"Nothing important," she replied.

"You appear not to understand our language," Amenhotep observed. "The scroll spirits must have..."

"You will touch him when it is time, my dear Amenhotep," Rachel interrupted. "We must get to the Library of Scrolls now."

The Egyptian nodded and turned to his kinsmen. "Now we proceed to the Library of Scrolls," he announced before turning towards the door of carved Egyptian symbols to manipulate a lever-like handle attached to it. "Be on your guard, my friends, for the Christians have overwhelmed our brothers outside and are surely looking for other ways to enter Cleopatra's tomb and our most holy temple. We must resist to the end if we want to enjoy the afterlife."

His fellow worshippers yelled out their agreement in a resounding chorus as the heavy doors swung open to reveal a flight of stony steps leading down to a dimly lit passageway.

"Rachel, who're these people?" Aiden repeated in English, looking around him at the natives wielding spears, swords and spiked clubs as the group made its way down the rough steps.

"Th–They think we are from their gods," Rachel replied in the same language.

"Why?" Aiden asked.

"I lied to them the first time I came here."

"About what?"

"About who I am and where I came from," was the reply. "I told them I was the divine daughter of Isis and Osiris, and that I had come from the gods to restore their country to her former glory."

"So that you can easily find the white book?"

"No, so that they can gladly give me the white book," Rachel, or Princess Anippe, replied.

"I don't understand," Aiden confessed, as the group got to the foot of the steps.

"I came here without the book," Rachel told him as their Egyptian rescuers continued to stare at them. "It appeared in a library across from that hall we found ourselves in and I needed to go and get it, but the Gray Ones, who had followed me and the book to Egypt, will not let me if I did not agree to their demand that I give them the book, so I convinced them that I would give them the book and lied to these people so that they can allow me entrance into their Library of Scrolls in order for me to get the book. I also had to lie to the people so that the Booklords will not destroy them if they refused to help me."

"Wow," Aiden said, looking at the wooden club of a dark fellow walking beside him. "You've gone through a lot."

"Yes," Rachel said, turning to Amenhotep. She realized that the Egyptian had left them alone, for the moment at least, and gladly turned back to her 'divine brother,' Prince Ramses or Aiden, who appeared lost in thought. "That last time, the Booklords had arrived at the library, but could not break the book's heavenly protection," Rachel told him. "And when they appeared in the library to meet me, many natives, who had never seen these angels-turned-demons before, died."

Aiden could only stare at her.

"I had to lie again," she revealed.

"What now?"

"I told the people that the scroll spirits were guardians of the white codex who protected me and served the god, Osiris. That the deaths were necessary sacrifices for the sustenance of every other life in that library at that moment. Luckily, the Gray Ones did not kill any other person after that, and of course, I escaped with the white book after retrieving it from the library."

"Okay," Aiden whistled. "Now I know why we're in trouble."

Princess Anippe sighed.

"What now?" her travelling companion wondered aloud.

"We'll retrieve the book first, and then we'll know what to do," Rachel said.

"What of Kimberley?" Aiden asked. "I hope she's okay."

"I hope so, too," Rachel said.

The group had stopped at the foot of another flight of stony steps going upwards. Amenhotep turned to Rachel, pointing at Aiden with his head. "Can I touch him now, my princess?" he asked.

The place grew cold.

"The ankh!" Princess Anippe screamed, grabbing her brother's hand. "Bring out your ankhs!"

Many quickly obeyed this command. Many could not. The black forms materialized out of nowhere, screeching intolerably as some of the reed torches went out. They disappeared almost immediately.

Aiden realized his palms were moist.

"Nobody died," Amenhotep announced, looking around him as murmuring broke out amongst the sons of Osiris.

"That is good," Rachel said, turning to Aiden. "It means they really fear the ankh."

"Who fears what?"

"The Gray Ones fear the ankh."

"The what?"

"The ankh." Princess Anippe took one of the amulets from the nearest Egyptian and raised it up for Prince Ramses, or Aiden, to see. "It scares away the Booklords."

"Okay," a puzzled Aiden said.

Amenhotep came and stood beside Rachel, his expression one of urgency. Again, he pointed at Aiden with his head.

"Why does he keep doing that?" Aiden asked Rachel, staring at the Egyptian.

"Yes," Rachel told Amenhotep in his language. "You can now touch him."

"And what did you just tell him?"

*   *   *

Carl Bain stared at the hollow-faced shapes floating around him for a long time before cursing softly, his right hand shooting up to his head as soon as he felt another headache coming. "Strange," he muttered. "What the hell happened back there?"

His gray companions offered him nothing but silence.

He moved his muscular arms backward to the nape of his neck, trying to loosen the stiffness there. Whatever happened was not good, because it meant that the invincibility he thought his spirit friends had bestowed upon him did not exist. He had encountered a strange force in that ancient hall moments ago. One that could defeat him and his infernal masters if given the chance.

When his superhuman being felt the raw strength of this unearthly force, he'd been pulled back and thrown out of the ancient reality he had been occupying with his foe by the will of the gray forms now surrounding him. A brief time spinning around with his newfound friends in an unknown realm preceded a reemergence into the ancient land they all previously occupied, only that they were no longer in the hall, where he had fought the girl. Kind of like an escape sequence.

"Why did we run away?" he asked the closest demonic form before him. "I was about to make her talk."

"Rejuvenation," its empty face seemed to say as it floated higher up in the air, its previous position taken up by another horrendous shape.

"You agreed to help me first!" Carl Bain snapped, getting up in anger and gesticulating. "I almost had her!"

"Rejuvenation," the Gray Ones echoed as they faded away.

The American's eyes sparkled and he suddenly lost his rebellious attitude. He looked at his bulging arms and hands, feeling a new form of strength sipping into him. Knowledge he never knew flooded into his brain and he felt ultimately satisfied. Flames erupted from his hands and he controlled it by forming a ball. His eyes sparkled as he reveled in his awesome power.

"Khabawsokar," a Roman soldier called out to him from the door of his temple. "We need your help."

"I have nothing to do with Christians," Carl Bain, or Khabawsokar, said, looking at the soldier. The man was not wearing any symbols like the others.

"The Emperor will spare you if you help us enter the Hall of Isis and destroy the pagans," the soldier continued as if he did not hear the ancient healer.

"The Emperor cannot touch me," Khabawsokar said with a wave of his hand.

"And what of your family?"

"He cannot harm my family," Carl Bain whispered slowly. "They are in a safe place."

"Still, I command you to help," the soldier said, losing his patience. "The doors are unbreakable from the outside. We have cleaned out the guards before it, but we cannot get in."

"Then burn down the door."

"The Emperor wants to preserve the temple as it is, with the door in place, not burned down," was the terse reply. "Now, I command you to..."

The Booklords appeared in their gory form and the soldier slumped dead. The demons surrounded Khabawsokar and he nodded after awhile.

"Yes," he agreed with them. "The Christians can help us."

They communicated some more with him.

"Yes," he said again. "That is a very good plan. No symbols."

Picking up his two daggers, Carl Bain, also known as Khabawsokar, walked out of his temple as his infernal masters vanished. He stepped over the dead soldier on his way out.

Chapter 11
NANU & THE DAUGHTERS OF ISIS

KIMBERLEY opened the second door and peered into a large enclosure. Stepping into this brightly lit man-made cave, she felt like she'd been there before. The structure's hexagonal corners had reed torches burning on gold stands only fit for royalty. Golden traditional chairs dotted the place amidst tastefully decorated tables that made up the furniture. Life-sized human paintings and hieroglyphs covered the walls.

"Open this door in the name of God and the Emperor!" someone shouted outside the long antechamber above her. "Open this door in the name of God and the Emperor!" this person repeated, banging loudly on the huge door guarding the hall. "Open this door in the name of God and the Emperor!" More banging followed this repeated command and Kimberley wondered if the fellow behind the door was ever going to get tired. Good that the hall's exit appeared impregnable from the outside, else she would have been facing multiple confrontations by then.

The sergeant-turned-Egyptian-princess reckoned that a large crowd waited outside the great wooden door of the lengthy hall above her, judging from the noise they made. Unlocking the barred structure from within would have been the worst decision at that point. Entering the side tunnel Aiden and Rachel escaped into moments ago had looked like a better decision, until the Portwood sergeant realized that the structure was actually a tomb.

"Open this door in the name of God and the Emperor!"

Kimberley looked around her. She'd come to the conclusion that there were no escape paths from the vestibule above, only coffins and ancient relics, and this exorbitantly decorated room. So where did Aiden and Rachel escape into?

"O' Cleopatra, Queen of Egypt and daughter of Isis, you have returned just like you promised your children!"

"Cleopatra?" Kimberley asked the person whose voice she just heard behind her, before turning to gaze at the most beautiful woman she had ever seen, her eyes taking in every inch of the face before her.

Luscious lips formed a base for a slim nose that led up to emerald eyes embedded underneath dark brows. The woman's long hair created a smooth oval shape with her face as it cascaded down her neck to caress her shoulders. Despite wearing black flowing attire, this enchanting beauty never looked out of place in the opulently decorated room. "I am Nanu, daughter of Nephthys, my queen," she introduced, bowing. "You are welcome back from the dead."

Kimberley did not know how to respond. She had felt like she'd been there before, so there could be some truth in the woman's assertion, except the death part, that is. "Are you alone?" she asked instead.

Nanu appeared surprised by this question. She shook her head vigorously. "No, my queen," she replied, kneeling before the police officer. "The daughters of our revered goddess are all here with me, including your maidservants and all those who went into hiding after your death."

"Okay, I get it," Kimberley pointed out. "I died and now I'm back. So, where are those you mentioned? And how did you come to speak my language so well?"

"I am not speaking, my queen," the strange beauty highlighted. "I am using my mind to talk to you."

For the first time, Kimberley realized that their mouths had remained closed ever since they met. "Telepathy," she said in English. "Amazing."

"Yes, it is," Nanu agreed in a foreign language, which Kimberley understood, adding to her confusion.

"We both understand each other when we speak our different tongues," Kimberley realized. "Yet I cannot speak your language. How is that possible?"

"Very simple, my queen," the Egyptian said in her tongue. "I am speaking with my lips and communicating with my mind now."

"Okay, good to know that you're reading my mind as well," the Portwood police sergeant muttered. "So, where are the others?"

"All around us," Nanu said, clapping her hands twice.

To Kimberley's utmost surprise, the life-sized female forms in the paintings all around them started moving. One by one, these works of art stepped out of the wall, stretching their bodies as if from a long induced sleep. The police officer counted twenty-nine females in all, including the beautiful Nanu, who stood before her studying her expression. "But, how did they..." she began.

"We have copied the tricks of the chameleon using magic our forefathers thought us, my queen," Nanu explained as the new feminine faces gathered behind her. "This is to protect us from those who want to harm us."

"You mean the people outside this hall?" Kimberley asked.

"Yes, the Christians," Nanu said, drawing nearer her guest.

"Those people are Christians?" Kimberley asked her beautiful host, who nodded.

"Th–They want to annihilate us if we do not turn to their new deity, and we have resolved to pray and fast until help comes our way from our goddess."

"Surely, she has heard our cries and sent you to us, my queen," a blue-eyed girl in a white dress said.

"I don't understand you," Kimberley began.

"Chione cannot talk with her mind," Nanu explained, turning away from the girl in a white dress. She noticed the blood smear on Kimberley's dress. "I see you have already engaged another in battle."

"They call him Khabawsokar here," Kimberley said, "but I know him as Carl Bain."

"A priest of the god of death and mummification," Nanu revealed, frowning. "He must have joined the Christians." The women exchanged glances. "He is betraying his people."

"He knows the ways of our forefathers," someone telepathized in the crowd.

"You bet," Kimberley whispered, thinking of the Gray Ones.

"But we can defeat him and the Christians," Nanu assured. "With your help, my queen, and the strength of our brothers."

"Your brothers?" a curious Kimberley noted.

"Yes, my queen," Nanu revealed. "Our men, who revere Osiris just as we adore Isis, have rescued your cousins from the scroll spirits."

"The scroll spirits?" Kimberley wondered aloud. Sounded like the Booklords to her.

"Princess Anippe and Prince Ramses are safely with our brothers as we speak," another woman telepathized.

Kimberley smiled when she heard this. Obviously, Rachel and Aiden were the mentioned prince and princess. "Can I go to them right now?" she asked Nanu.

"We will meet them at the Library of Scrolls if we leave now, my queen."

"The Library of Scrolls?" Kimberley's frown deepened. "What are you trying to tell me?"

Nanu's piercing eyes remained unwavering. "The Library of Scrolls, my queen," she repeated with confidence. "Where we must retrieve the white codex as Princess Anippe had promised us, and reclaim Egypt from the Christians and Romans."

"The white codex?" Kimberley started. "You meant the white book, right?"

"Come, my queen," Nanu rather urged her guest, taking the foreign woman's hands. "I must take you to your cousins."

The change in Kimberley's eyes lasted only seconds. What had gotten into her this time? She looked at the women standing behind Nanu and nodded without a word. Was she really Queen Cleopatra back from the dead? She still didn't think so. "Follow me," she said in a language she had never used in her life and turned on her heels, only to notice the dropping temperature.

The men stormed the enclosure, yelling at the top of their voices. Kimberley drew her short swords as their weapons dropped two daughters of Isis. She side-stepped and stabbed an attacker before turning twice to slash open the stomachs of two other intruders in quick succession. The women behind her revealed various weapons and clashed with the aggressors. She dodged another man swinging a broad sword and sank her two swords into his back.

"Kill them all in the name of God!" an unknown soldier bellowed as he jumped into the fray. "Kill them for the Emperor!"

"They are a distraction!" Kimberley warned her new friends, pulling out her ankh necklace before engaging another angry fellow. "Show your amulets if you have one!"

Seeing the beautiful Nanu struggling to pull out a necklace while blocking the swings of a huge soldier, the Portwood police officer silenced her present opponent with a decisive stroke and jumped over to help.

"Die in the name of God!" the bearded Roman cried, coming at his Egyptian opponent a fifth time.

Nanu fell when the rough-looking fighter brushed her off her feet and rolled away before he could sink his weapon into her. Kimberley slashed at the man's right arm as he was about to repeat the downward jab and he dropped his weapon, shouting in pain.

Dodging the sergeant-turned-Egyptian-queen's second swing, the Byzantine soldier landed a fist on the sergeant's left flank and knocked her off balance using his right knee.

Kimberley fell forward, losing her swords in the process. She cushioned her fall with both hands and rolled away before a huge foot slammed into the ground she previously occupied. Blood splattered her face and the big man fell on his face beside her, Nanu towering over his dead body.

Kimberley picked her short swords and Nanu pulled her up. "Thank you," she told the Egyptian girl.

"It is useless, my queen!" Nanu cried, retrieving her weapon from the fallen soldier's back. "They are too many, we must leave now!"

Kimberley kicked someone in the groin, turned away and downed another advancing fighter. "I know," she said, watching the battle. More Byzantine soldiers forced their way into the large hexagonal cave, shouting at the top of their voices. The dead soldiers were more than the female bodies lying on the cold floor, but Nanu was right. They couldn't hold back the enemy forever. "We must go now!" the Portwood sergeant shouted, edging closer to the back of the cave as she fought. How she knew whatever secrets lay there was beyond her.

"Follow your queen!" Nanu rallied as she pranced about behind Kimberley. The daughters of Isis heard her and started falling back behind her, the enemy pushing forward at the same time.

"Kill them all!" another Byzantine fighter growled, swinging his sword at the retreating women.

He was silenced.

"Here lies the route we must take!" Kimberley cried, getting to the cave's back wall by plunging her weapons into another man.

Nanu pushed away the dead man and pulled down the hidden lever she knew where to look for. The reed torches went out and darkness befell both parties.

The Emperor's men hesitated when the sense of sight failed them, and Nanu pulled another stick.

The wall cracked open in the darkness, revealing a partition the size of one person. The beautiful maidservant helped the women slip through, one at a time.

Their appearance was as sudden as the death it caused. Khabawsokar and the scroll spirits brought light with them, but killed many on both sides of the warring divide before the amulets that fell out of dead hands forced them to retreat.

Kimberley grimaced as she pushed away a dead woman and pulled herself out of the bodies lying about. A man whimpered like a child to her left.

"Help me!" Nanu cried in the darkness.

Kimberley reached out blindly to grab a flailing arm. She pulled up the Egyptian woman, who appeared flustered.

Nanu reignited the reed torches by finding their wooden control on the cave's wall. All around her, survivors picked themselves up amongst the dead. "My sisters!" she cried, staring at the dead women.

"We cannot help them anymore, my friend," Kimberley pointed out sadly. "They are now at peace with Anubis."

"Anubis!" Nanu's blood boiled at the mention of that name. "His priest caused this!" She spat at a dead Byzantine soldier lying at her feet and turned towards the wall partition. "We must avenge our dead sisters, my queen."

"Aye," Kimberley agreed, following her. "That we must do." Through the hexagonal cave's main entrance, she saw fighters cowering and praying outside. The men must have lost their will to fight after witnessing the carnage their allies had caused.

Nanu's cry brought Kimberley out of her thoughts. She quickly slipped through the secret door on the wall and gaped at the heap of bodies before the maidservant.

*   *   *

Khabawsokar looked himself over and walked on down the long hall, noting how impeccably normal his appearance was. Despite the enormous power those symbols mustered, he and his infernal masters had come out of the last battle unscathed. Their human minions, however, could not claim such a victorious state of affairs judging from the dire aftermath of that particular skirmish.

"The Emperor has decreed that the pagan buildings be destroyed, Khabawsokar," the Roman centurion following Carl Bain began.

"That was not part of our agreement," the American-turned-ancient-Egyptian-priest said.

"It is a decree from the new emperor, pagan priest," the soldier returned. "After all, you told me no harm would come to my men, yet you killed all of them. You lied to Emperor Theodosius."

"I did not lie, my friend," an annoyed Carl Bain emphasized. "I opened the temple doors from within as we agreed, and then I allowed your men to do what they must do for the period we agreed on."

"Then you killed them, Khabawsokar," the officer snapped, clenching his fists.

"My masters grew tired of their incompetence against mere women," the Egyptian priest retorted. "They had to do what they did."

"The Cave of Isis can only fit few men at once, Khabawsokar," the Roman said coldly. "I could only send in a few of my best fighters at a time, since that tomb was not made for fighting battles."

Both men walked on in angry silence.

"No wonder you told us to remove our symbols," the Roman officer said.

"Your symbols are more pagan than Christian," Carl Bain replied dryly. "Trust me, they cannot harm me."

"You have betrayed the Emperor by killing his best men," the angry soldier continued. "After all, you serve the god of death."

"We both serve gods of death, my friend."

"You traitor," the Roman bellowed, drawing his sword and stopping the priest with it. "Many refused to volunteer for the attack when they saw that you were an ally. Many who feared your pagan rituals and dark magic, Khabawsokar," he cried. "Now, you must die for your sins, pagan!"

No sooner had the officer finished talking than he fell dead at the feet of the Egyptian high priest, a pool of his blood slowly spreading underneath him.

"Our enemies prepare to fight us after fleeing from your men and yet you mourn these same lazy men?" Carl Bain asked with a sigh. For the second time that day, he walked over a dead body, shaking his head.

The priest of death and mummification emerged onto a balcony overlooking the courtyard of the Temple of Isis. He now had on a new face as well as the robes of a Christian priest with the associated ineffectual symbols. A cheering crowd of Roman soldiers, peasants and Christian scholars from the Church of Alexandria greeted his raised arms. No one had noticed the mysterious transformation of his attire and appearance as he stepped out of the temple. No one but his infernal masters.

Carl Bain grinned for all to see. "We have successfully pushed them out of their pagan temple!" he declared to more cheers. "Now, we will burn down their buildings as decreed by God and our new emperor, and destroy all their scrolls and manuscripts with these pagan structures!"

The crowd went wild, and rushed into the temple through its open doors, shouting and condemning the pagans as they went. Many held up reed torches alongside the Christian symbols Khabawsokar and his spiritual masters knew were useless.

Carl Bain looked out across the large square, at the iconic Library of Scrolls, within which the Booklords had already started destroying the protections of the white book, and within which the final battle against the traveling trio and their pagan allies must be fought and won.

The American hustler knew he must retrieve his package right there before it was lost forever in time. There might never be another chance like the one before him now.

Suddenly, he spotted the dreaded symbol amongst the raucous crowd rushing into the temple below him and quickly looked away before its unknown magic got to him. He knew that he and his masters would soon leave that pitiful city, so the sign's effect on him would soon be a thing of the past. How the Christians and those they persecuted came to love that particular sign so much he might never know.

The new priest turned to one of the three military officers standing beside him on the balcony. "You know the plan," he said. "Proceed."

The men nodded silently and left for the task ahead.

Chapter 12
THE LIBRARY OF SCROLLS

ANKHS drawn, they burst into the revered edifice when the secret door fell. All the scroll spirits in the library vanished and eerie silence prevailed.

"That must be where they found the white codex," Rachel, or Princess Anippe, said as she pointed towards the area where the Gray Ones had been floating around.

"Then we must go there immediately," Amenhotep announced, quickly moving towards the said spot with his princess and fellow brothers.

"Amazing," Aiden, or Ramses, whispered as he walked in-between the neat stacks of papyrus scrolls packed in wooden racks that lined up in all directions as far as he could see. Aiden had become Prince Ramses after Amenhotep touched him, but unlike Rachel, he couldn't recall his old memory and had no inkling of the alternate reality the white book had thrown him into.

Rachel, on her part, knew exactly what was going on and had an eye on Aiden should the need arise to reverse the white book's 'spell' on him through touch. She hoped to do so in any dire situation before he did anything stupid as an Egyptian prince.

Rachel and Amenhotep got to the spot together. The cold emanating from the white codex helped her locate its position beneath a stack of scrolls. Its book-like appearance gave it away when she got to this position. "Its inscriptions have frozen," she said, feeling the cold blue lettering on the ancient book's pages.

"And what must we do now, my princess?" Amenhotep asked her.

"Well, eh, we must wait for...the queen's sister?" Rachel stammered, wondering how she knew that.

The library's designers had made it possible for natural light to illuminate the building from many open circles on the walls. These windows could be shut to keep out bad weather. The noise outside drew some brothers of Osiris to these circular openings, and from here, they could see the crowd gathered before the Temple of Isis on the other side of the yard.

"They are heading for the wooden doors of the Temple of Isis," an Egyptian pointed out. "They want to burn down the temple!"

"It has already begun," Princess Anippe said, turning to the openings with dismay.

"Yes, it has, my princess," Amenhotep agreed. "We must stop this madness right now before it destroys us all."

"Who is the man on the balcony?" Rachel asked those watching.

"He looks like a Christian priest," one of the Egyptians replied. "Maybe he is the man leading this madness."

Amenhotep appeared impatient. "What is keeping our guest?" he asked, clenching and unclenching his fists. "What is keeping the queen?"

"I will be representing her," a voice behind him said.

"Kim!" Rachel exclaimed when she turned and saw the familiar face grinning at her. A hug and a pat on the head followed. "Oh, Kim! I'm so glad to see you alive!"

Kimberley had emerged into the Library of Scrolls from another secret entrance with several women and two girls.

"Nanu!" Amenhotep cried on seeing one of the women with the dead queen's sister. "Nanu, you are alive!" The woman rushed to him and they hugged each other before he turned to Kimberley and bowed to her. "Welcome back from the dead, my queen," he said in his language.

"Here we go again," Kimberley said in English. "I am not Cleopatra," she told Amenhotep in his language.

"Then, who are you?" Nanu asked her.

"I am...her sister?" Kimberley replied, wondering why she just got that information from wherever it came from several minutes into being someone else.

The Egyptians surrounding her appeared confused.

"Our queen has no living sister," Amenhotep reasoned. "You must be mistaken, my queen."

"Yes, your queen had a sister," Kimberley replied. "We were separated at birth and I was taken to Mount Olympus by the gods?" She marveled at her answer.

"It is possible," the boy with the brothers of Osiris said. "Our queen had so many secrets." Those around him nodded in agreement.

"You look so much like her," Nanu observed. "No one can tell the difference, my queen."

"Actually, I am her twin sister, sent down by the gods of Greece," Kimberley revealed, frowning.

"You are still my queen," Nanu said.

"As you wish," Kimberley muttered in English and turned to Rachel. "Where's Aiden?" she asked the little girl in the same language.

"Welcome, sister," Aiden, or Prince Ramses, said behind her as he came over to hug her. His facial expression changed when he did this. "What's going on?" he asked in English, and Kimberley turned to Rachel, a questioning look on her face. Apparently, Aiden couldn't maintain a dual identity like his fellow time-travelers.

"He's not himself anymore," Rachel supplied in English, nodding towards Aiden. "I was waiting for you to show up before changing him back when we want to leave with the book." She held up the revered codex for the sergeant.

"So, what are we waiting for?" Kimberley wanted to know.

"We need to leave without alerting these people," Rachel said. "And we must help them if we can."

"And how do you think we can do that?" Kimberley asked.

"You want to leave us?" Nanu began and Kimberley turned to her. She'd forgotten the mind reader could also understand English.

"No, we…" Rachel began.

"We will save Egypt before we leave," Kimberley said.

Nanu nodded.

"The Temple of Isis burns!" an Egyptian watching the temple from the circular windows shouted. "The Christians are coming!"

The library's main doors flew open and a throng of irate men and women rushed into the building, chanting Christian songs of war and wielding weapons they modified from home implements.

"Quick, protect Queen Cleopatra's twin sister and her relations with your lives!" Amenhotep urged his brothers. "Use your swords and clubs if you must!"

Weapons drawn, the brothers of Osiris and remaining daughters of Isis surrounded Kimberley and her 'relations.' Amenhotep stood before Rachel who held the white codex. "What must we do now that we have the white codex?" he asked her.

"I need a reed pen," Princess Anippe replied.

The Egyptian boy with Amenhotep reached out into a set of papyrus scrolls separated from the rack beside them by a wooden partition. He brought out a reed pen and gave it to Rachel.

The Christian crowd clashed with the brothers of Osiris who pushed them back with deadly force. Many lay dead, and those before the pagans hesitated, but kept up their angry chants.

"Kill the pagans!" someone in the crowd raised.

"Kill them all!" another added.

"Tie your ankhs to your hands if you have one!" Kimberley ordered everyone. "Something tells me this is just beginning." She obeyed her order before drawing her short swords. Thankfully, she saw Nanu face the library's door with the remaining sisters of Isis and turned to the little girl beside her. "Don't know what you're thinking right now, Rachel," she said in English, "but we need to leave now?"

"I know," Rachel said.

"Find a place and time with someone who can help us," Aiden advised her. "One of your father's friends like we agreed."

"I know," Rachel repeated, her right hand poised to write with the reed pen on the cold open codex.

"How do I help, my princess?" Amenhotep asked her and she turned to the Egyptian.

"I need the names of those you have seen in the crowd before us."

"What are you doing?" Kimberley demanded, staring at Rachel.

"We need to act like we're helping these people," Rachel explained. "Until we can leave."

"And who will help us?" Kimberley asked, frowning.

"They're already doing that."

"Guess you're right," the sergeant said. "But these things have happened, you know, there's no need to help them, since they will all still perish?"

"Just give me a few minutes, Kim," Rachel begged.

"There won't be anyone left to help if you waste more time," Kimberley said, wondering why the little girl had become philanthropic all of a sudden. How she wished the library had ankhs drawn all over its walls.

The Egyptians had left Aiden alone ever since he hugged Kimberley, but now he risked another memory-changing touch as he drew nearer to his traveling companions in order to know what had gone wrong. "Can we leave now, please?" he begged.

"What is going on, my queen?" Nanu demanded as she turned back to the woman she'd come to respect after the fight in the burial chamber.

Kimberley hoped the Egyptian woman did not capture the content of their last conversation. "Okay, Rachel," she told her fellow time-traveler. "Let us help them."

Nanu frowned. "You speak in the tongue of kings and queens, my mistress."

"Yes," Kimberley told her. "I do that when I'm under pressure."

The Christian crowd had picked up courage once again. They moved closer to the armed pagans before them. Those holding weapons among them stepped forward and maneuvered the scroll shelves to surround the smaller group. Princess Anippe looked at Amenhotep.

"There stands Jasiah, the Jew," the Egyptian pointed out in the livid crowd before them. The princess quickly wrote on the codex and Jasiah disappeared from the crowd. Amenhotep was as surprised as his brothers and sisters as well as those on the opposite side of the divide, who drew back in fear, murmuring amongst themselves. "My gods!" he blurted out. "This is power from the gods!"

"Power from the gods!" someone picked up in the crowd surrounding the pagans, and this message was dissipated until palpable fear descended on these angry Christian men and women.

"And there is Aristides, the Greek," Amenhotep resumed with glee. "He used to be my neighbor until he became a Christian."

The Greek guy disappeared and a second fellow followed him. Chaos ensued around where both men once stood.

"Flee for your lives!" a panic-stricken man shouted as he headed for the library's wooden doors. Many fell and were trampled upon as the large crowd surged towards the exit. In their confusion, some even ran towards the pagans in the middle of the large hall and were struck down.

"Don't kill them!" Princess Anippe cried, but the brothers of Osiris and daughters of Isis ignored her.

"There goes the people you thought were good people," Kimberley muttered after making sure that no daughter of Isis stood near her. "See them killing without mercy."

"Please, stop killing them!" Rachel shouted again. "Have mercy!"

"We've done enough already, Rachel," Kimberley warned. "Now, let's leave before it's too late!"

Rachel stared at the white scroll as she tried to write on it again.

"What's the matter?" Kimberley demanded.

"I-I cannot write on the book any longer!" the little girl stammered.

"Then get us out of here, first," Aiden aired in fear, looking around him at the unsmiling faces surrounding them. "This people don't like us."

Rachel touched a previous destination on the white codex, and looked around her in fright. She repeated this action with other fingers, braving the biting, icy cold surface of the ancient artifact. Finally, she looked up in alarm. "It's not working," she cried.

"The ice must be preventing you from writing or touching the book's surface," Kimberley pointed out. "Now, we're toast."

Hesitantly, Rachel turned to write again on the white codex, and dropped it in pain.

"What's the matter?" a bewildered Kimberley asked.

"What is wrong, Anippe?" Aiden demanded as he supported his little sister. "Why do you drop the codex of the gods, which is about to give us victory?"

"It's...It's too cold," Rachel cried, holding her hands. She noticed Aiden's change in language. He must have become Prince Ramses after skin contact with the many Egyptians around. "It has never been this cold before."

Kimberley knew why. "Told you we could have left earlier," she said.

Princess Anippe tried to touch Prince Ramses, or Aiden, as he turned away from her.

Too late.

A brother of Osiris slumped before Kimberley and she saw them on the circular openings. "Down!" she shouted, crouching low herself as the arrows flew past. Nanu fell before her clutching a bloody leg with a protruding shaft.

"Nanu!" Amenhotep cried, crawling towards the fallen woman. He supported her head and she looked at him.

"It is...poisoned!" she stammered. "I will die."

"Have faith," Amenhotep said. "You will be with the gods when you do."

He teared up.

The Emperor's soldiers jumped into the pagan building through the circular openings on its walls. Some had bows and arrows while others drew their swords, cutting down everyone in their way.

"They will kill us all if we do not fight," Prince Ramses, or Aiden, declared and stooped to pick up a dead sister's sword.

"Fight we must," Amenhotep urged his people, leaving the dying Nanu to stand up and ready his sword.

"Our victory is assured for the gods are with us," Ramses cried, raising his sword amidst the deadly arrows flying past him. He stepped forward.

"Aiden, no!" Rachel grabbed his left leg, holding him back, and he turned around angrily.

"Let me fulfill my destiny by freeing my people, sister," he snapped before going blank and falling backward on Rachel's outstretched arms.

"You'll kill yourself first," Kimberley chided him, and noticed the change coming over him with satisfaction.

The remaining brothers of Osiris and sisters of Isis stood up with Amenhotep and charged the incoming attackers. The crowd making for the great doors swayed back towards the pagans once they realized what had happened. The power of the gods had been broken by the Emperor's elite soldiers.

Both parties clashed viciously with deadly results.

"Where's the reed pen?" Rachel demanded beside the reoriented Aiden.

"English, please?" Aiden urged her.

"The Serapeum is on fire!" one of Amenhotep's brothers shouted near Rachel. "They will destroy the temple with the library!"

Kimberley frowned when she heard this. Was the library part of a temple? Two Roman soldiers ran at her and she struck them down with ease. Something caught her attention as a Roman archer attacked an Egyptian pagan some feet away. "The soldiers are pulling off the ankhs from the wrists of our dead and wounded and breaking them!" she realized, turning to Rachel.

"That could mean only one thing," Rachel said. "They're working with the Gray Ones!"

Using one of her swords, Kimberley dragged the cold codex back to Rachel. "Get us out of here," she told the little girl and grabbed Aiden by his right arm. "Hold me," she told the Jewish girl, reaching out a free hand.

"I don't have the reed pen," Rachel revealed.

Still holding Aiden, Kimberley engaged a Christian rioter and wounded him before kicking him away. "We must find that pen, and quickly, too," she said, letting go of Aiden to crouch low and join the search. "Should be lying around here somewhere."

"I–I dropped it when I dropped the codex," Rachel said, turning to the cold ancient book lying on the floor. Someone had set a rack of distant scrolls on fire and this brought a new urgency to their search.

"Found it," Aiden announced, holding up the reed tool.

"Exactly when we thought you were dead," Kimberley joked, smiling.

Rachel saw with trepidation that a thin film of ice had covered the white book's fragile surface despite the searing heat from the burning shelves of dry scrolls in the library. "And how do we use it now?" she asked, trying to write on the frozen codex lying on the floor. "The ink will never write on ice."

"Just keep trying," Kimberley said, standing up to guard both kids. She faced another soldier, slashing away before stabbing him in the forehead. Another fighter ran up to her and she dodged his swing before slashing his leg open. "Aiden, hold my leg and Rachel's arm. We must always be linked from now on," she breathed as the kneeling man whimpered before her. She kicked him on the head and into oblivion.

The battle petered out. The Christians and their military allies had the upper hand.

"It's all over!" Aiden cried, staring at the discouraging scenario all around him. "Our side is losing badly!"

A crowd gathered around the three time-travelers, but kept their distance.

"Yeah, just keep off if you don't want to die, you hear?" Kimberley warned them, menacingly brandishing her two swords as she surveyed the violent scenario around her. Flames leaped high into the air from many burning shelves of priceless scrolls, forming a glowing background to the mayhem unleashed in the Library of Scrolls by the two clashing religions. Many brothers of Osiris and daughters of Isis lay dead, the soldiers and angry mob having pulled these dead pagans' ankhs from their arms and wrists and, either broken or thrown said amulets into the fire now ravaging many scroll shelves. The few remaining traditionalists were surrounded on all sides by the Emperor's men and the Christian crowd, and they still chose to fight to the death.

A man stepped out of the crowd and quickly drew back when Kimberley turned to him. She knew they feared her. All through the skirmish, very few civilians had attacked her owing to the ferocious manner she downed her foes. Now, all that was about to change. "Anytime now, Rachel," she called out.

"I still can't write on the codex," Rachel stammered.

A group of soldiers surrounded and killed Amenhotep. An officer pulled off the wooden ankh the Egyptian tied to his right arm and broke this symbol into two. The man turned to Kimberley with his comrades and an archer, who had just finished another assignment. "Anytime now, Rachel," Kimberley repeated, taking up a fighting stance. "I will die fighting if I must."

She flung one of her short swords at the archer through a gap the surrounding crowd had created for the Roman soldiers, and watched the weapon sink into the man's forehead with satisfaction. Picking up a dead man's sword at her feet, searing pain pushed her back before she realized an arrow had buried itself in her right shoulder. "This is futile," she muttered and crashed to the ground.

The crowd surged forward as if her fall was a signal. Some grabbed Rachel and some held Aiden.

"Kim!" Aiden cried in alarm before reverting back to his Egyptian identity. Someone knocked him out cold.

"No!" Rachel screamed, kicking away as two angry folks held her up.

The soldiers forced their way to Kimberley's body and threatened those holding her to leave her alone. Slapping a man who had brought out a dagger, their officer turned to the dying woman in royal Egyptian attire and pulled off the golden necklace around her neck as she lay on the floor.

He broke the brittle ornament and slumped with all his men in the library as the Gray Ones appeared in their gory glory. Everyone fell dead except the Bookbearer and her fellow time-travelers.

Carl Bain, or Khabawsokar, walked over to where Rachel lay near the white codex and stooped to pick it up.

"Give that back!" the brave girl cried and grabbed the slippery codex from one end. The priest of death and mummification simply pushed her hand away and stood up with the revered prize.

"You had this all this time and you never knew what to do with it, little one," he said, grinning. "Now, it is too late. The Breath of Lucifer has failed you."

Prince Ramses came round and crawled up to his dying relation. He pulled off the arrow embedded in her shoulder. "Oh, Kim," Aiden cried, looking around him once he'd changed back to himself. "We have failed."

"No–No we haven't," Kimberley whispered, breathing hard.

"Yes, you have, my dear," Carl Bain said, and handed the white codex to the entities hovering above him. The artifact froze up again, but the scroll spirits took it without incident and started floating up into the library's higher structures.

"How is that possible?" Rachel cried. "You can't take it against my will!"

"Maybe you're too tired to allow the powers your father bestowed on you to fight back, my dear," Carl Bain suggested. "Now, where is my package?" The American tormentor walked up to where Kimberley lay and looked down on her pitiable figure.

The Portwood officer laughed despite her pain. "You came all this way just for coke?" she joked.

Khabawsokar became livid. "You know what I'm talking about," he snapped, stooping and reaching out beside the female cop to grab Prince Ramses by the neck.

"Uuugh!" Aiden let out, struggling to breathe.

"Leave us alone!" a helpless Rachel screamed, remaining where she lay.

For good measure, the American thug placed a foot on Kimberley's injured shoulder and pressed down hard. "Now, where is it?"

"Don't…Don't have it with me anymore," Kimberley confessed, grimacing in pain as she tried to lift the foot on her shoulder, to no avail. "Let–Let him go!"

"Not until you give me what is mine," the maniac causing her pain muttered. "I will kill him if you don't." His grip tightened around Aiden's throat as he lifted the boy into the air.

"I didn't see it when...when we came here," Kimberley stammered. "You must...must believe me!"

"You lie, bitch! Where is it?" Carl Bain shouted. "Where is my package?!"

"I–I don't have it!" Kimberley cried, tears flooding her eyes. "Please, don't...don't kill him."

"You will all die now!" Carl Bain growled, lifting Aiden higher as he tightened his grip on the boy's throat.

Aiden's face turned blue.

"You'll kill him!" Rachel screamed. "Please don't!"

"You're all dead already!" the furious Carl Bain whispered. He heard a strange sound behind him and turned to see what had made this noise.

The blast pushed him and his infernal masters out of the Library of Scrolls at the same time another explosion rocked the pagan building's higher structures.

The white book fell back freely, down to the floor. It landed beside its current Bookbearer.

Only the noise of the leaping flames could be heard in the library.

Nanu held up the wooden cross a bit longer before dropping it in death. She had retrieved it with her failing strength from within the cloak of a dead Christian lying beside her.

"The book is dry!" Rachel discovered, dragging herself towards it. She picked up the reed pen and grabbed Aiden's hand. "Hold Kim," she told him.

They disappeared as Carl Bain and his masters reappeared in another part of the burning library. The American hustler surveyed the destruction he'd brought upon the Christians and pagans by the might of his newfound power and cursed softly.

He gave chase.

Chapter 13
GERMANY

KIMBERLEY woke up with a start, her right hand feeling her left shoulder for signs of injury. Her eyes tried to accommodate the single light bulb shining down from the ceiling through apertures frequently created between two faces she saw staring down at her. These faces were familiar ones and this knowledge made her feel better. "Where're we?" she asked.

"No idea, Kim," Aiden said. "Good that I'm no longer wearing a skirt, though."

"Very funny," Rachel said.

Explosions went off outside, far away from the room. Machine gun fire followed these loud noises. Kimberley sat up from the bed she'd been lying on; a Victorian-styled one with high poles at the corners. "Must we always show up in a war zone?" she grumbled. "Those sounded like bombs, and gunfire."

"What must we do now?" Aiden asked.

"The Bookbearer should know," Kimberley said, turning to Rachel.

"We–We will find one of Father's friends here," Rachel stammered. She seemed frightened by the explosions rocking the vicinity. "Hopefully, this person will tell us what we must do with the white book."

"And how to stop the Gray Ones," Aiden added.

"We can use an ankh like we did in Egypt," Kimberley pointed out. "They're scared of that symbol."

"We don't have any, remember?" Aiden said.

More explosions and machine gunfire.

"We could make one," the sergeant continued. "Using wood."

"We don't have the time?" Aiden objected. "And the materials?"

"We could draw them," Rachel suggested.

"And where's paper and pen for that?" Aiden asked.

"Some...Somewhere around?" Rachel thought. "Or on the book's pages?"

"First, we have to go outside," Kimberley said.

"Too dangerous," Rachel said. "We should remain here."

"We need to know where we are, girl," Kimberley told her. "We won't know if we don't look around."

"Rachel's right, Kim," Aiden decided. "What if we look around in this room for clues first?" He didn't like the thought of going outside.

"Nothing in here," Kimberley said, looking around her. "Nothing, but old boxes and...and this bed." The room had the wooden bed as its only furniture. Kimberley's younger companions stood beside two of the six wooden boxes lying around. "Wonder if there's anything in those boxes," she thought out loud.

Three new explosions rocked the distance and the two kids drew closer to the bed. The gunfire stopped.

"What now?" Aiden asked in the silence that ensued. He turned to look outside from a window and realized there was none. "Okay, who forgets to put windows in a bedroom?"

"Depends on what this place is used for," Kimberley reasoned.

"Could be a prison," Rachel whispered, standing beside Aiden.

"Oh, please," Aiden began.

Kimberley sighed. "Only one way to find out," she said, getting up and reaching for the only door in the room. "Locked," she announced moments later while shaking the door's handle. "Means we're prisoners."

"Not good," Aiden said. "We can still leave with the book, right?"

"What's with the boxes?" Kimberley asked again. "Let's open one." Her young companions had already done that. The crate they chose contained only a peculiarly red flag with a funny black cross in the middle. Kimberley's face lost all expression. "Christ," she muttered.

"What's wrong, Kim?" Aiden asked her in surprise.

"That's a Swastika," his police companion told him. "Could mean only one thing with certainty. This is..."

They heard heavy footsteps and the door burst open. Five soldiers stared into the small room. These men had the American flag sewn onto the long sleeves of their jackets.

"Quick!" their sergeant snapped. "Out the door if you want to live!"

"Okay," Kimberley said.

One of the men pulled Rachel out of the room, her precious book clasped underneath her right armpit.

"What's going on?" Aiden asked, stepping forward like his younger companion.

"They're coming, serg!" a voice called out from behind the soldiers.

"Collins, Danny, cover us!" the sergeant yelled back at this person, taking Rachel's free hand as Aiden and Kimberley followed behind the little girl through the door.

The machine gun fire resumed ahead of the party as they hurried away from the room through a passageway. A yelp and a thud prompted the men to ready their firearms while approaching an exit door on the building.

"Medic, Danny's down!" someone shouted near the exit and Kimberley frowned.

"I can shoot, you know," she told the sergeant.

He handed her his sidearm.

Danny lay near the exit, and Collins covered him, releasing bursts of gunfire from his M1 Garand rifle while dodging the return fire that smacked into wood and ricocheted off concrete all around him.

A medical officer knelt beside Danny as Kimberley joined his comrades in taking up positions behind the door and a nearby window. Their combined firepower pushed the opposition back behind some trees in the courtyard spread out before the exit door.

"We'll move out in twos," the sergeant said, taking aim with his rifle and pulling the trigger. A scream at the other end of the large court greeted his effort. "Those waiting should give covering fire."

The man holding Rachel sprang out from the door, shooting sideways as he hurried along with the little girl. Next, Aiden briskly followed another soldier, bullets zinging past his stooped figure. Those behind concentrated their gunfire on the trees with varying results. Kimberley's marksmanship remained excellent and she felt pleased with herself. Her shots took out four enemies before she raced out of the building with the three men carrying the wounded Danny.

The others gave covering fire from four Jeeps packed beside the buildings. The peculiar design of these military vehicles strengthened Kimberley's shaky assertion that the book had brought them into World War II.

"Where are we going?" she asked the soldier sitting beside her in the last Jeep.

"Back to our lines, miss," the man replied her, shooting at the receding enemy as the vehicle sped off.

"Are we behind enemy lines?" she wondered aloud.

"Yes," the man replied, curiously looking at her. "Didn't you know?"

"Of course, I did," Kimberley lied. "Just trying to confirm that. Thanks." She noticed that the other men in the Jeep were throwing glances at her. "We just–just didn't know where we were," she added.

"Yeah, sure," one of the soldiers in front said. "They must have covered your eyes before bringing you here. Good that we found you three when we did. Nuclear experiments never go well for test subjects."

Kimberley frowned. Maybe touching the man beside her would help her realize whose life she'd taken up, yet she hesitated. "What do you mean, exactly?" she asked the soldier in front.

"Ever heard of the Alsos Mission?"

"She's not been debriefed, Johnny," the Jeep's driver interrupted.

"Right," Jonny said, turning to Kimberley. "HQ will give you details when they decide you should know, miss."

"Am I a spy?" Kimberley wondered.

"You don't know, miss?" Johnny seemed surprised.

"Maybe she's still dazed by the torture they gave her, Johnny," the driver reasoned. "She'll come round once we get to HQ, but right now we need to keep a lookout for Germans out there." The soldier scanned the landscape to his left as the vehicle raced on. "We aren't out of the woods, yet."

Kimberley touched the private sitting beside her and the needed information flooded her head. The man stared at her. "It's cold," she told him. "Sorry."

The weather had actually turned cold, and Kimberley realized what this implied.

"Someone's on the road!" the radio beside the driver crackled.

Kimberley saw the man step onto the middle of the road before the first Jeep speeding ahead of the group. Aiden was in that Jeep. "No!" she yelled before the first Jeep's rear sprang up into the air, its occupants falling off like toy soldiers dropping from an upturned toy car.

"Number one's under attack! Take evasive action!" the radio coughed out even as the driver swerved to the right, avoiding the Jeep in front by inches. He screeched to a halt and everyone scrambled for cover beside the car.

The lone German standing in the middle of the road shot the first Jeep's occupants where they lay, one after the other. Kimberley and the soldiers from the remaining three Jeeps opened fire on him.

"What the hell?" Johnny complained beside her. "Nothing's getting to him."

"He just stands there," another soldier added.

"Like he's wearing something bulletproof," their sergeant deduced. "Maybe we could wear it down, though. Keep shooting!"

Kimberley aimed for the German soldier's forehead. When the bullet deflected off nothing, she looked more closely at the face underneath the helmet.

Carl Bain.

"Not again," she muttered.

"What?" Johnny asked her.

"It's not his armor," she said to herself.

"What?"

Before Kimberley could say something, she saw Aiden get up from the ground and fall back again after the enemy pointed the pistol at him. "Oh, my God!" she whispered.

Aiden had been shot.

"Aiden!" Rachel screamed behind the second vehicle, getting up only to be pulled back down by the soldier holding her. Their assailant noticed this reaction and briefly turned to Rachel's direction.

"You'll get yourself killed, girl," the man with Rachel warned her, but she wasn't listening. She turned to Kimberley.

"We must do something, Kim," she cried, staring at her fellow time-traveler.

Kimberley nodded, but remained transfixed. She saw the pool of blood spreading underneath Aiden and wondered whether she was dreaming.

It was no dream.

The man with the Luger stepped around the upturned Jeep in front of the column, his invincibility demonstrated by the bullets bouncing off his body, limbs and head. He shot two more US servicemen before turning his side arm towards Rachel's distant position.

"No!" Kimberley shouted, seeing the impending disaster.

Carl Bain fired two shots in quick succession. Shots that careened off the white book's protective dome, which materialized in the nick of time. This icy sheet quickly enveloped the last two vehicles and everyone behind them, the reason for its sudden appearance visible high above the road for all to see.

All except the dead.

"My God!" Johnny cried, looking around him and upwards. "What's going on?"

The Gray Ones had almost swarmed out the Sun's light with their number, putting those below into an environment of forest-like shade.

"It's the devil, that's what!" Johnny's sergeant cried a few feet away.

"Yeah," a fellow private lying next to the sergeant said. "Satan's come to collect his own."

"And we're all going to hell 'cause of these damn Krauts," another private complained.

In addition to the goings-on outside the infernal dome, many of the soldiers kept turning to stare at Rachel's book owing to what it had achieved for them a few moments ago.

"And what's with the book, miss?" the US Army sergeant asked Kimberley. "Some kind of new German weapon you were protecting?"

"No, of course, not," Kimberley said, her eyes fixed on Aiden's still figure across the road. "You don't have the slightest idea what it is."

"I know your little friend over there had it with her when you three were in that holding cell," the sergeant pointed out, "so figured they knew you had it with you, and must have decided to leave it with you."

"I'm not a double spy, sergeant," Kimberley said, her teary eyes still on Aiden's body stretched out on the dusty road behind the maniac now trying to break the dome with shots from his Luger.

"Whatever you are, Alsos leadership will be very interested in that book, or whatever it is," the US Army sergeant said. "And I must get it to them."

"Pray we leave here alive first."

Carl Bain stopped shooting and walked over to the third Jeep, behind which crouched the female police sergeant and three US soldiers. Kimberley looked up from inside the white book's cursed dome as the tenacious man approached her.

"Stop shooting!" the US Army sergeant with Kimberley ordered his men. "Conserve your bullets."

"About time you did so, Sergeant Bradley," Carl Bain told him. "Even though your weapons are no match to the power behind my invincibility,"

"H-How did you know my name, mister?" The sergeant and his men wore no tags. "Lucky guess," he scoffed.

"What do you want?" Kimberley asked the maniac standing outside the dome. She spoke another foreign language.

"You know what I want," he replied in the same language. Sounded German.

The American soldiers could only look on.

"I don't know what you want," Kimberley said.

"Give me the book, and my package," Carl Bain said. "Haven't you gone through enough trouble for that little box, already?"

"Can't give you the book, you know that," Kimberley said, shaking her head. "And I don't think I still have your package."

The American outlaw smiled. "You can do better than that, sweetie," he said.

Kimberley frowned. "You don't believe me."

"Your friend is still alive."

"What?"

"Your friend is still alive," the German officer repeated in English, turning away to walk back up the road. "I'll kill him this time if you don't comply with my demands."

Kimberley started. "Aiden."

"No, please don't!" Rachel cried.

"He's threatening you?" Johnny's face reddened. "Sniffling Kraut! Just wait till I get you!"

"Nazi scum!" another soldier behind the last Jeep shouted.

"Give me what I want, girl, or I'll kill him this time," Carl Bain repeated, pointing his Luger down at Aiden. A pool of blood had spread out underneath the boy's right arm and the American hustler shifted his left foot in order to avoid the fluid staining his polished boot.

"Give him his package, Kim!" Rachel cried. "Don't let him kill Aiden."

"You know he wants the book as well," Kimberley started.

"Just give him one, already," the little girl cried. "Aiden's life is at stake here!"

"Okay, okay," Kimberley said, reaching into her inner jacket pocket and hoping she still had the little silver box after their last time travel. What she found there in addition to the box filled her with renewed hope. "Come and take your package," she told Carl Bain.

"Very good," the man standing over Aiden said. "You've changed your mind."

"Yes," Kimberley said, smiling sheepishly.

Carl Bain returned his gun to its holster, grinning. "You see, it's not so difficult, eh?"

"Yes," the Portwood police sergeant said. "It's not so difficult."

"Can you tell us what's going on, miss?" Sergeant Bradley demanded.

"It's a long story," Kimberley said. "You're never ever going to believe me."

"Then I guess we will have to force it out of you once we get to HQ," the US Army sergeant grumbled.

"Where is it?" Carl Bain asked Kimberley when he got to her position.

"I'll give you your package for the boy's life now," Kimberley said. "Later, you will talk to the Bookbearer about the book; heaven knows I've tried about that."

"Deal."

"Take it now." She stretched her hand out of the white book's magical dome and placed something on the palm of the man's gloved right hand.

Carl Bain's expression quickly changed and his face became contorted in pain. "You bitch!" he snapped. "What did you give me?"

"Your package, of course," Kimberley said with all innocence.

The man opened his right palm and vanished with the gray mist covering the Sun.

The books protection disappeared and Kimberley sprang up from her position, Aiden's condition in her mind. "Medic!" she screamed as she raced up to the boy. "Someone's alive here!"

The military doctor with the party had already come up. "I'll bandage the wound," he said, dropping his first aid kit and going to work. "Don't worry; I think he'll be fine."

Some of the men had surrounded the group while others removed the dead.

"What did you give that Kraut, miss?" Johnny asked Kimberley. "Funny how he just disappeared."

"You will never believe me if I tell you," Kimberley said.

"Guess we're all eager to know."

Kimberley looked at him and frowned. His comrades nodded in agreement. They were curious to know. Kimberley smiled. "I gave him a tiny gold cross," she said.

"I believe you," Johnny said. "Krauts need Jesus."

His comrades laughed with him.

Kimberley rolled her eyes and turned back to Aiden and the medic working to save his life.

"Johnny," Sergeant Bradley began as he came up. "Take that woman and her companions into custody and confiscate that book. They're our prisoners now."

Chapter 14
THE ALSOS MISSION

COLONEL Boris Theodore Pash looked up from his papers and studied his cabinet members seated round the large oak shoe-shaped desk in his equally large office. "You're telling me the Germans have a powerful new secret weapon?" he repeated, trying to appreciate the enormity of that statement.

"Yes, sir," Captain Wayne Stanard said. "The sergeant with the team reports invincibility unrivaled by any of our most advanced scientific research projects."

"What exactly do you mean, captain?" Colonel Pash asked.

"They were held up for two hours by only one man, sir," a Counter Intelligence Corps agent said. "This soldier had…" he looked at papers before him, "only one Luger."

Colonel Pash frowned. "Did he have a bulletproof vest on?"

"Perhaps they have developed a new kind of vest?" Captain Stanard suggested.

"None that we're aware of, sir," the CIC agent replied.

The colonel sighed. His job was hard enough without this kind of news. Alsos had encountered numerous roadblocks in the past few hours that deserved his unreserved attention, chief amongst them being that the French First Army had captured Stuttgart from the Germans the day before, something that the Americans and British had never envisaged and planned for. "Any news from the French?"

"General Devers of the Sixth Army Group is threatening to cut off supplies to de Lattre if the French did not relinquish Stuttgart," Captain Stanard said.

"We don't need that now," Colonel Pash said. "We need to work with the French, even though their present action is threatening what we intend to do at Hechingen."

"We could send in a ground force instead, sir," Major William Allis, a War Department staff, suggested. "A small force like we used in Stuttgart could get in and out without the French knowing about it."

"Good," the colonel said. "CIC Agent Joana here reports that Otto Hahn is at his laboratory in Tailfingen, while Werner Heisenberg and Max von Laue are at Heisenberg's laboratory in Hechingen. We could scrap Operation Effective and use a smaller team."

"What about Sergeant Bradley's report, sir?" a CIC agent asked the colonel, who nodded and looked at the woman sitting quietly all this time on a chair placed in the middle of the room.

"And where is the book now?" the colonel asked the CIC agent.

"Right here, sir," the agent replied, holding up the white book for all to see.

Colonel Pash turned to Kimberley, who sat straight on the single chair in the middle of the room. She had her small cross necklace with her in case the Gray Ones and their American minion decided to show up.

"And what do you have to say about this, Agent Joana?"

"Eh, what?" Kimberley had forgotten her alternate Counter Intelligence Corps name, but now remembered. "Well, sir," she began, "the story of that book is bigger than all the wars the world has ever fought in history put together." She smiled when she saw the confusion plastered on the many faces surrounding her. The colonel before her had a frown on his face instead.

"This is no joking matter, agent," the Alsos leader warned. "Is this book a secret weapon?"

"What? Of course, not." Kimberley shook her head. "Not in my knowledge, no, sir."

"Sergeant Bradley reports it protected the Jeeps from the lone German with a 'dome of ice'?" the first Counter Intelligence Corps agent pointed out, and Kimberley scoffed.

"That must be a figment of the sergeant's imagination, sir," she replied. "What, with his men under attack and all that, anyone could flip in that situation."

Sergeant Bradley stiffened where he stood. "I know what I saw, agent," he said. "You were there, why are you now lying all of a sudden?"

"Am I, sergeant?" Kimberley asked him. "A lone super soldier? A dome of ice from a child's book? Really, sergeant, which sane person would believe all that fairy tale?"

Those gathered laughed at this, but Colonel Pash remained silent.

"So, why is the book wet, agent?" he demanded. "Always wet, I mean."

Kimberley made light of this question as well. "I don't know, sir," she said. "Someone must have thrown it into a bathtub, you know."

This time, Colonel Pash laughed with his cabinet. "Sergeant Bradley's men must be very exhausted to be reporting sighting ghosts and lone German super fighters during this expedition beyond enemy lines," he reasoned. "Nonetheless, I'm assigning Dr. Carlton the job of investigating this. If the Germans have a new weapon and this...this book defends against it, please find out, doctor, and if Sergeant Bradley's men are having some kind of psychological breakdown, doctor, please don't hesitate to let us know as well."

"Yes, colonel," Dr. John Carlton said with a chuckle. "I seriously doubt the veracity of this story," the Cornell University scholar and scientist added. "However, I'll thoroughly pursue my duty to its conclusion, sir."

"Okay, gentlemen," Colonel Pash said in conclusion. "You can go now, Agent Joana. Sergeant Bradley."

"Thank you, sir," Kimberley said, getting up. A private led her and the sergeant towards an exit. "What of the book, sir?" she asked. "Eva will be distressed if she doesn't get it back."

"I will return it to your friend once I've given it a thorough check, agent," Dr. Carlton said. "No need for her to be distressed, dear."

But Kimberley wasn't convinced she had succeeded in taking everyone's suspicion away from the ancient relic. She could only hope for the best now.

"Back to our pressing work," Colonel Pash resumed as she was being escorted out. "And first stop, Hechingen."

"We have taken delivery of two armored cars, four Jeeps with machine gun mounts, and two .50 caliber machine guns, sir," someone stated as Kimberley went out of Colonel Pash's office.

"Whatever you're hiding, agent, I'm going to find out," Sergeant Bradley said behind her.

*   *   *

Carl Bain watched his men unpack equipment from three Tiger II tanks. He admired the professionalism of the German army at a time he knew that they had lost their petty war. If only they had a better commander-in-chief than Adolf Hitler, he thought, winning would have been very easy, since he'd confronted the enemy and knew that these so-called 'allies' had many weaknesses. Shaking his head, he turned to look at his invisible companion again. The infernal war he'd found himself in mattered more to him at the moment.

The American hustler flinched and looked at his right palm. He looked at the cross sign that had burnt into his black glove where the police sergeant had placed the cursed symbol. He wondered why his masters feared a simple cross sign.

"We need a new plan," he told the ashen form floating beside him. "This one is not working."

The demon remained expressionless and Carl Bain cursed softly. "Have you lost your tongue?" he snapped, but the gray entity did not react. Their silent presence could be frustrating, the American thought, and what use was the power they had given him if he could not get back his package with it?

Carl Bain cursed again. He stood up and looked out at the terrain before him. The battalion was preparing to move out of the vicinity, having been pushed back by the French First Army. The American, however, intended going the opposite way.

A new plan had emerged.

"Yes," he told the demon beside him. "It's good that you've found her. We will manipulate her before they get to her."

The demon's face remained blank.

"This will work," Carl Bain told himself.

*   *   *

That evening, Aiden brightened when he spotted Kimberley entering the clinic block with Rachel right behind her. He had recovered some strength after the military doctor removed a bullet from his shoulder, stitched him up, gave him pain pills and adequately fed him.

"Hey," he said, reaching out his right hand when they came up to his bed.

"Hey," Kimberley returned, taking the outstretched hand. "Glad to see you awake."

"I'm okay now, Kim," Aiden assured her.

"Good to hear," Rachel said. "We almost lost you."

"We should stick together from now on," Kimberley whispered, looking around. "And I think it's time we moved on."

"What about the book?" Aiden began.

"It's here, somewhere," Kimberley said quietly. "We just need to find it without raising suspicion. Good that we're not confined."

"And our contact?" Aiden asked.

"I am yet to find her here," Rachel said. "I hope I find her soon."

"Just keep looking," Kimberley said. "Keep looking while I look for the book."

"Won't it reveal itself when the Booklords come for it?" Aiden asked her.

"Of course, it will, but we can't wait for that to happen, right?"

"Those things haven't been able to take the book, you know," Aiden pointed out.

"Not for trying," Rachel said. "Remember they almost succeeded last time? They..."

"We just have to find a way to end this and...and return home," Kimberley cut in.

"Will we ever do that, Kim?" Aiden asked. "Return home, I mean?"

"Yes, why not?" Kimberley snapped. "We just have to find one of Rachel's father's friends who know what we must do with the book. We can go home afterwards, right Rachel?"

The little girl nodded silently, looking down at the floor.

"Or we can just go back now with the book?" Aiden proposed and Rachel looked up anxiously.

"Aiden," Kimberley whispered as a military doctor passed the bed. "We promised to help Rachel, remember?"

Aiden nodded, and then shook his head, staring at her. "Dunno what's happening anymore, Kim," he whispered back. "It's like we've lost our way."

Rachel turned white. "No, we haven't," she said quietly, frowning. "I–I just need to...to find our contact here."

"If she's here, that is," Kimberley whispered. "She could be anywhere, for all we know."

"If she's not here, then we won't be here," Rachel said.

"And how did you know that?" Aiden asked her.

"Experience?"

Two sentries stopped outside the military clinic. "You need to come with us, miss," one of them told Kimberley.

"Okay," she said. "Stay with Aiden," she told Rachel, who held her right hand.

"Please, don't go," the little girl begged her. "They are not our friends."

"She has to," Aiden said. "You'll come back, won't you, Kim?"

"Yes, I'll come back," Kimberley said. She had her doubts, but could only keep these to herself at the moment.

They took her to a separate cabin in the Alsos camp. A familiar face greeted her from behind a small desk on which lay the white book. Kimberley noted the presence of Sergeant Bradley and Private Johnny among the men standing beside the door. She studied the ancient codex as she sat down on the seat offered her by her guest. The artifact appeared not to have been tampered with. Yet.

"It appears you have not been truthful with us, CIC Agent Joana," Dr. John Carlton began, sliding the book towards his end of the desk. "I have been examining the nature of the material used in producing this book and it seems quite remarkable."

"What do you mean, sir?" Kimberley asked, feigning ignorance. "That's just a book, right?"

"Wrong, my dear," the learned doctor said, standing up to walk towards a rack of books. He picked out one with a red cover and brought it back to the desk. "The History of Ancient Rome."

Kimberley's heart skipped. "What has that got to do with anything, sir?" she asked.

"Everything, agent," the doctor said. "Everything."

"I'm all ears, sir."

A short pause followed. Kimberley braced herself.

"Ever heard of papyrus?" Dr. Carlton asked her.

"Yes, sir," she replied. "The Egyptians used it for their manuscripts, I think."

"Well, Agent Joana, this book was made from a very tough papyrus-like material," the doctor revealed. "I think it was even made before the earliest form of the codex came into use in ancient Rome."

"Okay, sir," Kimberley chuckled. "I guess Eva never knew she'd been carrying around ancient treasure."

"You really think this is a joke, agent?" Sergeant Bradley asked her. "You'll soon think otherwise."

"Right," Private Johnny said, and the men at the door started murmuring.

"How did you come across the children?" Dr. Carlton asked Kimberley.

"They were part of a group our targets prepared for a nuclear experiment," Kimberley replied. "I was forced to join this group when the Germans discovered what I was actually doing. It's all there in my report." She wondered where all the questioning was headed.

"Good intel, by the way," Dr. Carlton commended. "We now know where Otto Han is, thanks to you."

"Thank you, sir."

"But you haven't been truthful about this book, and Sergeant Bradley's report."

"To the best of my knowledge, I have been, sir," Kimberley lied.

"Liar!" Sergeant Bradley exploded. "Can't believe you made

mockery of my report before my superiors. Just wait and see, miss. Dr. Carlton will expose you and your lies."

"And you'll have to tell us about that lone super soldier when we finally break you," Johnny added. "Right, serg?"

The doctor studied Kimberley briefly. He sighed and opened the white book. "Whose names are these, agent?"

"I don't know, sir," Kimberley replied. "It's possible Eva writes on it, after all, it's her book, right?"

"Are you saying this is Eva's book?"

"Exactly, sir."

Dr. Carlton turned to a guard stationed at the door. "Bring the girl," he directed.

"I hope you'll take it easy with her, sir," Kimberley pleaded. "She's been through a lot, really."

"I don't understand, agent."

"That little girl's the one with the book, doctor," Sergeant Bradley pointed out. "She knows more than she lets on."

"She lost her parents in Warsaw," Kimberley revealed, glaring at the US Army sergeant.

"I see," Dr. Carlton said. "Don't worry, agent."

Rachel entered the room looking distressed. She walked over to Kimberley and the woman took her hands.

"Eva, how are you, my dear?" Dr. Carlton began.

"I'm fine, sir," Rachel replied.

"And this is your book?"

"Yes, it is."

"Eva, why did you write these names?" she was asked.

"I–I was whiling away time with it, in...in the room?"

"You were provided different mediums for writing while you were...incarcerated?" the doctor asked, flipping through the book's pages. "Even charcoal and...and ink?"

"I think she used whatever she saw, sir," Kimberley said.

"Is that correct, my dear?" the doctor asked Eva.

"Yes, of course," Rachel replied.

"Well then," Dr. Carlton said. "This means that you're Agent Joana's accomplice, little one."

"I don't understand, sir," Kimberley started. "What are you saying?"

"I have investigated this, my dear, and I've come to the conclusion that you're both lying."

Both accused individuals had blank faces.

"I have looked at Sergeant Bradley's report and I've spoken to the men who volunteered for the mission he led in order to get you out?"

"And what did you find?" Kimberley asked the man.

"Their narrations corroborate," Dr. Carlton said. "They appear to be telling the same story, and it's obvious that the first Jeep did not flip over from a road mine. I examined the pictures they brought back."

"That is not enough evidence to conclude that I've been lying, sir," Kimberley objected.

"Yes, well, that coupled with the fact that the book before me is unlike any I've ever seen," the scientist said. "I also have with me an individual who had been telling me a purely fantastic story about this...this white book." Dr. Carlton noted the stark surprise on the face of the little girl with the agent, but continued like nothing was out of place. "She was also rescued from the Germans in the raid that brought you back."

New information.

"I don't remember seeing any other civilian among the soldiers that rescued us, sir," Kimberley said, trying to hide her alarm.

"But you must believe me, my dear, knowing that I just used a name no other individual in this room knows for Eva's book," the scientist interrogating her argued.

The white book.

Kimberley wondered if Dr. Carlton had really found the woman Rachel had been looking for.

"We don't believe you," Rachel said, and the doctor smiled.

"So, it's true then," he said, getting up from his seat. "I'm afraid you've been found out, my dear," he told the little girl, and turned to Sergeant Bradley. "Bring in Mrs. Hannah Braun."

The US Army sergeant nodded and left. He soon returned with a middle-aged woman dressed in a black blouse and a gray skirt. Her blonde hair was cut short and her facial features had sharp lines as if chiseled out from stone. Her firm steps conveyed the impression that she could soak up pressure. Her piercing eyes took in every little detail as she walked into Dr. Carlton's office, and they widened when they rested on Rachel's face.

"Aunt Shira!" Rachel exclaimed, wringing her hands around Kimberley's.

"Rachel, is...is that you? It cannot be," the woman said, moving towards the little girl and her companion.

"Rachel?" a puzzled Dr. Carlton demanded. "But, of course, your name is not Eva. Rachel is all over the book's pages. Fascinating."

"Her name's Eva Rachel Braun, sir," Kimberley lied. "Looks like you found her aunt."

Dr. Carlton stared at the Counter Intelligence Corps agent.

"Okay, this is getting interesting," Sergeant Bradley told his men.

"More lies, Agent Joana?" the doctor wondered aloud. "Mrs. Braun here has already told me that she has no living relative here in Germany."

"But you just saw how she reacted when she saw Eva?" Kimberley pressed on.

"You don't need to do that anymore, Kim," Rachel said, looking at her aunt with tears in her eyes as the middle-aged woman drew nearer.

"What are you doing?" Kimberley whispered.

"We don't need to hide anymore," the little girl sobbed, taking her aunt's outstretched hands.

"And she's right, agent," Dr. Carlton said. "You don't need to hide anymore."

Kimberley stared at Rachel's aunt while holding her forehead. "You had to be a German Jew," she grumbled, looking away in frustration. It was all in the open, now. No need to hide anything anymore.

Mrs. Hannah Braun hugged Rachel before looking the little girl over. She touched Rachel's face with her right hand and patted her body. "You–You survived the Mine, child," she exclaimed. "Is this really you, Rachel?"

"Yes, Aunt Shira," Rachel replied. "I survived, but they're after me."

The woman frowned as she hugged her niece again. "I knew something was wrong when I saw the white one."

Rachel leaned in towards her and spoke in a foreign language.

"What're you telling her, Rachel?" Kimberley wanted to know.

"Nothing," the Jewish girl replied, looking up. "We're just speaking Hebrew."

Kimberley felt ostracized.

"You will need the second book to achieve what you seek," Hannah Braun told Rachel in English.

"What is she saying, Rachel?" Kimberley asked the little girl, coming forward.

"The black one?" Rachel asked her aunt. "But Father said we can defeat them without…"

"No," Aunt Shira said. "You'll need the second book."

"Is there another book?" Dr. Carlton wanted to know.

"Yes, there is," Kimberley said. "The black one."

"Aunt Shira says we have to find it," Rachel said.

"No," the woman said. "I said you'll need it to achieve what you must achieve. Unfortunately, you will never find it now."

"Why?" Kimberley asked. "Why can't we find it?"

"The Booklords have already found it," Aunt Shira said. "It is in their custody as we speak."

"Oh, God," Rachel exclaimed, covering her mouth with both hands.

"And how did you know that, Aunt Shira?" Kimberley felt a funny feeling in her stomach. "Have you been in contact with the Gray Ones?"

"No, of course, not," Rachel's aunt replied. "I practice Shurabi, so I know what has happened to both books since their creation."

"Shura what?" Kimberley frowned. She hated new words. They implied new meanings and new twists in the narration.

"Shurabi," Mrs. Braun repeated. "Ancient Jewish magic. It has helped me to be ahead of the Booklords all these years."

"Okay, I get that," a lost Kimberley said. "Which other option is there, then?" she asked Rachel's aunt.

"Returning the book to the Gray Ones," the woman replied.

"Ok, that's not an option," the Portwood police officer quipped. "We can't trust them."

"You don't need to," Aunt Shira said. "This is the only available option left for you now, my dear."

Dr. Carlton cleared his throat. "So, your fantasy-filled story notwithstanding, Mrs. Braun, we've established that this white book has a black copy," he said. "We've also agreed that you lied in your report, Agent Joana."

Kimberley said nothing.

"We've also discovered the veracity of Sergeant Bradley's report," the Cornell University scientist added, and Sergeant Bradley grinned. "Which leads us to the one question I need answered, Agent Joana: Do the Germans have a new secret super weapon? A super soldier only this book can defeat, and how does the book do that? Please be patriotic for once, agent. Alsos needs to know the truth."

"There's no secret weapon, sir," Kimberley replied. "What we have is a man who had been following us from our time, because we have something he wants."

"From your time?" Sergeant Bradley asked. "Do you think this is all a joke?"

"I don't believe that, agent," Dr. Carlton said.

"You believe this pile of paper can defend against a super soldier and yet you don't believe it's a time machine?" Kimberley asked him. "Okay."

"I don't believe you, Agent Joana," Private Johnny said. "That's not possible."

"I don't care what you think, private," Kimberley returned.

"Unbelievable," the private chuckled. "So, where're you coming from, the past or the future?"

"Actually, we're coming from the past, because we had to go back in time while escaping from the Booklords," Kimberley replied. "Now, we intend moving forward into the future, into our time."

Private Johnny's face turned white. "How you lie with a straight face is beyond me, miss," he said coldly.

"You forget she's an agent, private," Dr. Carlton said. "For all we know, she could be working for the Germans right now, judging from all the lies she's been telling us."

"But it's true," Aunt Shira said, and all eyes turned to her. "Both books are time machines, doctor."

"Are you sure of this, Mrs. Braun?" Dr. Carlton asked, and the woman nodded. "Incredible," he exclaimed. The middle-aged woman had sounded convincingly truthful all evening, so he had no reason to disbelieve her, yet. "Get Colonel Pash," he directed a guard.

"The colonel has left with the contingent drafted for the Hechingen mission, sir," the guard reported.

"Then get him on the phone, damn it!"

"Yes, sir."

Kimberley noticed a drop in the room's temperature and moved to pick up the white book from Dr. Carlton's desk.

"Hold it right there," the man interrupted her. "Alsos will confiscate this…this white book and…and will investigate whether it's really a time machine like you said, agent."

"I told your superior that this book's story is bigger than all the wars the world has ever fought in history put together, sir," Kimberley reminded him. "You still don't get it, do you?"

"It's possible that the Germans have acquired a new biological technology and are strengthening their soldiers with this weapon," the scientist rather continued, deep in thought. "This book must be defensive in nature, if one must believe the fantastically unbelievable story you, the little girl and Mrs. Braun just told us. Obviously, the Germans want to get it at all cost, since it's…mysticism could unravel their biological weapons technology, right?"

Kimberley rolled her eyes.

"And if it turns out that you're right about this…pile of paper being a time machine, agent, then we have our own super weapon right there, my dear."

"That will not help anybody, doctor," Mrs. Braun, or Aunt Shira, told Dr. John Carlton. "Like the nuclear weapon your government is seeking to develop, another super weapon will only cause more destruction."

"Let the generals decide that, Mrs. Braun. I'm just doing my job," Dr. Carlton replied.

"It's getting cold in here," Sergeant Bradley observed.

"You know what that means, Rachel," Aunt Shira told her niece.

"They're coming," the little girl said, cleaning her teary eyes.

"And what do you mean by that, little one?" Sergeant Bradley demanded, looking out of the room with his men.

"It means we have to leave right now with the book, sergeant," Kimberley said, "or else everyone in this camp will die."

Sergeant Bradley panicked when he remembered what happened to his men on the road from Stuttgart, but refused to say anything that would help the double agent.

"You're not going anywhere, Agent Joana," Dr. Carlton said. "And no one's going to die. Take them away, sergeant."

The US Army sergeant moved to obey his superior.

"We've lost all hope," Rachel said, beginning to cry again as the soldiers surrounded her and her companions.

"No, we've not, Rachel," Kimberley told her while her aunt consoled her.

"No need to be afraid, my dear," Aunt Shira, or Mrs. Hannah Braun, said. "You just need to give back the book."

"Stop saying that, woman," Kimberley snapped. "Can't you see you've done enough damage already?" She searched frantically for her tiny cross before Sergeant Bradley's men forced her hands behind her back. Unfortunately, she could not find it. "You don't know what you're doing, Dr. Carlton," she pleaded.

"I know exactly what I'm doing, agent," the doctor said. "Unlike you, my dear, winning this war at all cost is the priority of everyone in this camp who volunteered for the Alsos Mission."

A slow wind picked up as the room's temperature fell drastically. Kimberley moved to pick up the white book a second time. Sergeant Bradley held her back by grabbing her waist. She managed to touch the ancient codex before the lights went out.

The soldiers could only shoot sporadically.

Their screams were gut-wrenching.

And within seconds, it was all over.

Chapter 15
PRISONERS OF WAR

THE book's dome started radiating a bluish hue that aided the sense of sight. Kimberley's thumping heart slowed down when she realized that Rachel and Aunt Shira were also inside the unearthly protection. The icy support spiking out from the book restricted her movements and she didn't like that.

"W-What just happened?" Sergeant Bradley demanded behind her.

"What I've always feared," she replied. "And I don't think it's…"

Gray hands penetrated the dome and grabbed her neck, pulling her towards the icy layer forming the hemispherical structure. The heat from these demonic extensions burnt her skin as she struggled to breath. Suddenly, she was free, panting and feeling her scorched neck. She turned from the strange, ash-like material on the floor before her to see Mrs. Hannah Braun, or Aunt Shira, swinging something around at the flailing infernal hands trying to get at the white book, or any living thing, through the dome's icy layer. The middle-aged woman had turned a fragment of the icy extensions supporting the book's magical dome into a weapon. More ash-like substance fluttered to the room's floor.

The Gray Ones withdrew and the magical dome disappeared.

Kimberley stared at the middle-aged German woman.

"You can fight them with a piece of the book's defense if you can break out a part of it," Mrs. Hannah Braun, or Aunt Shira, told her.

"Never knew that," Rachel said, wide-eyed.

"Now you do, my dear," her aunt said.

"They can now withstand the book's defense for longer," Kimberley noted. "I wonder why this is so." Rachel's aunt wanted to say something, but thought better of it. Kimberley noted that as well. Despite the defensive information she just got about the white book's icy extensions from the German Jew, Kimberley still felt that the woman knew more than she had revealed to the Alsos team investigating Sergeant Bradley's report.

The Portwood police sergeant looked around. Chaos ruled Dr. Carlton's small office. The man, himself, lay dead near Kimberley's feet, killed the instant his infernal visitors came calling.

Sergeant Bradley dropped down beside Private Johnny's body, sobbing. His men lay strewn around like ragdolls, smoke still coming out from the muzzles of their hot M1 Garand rifles in the cold environment the white book continued to sustain within and around the small office. "Why?" the sergeant cried. "What killed them all?"

Kimberley had nothing to say. She searched her pockets for her cross necklace a second time. She frowned when she could not find it. Using a pen she saw on the dead Dr. Carlton's desk, she drew a cross on a piece of paper, and handed Rachel the pen.

"Who did this, Agent Joana?" Sergeant Bradley asked her.

Kimberley walked to the door without saying anything. Sergeant Bradley cocking his sidearm stopped her cold.

"What is it, young man?" Rachel's aunt asked the soldier. "What more do you want from her?"

"She caused all this," the man shouted. "You all caused this mayhem."

"Your superiors never listened to me," Kimberley said quietly. "None of this would have happened if they did."

"They...They were doing their job," Bradley pointed out.

'Just as I was doing mine back in Portwood,' Kimberley thought. "What do you want, sergeant?" she asked.

"Where are you going?" the man demanded, sniffing.

"To see if my friend is still alive in your clinic facility."

"Aiden," Rachel exclaimed, moving towards the door. "Please, God, let him be alive!" she prayed. Events of the past few minutes had kept her from remembering her wounded friend. "Please, God, let him be alive!" she repeated at the door.

"Stop!" Sergeant Bradley ordered her and she froze. "I'm...I'm coming with you two."

"Me, too," Aunt Shira said, stepping over a dead soldier.

"Protect us, Rachel," Kimberley told the little girl and turned to the others. "I can't hope on a piece of paper to do that," she said, raising the sheet on which she had drawn a cross for all to see. "It's a joke," she added when no one laughed.

Rachel picked up the white book as she passed Dr. Carlton's desk and

Kimberley made way for her to take the lead as they left the doctor's office.

Outside, the camp appeared lifeless. Dead bodies lay everywhere.

"Who did this?" Sergeant Bradley repeated. "Who would do such a thing?"

"Alsos Spear HQ, Alsos Spear HQ," a radio crackled somewhere in the compound. "Alsos Spear HQ, please respond."

Bradley moved away to investigate this at the same time a familiar figure appeared at the door of the Unit Clinic in the compound.

"Aiden!" Rachel shouted, racing up to his tired-looking figure. "Aiden, you're alive!"

"Aiden, did they touch you?" Kimberley wondered aloud as she came up to the two kids. "You survived again."

"I know, Kim," Aiden said. "They met me on my bed, and just…just left me alone."

"We've all been with the book for some time now, Kim," Rachel said. "That gives the three of us some protection, you know."

"Are you saying we're all now Bookbearers?" Kimberley asked her.

"No," the little girl said. "But it is possible that the Bookbearer's protection from the book could rub off on those bearing the burden of the book with him or her." She looked at her aunt for support.

Aunt Shira nodded. "That protection wanes off if the strife is not quickly resolved, though, so we're lucky your friend here is still alive," she added. "The same goes for you, too, my dear," she told Kimberley.

"Okay." For some reason, Kimberley didn't like what she just heard.

"And your friend here appears wounded already," Mrs. Braun, or Aunt Shira, continued. "The Booklords don't attack the wounded, or the diseased, if I remember correctly."

"That really works?" Kimberley asked. "Glad to hear that."

"Everyone is alive except the doctors and nurses working shifts here," Aiden announced, and Kimberley brushed past him to enter the clinic.

True to the boy's report, only the clinic's staff lay dead on the building's floor.

The soldiers on the beds appeared perplexed.

"What's going on, miss?" one of them asked Kimberley, but she had no ready reply.

"Back at the Mine, Barak was wounded by the Romans and when the demons came for the books, he wasn't killed," Aunt Shira said behind Kimberley on entering the clinic.

"Wasn't he associated with the book, Aunt Shira?" Rachel asked.

"No, he was visiting his relation at the time. He had travelled all the way from Rome."

Sergeant Bradley entered the clinic. He'd been at the communication block for some time. He pointed his sidearm at Kimberley and her group standing in the middle of the room.

"Not again," Kimberley said.

"Task Force A wants us to hold these four individuals as prisoners of war until they get back here," the US Army sergeant announced to shouts of approval from some of the wounded men in the room. "Now, who's with me?"

Some of the patients stood from their beds.

"What's happening, Kim?" an alarmed Aiden asked.

"I thought you were with us," Rachel accused Sergeant Bradley.

"Don't do this," Kimberley pleaded with the man.

"Orders are orders," he said. "The colonel will know what to do with the four of you."

"Step back," Kimberley warned the injured soldiers taking positions around them. "I don't want to cause you more pain."

"And I don't want to put a bullet through you," Sergeant Bradley warned her. "Now, hand over that cursed book, child," he told Rachel, his left hand stretched out towards her.

"No, I won't," Rachel said, tightly clasping her precious book to her bosom.

Sergeant Bradley placed the pistol's muzzle on Aiden's head and the young Jewish girl gave him the book.

"Did you have to do that?" Aunt Shira asked the soldier. "You could have just taken the book from her, you know, seeing that she's just a child?"

Murmuring broke out among some of the wounded soldiers in the hospital block as they voiced their agreement to this.

"Desperate times call for desperate measures, ma'am," Sergeant Bradley said, trying to regain the men's support. "Now, we must tie you all up."

Ropes appeared from nowhere and the clinic's strongest patients secured Aunt Shira, Kimberley and her two companions to bed posts under Sergeant Bradley's watchful eyes.

"What do you even have in this book?" the US Army sergeant wondered aloud, flipping through the ancient codex. "Nothing but names?" His right hand moved over an open page.

"Don't you dare touch any names in that book," Kimberley warned him. "You'll never see your family again if you do."

"You will die if you do," Rachel threw in.

The man closed the book. "And why is that?" he asked. "You told Dr. Carlton it was a time machine. Why will I die if I touch the names?"

"You'll die because…because…," Kimberley fumbled. She had Rachel to thank for mixing things up.

"Because, you'll never survive the changes that will transport you to another place and time if you do not know the secret word," Aunt Shira rescued her with.

"And what's the secret word?"

"We're not telling you until you let us go," Aiden said.

Sergeant Bradley frowned. He didn't believe the boy, but he still couldn't get himself to touch a name in the book without the necessary precaution, if there was any, that is. "Colonel Pash will know what to do with the four of you and your book," he concluded.

"You know they'll come back for it," Rachel said and the US Army sergeant smiled. "The book will protect me, remember?" he said.

"Wrong," Kimberley said. "The book can only protect when its Bookbearer is holding it."

"Then the little girl comes with me," Sergeant Bradley said.

"No, I won't," Rachel protested.

"Take me instead," Aunt Shira began, surprising Kimberley, Aiden and her niece. "I am also a Bookbearer, as well as a Bookmaker."

"I don't believe you, ma'am," Sergeant Bradley said, untying Rachel. "She is coming with me, because I've seen what she can do, but for the rest of you, until Task Force A returns, we will see you as our prisoners of war."

"Really, serg?" a short man with greedy eyes began. He had tied up Kimberley. "We could do with a little rest away from the front, you know. If this here book could take us out of this war with all the killing and blood-letting, why don't we take that chance?"

"We'll do no such thing, Private Gus," Sergeant Bradley said. "Now, get some guns with Ralph and Fred and guard these prisoners. The rest should come with me."

"Yes, serg," Gus obeyed, stooping to withdraw a dead medic's sidearm just as Ralph and Fred separated from their comrades to look for weapons.

Kimberley thought the short fellow had other intentions when she looked at his face, but the moment passed and he just walked over to where she squatted. He sat on the bed he had tied her to.

"What if those things come back, serg?" a severely wounded soldier lying on a bed asked Bradley in a faint voice. "What will be our fate, then?"

"You're wounded," Kimberley told the man. "They won't hurt you."

"Okay," Sergeant Bradley said. "One less thing to worry about, right?" He left with Rachel, the white book and the wounded who were able to follow him.

Kimberley felt defeated. Beaten.

"It doesn't need to be a cross, you know," Mrs. Braun, or Aunt Shira, began.

"What?" Kimberley asked her.

"Your drawing," the older woman clarified. "It could be an ankh; an 'X' or a 'T.' Any sign that indicates two lines that intersect scares the hell out of the Booklords."

"I see," Kimberley claimed. Of course, they'd used the ankh back in Egypt. "Does it have anything to do with the crucifixion of Jesus Christ?"

"I don't think so, but I really don't know," Aunt Shira confessed. "It's a temporary measure, by the way."

"And what do you mean by that?"

"It only scares those demons," Aunt Shira replied. "It doesn't stop them from repeatedly coming back for the book."

"I see," Kimberley repeated, still trying to understand where the German Jew was going with her explanation. "So, what's the permanent measure?"

"The Ice of Masada weakens with time," Aunt Shira said. "Sadly."

"The Ice of Masada?" Kimberley frowned in thought. "I've heard that before. Is that the name for..."

"The book's ice dome," Aunt Shira supplied. "The Ice of Masada protects the white book against the Gray Ones, while the Fire of Masada protects the black book from the Black Ones."

"The Fire of Masada?" Kimberley frowned again. "Fire and Ice?"

"That protects the third book," the German before her said.

"A third book?"

"A combination of these elements produces an indescribable force that can only protect the ultimate determiner of one's destiny," Aunt Shira pointed out.

"The third book?" Aiden asked her, visibly puzzled. "Is there a third book, ma'am?"

"No, there isn't, my dear. Not yet," Aunt Shira revealed. "We were trying to figure out how to make it before the Romans broke into the Mine and took away the black book."

Kimberley let out a silent sigh of relief. A third book was the last thing she wanted to hear about in this weird tale trying to spiral out of control.

"Is that a fairy tale or something, ma'am?" Gus interrupted. "Couldn't help listening to your conversation."

Kimberley saw an opportunity in the soldier's ironic remark. "Help us get the book your sergeant took away from us, Gus," she urged the private. "Help us get it back and we will help you leave this war."

"And where will I go?" the private wondered aloud. "Where will you take me to?"

"Back home?" Aiden told the private. "With your family in a better future?"

"Okay, I'll help you."

"You heard the sergeant, Gus," Fred said. "Don't listen to them."

"I'm not listening to them," Gus said. "I'm just trying to survive this war. Who's with me?"

"Sure, I'm in," Ralph said. "Better to leave now alive than in a box, on a later date."

"Of course," Kimberley agreed with him.

"You two better know what you're doing," Fred warned his comrades.

"You won't regret this, Fred," Aunt Shira told the doubting soldier. "Just help us."

"Yes, Fred," Aiden contributed. "Just help us."

"Come on board, Fred," Ralph urged his mate, who appeared to be hesitating.

"What do you want to do, Gus?" Fred finally asked his comrade.

"Untie them, Fred," Gus ordered him.

"Why me?" Fred wanted to know. "Why not Ralph?"

"Because you're nearer, dammit," Gus snapped.

Fred untied the three prisoners Sergeant Bradley had ordered him to guard with his comrades. Gus and Ralph had their guns trained on the two women and one boy as he worked to free them.

"I'll go check on the sergeant," Private Gus said afterwards. "You too should remain here and watch over them. Shoot them if they try anything funny."

"Thought they would have been better off tied to the posts," Fred said.

"They're our way out of here, Fred," Ralph said. "Let's try and show them some respect."

"Exactly, Ralph," Gus agreed.

When he left, Kimberley turned to Rachel's aunt. "Why did you volunteer yourself in place of Rachel?" she asked.

"I was just trying to protect my niece," Aunt Shira said.

"Are you a Bookbearer as well?"

"All Bookmakers are Bookbearers," the woman replied. "But not all Bookbearers are Bookmakers."

"I see," Kimberley said quietly, deciding to let the issue rest for the time being, though she still had her doubts.

She thought of the Gray Ones. They had failed to attack a second time and she wondered why.

Ralph started whistling.

"We can't wait for your friend, Ralph," Kimberley told the man. "This is what we must do."

"I'm all ears," Ralph said, drawing closer.

Aiden, Fred and Aunt Shira drew closer as well.

*   *   *

Private Gus Carrington walked to the army mess hall. He knew that Sergeant Bradley and almost all the injured-but-able-bodied men of Alsos Unit Spear were stationed there waiting for Task Force A to return. He thought about what he'd done and shrugged it off. If the rumor circulating a few days ago, after Sergeant Bradley and his team returned from Stuttgart with the little girl and her book, were true, then what he was already doing could mean the difference between life and death for him, and Ralph. And Fred, if that lazy fellow wasn't having cold feet already.

The private met a sentry at the double doors of the mess hall. "I need to see the sergeant, Pete," he told the man. "It's urgent."

"He won't like it if you left those prisoners unguarded, Gus," Corporal Pete told him. "That's a priority, you know?"

"Of course," Private Gus said. "Know where he kept the girl?"

"Is that why you're here, private?" Pete frowned and brandished his rifle.

"No, of course not," Gus said, grinning. "Just wanna see the sergeant, that's all."

"Okay, you can go in," Pete said, lowering his weapon. "I hope you know what you're doing."

"Yes, I do, Pete," his comrade said. "Just wanna see the sergeant, that's all. Fred and Ralph can handle the prisoners."

"Can they?"

"What do you mean by that?" Gus snapped.

"They're right behind you as hostages."

"What?" Private Gus spun round and gaped at the five individuals making their way towards the mess hall. Corporal Pete raised his gun again.

"They die if you open fire," Kimberley warned, using Fred's service rifle to steer him towards the mess hall. "Now, drop your weapon."

The sentry obeyed and raised his hands like Gus, who drew back when the five from the clinic got to the hall's double doors. Aunt Shira had Ralph covered with his Garand rifle, while Aiden had ropes with him just in case. The boy took Pete's gun and pointed it at the guard.

"What do you want?" Pete asked Kimberley.

"Open the doors and step inside first," the Portwood police officer ordered him. "Don't try anything stupid."

Those inside were startled by the group when the corporal obeyed her. They raised their guns before realizing the futility of such an attempt.

"Do no such thing," Kimberley advised them. "As you can see, your comrades are not in the best of situations." She directed Corporal Pete to move over to Sergeant Bradley's group. "Now, drop your guns."

"You know that's not possible," Bradley told her. "Task Force A will be here any minute now and you'll be…"

"Drop your weapons, I say!" Kimberley shouted.

"Do as she says, serg," Gus urged Bradley.

Grumbling, the men behind the sergeant started obeying the order. Bradley saw this and did the same thing.

"Now, step back," Kimberley told them, and they obeyed her. Aiden collected the rifles and pistols on the floor and returned to the safety of his group. "Where is Rachel, and the book?"

"Right here, Kim," the young Bookbearer said, stepping forward from behind the Bradley group.

"Oh, child," Aunt Shira began. "Did they hurt you?"

"No, aunt," Rachel replied, walking over to Aiden with her book tucked under her armpit in her usual manner.

"She's okay," Sergeant Bradley said. "I just didn't allow her to open the book."

Kimberley grinned. "Because you knew what might happen," she told him. "Good to see you're learning fast, sergeant."

"What now?" Private Fred asked no one in particular.

"We need a Jeep," Gus said, moving towards Aiden and his stockpile of guns.

"Don't do that, Gus," Kimberley ordered him.

"Why not?" the private asked her, stopping in his tracks.

"You fools," Bradley snapped. "I should have guessed how you were overpowered."

"They're our hostages," Kimberley tried to ascertain. "They will continue being our hostages."

"But you promised to…" Gus began.

"Until a time when the arrangement will no longer be needed," Kimberley concluded, glaring at the short private. "Now, Private Gus, we need a good Jeep."

"You won't get far," Sergeant Bradley warned her. "We'll radio for aerial search and destroy."

"Can't wait for that, serg," Kimberley said with a smile as she withdrew with her group. "Right now, we really have to go."

"We will find and stop you before you go far," Bradley said coldly.

"In your dreams," Kimberley whispered, opening the structure's double doors.

Bradley and his men filtered out of the mess hall after Kimberley's exit. Luckily, a GMC CCKW truck sat at the corner of the radio building near the hall. Ralph took the steering wheel while Gus entered in front beside him. Fred entered the back with Aunt Shira, Aiden and Rachel. Kimberley covered Sergeant Bradley and his remaining men, waiting for the truck to start.

As the heavy-duty vehicle groaned into life, she joined Gus and Ralph in the front seat, her rifle still pointing at the soldiers standing helplessly before their mess hall. "Nice meeting you, sergeant," she quipped and banged her door shut.

Sergeant Bradley and his team watched in frustration as the fugitives rumbled away. They yelled curses at the escapees when the truck stopped and Aiden got down to dump all the guns he had collected into an empty shallow well near the road.

"Why am I doing this, Kim?" he demanded as he worked.

"Because those men still need protection in this war," Kimberley replied. "We can't just take away their guns in the middle of a war."

"Good point," Private Gus said. He felt happy. After all, he'd been promised an easy way out of the war.

Bradley raced to the shallow well, being the only one fit to run in the company of assembled survivors of Alsos Unit Spear. He jumped into the structure as the truck pulled away. When he got out of it with a rifle in his right hand, the escaping prisoners had become a speck in the distance. "Damn it!" he muttered. "Radio for air support," he ordered those doing their best to come up to his position despite their battle injuries.

"What do we tell them, sir?"

"Tell them we need a search and destroy in the area. A lone 'Jimmy' truck filled with prisoners of war and heading back to the front. Quickly!"

Chapter 16
AUNT SHIRA

RALPH floored the gas pedal and the GMC truck surged forward. A dense forest of giant fir trees raced backward on both sides of the narrow dearth road he'd decided to take once he left Alsos Mission's forward camp in Germany. There were so many such roads around the secret mission's German barracks, but the US Army private had chosen a particular one, because he thought it could not be monitored from the sky due to the canopy the fir trees provided for the road's occasional users.

"Where're we going?" Rachel asked Aiden.

"No idea," he replied.

"No where in particular," Kimberley told them from the front. "We just need to make sure we're not being followed, then we can stop and do what we need to do."

"Right on," Gus enthused beside her.

"They're not following us," Mrs. Hannah Braun, or Aunt Shira, said from the truck's cargo area.

"Obviously," Kimberley said, staring at the receding road behind them through the side mirror near her.

"Bradley won't risk putting a bunch of wounded men in a truck to go after losers like us in German territory, would he?" Gus pointed out.

"We still have to be careful, though," Kimberley warned. "Remember Task Force A."

"They won't use the road," the ever-hesitant Fred said from the back of the truck.

"Sure thing," Ralph agreed. "They won't find us easily from the skies, though."

"Hope you're right." Kimberley looked up at the massive trees

154

shooting up into the sky from all directions near the narrow track road. She felt safe, despite the ordeal she'd just gone through with her fellow time-travelers. At least, they had found their contact, even if the woman's instructions on the white book were not palatable. She could hear Rachel conversing with her aunt at the back of the truck. She wished she knew some Hebrew. "Stop the truck," she told Ralph, satisfied that they weren't being followed.

"Did you hear that?" Fred asked from the back.

"Hear what?" Kimberley frowned. She could hear a faint sound like a whistle coming from up above. It sounded like…

"An aircraft," Gus said.

"A P-51," Ralph added. "And it sounds low."

"Get off the road!" Kimberley yelled. Ralph swerved to the right seconds before the ordnance exploded on his left. Another explosion followed the CCKW truck as it sprang into a jungle of giant randomly positioned fir trees, Ralph maneuvering the mobile 2.5 tons with some expertise and daredevilry. "Everyone alright?" Kimberley called out.

"Yes," Aiden shouted back, Rachel holding on to him for dear life as the heavy truck bumped up and down in motion. His heart was in his mouth.

"It's a Mustang, alright," Gus said, watching the fighter-bomber fly by through the windshield. "I think he's got HAVRs and intend using them."

"He's coming round," Kimberley warned. "We won't survive those rockets."

"Everybody out!" Private Ralph yelled, killing the engine.

Kimberley jumped out with the two in front and ran back to see Fred lifting Rachel out of the cargo bay, while Aiden helped Aunt Shira step down in her pace. "Move away from the truck!" she told them, doing so without delay.

Fred carried Rachel away from the CCKW as fast as he could, Aiden and Aunt Shira on his heels. The whistling sound of the Mustang's British Rolls-Royce Merlin engine could now be clearly heard above the fir trees.

"Hit the ground!" Kimberley shouted, and dropped down before Fred covered Rachel on the ground beside her. The HAVRs decimated the Jimmy truck in two explosions that raised massive dust and sent debris flying at high velocities across a wide radius around the vehicle.

As the aircraft flew past, it fired more rockets at the site, spewing up more dust and forcing the escapees to hug the ground a little bit longer. One by one, they picked themselves up as the P-51's peculiar whistle receded.

"He will make a sharp turn," Ralph warned, turning to survey the landscape around them. "Luckily, he can't fly low enough to use his machine guns on us, because the trees won't let him. So, our best chance is to hide behind those shrubs." The others followed him as he moved to the said shrubs.

Moments later, the escaped prisoners heard the Mustang's whirring engine as it scaled the tree tops, its pilot probably trying to see through the dense mass of fir leaves blocking his view for signs of life. More rockets exploded near the wrecked truck, but none did so near the hidden escapees.

"We should wait and see if he comes back," Kimberley suggested as the sound of the aircraft's engine became faint again.

"A unit will soon be here behind that fighter," Gus reasoned, standing up as he dusted off his uniform. "We can't remain here."

"No, we can't," Kimberley said, helping Rachel to get up.

"Can't we leave with the time machine?" the short private asked her.

"Not yet," she said.

"You should keep your deal, miss."

"I can't keep it here, private," Kimberley returned.

"The book doesn't work in the present circumstance," Aunt Shira helped Kimberley with. "It needs some quiet."

"But we have some quiet now, don't we?" Private Ralph wondered aloud. "We've done our part of the deal, right?"

"We can't risk distraction while performing this ritual," Aunt Shira told him, and Rachel nodded in agreement. "First of all, we have to make sure the fighter is not coming back."

"Okay, we can leave this place since we're not sure of the Mustang," Fred said in order to calm things down. "But we need guns to protect ourselves with in case we meet any unit."

"Sadly, we've only got one left," Private Gus said, eyeing the M1 Garand hanging from Kimberley's shoulder. "We'll need more than that when Task Force A gets here."

"Dear me," Aunt Shira said. "I must have forgotten the gun in the truck."

"Now it remains one," Gus said, still eyeing the rifle Kimberley held. He'd thought of seizing the weapon from its present handler. "We shouldn't have left those guns behind."

"Can we look for the gun in the wreck?" Fred asked, rather foolishly.

"No need for that now," Aiden said, looking at the wreckage that was a 2.5 tons GMC CCKW truck a few minutes ago. "No one can differentiate the gun from this mess now." He heard aircraft engine and looked up.

"The plane's coming back!" Ralph announced, pointing upwards. "And he's headed this way. I think he has seen us!"

"Spread out as you run!" Kimberley suggested, pulling Rachel along. "That way he won't know who to pursue or fire his remaining rockets at." She dashed off with Rachel in tow as the others ran in different directions.

*   *   *

High above the scampering figures, First Lieutenant Howard Royd frowned as he steered the Mustang upwards for another turn. "I think I got them, Nick," he said into his radio.

"Good one," Nick replied. "How did you do that?"

"I dropped my bombs to scare them in my first run, then I saw them get out of the heavy vehicle through the trees as I came in for my second run," Howard explained. "I couldn't see them the second time, though, when I used rockets on their truck. They must have hidden in the undergrowth back then. Just saw the truck's wreckage as I flew by."

"Are they still alive?"

"Yes, confirmed alive," the Mustang pilot said. "I see them running below the trees now." Colonel Pash had specifically directed him to make sure of this. "Didn't use my Brownings. Could have mistakenly killed someone if I had decided to."

"Okay, good job, man," the man at the other end of the radio aired. "The colonel just sent Sergeant Bradley and a volunteer to the area. You can come on home now, boy."

"Okay," Howard said, completing another fly-by of the destruction he'd earlier caused. His mission now accomplished, the homebound first lieutenant checked his compass.

The instrument's needle appeared motionless.

Howard glanced at his control monitors. He stared at the glass circles the second time he looked. Something seemed out of place, but he couldn't figure it out. The Mustang had a steady speed of 280 mph. Its fuel gauge indicated full main tanks and a half-filled fuselage tank, yet the plane seemed to be slowing down. No engine noise or sputter, just a drag that refused to go away.

Then the fighter-bomber pilot realized what had happened.

Everything had started moving in slow motion, even his hands and the needles on the control gauges. He could clearly make out the plane's propeller blades in front of him. Even the inward and outward movement of his chest as he took his breath were slow.

First Lieutenant Howard Royd panicked for the first time on a mission. He felt he no longer controlled his thought processes, and realized that even his mind had slowed down.

"Still there, Royd?" Nick's voice jolted him from the slumber he had fallen into.

Nick's voice?

"Still here, Nick." Spoken at the normal speed. Not slow, like his arm movements and the gauge needles. Surprisingly, his eyes still moved normally, so he saw the black speck as soon as it appeared on the horizon ahead of the Mustang.

"What's the matter, Royd? Your fighter okay?" Nick's voice seemed to be sailing in and out of his consciousness. His drowsiness. He felt lethargic. Like he'd been sunk into lead.

"I think I have a problem," he said normally. "Trying to figure it out." He lost whatever Nick continued with, because his attention went back to the black speck, which had become larger and more distinct. Or more indistinct. What was it? A shapeless entity on a head-on collision course with his fighter-bomber? He tried to steer away from it, but his plane refused to obey him. "What the hell?" he cried in desperation.

"Royd, are you okay?" Nick's concerned voice again.

Bigger and bigger it grew, until Howard could see its hollow face and tangled arms. Again, he tried to veer off, to no avail. The apparition swiftly ate up the distance between his plane and its position, and the fighter-bomber pilot looked on helplessly.

"Noooooooooo!" he shouted, crossing his arms before his face in hopeless defense before the gray form went through his propeller and windshield, piercing his chest and tearing through his kapok-filled seat without slowing down. It burst out through the mustang's sliding canopy and vanished into thin air.

The first lieutenant felt raw inside. His stomach churned and he started gasping for air, sweating profusely before losing consciousness.

The Mustang P-51D went into a diving spiral.

*   *   *

Kimberley heard the plane explode as she held Rachel beside Aiden and Mrs. Hannah Braun, or Aunt Shira.

"Now, we have some quiet," Private Gus said, emerging from some undergrowth to her left. "We've brought you this far, agent. Time to get us out of here with your time portal as you promised."

"Of course," Kimberley said. She knew what she had to do. "We lied to you," she said. "The time portal doesn't exist. This is just a book of codes and we mustn't let it fall into enemy hands."

"What?" Ralph began. "What are you saying, miss?"

"We have to take the book to Heidelberg, private," Kimberley told him. "We feared there had been an infiltration at Alsos Unit Spear, so we lied to you in order to escape from the camp and get this book of German nuclear codes to General Groves, who would know what to do with it."

"German nuclear codes?" Fred asked no one in particular. "The Germans have developed nuclear weapons?"

"Who's your suspect?" Ralph asked Kimberley.

"You guessed right," she told him.

"Sergeant Bradley?"

"It's not true," Gus cut in. "What about the attack at the camp?"

"A German biological superweapon designed to cause hallucinations, fear and a killing spree within the enemy ranks."

"My God!" Ralph exclaimed. "But this is possibly true. Nobody has examined the dead at the camp to know how they were actually killed."

"I couldn't get myself to tell you all this at the camp," Kimberley lied, "because Sergeant Bradley was there."

"A lie!" Private Gus exploded, stepping forward.

Kimberley raised the M1 Garand's muzzle, covering the three deserters before her.

"What are you doing?" a startled Gus began, taking a second step.

"Stand back," the Portwood police officer warned him, pulling Rachel behind her and signaling Aunt Shira to follow the little girl's example with a slight jerk of the head. Aiden moved behind her without being prompted. "I won't warn you again."

Private Gus moved towards Kimberley and she cocked the rifle. The single shot brought him to his senses and he stepped back, grumbling. "You lied to us," he snapped. "We risked everything for you."

"You must know that we can't go back now, agent," Ralph said. "We can at least go with you to Heidelberg."

"No," Kimberley told him. "You did all this for your country."

"Can't you take them with you, Kim?" Aunt Shira began.

"America needs them now, Mrs. Braun," Kimberley said, wondering how the German woman came to know her name. Rachel and the Hebrew language? "We need them to stall Task Force A lest they catch up with us before we can get to the General."

"This is not fair," Fred said.

"But America needs you to fight this war right now," Kimberley repeated. "We have a different obligation, and we have to part ways here. It's not right if you follow us, because the men of Alsos Unit Spear still need you."

"They don't anymore," Ralph pointed out. "We'll be court-martialed if we remain here."

"No, you won't be court-martialed after the truth becomes known. You won't forgive yourselves if you don't remain here."

"We'll be punished," Fred said, turning to Gus. "Told you this was a bad idea. This will..."

"Shut up," Gus cut in.

"She's right, Gus," Ralph began, nodding. "I know I won't forgive myself if I left now after what I just heard."

"Why? What for?" Private Gus snapped, clenching his fists. "Y'all changing your mind all of a sudden?"

"I haven't changed mine," Fred noted. "Though I still think this was a bad idea."

"No, it wasn't," Aiden said. "You guys helped us to resume our journey."

"And which journey is that, exactly?" Private Ralph asked him.

"We're...We're yet to find out," Kimberley replied. "It could end in Heidelberg or take us back to the President, but the sooner we move on, the sooner we find out where it will end." Silently, she thanked Aunt Shira and the kids for playing along with the bogus story.

They heard the rumbling of a single vehicle.

"Task Force A," Fred guessed. "Your gunshot has given us away," he told Kimberley.

"You forget the smoke from our wrecked truck and the P-51 did that long before she fired that shot, dumbo," Ralph said. "Besides, that sounds like just a Jeep. Maybe a forward party."

"One Jeep won't be a problem," Gus told his comrades. "Let's seize this gun and teach this woman a lesson right now. Who's with me, huh?"

"No, Gus," Ralph said. "We need to turn ourselves in now. It's the only way."

"And I thought Fred was the weak one," Gus said, eyeing Kimberley's gun. "Come on, Ralph, let's face her. She can't shoot us both at once, right?"

"Don't be foolish, man," Ralph warned his friend. "After what you just heard, how sure are you that this time portal even exists?"

"As sure as the rumors going round back in camp about that little girl and her book," Gus replied, stepping towards Kimberley again. He brightened when Rachel drew back behind the agent.

"I'll shoot you if I have to," Kimberley warned Gus, taking a backward step with her group.

"You're scared already, miss," the private told her. "I can smell it."

"Then smell this," Kimberley said, taking aim.

Gus lunged for the gun, dodging her shot. Ralph pulled him down by grabbing his legs before he could touch the rifle. Both men fell on the ground as Kimberley drew back with Aunt Shira and the children. Ralph was clearly on her side now.

Another resounding shot came from the narrow road outside the jungle of fir trees. It zipped past Kimberley and she recognized the dangerous situation they'd been thrown into.

"Run!" Ralph yelled at her, struggling with his comrade on the ground. "Run before it's too late. We'll try and slow them down." The female CIC agent lifted the little girl behind her and made to move away before he remembered one thing. "Drop the gun! We need the gun!"

Three more shots zinged through the surrounding shrubs. A fourth one struck the trunk of a nearby tree.

"We need the gun!" Ralph repeated.

Kimberley nodded and dropped the weapon. She ran after Aiden and Aunt Shira while carrying Rachel.

"Get the gun, Fred!" Gus snapped at his fellow private, who had been lost all this while. "Get the gun, you fool!"

Fred picked up the M1 and made to follow the fleeing Kimberley before another shot from the new assailants forced him to change his mind. Crouching, he turned around and put the Garand rifle into better use.

"Idiot!" Gus railed from underneath Ralph. "You're letting them get away!"

*   *   *

Far into the forest they ran, until the distant gunfire sounded faint.

"Never knew you could run that fast," Kimberley told Aunt Shira, putting Rachel down on her feet.

"I was a long-distance runner for my school," the middle-aged woman replied. "I won gold, twice."

"Not bad," Aiden said.

"She can run, you know?" Aunt Shira directed at Kimberley.

"Who?"

"Rachel, you carried her all the way here," the older woman clarified.

"Oh," Kimberley said. "She would have slowed us down."

"And I'm tired," Rachel said, swinging her arms.

"Poor child," her aunt exclaimed. "Let me bear this burden for you while you regain your strength. Let me bear the book for awhile now."

Kimberley started. "Is that alright?" she asked. "Is the book the reason you're tired, Rachel?"

"Yes, Kim," the little girl replied. "Aunt Shira can do a better job of holding the book, you know."

"Yes, of course," Kimberley grudgingly agreed, wondering if her suspicions were correct. "Now that we're temporarily safe, we need to know what to do with it."

"I gave you two options, Miss Kim," Aunt Shira said.

"It's Miss Reyna, Mrs. Braun," Kimberley corrected. "My friends call me Kim."

"Well, Kim, either you find the first book, which you cannot do right now, or you hand this book back to the Gray Ones, which is the best option from the situation of things."

"And how did you know that?" Aiden asked the middle-aged woman.

"Know what?"

"That that's the best option?"

"You have been through a lot, dear," Aunt Shira told him. "Imagine if everything you've been through could be reversed by just handing this back. Won't you do that?"

"And what does the Bookbearer have to say about this proposal of yours?" Kimberley asked, trying to forget the possibilities the said proposal offered to her situation.

"I've already made up my mind, Aunt Shira," Rachel said, rubbing her hands. "Thought I told you."

"Returning it is the only option there is," her aunt emphasized. "I think you have to make up your mind again, or if you want us to decide for you?"

"No," Kimberley said, faster than she had wanted to. "We'll stick with Rachel's decision." She saw gratitude in the little girl's eyes.

"Fine," Mrs. Braun said, stomping off ahead of the group.

"Do you think she's angry?" Aiden whispered.

"Aunt Shira gets ticked off by the slightest thing," Rachel said. "Once she refused to eat at the Mine, because the food wasn't cooked her way."

"Okay," Kimberley said, frowning. "Are there only two options left in this story for us? What if she's not laying everything out for us as she should?"

"Meaning?" Aiden asked. "She's lying to us?"

Kimberley nodded. "Maybe," she said. "Sounds like she's trying to persuade us to do a particular thing." This line of thought encouraged another line of thought and she turned to Rachel. "You said the Gray Ones usually killed your targets as soon as you make contact with them?"

The little girl nodded.

"Then, why is your Aunt Shira still alive? Why have we not seen those things and that crazy guy for some time now? We're sitting targets, right?"

"You're saying they must have met her before we got to her, Kim?" Aiden wondered aloud.

"Yes," Kimberley said. "I think they even struck a deal with her."

"Which deal?" Rachel asked.

"To lie to us in exchange for her life?"

Aunt Shira had stopped ahead of them. She made to raise the book, but stopped midway and turned back. "There's one other thing I forgot to tell you. You could strengthen the Ice of Masada."

"Is that the name for a place?" Aiden asked her.

"No, that's the collective name for the book's protection against the Gray Ones," Kimberley enlightened him with. She turned to the German Jew before her. "Are you saying the Bookbearer could make this protection stronger?"

"Yes," Aunt Shira said.

"But I'm doing my best, Aunt Shira," Rachel protested. "I can't do more than I am doing.

"That's because you're a weak Bookbearer, my child," Mrs. Braun, or Aunt Shira, told her niece. "You need a stronger Bookbearer or...or Bookmaker in order to unleash the full strength of the Ice of Masada."

"Which is you," Aiden said. "You can now help us unleash the full strength of this Ice of...Masada."

"No, my dear," the middle-aged woman said. "If you let me, I will give the book back to its original masters. That's the only way to end this madness and...and be freed from the chains I've borne these many years."

Kimberley gaped at the German Jew. Rachel's uncle, Ezra, had said the exact same words in a different situation. "Give her back the book."

"What?" Aunt Shira didn't expect that.

"Return the book to your niece, Mrs. Braun," Kimberley repeated. "It is hers to decide what to do with."

"I'm a Bookbearer as well, Miss Kim," Aunt Shira said.

"It's Miss Reyna, Mrs. Braun," Kimberley corrected with a sigh.

"Okay, young woman, I get that," Aunt Shira said. "But what if I don't want to return the book? What if I am right and would have to take the book by force?"

"Aunt Shira, what are you saying?" Rachel began.

"I won't do that, dear," her aunt allayed.

"Then, why are you saying it?" Kimberley demanded.

"I may have to do that if you three do not agree on what to do about this dire situation very soon, Miss Kim," Aunt Shira said coldly, glaring at Kimberley.

Both women moved at the same time, Kimberley putting out a foot for the older woman, who wanted to distance herself from her younger opponent, but could only crash to the ground instead.

"What are you doing, Kim?" Rachel shouted, going down beside her aunt. "She did nothing wrong!"

"Can't you see she wanted to run with the book?" Kimberley told the surprised girl.

"Or she's just trying to avoid what you just did to her?" Rachel put forward.

"You always trust people blindly," Kimberley berated. "Can't you see that this has been her plan from the day we first met her?" She looked at Aiden for support and he nodded in agreement, visibly not sure of his position.

"Maybe," he said.

"She has been helpful to me, to us," Rachel cried. "She's just trying to help us. Please don't treat her like this again." She helped her aunt to turn on her back.

Panting, the middle-aged woman spat out earth. Her new foe towered over her.

"I'm sorry for this," Kimberley said, her right hand outstretched. "Just hand over the book to your niece and I won't do worse things to you."

"The book is not yours to decide who holds it or what happens to it," Rachel said angrily.

Kimberley said nothing. She looked at Aiden, who could only look on.

"I'm sorry, too," Aunt Shira said, stretching out her own hand. "I don't know what got into me. Please help me up?"

Kimberley stooped and obliged the middle-aged woman. A big mistake, because the next instant, her feet were brushed off from underneath her and she fell on her left hip.

"Aunt Shira, don't!" Rachel screamed, drawing back with Aiden.

The woman Kimberley had tried to help picked up a fir branch and struck the Portwood police sergeant on the head. Luckily, Kimberley blocked her face with her crossed hands the second time the branch came down.

The loud crackle of gunfire stopped this assault, Aunt Shira falling backward with the force of the bullet.

Kimberley flung the fir branch at the lone soldier turning to aim his rifle at her, and charged him as soon as the wooden weapon confused his aim. She brought him down with her momentum and knocked him out with an uppercut.

Dizzying pain numbed Kimberley's forehead and her hands came out from this part of her head blood-stained. She had an ugly gash from the fir branch attack.

More bullets whizzed past from a group of shrubs forming a thick wall through which the first American soldier had emerged, and Aiden pulled Rachel down with him in a squat. Kimberley seized the knocked-out US soldier's M1 Garand, rolled over on her stomach and returned fire.

The shooting stopped all of a sudden and someone cried out on the other side of the undergrowth blocking Kimberley's view. She crawled on all fours to the thicket and parted it. The person she saw on the other side holding his right flank while lying on the ground she had expected to see after hearing his familiar voice.

"Sergeant Bradley," she confirmed. The man made to go for his gun and she cocked her Garand. "Don't try it, dear. You've already lost the fight. Now, throw your guns over to my side, nice and slow."

The US Army sergeant obeyed her and fell back on the ground, panting. "I need help!" he screamed.

"Which you'll have to get yourself," Kimberley said coldly. "What did you do to Private Ralph and his mates?"

"Gus is dead," Bradley said flatly. "The other two surrendered and are chained to the Jeep, waiting for my return."

Kimberley tried to hide the gratitude in her voice by sounding curious. "Whatever happened to search and destroy?"

"The colonel is still busy at…."

"Told you not to follow us," the Counter Intelligence Corps agent admonished him.

"You killed my man," Bradley accused, struggling as he got up.

"I didn't," Kimberley said. "I just knocked him out. Now, turn round and leave this place, or I'll make sure I plant a bullet in your head next time we meet, okay? Am I clear on this?"

"Crystal," the man replied as he dragged himself away. "What about my man?" he called out after some silence.

"I'll make sure I tell him the same thing when he comes round," Kimberley assured the sergeant. "Now, move along, please."

"Sure thing, agent."

Kimberley watched the obstinate army officer disappear in the direction they had all come from before breathing a sigh of relief.

"Aunt Shira!" Rachel cried behind her.

"She's trying to get away, Kim!" an exhausted Aiden shouted beside the little girl. He lacked the strength to do anything.

Kimberley turned her attention to the woman lying on the floor a few feet from her current position. She'd forgotten all about the drama that had played out minutes before the two US soldiers from the Jeep attacked, since she thought that Rachel's aunt had already died.

This could not be farther from the truth.

Mrs. Hannah Braun, or Aunt Shira as her niece fondly called her, had the white book raised above her head while whispering some unintelligible words.

"What's she saying?" an alarmed Kimberley asked Rachel, covering the short distance between her and the dying woman without waiting for the little girl's reply. She went for the book, but it was too late. Glaring light shot out from the ancient codex and the Gray Ones appeared with their human minion.

This time the book did not produce an icy mesh for those it protected. If not for the long relationship Kimberley and her two time-traveling companions have had with it, they would have lost their lives there and then.

Instead, two apparitions held Kimberley, scorching her wrists in the process, while three faceless fiends surrounded the two kids time-traveling with her.

"What have you done?" Rachel asked her aunt. "You betrayed us!"

"She did no such thing," Carl Bain said, taking the book from the dead Aunt Shira's rigid right hand. "She did the right thing."

"How?" Aiden asked.

Carl Bain paused briefly, looking directly at the boy. "She could have given my masters the book as soon as she took possession of it," he said, "but she took time out of love for your friend here to inform you guys of the futility of your quest before urging you to hand over your possession to my masters without delay."

Rachel closed her eyes and whispered some words, clenching her fists.

"Sorry, my dear," Carl Bain told her, "but this time, your chants will not work, because a Bookmaker and superior Bookbearer handed us the book willingly. Save your magic for another day."

"You will never succeed," Kimberley said, gnashing her teeth against the pain her two captors were inflicting on her. "Your friends will never leave this world with the book."

"Wrong, my dear," Carl Bain countered. "Watch me succeed."

Kimberley twisted and turned to no avail. Her wrists were on fire. She looked at Sergeant Bradley's man, who must have died when the Gray Ones appeared. He still lay in the position her uppercut had forced him into.

"My masters will go now, and I must do so with them," her tormentors' human servant said. "But first, where is my package, my dear? I need it right now."

"Go to hell."

Carl Bain boiled. He exploded in rage, unleashing a blistering volley of fire at the woman struggling between two demons. This natural element engulfed his target, causing her more pain than she had ever felt in her entire life as her horrendous persecutors released her and she crashed to the ground.

"No!" Rachel screamed, stepping forward and tearing up. "Kim, no!" Her voice shook as she cried.

Aiden held her back with tears in his eyes. He knew that confronting the Booklords guarding them would be a dangerous thing to do in the situation they'd found themselves in.

"You monster!" Rachel shouted at Carl Bain as Kimberley's body burned between them.

"You should be happy I didn't kill you as well," the American hustler said, strolling up to the Portwood police sergeant's corpse. He extinguished the flames with a wave of his hand and bent down to search for his package in her pockets. Smiling, he brought out the small silver box from her left pants pocket.

Something familiarly tiny also came out with the silver box.

"Damn it!" Carl Bain muttered and disappeared with his infernal masters.

The white book, the American hustler's silver box and this familiarly tiny object fell to the floor right where he previously stooped.

Now unhindered, an exhausted Aiden forced himself to get to this spot with Rachel.

"What do we do?" the confused Bookbearer asked him.

"Quick, take us out of here," he said, pocketing Carl Bain's silver box.

"With her body?"

"Yes, with her body." Aiden failed to notice the other object on the ground since the grass had hidden it from his view.

Rachel pulled out her pen, picked up the book and flipped it open. She scribbled on it and held Aiden's left hand as he took Kimberley's burnt right hand.

They all vanished into thin air, but Kimberley's tiny gold cross remained where it fell from Carl Bain's right hand.

Chapter 17
CHORNOBYL

CARL BAIN felt his head squeezing as his floating body kept whirling in what he knew to be an infinite abyss. Inhuman voices coming from the deepest part of this void had all but turned him deaf from their incessant clamor for his death. These strange vociferations blamed him for failing to retrieve the white book from its Bookbearer during the last attempt at this apparently simple task. The debacle in Germany, according to his infernal masters, was clearly his fault, and he must suffer the consequences, just as he had done immediately after every other previous failure.

Fear gripped the American hustler as he continued to spin in the unearthly haze these demonic apparitions had thrown him into. Unlike the other times this horrible experience had occurred to him after an unsuccessful campaign to seize the white codex, the intensity of his suffering had increased twofold. His head ached like crazy and he could only shut his eyes in response.

These were now forced open and the demon leader filled his view.

"Why are you doing this to me?" he cried. "What have I done to deserve this?"

"Your fault," the spirit being appeared to say. "Death awaits you."

"How is it my fault this time, huh?" the suffering man snapped, glaring at the hollow face before him. He got a higher dose of hellish headache for his trouble. "Please stop," he begged.

"One more chance," the shifting form torturing him conveyed.

"Yeah, you keep repeating that," Carl Bain said. His headache became unbearable. "Just wanna go home with what's mine," he cried and the throbbing pain reduced. He cursed the misfortune that had befallen him, breathing hard.

The spirit entity stared blankly at him with invisible eyes. "One more chance," it repeated. "A new plan."

"Whatever," the American thug said. "Hope it doesn't fail again this time."

The demon before him remained unperturbed. "Success, failure or death," it conveyed. "One choice only. Do not frustrate effort."

"I do my best," Carl Bain said, wishing he could see beyond the hollow representing a face before him.

The Booklord communicated some more and, for once, the American it had been torturing smiled.

"Can't wait to do more of that," he said. "The boy is next."

*   *   *

"Aiden, what's happening?" repeatedly wafted into his dream, until he grudgingly opened his eyes. He rubbed them and the blur cleared. Rachel standing over him got his attention.

"Where's Kimberley?" he asked her, sitting up. The little girl had the white book with her, and held it as if her life depended on it. Her sad look told Aiden what he needed to know. "She's not here with us," he concluded.

"Do you think she's dead?" Rachel asked.

"I don't know," her fellow time-traveler said. "Maybe she made it, but got separated from us."

"How is that possible?" Rachel asked.

"Everything is possible right now," Aiden said. For one, his wounds from his last journey had all disappeared, and he knew that the time travel they'd all been subjected to must have had a hand in that miracle. He just hoped that his dear police friend had undergone a similar transformation, despite her having lost her life before his very eyes during their German journey. He didn't want to believe the impossible...yet. Kimberley wouldn't leave them in this timeless void of nowhere the book had remanded them in, would she? Of course, she was still alive. He didn't want to believe any other thing. "Where are we?" he asked his younger companion, looking around with a frown on his young face.

Aiden sat on a couch in what appeared to be a tastily furnished living room. Five armchairs were arranged with this couch around a low wooden table, and before this arrangement, an old-fashioned box TV set sat on a table near the room's wall. "Where is this place?" the young boy wondered aloud, getting up. To his right, near a staircase, plates of unfinished meals lay out on a dining table having four identical chairs around it. "I feel like I just finished eating, Rachel, with you...and...and some other people?"

"Feel so, too," Rachel agreed. "Who are these people, and...and where are they?" she asked.

"We'll soon find out," Aiden said. He noticed the open entrance door first and moved towards it, knowing that he could be in for a nasty surprise.

Rachel hesitated before following the boy from Portwood. "You must be missing your parents like I do," she said.

"I don't have any," Aiden said. "Lost them when I was younger."

"I-I'm so sorry," his companion stammered. "Shouldn't have brought that up."

"It's okay."

The little girl calmed down. "I-I hope to see Father again, someday," she said.

"Sure you will," Aiden assured her. "Everything is possible right now."

"Including that?" Rachel asked him, pointing at the window near the main door. Outside, a dark sky prevailed above a bald man who slammed the trunk of his car and turned towards the door.

"Aleksandr! Kateryna!" this man called out in a foreign language. "Where are you two? We have to go now!"

"Can't understand a word apart from the names," Aiden said, having stopped to listen. "Wonder who he's talking to?"

"Us?" Rachel suggested. Could she be Kateryna?

"Here you are!" The tall woman coming down the stairs spoke the same foreign language. She seemed quite angry with the two at the entrance door.

"Hi," Aiden began. His new acquaintance disregarded this greeting and grabbed Rachel's right arm before getting to him. Once she took his right arm, a wave of change zapped through his body and he became someone else without knowing it. "Mama, where are we going?" he asked the woman in Ukrainian.

"Slavutych," she said, pulling him and Kateryna towards the door.

"Mama, why are we going to Slavutych?" Rachel, now Kateryna, asked her new mother.

"Something about pollution from a plant," the tall woman replied as she opened the door. "I hope you have your school bags?"

"In the car," Aiden, who now knew himself to be Aleksandr, said.

"We must hurry, Paul," his 'mother' told the baldheaded middle-aged man now opening the car doors as they came out of the house. "The buses should be leaving by now."

"Not yet, they have not," Paul said. "They came late."

"But still, we must hurry."

"I know, let them get into the car," the man said.

"Why are we living, Mama?" Rachel, or Kateryna, asked her new mother.

"I told you, it's because of a minor accident at a factory downtown."

"We have to go to Slavutych and live there until things are cleaned up," her new father said, staring at the book she still clasped underneath her arm. "Is that your school book?"

"Yes, Father."

"You should have left it in your school bag."

"Let her be, Paul," the man's wife said. "She loves this book, remember?"

"Okay," Paul Yuvchenko said, entering the car. "We can talk about your books later, but right now, get into the car. We have a journey to make."

Kateryna entered the car behind her brother and looked at the book her mother said she loved. She could not recall having such an old school book. She wanted to say something before her brother's left hand accidentally touched hers and she stared at him the next time she looked at him.

Aiden had also realized his dual identity as soon as he had touched Rachel's right hand. Fortunately for him, he still retained Aleksandr's knowledge and knew everything about their present situation in addition to being a fluent speaker of the local language. "What's wrong with the plant, Father?" he asked the man in the car's driver's seat.

"I really don't know, boy," his 'father' said, starting the vehicle and turning on the radio. "We must go away for some time."

Understandably, Aiden knew the man could be hiding something, but he wondered whether this incident at the said plant would have anything to do with their peculiar situation and the Bookmaker Rachel needed to meet this time around. He tried to recall any historical pollution involving a plant or factory from History class and the only one he kept remembering was the nuclear disaster in a Ukrainian town called...

"Chornobyl...," the news presenter said on the radio.

"Is it the nuclear energy plant, mother?" Aiden asked his 'mother' and she glared at him.

"Mind what you say, young man," she said as her husband turned off the radio. Putting it on was a bad decision, for sure. "Nobody is sure of what happened and where, so we...we just have to move to another city. Could be a drill."

Or a nuclear disaster, Aiden thought. Chornobyl really struck a chord in his memory. The salon car had left their 'front yard,' heading towards the main road linking the streets of the neighborhood. "Who are we meeting here?" he whispered to Rachel or Kateryna.

"Another woman," Rachel whispered back.

"Quiet back there," their new father ordered them.

Aiden looked out the window. A clear sky crowned the day, with rays of morning sunlight beginning to radiate down to the surrounding streets. School buses lined these streets amidst people carrying luggage, baby trollies and other personal items out of their houses. Many were trooping into these vehicles with their handbags tucked underneath their arms. A gay atmosphere persisted despite the confusing news surrounding the evacuation.

Suddenly, people started running far behind the car as pandemonium broke out in the human lines snaking into the buses on both sides of the road.

"What's happening?" Paul demanded, looking at his side mirror. His wife and kids turned to look through the car's rear window.

"Why are they running?" Rachel, or Kateryna, asked in Ukrainian.

"Something is not right," Aiden, or Aleksandr, said in Ukrainian.

Mr.Yuvchenko accelerated the car. People were running away from the road and some were jumping down from the buses through windows.

"Why are they running, Paul?" Mrs. Yuvchenko asked her husband, looking back now and then. "Is it about the pollution?"

"Doesn't seem to be,"Aiden said, staring at the rear windshield with Rachel.

Something in the buses started grabbing the people running near these vehicles one after the other.

"Did you see that, Rachel?" Aiden exclaimed, pointing at the spot a little boy previously occupied.

"What did you just call your sister, Aleksandr?" his 'mother' demanded.

"Um, did you see that, Kateryna?" Aiden rephrased.

"Yes, I did," a nervous Rachel, or Kateryna, replied, her eyes darting about. "They're here."

"Who are they?" her 'father' asked her as the car approached the main road linking the streets. "What do you think is happening there, Kateryna? People are just running out of fear. Someone must have said something to cause the commotion."

"Then why are we speeding?" Aiden wondered aloud.

"Now, look here, young man," Mr. Yuvchenko began, turning now and then to glare at his 'son.' "You shouldn't question my explanations, are we clear on that?"

Aiden understood why his 'father' had tried to explain the situation away, but that was not necessary, since he and Rachel had come a long way and were not the innocent children the Ukrainian man thought them to be.

"Are we clear on that, boy?" Mr. Yuvchenko repeated, momentarily taking his attention away from the road. "Stick to your books or I will…"

"Look out, Paul!" his wife warned him and he turned back to the steering wheel, in time to see a lone figure standing in the middle of the road.

The vehicle swerved off the street into the last yard before the main road and hit a post office box. Mr. Yuvchenko's head slammed into the car's steering wheel and he sat up with a bloodied nose. His wife's seat was empty. "Leyla," he cried, looking around in fright. "Aleksandr, where is your mother?" he asked Aiden, who still sat in the back seat with Rachel.

"They've taken her," Rachel said.

"What?" her 'father' asked confusedly.

"And here they come," Aiden said, his knuckles turning white as he tightly held Rachel's hand.

Mr. Paul Yuvchenko slumped on his steering wheel.

"He's dead," Rachel realized in panic. "Aiden, the book is not protecting us!"

"I know," Aiden cried, looking out the closest window. People running helter-skelter were dropping dead around the car, as well as on the street. "I cannot see them," he whispered in fright.

Thumping on the car's roof. The children looked up, breathing hard. The noise stopped. They could hear their heartbeats in the silence that ensued in the small cabin.

The car's roof tore open and Rachel started screaming. The book's protection appeared in time to block Carl Bain's right hand from reaching for Aiden in the car. The Portwood thug ripped off the car's roof and flung it away before repeatedly landing his fists on the magical dome. It held.

Carl Bain rose up into the air and closed his eyes, drawing intense energy from his infernal masters now fluttering about. Energy strong and hot enough to ignite the gasoline in the car's fuel tank.

The explosion blew up the car, its parts landing as far out as the main road. Still, the cold dome surrounding the two kids remained as solid as the supernatural ice it came from, its filaments from the book growing in size and strength to form very hard extensions. Aiden and Rachel waited in it, shivering and holding their breaths as they stared through its transparent structure at the vile human servant of their incessant tormentors.

"Give me the book, Rachel," Carl Bain said, softly landing on the ground beside the book's icy defense. "And Aiden, I need my package."

"I don't have it," Aiden said. "You must have left it back in Germany."

"It's in your pocket, boy," the minion said dryly. "You can't lie to me, remember that when I snuff out your life."

"You can't get in here," Aiden said with uncertainty. "You won't succeed this time."

"We'll see about that," Carl Bain whispered, standing back for his demonic employers to race in and stack themselves on the dome, blocking daylight from those inside it. Fortunately, the bluish light from the icy layer returned and flooded the hemisphere's interior as the long hands piercing the crystalized structure started groping for the children.

Rachel tried to break off a piece of the icy projection emanating from the book, but stopped when her hands could no longer bear the cold coming from the magic extension.

"What now?" Aiden cried when a thin grayish hand caught his left arm. The pain was unbearable. "They're so many," he shouted, pulling his arm away. "We're doomed!"

"No, w–we're not," Rachel stammered, her hands trembling. More horrendous hands grabbed hold of her legs, burning their shapes into her skin. Others went for the book, and she resumed the task she had set for herself, ignoring the thought of failure sounding off in her head, as well as the unbearable pain coming from the ugly hands pulling her in different directions.

The white book's projections were now strong enough to hold the ancient artifact, as well as prevent any external aggressor from retrieving it from its present position, at least for some time. Remarkably, the demonic hands going for the codex were turning into ash and fading away.

And satisfied with this occurrence, Rachel concentrated on breaking off the filament-turned-extension, despite feeling a bit drowsy.

"What are you doing?" Aiden asked her, struggling to remain where he stood while keeping his eyes open, even as the grotesque hands from one side of the dome started pulling him towards the hemisphere's magical wall.

Rachel pushed and pulled one last time after a quick reprieve for her freezing hands and the extension broke off.

Immediately, the little girl felt a warm, fussy feeling inside, which adequately buffered her from the cold surrounding her. Swinging the weapon around like Aunt Shira, she cut through the long arms and hands holding her captive, surprisingly passing through the other extensions supporting the magical dome without causing them any damage. As the Gray Ones turned into ash and vanished, the Ice of Masada replenished its shape by filling up the holes created on its surface by the ghostly arms of these unearthly entities.

Rachel freed Aiden from the long ugly hands trying to pull him out of the dome using the same tactic she'd used to free herself. "Cool," he cried, feeling his blistered arms and legs. "How did you know about that?"

"Aunt Shira."

The demons started peeling away from the infernal dome guarding the book when the fluttering ash of their defeated colleagues reached them outside the book's hemispherical defense. Daylight flooded into this structure once again and the bluish light within it vanished.

Rachel surveyed the surrounding street through the ice dome. People lay dead everywhere she looked.

"Felt sleepy back there," Aiden told himself, blinking.

"The Gray Ones," Rachel said. "They want us to lose focus." She glanced at the book in the middle of the dome to assure herself of its safety. Its projections were like strong struts holding up the hemispherical structure protecting them from their attackers.

Carl Bain saw his masters retreat. He cracked his knuckles and walked over to the dome, wondering why his hands could not penetrate the infernal structure like his demonic lords. These apparitions now surrounded him and the mysterious dome, their number flooding the street and its many neighborhoods. Carl Bain understood what this meant. "This is the final battle, kids," he assured the two obstinate individuals inside the icy prison. "And don't worry, you'll soon be freed."

"Aiden, we mustn't let him break in," Rachel cried, fearing the worst and thinking of Kimberley, who she might never see again. "He's going to kill us if he does."

"We must be strong," Aiden said, taking the book's weaponized projection from his younger companion.

"You come to me with a stick?" Carl Bain mocked. "That's all you can think of?" He noticed an encouraging sign on the icy phenomenon before him. Cracks had appeared on its surface. His masters had done well.

The American slammed his right fist into the dome. He followed this with his left fist. He repeated the sequence, and resumed a continuous barrage with both fists in repeat fashion. He noticed Rachel looking at the book. "Pity you can't produce your petty symbol this time," he told her.

"You will not win this time," Aiden stressed, both hands holding the book's broken icy extension like a baseball bat. He flinched every time the dome shook.

"We'll see about that, boy," Carl Bain said, landing blow after blow on the dome before him. Obviously, the white book's hellish defense had been weakened owing to the barrage from his demonic masters. This opportunity to seize it he knew he must not frustrate with his own hands, else death awaited him.

Another crack announced itself with a splinting sound.

"The ice is no longer freezing up as quickly as it used to!" Rachel cried, feeling the projections holding up the book. "What's happening?"

Aiden turned to her, frowning. "How can I help?"

"Maybe we can control the book together like we did in Sierra Leone," Rachel said.

Aiden placed his right hand atop Rachel's hands on the white codex just as Carl Bain slammed another fist into the cold structure protecting them. Another blow shook the dome, but it started freezing up again, and the cracks on its surface slowly began to disappear.

Angrily, the Gray Ones' human minion increased his tempo, landing blows on the dome in quick succession. His knuckles had become bloodied, but he did not feel the pain. He could not feel the pain.

A loud crack crowned his effort.

"Any moment now," Aiden realized. The mysterious hemisphere could not sustain itself anymore. He felt the watery surface of the icy extension he still held in his left hand. The 'rod' had served Rachel well against the Gray Ones. Whether they would serve him well against another stronger human being remained to be…

The dome shattered into smithereens, and the whitebook's extensions broke off, while Rachel fell on her knees in shock. She snatched the mysterious artifact before it reached the floor of Mr. Yuvchenko's burnt car.

Carl Bain grabbed Aiden's neck with his left hand. He lifted the boy high up in the air and tightened his grip. "Now you die, fool!" he snapped.

Aiden stabbed the man's side with the icy pickle and crashed to the burnt car's back seat in the confusion that ensued. The fellow staggered backward, shaking his head and Aiden spun round to help Rachel, who struggled with two Booklords for the white book.

Carl Bain pulled out the white book's icy projection from his side, staring at its bloody end and wondering why the jab had made him so weak. Seeing his attacker reaching out to the little girl in her attempt to stop his dark masters from taking the book, the American hustler boiled. "Die, you fools!" he shouted, stretching out his hand to send a volley of flames in the children's direction.

Aiden touched the book as soon as the deadly flames left the towering figure raging behind him and Rachel.

What happened next had never happened before.

Chapter 18
AMNESIA, DEAD BODIES & RADIATION LEVELS

IVANNA heard the boom and felt strong wind on her left as she turned to look in this direction. The loud noise had come from beyond a line of trees bordering a recreational park she could spot from her vantage point up on the hill. This park sat near a residential area, which sprawled out beside a business district very close to where she had stopped her bike. The young woman knew about the park, because she had earlier cycled through it on her way to nowhere.

Spinning the bicycle around, Ivanna pedaled down the road thinking of the shortest possible route to this public leisure ground. The absence of any human being in the vicinity worried her, but she tried to focus on the new objective she just identified for herself. An old woman she had earlier met sitting on a bench at the park had told her that the government wanted people to leave the area without giving them any reason for the evacuation order. Could an impending natural or human-engineered disaster be the reason for the government's drastic decision? If this was correct, then investigating the boom she earlier heard, which could be part of the unknown catastrophic event, might give her a clearer picture of the situation she'd suddenly found herself in.

As she cycled down the road, meandering her way through some vehicles she thought had been left in a hurry, Ivanna realized that the wind coming from her intended direction had subsided. Her current route went through the business district; hence most of the buildings she passed along the way housed offices. That notwithstanding, the absence of any individual in the area was quite telling. The doors left ajar gave the bold young woman no clue as to where everybody had disappeared to, but the entrances and exits left wide open told her a different story. Many must have fled through these apertures a few minutes ago.

Of course, a land evacuation could never be that thorough within such a short period of time following the said government announcement. For all she knew, the people could be hiding somewhere, perhaps in underground bunkers or strong housing structures sited in strategic parts of the city. Sadly, even if that explained their absence, one or two individuals, who must have missed the evacuation announcement and directions to the bunker like she did, would have been a welcome sight in that eerie environment of empty concrete blocks.

Papers fluttering in the wind caught Ivanna's attention, and she noticed a child's toy lying near a small newspaper kiosk. The mother of the toy's owner must have hurried him away before he could grab it, she thought, wondering what would have caused this desperate situation as she rode past.

Ivanna forgot the poor child's toy in the face of what she saw lying around her when she got to the road junction near the newspaper kiosk. While crossing the junction, she could not explain the traveling bags left on the sidewalk leading to the residential part of town, nor could she ignore the abandoned car parked beside the road, its front doors wide open. She stared at the red high-heeled shoes placed on a sidewalk bench beside some newspapers obviously belonging to the same person.

Then she saw the bodies as she rode into the residential district.

"My God," she said, covering her mouth with her right hand as she stopped the bike. The dead people lying around her had facial expressions of terror-stricken surprise and inevitable doom, their limbs positioned in awkward angles and directions.

They were scattered about just as she had witnessed in her dreams.

"Hey. Over here."

Ivanna spotted the slender woman kneeling beside a dead girl and rode up to her. Blonde hair, sparkling eyes and a straight nose were the features she quickly picked out from the individual smiling at her near a corpse.

"It all looks surreal, right?" the woman began.

"What happened here?" Ivanna asked, noting the reading instrument hanging from the blonde woman's neck.

"I am still not sure, but I don't think it has anything to do with the pollution," she replied.

"Pollution?" Ivanna held her breath.

"Yes, the disaster at the nuclear plant?"

"Oh, no," the girl on the bicycle said, realizing the reason for the evacuation. "Is it bad?"

"Yes, dear," her new acquaintance replied. "Many have already died in Pripyat, and we shouldn't be here, for sure."

"The evacuation?"

The woman nodded.

"Did you miss it?"

"Yes," the woman said. "Came back from work in the morning, so I have been sleeping all through the day, and it feels very strange, because I was at the plant yesterday and they were talking of this test they needed to run on reactor 4."

"Test?" Ivanna asked.

"They wanted to see if the cooling pump system could still function using power generated from the reactor under low power should the auxiliary electricity supply fail," the woman explained. "They must have disabled the automatic shutdown system at some point if the reactor must run at low power during this test," she told herself.

"Do you work there?" Ivanna asked,

"No, I have an office here in Chornobyl, but my work takes me to the plant from time to time. By the way, I'm Oxana." The blonde woman stretched out her right hand. "And you are?"

"Ivanna Viktoriya," Ivanna said. "I'm an artist."

"Oh, good," her new friend said. "I am a nuclear scientist working for the government at the ministry here in Chornobyl. Just got up to hear the news on the BBC, and when I came out from my flat, I saw the bodies."

"You see no connection with the pollution?"

"No, dear." Oxana looked at the instrument hanging from her neck. "Radiation levels are not fatal," she said. "Whatever caused this is not from the plant."

"Why do you say so?" Ivanna asked. "What do you think caused this? Someone?"

"Something, I think."

"Something? What is it, then?"

"You heard the loud noise?" Oxana rather asked.

"Yes." Ivanna said, remembering her original mission. "I wanted to go and see what caused it."

"What are we waiting for? Let's go and investigate," Oxana said. "Your bike is not built for two people, though."

"We can take a car," Ivanna said. "I saw one on my way here, near the junction."

"But of course, you're right," the other woman said. "There are so many left on the road ahead. We can choose any one we want."

A cold chill went up Ivanna's spine when she heard this. "Who did this?" she wondered aloud, alighting from her bicycle. "What caused these people to abandon their cars and…and belongings as they fled?"

"There is only one way to find out," Oxana said, looking around. "The authorities will soon be here, so we must hurry."

They started off towards the vehicle near the junction, Ivanna pushing her bike along. The instrument hanging from Oxana's neck made her curious. "What's that around your neck?" she finally asked.

"A dosimeter," Oxana replied.

"What does it do?" Ivanna propped her bike on the bench hosting the red shoes. She approached the lonely car with her new companion.

"I use it to check for radiation levels," Oxana said, getting into the vehicle's driving seat. The car's owner had left its key in the ignition keyhole. "Right now, the level is not fatal."

"And what is the fatal level?"

"Four to five Sieverts." The car started without any problem, its engine sounding as good as new. Oxana revved it up a bit and slammed her door.

Ivanna entered the car and closed the door. It had a sparsely furnished interior. "What level of radiation are you getting now on your instrument?" she asked.

"302 millisieverts." Oxana changed gear and drove onto the road, heading into the residential area.

"Is that bad?"

"Yes, but it doesn't kill," the blonde scientist said, avoiding the bodies lying on the street as she drove. She slowed down whenever she had to tread carefully.

"I-I must tell you this," Ivanna began.

"Tell me what?" Oxana asked her, eyes on the road.

"Can't remember yesterday, or the day before yesterday," the artist revealed. "I can't remember how I got here."

"But you said you're an artist?"

"Yes, I know I'm an artist." Ivanna felt uncomfortable. "I just don't know how I became one."

"You mean you've forgotten your past up until yesterday?"

"Yes."

"You have amnesia."

"Yes."

"Have you been sick?"

"Remember I can't remember anything," Ivanna reminded her companion, smiling sheepishly. She looked at the concrete living quarters lined up beyond little green gardens through her side window. The serene atmosphere contrasted sharply with the dead people lying on the street. Bags and personal items littered the road, left were they fell as their owners fled to their deaths. The female artist looked away when she started seeing smaller bodies lying beside their parents and stifled the tears rushing out of her eyes. Suddenly, she saw a sight she could only gape at. Living people standing at their doorways and trying to comprehend what she still couldn't understand.

"Sick and aged."

"What?"

"Those people are sick, and some are old," Oxana repeated. "They don't attack the sick."

"They?"

"Yes," Oxana said. "They don't go after the sick, because they avoid diseased tissues, and they don't go after old people as well, probably because their tissues have started failing, too."

Ivanna stared at Oxana. "I-I don't understand," she stammered. "What are you saying? Who are 'they'?"

"The Booklords," the scientist replied. "I think they caused these deaths, and if it turns out to be true, then their presence in this town means that something of importance happened here today. Maybe the sound we heard earlier today?"

"You're not making sense," Ivanna pointed out. "I'm not sick."

"You said you have amnesia."

"I-I know, but I'm not sick," Ivanna stressed. "I'll remember my past very soon."

"How sure are you about that? Having amnesia means that you could be sick, or you…"

"I know I'm not sick, and neither are you."

"Actually, I am," Oxana revealed. "I've been getting some dose of radiation over the years in order to be safe from them."

"Safe?" Ivanna couldn't believe her ears. "You mean you've been deliberately harming yourself just to be safe?"

"Sure, just 60 millisieverts a year," Oxana said. "After all, we are not going to live forever, right?"

"Well, maybe, but what if you get cancer or something?"

"Then, I'll die, won't I?" the nuclear scientist asked her companion. "I've lived long enough, haven't I? And Shurabi might just take me to another time and place after this life."

"Shurabi?" Ivanna couldn't believe her ears. "Is that another word for madness?"

"Never mind about that, honey," Oxana aired, approaching a line of buses parked beside the street. "Just know that this could get dangerous a lot sooner than you think."

"What were you saying about having amnesia?" Ivanna asked. "You wanted to say something before I interrupted you."

Oxana became grim-faced. "I know you won't believe me, but losing your memory could also mean that you're not from this time and place."

Ivanna stared incredulously at her companion. "I can see that you're not yourself," she said.

"You say you can't remember what happened yesterday," Oxana continued, ignoring the accusation. "Can you remember what happened last night?"

"Well, yes...I-I had several dreams."

"Can you remember any of those dreams?"

"Yes," Ivanna said, frowning. "I dreamt I was dead."

"Strange." Oxana kept her eyes on the road.

"You say you've been getting radiation doses of 60 milli what?"

"Millisieverts."

"From where?" Ivanna asked.

"From the plant."

"If this is so, then why would these 'Booklords' attack and kill people whose environment has been polluted with higher radiation levels?"

"It builds up," was the succinct reply. "I've been exposing my cells for five years now. The people here just got exposed from yesterday."

Trees lining the edge of the district park stood on one side of the road like sentries guarding priceless grass. Ivanna searched for the old woman she had earlier seen sitting on the wooden bench in the park, but could not find a soul in the area.

"Looking for someone?" Oxana asked.

"Yes. Met her earlier today sitting over there," Ivanna replied, pointing at the particular bench.

"She must have left."

"You're not stopping," Ivanna observed.

"Can't see anything around here," Oxana explained. "Our best bet is to investigate the street after this park."

Ivanna did not object. The car moved into the next street, where residential concrete blocks lined the road again. More buses waited on both sides of the street, and more corpses littered the area, especially near these buses.

"They were to be used for the evacuation," Oxana began.

"I know," Ivanna said. "Wonder what really happened to these people."

"You still don't believe me, do you?"

"Yes," the artist replied. "You don't sound convinced, yourself."

"I'm still not sure about the 'why,' but I'm sure about the 'how.'"

Oxana stopped the car. "These people were killed by the Gray Ones, a group of Booklords looking for a particular ancient artifact."

"Why did you stop?"

"Those two kids lying near that bus need help," the scientist replied, opening the car's door.

"From your assertions, they should be sick, right?"

"Either that or they're from another place and time, like you."

Ivanna shook her head, but said nothing. She got out of the car and, avoiding the dead bodies on the ground, followed the blonde woman towards one of the buses parked on the left side of the road. She gladly saw that people had started coming in from the junction between the street and a major road leading to other parts of the city. Living people.

"They'll call the authorities now," Oxana pointed out. "We have to leave this place before then."

"But we didn't do anything," Ivanna said. "Why can't we stay and help them?"

"The Gray Ones will return."

The men and women now looking at the dead bodies were drivers and evacuees who saw the disaster from the main road and stopped their vehicles to see what had actually happened for themselves. Some drove into the street, passing the two women walking towards the line of buses packed beside the road.

"What happened here?" a young man, who had stopped nearby, asked Oxana in Ukrainian.

"We really don't know," Oxana replied in the same language. "We're just as shocked as you are."

"Let's hope it's not the pollution from the plant," the man said in a shaky voice, making a cross sign across his chest and going over to another dead body.

"Why can't they just leave as they were told?" Ivanna aired, walking quickly in order to catch up with her companion. "I mean, they should know it could be the pollution from the plant, right?"

"But we know it's not the pollution," Oxana said. "Believe me, if it was, I won't delay warning them."

The school logo on the bus they approached indicated that the car came from Kyiv. A boy and a girl rested on the vehicle's front right tire, supporting each other as best as they could. This pair stared at the two women approaching the bus. Ivanna thought she had seen the boy in one of her dreams.

"Kimberley, you're alive," the boy shouted, getting up with the tire's support.

"You see, they know who you really are," Oxana told Ivanna,

beaming.

"We thought we've lost you," the little girl still resting on the tire said.

"Who is Kimberley?" Ivanna asked the two children, stopping before them alongside Oxana.

"They're talking to you," an elated Oxana told her. "You are Kimberley, and I was right about you."

"I am Ivanna," Ivanna told the children, ignoring the nuclear scientist. "I don't know who you're talking about." Both kids looked at each other and the boy stepped towards the artist and took her hand. A wave of familiarity rushed through her brain, and all the memories she'd been longing for flooded back into her head. Ivanna's pupils disappeared as she gradually became someone else.

Oxana felt overwhelming excitement as she watched this dramatic change. "She's this Kimberley, isn't she?" she asked the kids standing before her.

"She'll soon realize that," the boy said.

"Aiden?" Ivanna, a.k.a. Kimberley, asked the boy standing before her.

Oxana turned to the artist with relief. "Your memories are back," she said.

"What happened?" Kimberley asked Aiden, ignoring the blonde woman speaking English with a foreign accent. "How did we get here?"

"It's a long story, Kim," Aiden said. "Where do I even start? Oh, first, you died…"

"I died?"

"Yes, and…and we got here, and the Gray Ones attacked us."

"I know you," the little girl beside Aiden told Oxana, drawing everyone's attention to the blonde woman carrying a strange instrument.

"Rachel, is she the one?" Aiden asked his companion, and she nodded.

"Who is she?" Kimberley asked Aiden, nodding towards the blonde woman standing beside her.

"You don't remember me?" Oxana asked her with a smile. "We just came here together. How can you forget so soon?"

"Sorry, I can't remember meeting you?" Kimberley returned.

"She was at the Mine with Father," Rachel said. "I think she's a Bookmaker."

"You're saying she's our contact here in, where are we?" Kimberley asked Aiden.

"Chornobyl," Oxana told her.

"Yes, she's the one," Rachel told Kimberley.

"Where have you seen me before?" Oxana asked the little girl, taking a forward step. She noticed a book approximately the size of a standard hardcover tucked underneath the girl's armpit, and her curiosity grew. "Can I see that book of yours?"

"Can I hold your hand, Mariah?" the little girl proposed instead.

"Of course," Oxana said, stretching out her right hand. "Mariah, was that my name in the past?"

"You said you were attacked?" Kimberley asked Aiden.

"Yes," Aiden said, intently watching the blonde woman who gave Rachel her right hand. Her pupils had disappeared. "We were also attacked by Carl Bain."

"So, how did you get here?" Kimberley asked him.

Oxana took her hands from Rachel, looking around her. "Yes," she said. "How did I get here?"

"Aiden saved us," Rachel told Kimberley. "He destroyed the Booklords when he created a strong wind by just touching the book."

"The boom," Kimberley remembered, turning to Oxana. "I'm beginning to remember now."

"I have no problem with that," Oxana said, staring at her hands before touching herself all over. "I can still remember who I am in this place, but I'm not sure it matters anymore, because I know I shouldn't be here right now."

"You're Mariah, Benjamin's assistant back at the Mine," Rachel told her.

"Strange," she said, smiling. "Wish I had a mirror."

Kimberley rolled her eyes and turned to Aiden. "Where did you face the Booklords?"

"Over there," Aiden replied, pointing at the smoldering skeleton of a burnt car sitting in front of an apartment block. "We came here after the Booklords had all vanished."

"And Carl Bain?" Kimberley asked him, walking over to the smoking car.

"He disappeared as well," Rachel replied. "He could have killed us, if not for Aiden. He destroyed the dome and..."

"He destroyed the dome?" Kimberley frowned.

"Like he did in Africa," Aiden said.

"So, tell me about this strong wind you created by just touching the book," Kimberley began, turning to Aiden.

"I think Aiden will become a good Bookbearer if he's given the chance," Rachel said. "He only thinks I'm crazy."

"You're not making sense, for sure," Aiden told her.

"You three have been traveling with the books?" Oxana, now Mariah, wondered aloud.

"No, Mariah," Rachel said. "Just the white one."

"Was Mariah my original name?" Mariah asked her. "You brought me here through the white one?"

"Yes," Rachel said. "I had no choice than to look for you with the book, just as I have done for the others."

"And how many of us have you found so far?"

"Only Uncle Ezra and…and…"

"You met Ezra?" Mariah asked the little girl, brightening up temporarily. "The Booklords killed him, right?"

Rachel nodded dejectedly.

"Are you in trouble?"

"Obviously," Aiden said.

"We were hoping you could help us stop them?" Rachel said, frowning.

"Are they after you?" Mariah asked her and she nodded. "Then you must find the other book."

"Aunt Shira said it's too late for that," the little girl said.

"You met Shira?" An unexpected question.

"Yes," Kimberley said.

"Not true," Mariah said.

"Not true about what?" an annoyed Kimberley demanded.

"About the other book," Mariah said. "I know the Black Ones are still after the Bookbearer with that book."

"But Father said we must defeat the Booklords first before performing the ritual with the other book," Rachel began. "This means we don't need the other book to defeat the…"

"Your father was wrong," Oxana, now Mariah, interrupted. "You can only defeat the Booklords by performing the ritual with the other book, and Shurabi tells me the Black Ones are still after the Bookbearer with that book."

Kimberley started. Shurabi. That magic word again.

"You can do Shurabi?" Aiden asked Mariah.

"I practice Shurabi," Mariah corrected.

"All Bookmakers practiced Shurabi, Mariah," Rachel began.

"You keep calling me that," Mariah said.

"But that's your name," the little girl pointed out. "We just want you to…"

"I think I prefer Oxana," Mariah told her.

"Okay by me," Kimberley said, turning to Oxana, a.k.a. Mariah. "What's Shurabi?"

They heard heavy rumblings.

"Sounds like a military detachment," Kimberley said.

"Quick, get into the car before they get here," Oxana told the children, who obeyed her. "Keep your heads down."

"Why the hurry?" Kimberley demanded.

"Children are meant to have left this area by now," Oxana said. "Those soldiers will arrest us if they discover the kids."

The military vehicles entered the street from the main road. Kimberley and Oxana stood beside their car as the convoy quickly rolled past them into the street. The young soldiers on the trucks looked like they had never fought a battle before. They were armed with Kalashnikovs.

"What will they do now?" Kimberley asked.

"They'll probably examine the bodies before checking them for radiation levels," Oxana replied. "Other than that, they're useless here."

The last vehicle stopped before the two women and five men in white laboratory coats jumped down from it with the soldiers it transported. These men started examining the dead bodies lying about, while some of the soldiers assisted them by stuffing bodies already checked for radiation into body bags. The remaining soldiers simply stood guard.

A high-ranking officer alighted from the stationary truck's driver's cabin and looked at Kimberley and her companion with disdain. "You are not supposed to be here," he slowly said in English.

"But we're not the only ones who saw this tragedy, captain," Oxana said. "Many have driven into the street as we speak."

"Let us deal with them," the captain said, turning to his men. "Please be on your way."

"What do you think is the cause of the deaths, captain?" Oxana put forward in Ukrainian.

"This area is very close to Pripyat, miss," the officer said in the same language. "The scientists are working to know if the radiation levels here were as high as the levels recorded in Pripyat within the last 48 hours."

"I am a nuclear physicist, officer, and I have a dosimeter with me," Oxana told the soldier. "Believe me when I tell you that these deaths are not due to the pollution from the plant. I've checked most of these bodies with my instrument."

For a brief moment, Kimberley thought that the Soviet Army captain would lose it, but then he walked over to their car.

"Are you crazy?" she whispered to Oxana. "You might have just blown the children's cover by being too forward."

"I was just trying to appear normal," Oxana whispered back. "Relax, he'll find nothing on the car. I checked its radiation level even before you met me today."

The officer stopped before the car's trunk and brought out a pen-like instrument.

"What's that?" Kimberley whispered to Oxana.

"I can hear you, miss," the Soviet Army officer said. "Your physicist friend will tell you what it is."

"It's an indicator. Measures radiation levels," Oxana explained to her companion.

"Bah!" the Soviet Army officer shouted in frustration. "This one does not work!"

"The indicator must have expired, captain," one of the men studying the dead bodies lying nearby suggested.

"Check their vehicle for its radiation level," the captain ordered the young man, who went to work immediately with his dosimeter.

"200 millisieverts, sir," the military scientist finally told his superior. "They must have been passing by."

"Now, leave before I am forced to take you in for questioning," the captain threatened both women.

"Okay, officer, we're leaving," Oxana said, turning back to the car.

Kimberley turned as well. She felt chilly.

"They're coming back!" Rachel shouted from the car's back seat.

"Who said that?" the military captain demanded, turning back to the car.

"Eh, nothing, captain," an alarmed Kimberley told him. "Could be that person lying over there."

"Ivanov, check the backseat," the man ordered an armed subordinate standing nearby.

"There's nobody with us, officer," Oxana said.

"Yes, nobody," Kimberley stressed, intentionally blocking the armed private's view of the backseat.

"You're lying," the man's commanding officer snapped, walking back to the car.

"Get out of the way," the soldier ordered Kimberley, pushing her aside. Two gloomy faces stared at him from the car's back seat when he peered in through the right side window. "There are children in the backseat, sir!"

"Seize them!" his superior ordered him.

Kimberley kicked the soldier between the legs and he doubled over. The soldiers around turned towards the vehicle.

"I order you to freeze!" the officer behind Kimberley demanded.

"We need to go, Kim," Aiden shouted from the car's back seat.

"Get in, Kim!" Oxana shouted, entering the car.

Kimberley opened the car's front passenger door.

"Stop or I shoot!" the Soviet Army captain behind her ordered, his right hand pointing a service pistol in her direction.

The Portwood police sergeant froze and raised her hands, surprised by the number of Kalashnikovs now pointing her way.

The soldiers surrounding the car moved in.

"Get out of the car right now," their captain ordered Oxana, who still sat in the car. "Get out before I do something drastic."

She obeyed him, raising her hands like her companion.

"You have to let us go right now, captain, before it is too late," Kimberley said.

"Before what happens?" the man snapped, frowning.

"Before they come, captain," Oxana said.

"So you know something MDV does not know?" the captain said coldly. "Is there something I must know right now?"

Both women said nothing.

"Whose children are these two?" The captain pointed at the two young faces staring at him through the car's side window with his left hand. His men started murmuring and he angrily looked around him. Some of them were pointing their guns upwards into the sky. "What is it, Ivanov?" he asked the nearest soldier, who obviously did not hear him.

Kimberley looked up to see what the captain's men were pointing their guns at. She froze at the sight of the individual gaping at her from above.

The weather turned cold pretty fast.

She acted without thinking.

Chapter 19
DESTINATION PRIPYAT

CAPTAIN Vladimir Zhukov of the Special Motorized Military Unit 5402 from the Kyiv Red Order Decorated Military District frowned at the woman whose hands were in the air before him. He glared at her companion through the car's side window. "Get out of the car right now," he ordered this other person. "Get out before I do something drastic."

The woman in the car obeyed him and raised her hands like her friend.

"You have to let us go right now, captain, before it is too late," the first woman standing before him said.

"Before what happens?" he snapped, frowning.

"Before they come, captain," the other woman said.

"So you know something MDV does not know?" the captain asked coldly. "Is there something I must know right now?"

Both women said nothing.

"Whose children are these two?" The captain pointed at the two young faces staring at him through the car's side window with his left hand. His men started murmuring and he angrily looked around him. Some of them were pointing their guns upwards into the sky. "What is it, Ivanov?" he asked the nearest soldier, who obviously did not hear him.

The men opened fire without being ordered to do so.

"Hold your fire," Captain Zhukov snapped, but nobody obeyed him. He looked up at what they were shooting at.

A strange man floated in the air high above the men.

Captain Zhukov panicked. He started shooting at the floating man like his men. The two women he'd been interrogating rushed into their vehicle and zoomed off, but he didn't care if they had kidnapped the children in their back seat anymore. His biggest concern at the moment looked like a man and floated like a ghost above his men. "Fire at will!" he ordered them, emptying his service pistol on the motionless individual high above the street.

The bullets had no effect on the apparition in the sky. It followed the moving car as the captain's fear-stricken men kept up their shooting.

"Where is it going?" a terrified private wanted to know.

Captain Zhukov realized he was shaking and his palms were sweaty despite the cold weather. He reloaded his gun and resumed the futile attempt to bring down the strange entity confounding his sense of sight high above the street. One by one, his men stopped shooting at it, lowering their fatigued arms while gasping for badly needed air. "Keep shooting!" he snapped and the soldiers started murmuring amongst themselves.

The captain turned and shot a conspicuous hesitator and the others resumed fire in the direction the ghostlike man had taken. He and the car had all but vanished round a bend.

"Stop!" Captain Zhukov ordered his men, peering into the distant horizon. Screeching voices forced him to turn in the opposite direction, but he saw nothing except the other soldiers from Unit 3502 coming out from the inner residential areas, probably after hearing the eruptive sound of gunfire. He heard the horrendous noise again.

"What is that?" Ivanov demanded to his left.

"Probably the confusion in your head!" Captain Zhukov snapped, waving away the screeching sounds in his own head. "Notify MDV of the car with two women and two children. Who got their number?"

"Here, sir."

"Good. Make sure it gets to HQ immediately." The screeching sound increased in the captain's head and he could not help holding his head with both hands. Looking around him, he realized his men were undergoing the same experience. "Where is that damn noise coming from?" he wondered aloud.

Right before his very eyes, something pierced through Captain Zhukov's men all around him, bursting out from their backs without spilling any blood. His men now collapsing around him, the Soviet Army captain suddenly felt raw inside. His stomach churned and he started gasping for air, sweating profusely before losing consciousness.

*   *   *

Carl Bain could not believe his eyes when he saw the woman he killed in Germany standing beside the car below him. She also recognized him and rushed into the car, which started moving immediately.

Ignoring the bullets whizzing through him, he went after the moving vehicle.

His masters simply smothered all the soldiers he left in his wake.

*　　*　　*

Kimberley knew how explosive the already tense situation would become when the weather suddenly turned cold. She had seen the floating man when the soldiers surrounding the car started pointing their rifles upwards rather than at her. She rushed into the vehicle when their captain joined them in attacking the apparition high above them. "Get in," she ordered Oxana, whose eyes were glued to the sky above them. "Get in, dammit!"

Oxana got in and started the car. "What is that thing above us?" she finally asked.

"An old friend," Aiden quipped.

"Get us out of here," Kimberley urged Oxana, who started the car and moved it. "Aiden, what of my cross?" she asked, turning to the back seat. "I had a small one in my pocket back in Germany."

"I couldn't find it before we left," Aiden replied.

"Did you draw any cross on the book?" Kimberley asked Rachel.

"Haven't seen any pen since we got here," the little girl replied.

"You were in Germany?" Oxana asked Kimberley.

"Yeah, sure. World War Two." The Portwood sergeant opened the glove compartment in the car's dashboard. "We need to make a cross sign and I need something to write with."

"Like a pen," Rachel said.

"Yeah, like a pen." Kimberley looked up in frustration. "There's no pen here."

The car swerved into the main road from Chornobyl and picked up speed.

Oxana pulled a pen from her breast pocket and handed it over to Kimberley. "You have a pen now," she said, "but you can't use it on the book."

"Why not?" Kimberley asked.

"Both books are from the devil, himself," Oxana replied, concentrating on her driving. "Back in the Mine, we tried to draw many forms of the Christian symbol on them to no avail. The symbols never appeared on their pages as long as we tried."

"That's a new one," Rachel said.

"We could draw on something else instead," Aiden suggested.

"Great idea," Kimberley said. "Only that there's no paper in this ancient car."

"Ancient?" Oxana was surprised. "This is a 1985 GAZ-24-10 Volga. It's a classic for us Ukrainian citizens, you know."

"Yeah, more like a Spartan classic to me," Kimberley grumbled.

"You Americans have no taste, you know?" Oxana emphasized.

"Do we have to go into that right now?" Aiden cut in.

"Remember we've established that you're Jewish," Kimberley said, ignoring Aiden. "Not Ukrainian."

"Remember the flying man after us?" Aiden tried.

"Remember your name is Mariah," Rachel told Oxana, and Aiden glared at her.

"Thanks for the help," he said, to which the little girl raised both hands in mock helplessness.

Oxana had ignored them all. "Give Aiden the book, Rachel," she ordered the Jewish girl.

"Okay." Rachel handed the book to the Portwood boy.

"Okay," Kimberley said, frowning. "You could be right about Aiden."

"I know I'm right," Oxana said. "The Gray Ones are afraid of him, that's why they haven't attacked us yet."

"I thought they were afraid of his union with Rachel during fights," Kimberley pointed out.

"That is true, but they have every reason to be more afraid of him, since he made the boom possible. Very few Bookbearers can do that, including yours truly."

"I think Aiden will be a good Bookbearer," Rachel said. "I know that anybody with the book for a long time becomes a Bookbearer and has better control of the book, but I think he has a special connection with the white book and…and can do a better job than me if he begins to bear the book right now."

Aiden stared at the strange little girl. "You know you don't like people holding this particular book," he told her. "Sure you want this?"

"If you can do a good job, yes," Rachel said. "But if you fall short, then I'll take it back."

"Aiden, Rachel will help us if you can't bear the book," Oxana allayed.

"And what of Carl Bain?" Kimberley asked her new acquaintance.

"Carl who?" Oxana had never heard the name in all her nine lives.

"The flying guy?" Kimberley clarified.

"Oh, he should be scared as well," Oxana said.

The white book's filaments sprang out from its cover and pierced all sides of the car around its flustered occupants, shattering side windows and the two windshields in its way. The car's interior became warmer despite the frozen extensions emanating from the book.

"That was close!" Kimberley said, eyeing an extension that had broken the front windshield.

"Is the dome still a half moon?" Rachel wondered aloud, looking at a side window for signs of it.

"No," Oxana said. "The Ice of Masada has taken the car's shape."

"Cool," Aiden said. He could hold the book despite its very low temperature. "It's getting warmer," he said.

"It will be warmer to you," Rachel said, "but actually it's getting colder, and anyone who holds it with you will feel the bite of this cold."

"Yeah, right," Kimberley said. "Talk about bookbearing."

"I–I don't know anything about being a Bookbearer," Aiden reminded everyone, staring at the cold ancient artifact he now held in his hands.

"You can only learn from experience," Oxana assured him. "There's really nothing to teach, just bear the book and you'll be fine."

"You have to be with the book for some time like me," Rachel said. "Only then will you be grounded in the art of bookbearing."

"You were murmuring some words beside Aunt Shira in Germany," Aiden told the little girl. "What did you tell Mr. Bain when he took the book back then? Some kind of ancient chant?"

"I was praying to Yahweh," Rachel revealed. "Sadly, He didn't help me then."

"Like I said, the two books are not from God," Oxana reminded them. "No way Yahweh would have helped you."

"But the cross defends us," Kimberley pointed out.

"The symbol you call the cross will always protect against the devil and his demons," Oxana said. "Just be yourself, Aiden."

"And what will that do?" Aiden wanted to know.

"That's the key to unlocking most of the secrets in the books," Rachel said.

"Okay," Kimberley said. "Good to know you have a living Bookbearer's manual."

"That's the much I can do, Kim," Rachel said. "The rest is up to him."

"Things are getting pretty cold pretty fast," Aiden warned, feeling the book's warm surface turning cold.

"That means they're ready to attack us," Oxana deduced. "Hold on."

The strands around the artifact had frozen up to become strong extensions that could keep it suspended in the space before Aiden, so he wriggled out beside Rachel and tried to break off an extension as a weapon, to no avail. Lonely road stretched out before the car and he found himself wondering where they were going.

A thud above signaled the beginning of the attack, but the car remained steady, eating up the miles before it. The Gray Ones appeared on both sides of the moving vehicle, floating alongside as if they wanted to make the journey with the car's occupants. Another thud came from the roof, seconds after the first one.

"Carl Bain," Kimberley said, looking up.

"He must be trying to get in," Aiden said.

"Sure he's the one?" Oxana asked.

"As sure as hell," Kimberley replied, staring out her side window. "Here they come!"

The demons edged closer to the vehicle on both sides of the road, until their numerical strength prevented light from penetrating into the car's interior and the Ice of Masada gave out its characteristic bluish glow. The infernal beings formed a hollow shell around the car, blocking Oxana's view of the road as they did so.

"We'll crash into something," Rachel cried.

"The road is a straight one to Pripyat," Oxana said, flooring the brakes, "but I can't drive blind from here to Pripyat."

"Why are you going to Pripyat?" Kimberley began.

"You'll know when we get there," the nuclear physicist told her.

"They don't want to touch the car," Kimberley realized, looking at the demonic shell all around them through the magical icy structure surrounding the Volga. "Like they're scared of touching it."

"They should be," Oxana said. "The Ice of Masada is stronger now, thanks to Aiden."

"I didn't do anything," Aiden protested.

Another thud on the roof. This time louder and heavier than the last two.

"What's he doing?" Kimberley wondered aloud.

"Like he's flinging something at us," Oxana said.

"Guess he's throwing heavy rocks," Kimberley said. "He's run short of ideas."

"I hope he never comes up with any good ideas again," Rachel said.

"Time to create the boom, children," Oxana told the two at the back.

"What if we go deaf or something?" Kimberley warned.

"Nothing of the sought, Kim," Aiden assured her. "You'll love it."

He touched the book, feeling its fresh warmth rush through his body before Rachel's hand joined his on the thick cover as she braced herself for the cold emanating from the book. A feint whistle escaped from the ancient artifact and the next instant, a jarring boom reverberated in the car, shattering the Ice of Masada and blowing away the tightly knit shell of hellish demons blocking Oxana's view. Just as quickly, the book spewed out new strands that formed a new defense against its enemies around the car. Oxana floored the gas as a fourth thud hit the roof.

"You guys alright?" Kimberley asked the children behind her.

"Yeah," Aiden said, looking at Rachel lying beside him. "Just very tired."

"I think the boom drains energy from its initiators, especially if they're children," Oxana aired. "Next time I promise to help."

A fifth stone hit the mysterious ice protecting the car's rear windshield area.

"He's our only headache now," Kimberley noted, drawing a cross on her left palm. "And he'll never stop coming until he's stopped."

"Shelf whatever you have in mind until we get to Pripyat." Oxana kept her eyes on the road. "His friends will not be able to help him near the plant. We won't even need the boom there."

*   *   *

Carl Bain watched the car from a distance, his senses still trying to assess the damage his opponents' new strategy had caused his masters. The gale had dispersed the Booklords, freezing many into ash and reducing him to a mere mortal. This meant he could not fly anymore. This also meant he could not attack his targets the way he had been doing with his supernatural powers. Angrily, he lifted a heavy rock from the roadside and hauled it at the car, sweating from the effort. This huge stone struck the Ice of Masada at the rear windshield area as the Volga sped away.

The American hustler stopped a vehicle driving by and pulled out its female driver. He took control of the vehicle and went after his opponents. He had no weapons to fight with if he succeeded in stopping their car. He just hoped his powers would return as soon as possible like it did several minutes after the two kids first attacked his masters. He saw a pocketknife on the car's dashboard and took it just in case.

*   *   *

"Someone is driving like a madman behind us," Oxana observed from her side mirror.

"It's him, alright," Kimberley said. "And I'm ready for him."

"How're you gonna fight him, Kim?" Aiden asked. "We have no

weapons except the Ice of Masada."

Kimberley smiled. "That will do."

"He's not flying anymore," Oxana noted. "Something must be wrong."

"Maybe he has lost his powers," Rachel reasoned.

"That must have happened the first time we held the book together," Aiden said. "No wonder he didn't show up several minutes after that."

"If that is the case, then we won't need the Ice of Masada to defeat him this time," Kimberley said. "Fasten your seatbelts, kids."

"How come we've seen no cars?" Aiden asked, obeying the directive with Rachel.

"That is because the authorities completed the city's evacuation many days ago," Oxana replied. "Except for the soldiers on guard in the city, we're definitely alone here."

"Here he comes," Kimberley announced.

Oxana increased speed, but the car behind matched her speed and bumped into her rear. "Hold on tight," she urged her passengers, steering to avoid another hit. "I can't shake him," she complained.

"We're too heavy," Kimberley said. "The Ice of Masada is weighing down the car and reducing our speed." Their enemy's vehicle pulled up beside their car and she saw their headache grinning through the clean ice covering her side window. She placed her left palm on the ice in order to display the cross sign on it, but the human servant to the Gray Ones appeared to be laughing at her. "It's not working," she admitted in frustration, pulling back her hand.

"What do we do now?" Rachel cried as she held on to Aiden's left hand.

"Don't worry," Oxana said. "We will find a way."

Carl Bain swerved into their car, creating a jarring sound of metal on metal. He repeated the action and Oxana tried to control the Volga. She now slammed into the other car before its driver could perform his dangerous maneuver a third time. She watched with satisfaction as the crazy fellow almost went off the road.

The American thug caught up with the Volga once again. This time he edged ahead before leaning into the space before the other car.

Oxana swerved away from her opponent. The Volga careened off the road and went downhill for some time before it started tumbling. It tumbled eight times and pieces of the Ice of Masada broke off when it landed on its four wheels at the foot of a tree bordering a forest near the valley's flat floor.

Carl Bain got out of his car and looked around while listening to make sure that the road was devoid of any living soul. He started walking towards the edge of the route's asphalt surface.

Across the road and down below, inside the damaged Volga, Kimberley held her head with her right hand. She withdrew the blood-stained hand and felt the gash again. "Everyone alright?" she asked. "Aiden, still there?"

"Sure, Kim," Aiden replied

"We're both fine," Rachel said beside the boy.

"Just bumped up a bit," Aiden said.

"Okay." Kimberley turned to their driver.

"I'm okay, Kim," Oxana said, checking her dosimeter for signs of damage.

The Portwood police sergeant unfastened her seatbelt and tried to open her door. It didn't budge. "We need to get out now," she said, pushing the door with her elbow. Her third try broke off part of the icy sheet covering the door before she could fling open the structure.

"Yes, of course," Oxana said, effortlessly opening her door since the protective ice covering it had cracks already. Aiden and Rachel got out of the damaged Volga from Rachel's side. The boy had the white codex tucked underneath his right armpit.

"The car's gone," he said, looking at the wheels of the Volga, which faced different directions. "What now?"

"We must go on," Oxana urged. "We're very near our destination."

Up above them, their nemesis stopped at the edge of the road and peered down the valley's slope. He cursed when he realized that the car he had run off the road was empty. Spotting its occupants making their way into the forest, he unfolded the pocketknife and hurried down the valley in pursuit.

"Good that we had our seatbelts on," Oxana said, looking back now and then as she walked beside Kimberley and the children. "Can't even imagine the outcome if we hadn't put on our seatbelts."

"Serious injury?" Aiden helped.

Kimberley looked at the many trees covered in red leaves before them and sighed. "I don't even know where we are," she said.

"We are still in the outskirts of the city," Oxana said. "Very soon we will…"

"Listen," Kimberley interrupted, frowning. She turned and spotted the American hustler running down the valley. "He's coming," she said. "Aiden, get into the woods with Rachel and hide."

"What of…"

"Just go." Kimberley looked at Oxana. "We'll stop him together."

"Okay." The nuclear physicist picked up a stick on the ground and raised it with both hands. "I'll do my best." She watched Aiden run off with Rachel. "Just don't touch anything, Aiden."

"Right," Aiden said as he ran.

"Get ready," Kimberley told Oxana. "Here he comes."

The man they waited for stopped at the damaged Volga. "Hey, Kim," he shouted, stepping forward a bit more cautiously. "Must we do this over and over again?"

"Just leave us alone, Carl," Kimberley returned. "You don't have to be following us around, you know?" She didn't care how the fool got to know her name.

"You still have something that belongs to me," the thug said. "I intend taking it back; and then there's the little issue concerning the white book."

"I lost your tiny silver box in Germany," Kimberley said. "As for the other problem, we can't solve it now."

"Not true," Carl Bain pointed out. He stopped before the two women, pocketknife in hand. "I saw my package with the boy here in Chornobyl."

"You saw something else," Oxana said.

"Ah, the Bookmaker," Carl Bain began. "Count yourself lucky that my powers have refused to come back."

"Count yourself lucky that you're still standing right there," Kimberley returned.

Carl Bain lunged at her and she side-stepped. He swung his weapon as he rushed past, dodging Oxana's swing at the same time.

The American hustler kicked the nuclear physicist when he turned around and she lost her balance. He dodged Kimberley's intended right fist punch before drawing blood from her right flank with the pocketknife. A hard kick to the wounded area saw the Portwood sergeant crumble to the ground in pain.

Oxana attacked the thug again, swinging her dry branch in wide arcs. Carl Bain avoided these vicious swings, spun round and stabbed his attacker's side in one smooth movement. He followed this achievement by landing a blow squarely on her jaw, which sent the scientist crashing to the ground on her back.

The human minion rushed at Kimberley, his pocket knife ready to end it all. She interlocked her legs with his, twisting to her left and causing him to lose balance. The American hustler crashed to the ground, breaking his fall with his right hand.

"Oxana, now!" Kimberley shouted.

Despite her wound, Oxana stood up and stepped up to land a convincing blow with her dry branch on their sole enemy's head. The man with the pocketknife blacked out just as quickly.

Kimberley seized his pocketknife.

"Don't," Oxana said, having read her new friend's mind.

"Why not?" the other woman wanted to know. "He'll keep coming for us until he kills us."

"Don't kill him, I know that's not who you are," Oxana persuaded. "You can break his legs, though."

"What?"

"That will slow him down and give us a head start." The nuclear physicist turned and walked back to the Volga. She opened its trunk.

"What are you doing?" Kimberley asked, untangling her legs from the unconscious man's and standing up with some effort.

"Getting a leg-breaker," Oxana replied, pulling out the damaged car's battery from its trunk.

"And how will that do the job?" Kimberley picked up Carl Bain's pocketknife and Oxana's dry branch.

"Watch and learn," Oxana said, bringing over the battery. She knelt beside Carl Bain, turned him on his back and smashed his left knee cap with the heavy electric-generating device.

The man on the ground sprang out of his unconsciousness screaming expletives, and Kimberley knocked him back into it with a blow from Oxana's famous dry branch. Oxana broke his other knee cap and he woke up again, cursing everything in sight.

Carl Bain's two opponents towered above him as he sat on the ground in unspeakable pain. Smiling, he thought his powers were coming back. His disappointment showed when he tried to spit fire out of his hands. Nothing happened and his smile faded away. He only felt reenergized and nothing more. For some reason he could not ascertain, his infernal powers had not returned. He looked around angrily, wondering why his masters were yet to come.

"Looking for your friends?" Oxana asked him, spitting out blood. "They won't come. The radiation level is way too high, and since they avoid defects and disease, they cannot come near any of us right now."

"That's why you came to Pripyat?" a surprised Kimberley asked Oxana. "That's why we're risking our lives? Are you mad?"

"No, I'm not," Oxana replied. "You and the kids are currently getting 2 Sieverts of radiation and your bodies are no longer palatable to the Booklords. That's a win in my opinion."

"And what of the long term scenario for us?" Kimberley snapped. "Did you consider that in your scientific calculations, genius?"

"We won't be here for long, I promise."

"You want us to die here?" Kimberley was visibly angry. "Is that what you want?"

"That is not true," Oxana said. "I needed to talk to you uninterrupted by the Booklords. That is why I chose to bring you here."

"Okay," Carl Bain told the two. "Now that you're done arguing, prepare to die."

"With which power, fool?" Kimberley asked him.

"This time I'll go for your throat," he replied, feeling for his pocketknife on the ground.

"Looking for this?" Kimberley asked him, displaying the weapon.

Carl Bain tried to get up and his knee pain shot through his spine. "Curse you!" he muttered, realizing what his enemies had done. "I will heal and I will find you no matter how far you go and no matter how long you hide."

"Let me see you try," Kimberley returned. "No need for words."

She knocked him out again.

"Come out, children," Oxana said, and Aiden came out with Rachel. The boy immediately went to the man on the ground.

"What did you do to him?" he asked the women standing over the unconscious fellow.

"No need for that now," Kimberley said. "Let's leave this place."

"We need a car," Rachel said.

Kimberley bent down beside Carl Bain and searched his pockets. She withdrew a bunch of keys from one of them. "We have one now," she said.

Chapter 20
SHURABI

THEY got to the deserted city of Pripyat that evening. Aiden and Rachel hid under a pile of clothes on the back seat before Oxana stopped at a checkpoint. The nuclear physicist brought out her identification card for the soldiers on duty to scrutinize. The pile of clothes on the back seat got a cursory inspection from one of the soldiers through the car's side window.

"They let me through, because I told them we had a government assignment," Oxana told Kimberley as she pulled out of the checkpoint.

"I see."

"Funny they forgot to ask you for your identification."

"What?"

"Some people still have permission to remain in the town," Oxana quickly added. "Plant workers, policemen, doctors, scientists and military personnel."

"Right," Kimberley said.

"I have an apartment close by," Oxana said.

"Okay," Kimberley said.

"Is anything wrong?" Oxana began. "You don't seem to want a conversation with me."

Kimberley sighed. "You brought us to an empty city with very dangerous radiation levels. Why would I want to talk to you?"

"I thought I could give the kids something to eat before you leave my time," Oxana returned.

"I could do with a little bite," Aiden said at the back.

"Me, too," Rachel said.

"Guys, you know we are always full whenever we fill a new body after each travel, right?" Kimberley asked exasperatedly.

"Right," both kids chorused.

"So what are you two talking about right now?" she asked them. "We don't need to eat before we leave, right?"

No answer.

"Majority wins," Oxana quipped, stopping before an apartment block and getting out of the car.

"What did you want to tell us that you couldn't tell us on the way here, anyway?" Kimberley asked her guest while exiting the car with her two young time-traveling companions.

"200 millisieverts," Oxana checked from her dosimeter, which still hung from her neck. "Not too bad and...and not good either. Great."

"Oxana," Kimberley said slowly. "What did you want to tell us?"

The blonde scientist looked up from her instrument. "I..."

"Let's go inside first, Kim," Aiden proposed. "Rachel's feeling tired."

"It's the radiation, but she'll get better after you leave my time," Oxana said, getting a key to unlock the apartment block's main door. "Come in please. You eat, I talk to you and you go, nothing more."

"Okay," Kimberley agreed. "We eat, we leave."

Inside, the building had a flight of stairs that stopped at the last floor. Oxana led her visitors up to the fourth floor and unlocked a wooden door as plain as the other doors lined up after it in the single corridor. Cheap furniture and abstract art graced her living room, which had space for a dining table sitting four. "Feel at home," she said, waving her guests to a sofa facing a box TV set. "I have *agnautka* and some milk in the fridge."

"What's *agnautka*?" Rachel asked, sitting down on the sofa with Aiden.

"A kind of Ukrainian bread," Oxana replied as she headed to a small doorless room fitted out as a kitchen.

"And where's the fridge?" Kimberley wanted to know.

"I thought you were not hungry," Oxana said, standing at the entrance to her kitchenette with a plastic milk container on one hand and a plate of sliced *agnautka* on the other.

"Since I'm already here, no need to put it off," Kimberley admitted.

"Okay, fine by me." Oxana dropped the food items on a side table before going to get glass cups. "You can switch on the TV, you know."

"Not interested," Aiden said. "The sooner we go, the better."

Oxana returned with the cups and shared the milk. "You can call me Mariah now. I guess I'm beginning to like the name," she told her guests.

"What, exactly, is Shurabi?" Kimberley began, sipping her milk and munching a slice of *agnautka* bread.

"Shurabi is a spell the Bookmakers derived from black magic," the nuclear scientist replied. "Anyone can live so many times after each death and be sent back in history through these various places and times, and even beyond man's early days on Earth, whenever his or her name is written on a book enchanted by this spell."

"Are you saying that everyone whose name was written in this book, and had been killed by the Gray Ones in the course of our journey, is not really dead?" Kimberley's curiosity had peaked.

Oxana, or Mariah, sighed. "All Bookmakers practiced Shurabi back then so that they can have the ability to develop a tougher form of parchment for the two books," she said. "The use of Shurabi involved an ancient art that gave its followers the ability to wield the powers inherent in the codices guarded by the Sicarii Kabbalah Masada."

"Gracious," Kimberley exclaimed, holding her head. "Must there be a new group of words every ten minutes?"

"No," Rachel said in earnest. "The Sicarii Kabbalah Masada is the cult of Bookmakers responsible for making the books."

"So, all Bookmakers and Bookbearers are members of this…this cult?" Aiden wondered.

"Yes and no," Rachel replied.

Aiden stared at her. "Yes and no?"

"All Bookmakers are Bookbearers, but not all Bookbearers are Bookmakers," Rachel said.

Aiden didn't blink.

"All Bookmakers are members of the Sicarii Kabbalah Masada," Mariah tried to explain, "but not all Bookbearers are members, because the art of Bookbearing as a gift bestowed on the Bookbearer through his or her ancestry is more potent than that a Sicarii Kabbalah Masada learns as a skill. You could be a good example of this gift coming from your lineage, Aiden."

"Wait, we still don't know if that is true," Kimberley began. "Aiden might as well be a victim of circumstance here."

"We don't know if he has Sicarii Kabbalah Masada history, do we?" Rachel began.

"But if he has Sicarii Kabbalah Masada ancestry, doesn't that mean his ability to wield the book is not a gift?" Kimberley asked.

"Why did they choose such a long name?" Aiden asked.

"That's another day's story," Mariah cut in. "We'll just have to make do with the fact that Aiden has the ability to bear the book. Where he got that power, you guys are yet to find out."

"Probably from a skilled great great grandfather," Kimberley mumbled. "We'll find out soon enough."

"As I was saying," Mariah continued, "the use of Shurabi involved an ancient art that gave its followers the ability to wield the powers within both books. These powers include the Flame and Ice of Masada, which defends the books and their Bookbearers from the menace of the Booklords, or the demons we know to have sent Mr. Carl Bain after us."

"Now we're getting somewhere," Kimberley said. "What about the boom?"

"Oh that," Mariah began. "That is a phenomenon we believe only gifted Bookbearers can initiate with a fellow Bookbearer. We don't know much about it, but we know it is not a reliable means of defense, despite its devastating effect."

"And why do you say that?" Aiden asked her.

"The boom doesn't happen everytime a gifted Bookbearer joins hands with another Bookbearer during a Booklord attack," the nuclear scientist said. "We never found out why back at the Mine and had to eventually abandon it as a form of defense against the Booklords after so many casualties."

"Pity," Rachel said. "What we need is a weapon that can destroy the Gray Ones once and for all. I was beginning to think we'd found such a weapon in the boom."

"Maybe the Booklords are unbeatable after all," Kimberley said.

"You do know about these demons, right?" Mariah began.

"Of course, we do," Aiden replied. "They've been trying to kill us since we left Portwood."

"And where is Portwood?"

"Home?"

"I see." The female Bookmaker paused. "There are two kinds of these...these demons."

"We know that," Kimberley said. "Ezra told us."

"Did he now?" Mariah asked, deep in thought. "You know that the kind after the codex in your possession is the deadliest kind, right?"

"Yes," Aiden said. "I just told you they've been trying to kill us since we left our town."

"Of course, you just did, my dear," Mariah said, frowning. "Did Ezra also tell you that whenever these demons kill, not even Shurabi can save their victims?"

Kimberley shook her head, slowly. "No, he didn't say that." The Portwood police officer couldn't help thinking of Jim and the other victims of the Gray Ones they had left in their wake. "So," she said, trying to break off the thought, "how did you know that the other book is still with its Bookbearer?"

Some of the gloom left Mariah's face. "Shurabi was placed on the books using invisible Hebrew writing arranged by practitioners of the

Kabbalah," she revealed.

"And what, exactly, is this…Kabbalah?" Kimberley asked her.

"A form of ancient Jewish mysticism or Kabbalah Ma'asit," the scientist replied. "It is a branch of the Jewish mystical tradition that concerns the use of permitted white magic by its practitioners," she tried to explain when she realized nobody understood her. "In ancient times, its practice was reserved for the Jewish elite, who could separate its spiritual source from Qliphoth realms of evil if performed under circumstances that were holy and pure, until the Sicarii Kabbalah Masada started using it to engage the messengers from Yahweh in spiritual conversations."

"How does this all fit into the bigger picture?" Kimberley wondered aloud.

"We, the Bookmakers, were shown by our heavenly visitors that Kabbalah Ma'asit laden with Shurabi was a very potent tool in the hands of any mystic," Mariah explained. "I practiced Kabbalah Ma'asit and Oneiromancy with Shira for years while we were hiding in the Mine and I know that the other book is still out there."

"How, exactly, did you know that?" Aiden asked.

"If the Booklords have seized this other volume," Mariah said, "then the isolated Hebrew words now visible on the pages of both books through the Shurabi will be hidden from members of the Sicarii Kabbalah Masada still alive."

"You mean the remaining Bookmakers?" Kimberley asked her.

"Yes," Mariah replied. "Those the Gray Ones have failed to kill." She paused again. "Since these words are still visible to me, then the other book, which we call the black book, is still out there."

"I see." Kimberley fell into deep thought. "So, how do we find this other book?"

"You don't need to," Mariah said.

"Don't need to do what?" the Portwood sergeant asked her.

"You don't need to look for it," the physicist said. "It will find you."

"And how will it do that?" Kimberley asked, surprised by the Bookmaker's reply. "Through its Bookbearer?"

"No, as long as it is still in the hands of a human being," Mariah began, "it will seek out its other half across the vastness of space and time, as long as that other half is also in the hands of another human being."

"And what do you mean by its other half?" Kimberley asked.

"Didn't Shira tell you about the third book?"

"She did, Mariah," Rachel replied for her fellow time-traveler.

"Then, you must know that the two books now in existence form this third book, which doesn't exist right now," Mariah said. "This third book is more powerful than the halves that form it after the ritual, and makes any Bookbearer wielding it a determiner of his or her destiny."

"That's it," Rachel exclaimed.

"That's what?" Aiden asked her.

"Father often talked of the ritual's 'purpose' for our people," she said. "The third book is the tool with which this purpose will be achieved, right, Mariah?"

"I just said that, dear," Mariah said, sitting down on the sofa beside the children. "Make sure the Booklords don't get hold of your own book while you wait for the other book to locate you in time and space," she warned them. "Once the ritual takes place, then and only then will our people be truly free to determine their destiny."

"I don't think Israel is doing badly right now," Kimberley said after some thought.

"I meant every Jew on Earth," the scientist said. "Now, leave me to die in peace."

"You can come with us," Rachel pleaded.

"And be killed by the Gray Ones? No, thank you," Mariah said. "I would prefer dying and appearing somewhere else with the help of Shurabi."

"Okay, your wish," Kimberley gave in. "So, you say we can only wait for this...this black book to find us? Sure we cannot look for it ourselves?"

"Of course, you can look for it if you want to," Mariah said. "I only told you that you do not have to look for it. I never said you cannot look for it."

"So, that's settled then," Aiden began. "How do we find it?"

"There's no time, Mariah," Kimberley said. "We have to try and find this other book before the Gray Ones get to it."

"Sadly, I don't know how one can go about looking for the black book," Mariah said, "but I can direct you to one who may know."

"A Bookmaker?" Kimberley wanted to know.

"No," the nuclear physicist said. "A slave who had the privilege of practicing Shurabi with us in the Mine."

"Did I ever meet him, Mariah?" Rachel asked.

"No," Mariah said. "He knew and interacted with members of the Inner Circle."

"The Inner Circle?" Kimberley frowned.

"The Bookmakers entrusted with performing the ritual," Mariah explained, turning to Rachel. "Your father was one of them."

The little girl was wide-eyed. "My father?"

"How do we know this slave when we meet him?" Kimberley cut in.
"You don't," Mariah said. "He will find you."

*   *   *

Carl Bain woke up surrounded by his infernal masters. "About time," he grumbled, sitting up. "You guys failed to show up when I needed you the most." His windpipe narrowed and he gasped for air as his body left the ground. "Didn't mean to…to say it that–that way!"

The demon leader standing before the suffocating man conveyed a message.

"I get it, okay?" Carl Bain wheezed. "You couldn't come in time, because you were delayed by the Ice of Masada in the hands of the boy."

He collapsed on the ground, panting. His knees slowly healed and he moved his legs about, then flexed his knees just to be sure that they had really healed. His unearthly powers returned and he felt unbridled energy coursing through his entity.

The lead demon communicated further.

"They have left? Okay, Africa?" Carl Bain boiled. "What are we waiting for? A new plan? Great."

He didn't object. He hated the way they choked him at their whim.

Chapter 21
NIGERIA

DENSE forest filled Aiden's view when he woke up. He realized he was sitting on grass with his hands tied behind his back. Five or six other individuals, including Kimberley and Rachel, sat around him, their hands also tied behind their backs.

Aiden noticed the armed men surrounding the group. These masked folks wore military-styled attire and held AK47 rifles. Bullet magazine belts hung from their shoulders.

"Where are we?" Rachel began.

"Shut up!" one of these men snapped at her. This fellow had large lips that ruined his handsome face. He stared at Kimberley and spat out. "You people always come here to take our oil."

"Your oil?" Aiden asked him. "But this is not…"

"This small boy," Ugly Face began. "I go reset your head if you no keep quiet now."

"Godspower, leave him alone na," another bully interrupted. "Na small boy you dey follow talk?"

Aiden understood the English-based language he just heard. The white book made that possible. He remained quiet after Kimberley told him to do so with an eye signal.

"Yes, Oga don come," the second man announced in the same pidgin English, the reason for this statement walking up to stand before the bound people moments later.

The new fellow had an air of authority around him, as well as a wooden face sticking out in the middle of an encroaching forest of grays and whites. A black suit poorly hid his huge frame and his legs looked as if chiseled out of massive chunks of rock. He wore a Bluetooth headset on his left ear and a golden wristwatch on his left wrist. Shiny black shoes completed this outfit.

"Are these the hostages from the Shell camp?" he asked one of the militants guarding the kidnapped individuals.

"Yes, sir," the armed man replied, swinging his semiautomatic rifle over his shoulder and waving his other hand at Kimberley and the two kids sitting beside her. "We picked these ones from Mr. Arnoud's house, sir. Maybe we should use them as a lesson to others?"

"No, Godspower. We will follow instructions to the letter."

"Please, why are you holding us?" Kimberley asked the man in black suit, ignoring the stares thrown her way. "At least, we have a right to know."

"Will you shut up your dirty mouth?" the man called Godspower snapped.

"No, my friend," the black-suited man objected, glaring at the last speaker. "We must treat them with respect, always remember that." He turned to Kimberley. "Good day, miss," he said, straightening his suit. "My name is Bruno Gbomoh and I represent the Movement for the Emancipation of the Niger-Delta, also known as MEND. I must assure you that you haven't left Rivers State."

Of course, the name rang a bell in Kimberley's head, since according to the mysterious book; a new place meant new roles.

"So, what happens now?" one of the captives asked Mr. Gbomoh. "We are hostages until when?"

"Until the Federal Government agrees to our demands, madam," Mr. Gbomoh told the woman. "You all came to the Niger-Delta to steal our oil, and we have decided not to close a single eye until you all leave our land."

It dawned on Kimberley all of a sudden. As usual, the book had bestowed a schizophrenic personality on them with their original selves blending with other vague characters. This time, they were hostages kidnapped from a Royal Dutch Shell expatriate's house in Rivers State, Nigeria.

From what the Portwood sergeant could now recall, MEND wanted to drastically cut oil production in the Niger-Delta region of the West African nation of Nigeria. The organization aimed to eventually expose exploitation and oppression of Niger-Deltans, as well as the devastation of the region's natural environment by oil corporations.

"Our government and overseas oil firms promote massive economic inequalities, fraud, and environmental degradation on our lands," Mr. Gbomoh continued. "And due to this, we are fighting for 'total control' of the Niger-Delta's oil wealth, since our people have not gained from these riches under the ground as well as in our creeks and swamps."

Kimberley rolled her eyes. What the man would never say was that MEND's methods included kidnap-for-ransom of oil workers, staging armed assaults on production sites, pipeline destruction, murder of Nigerian police officers, and the sale of stolen oil to the black market.

"As I speak," Mr. Gbomoh continued, "other operations are rounding up on oil installations across the Niger-Delta, and more of your fellow expatriates will soon be joining you here."

Kimberley sighed. She could now remember the attack on the house at Bonny Island and their subsequent kidnap by armed men. Blindfolded and transported to an unknown destination, they'd met other kidnapped hostages at this location.

"So, we are hostages, Kim?" Aiden asked the Portwood sergeant and the MEND militants surrounding the hostages laughed at him.

"So na now you know?" one of them asked him in Nigerian pidgin.

"Una own don finish today," another grumpy fellow added in the same language.

"No, Peter," Mr. Gbomoh told this rebel. "Give them food and wait for my orders, understand? I'll give it when the others arrive or when those fools at Abuja have carried out our demands."

He left.

Kimberley looked at Rachel and heaved a sigh of relief when the little girl turned to stare at her with resolute eyes.

But where was the white book?

"Where's the book?" Kimberley mouthed, hoping the little girl would get the message.

"Quiet, I say! Keep quiet," the militant called Peter snapped at the Portwood sergeant. "Fine girl for face, no make me vex o."

"Oga don commot," Godspower said. "Now na me be presido."

"Who dash you?" a fat Nigerian hostage whispered, unfortunately generating raucous laughter from the militants.

An angry Godspower slapped the man hard across the face. "Who give you permission to talk?" he snarled in Nigerian pidgin. He lifted his weapon and brandished it at the hostages. "I go kill anybody wey open mouth again!" he said in the same English pidgin.

Kimberley turned to Rachel and the little girl nodded at a heap of items on the grass some feet away from the hostages. The white book lay atop this heap. If they would have any chance against the Gray Ones, they would have to find a way to get back the ancient volume.

The militants brought Spaghetti on plastic takeaway plates and untied the hostages. As they ate, Aiden and Rachel moved closer to Kimberley under the watchful eyes of the rebel guards.

"We must find a way to get back the book," Aiden murmured in-between mouthfuls.

"The Gray Ones will soon be here," Rachel whispered. "What do we do?"

"We must retrieve the book and look for the guy Mariah told us about," Kimberley outlined. "He must be around here somewhere."

"Hey, you three," one of the militants began, pointing at the three time-travelers. "What is going on there?" He walked over to the trio.

"Nothing, sir," Aiden said, looking up. "We're just enjoying the food."

"So be quiet while doing so," the man growled.

"Okay," Kimberley said. "What happens to us if the government doesn't do what you wanted?"

"Death na," the man said without hesitation. "*Ọnwụ*."

Kimberley appeared confused.

"It means 'death' in Igbo," the man grumbled.

"Okay," Aiden whispered, looking at the book lying on other personal belongings a few feet away. His mind was in overdrive, puzzling over the best way to make the armed men return it.

"What are you looking at?" the fellow hovering over them demanded, startling the boy. He went over to the heap of items and picked up the hardback volume. Turning it and flipping it open, he frowned.

"It must be clear to you now that the Nigerian government cannot protect you," the rebel whose comrades called Godspower said behind Kimberley. "We told you to leave our land while you can. Now you'll die in it...."

"And what about this book?" the militant holding the white book asked Aiden.

"It's nothing," Kimberley replied. "Just a scrap book I record names with."

"Names? Of who?"

"People I do business with," Kimberley lied, looking at Rachel.

The man looked through the book's pages. The scribbled names on these pages did not convince him. "It's not true," he said. "You dey lie." His fellow militants gathered around him and the three hostages he was confronting.

"Soothe yourself," Kimberley said, trying to sound like she cared less.

"What kind of business?" the man asked her.

"The kind that's none of your business?" she replied, frowning for good measure.

"Of course, it is our business," Mr. Bruno Gbomoh said outside the group of militants and hostages. "Kpakol, give me that book," he ordered the militant holding the hardback.

"Where did he come from?" Kimberley whispered, nodding towards the MEND spokesman.

"No idea," Aiden said.

Mr. Gbomoh flipped through the white book. He had a puzzled expression as he looked at his wet palms in turn. "Where is the water coming from?"

"It fell into a bucket of water this morning," Kimberley lied.

"No, Kim," Rachel opposed. "You must tell them the truth now."

"And why should I do that?"

"Because it's…it's getting cold now," the little girl blurted out.

Kimberley's heart skipped. How did she miss that?

"What are you talking about?" Mr. Gbomoh asked Rachel. "What do you mean by that?" His right hand went to the holster underneath his suit.

Kimberley glared at Rachel, but the latter ignored her and looked straight into Mr. Bruno Gbomoh's eyes.

"They are coming," the little girl told the rebel.

The militants erupted into roaring laughter.

"Who is coming?" the one they called Peter asked his comrades. "Soldiers? Them no dey fear?"

"Abi na police?" another rebel wanted to know in the same pidgin language. "Those ones sabi fight?"

The militants laughed for a long time afterwards.

"Still we must not let our guard down," Mr. Gbomoh said, turning to Kimberley. "What does your little friend here mean by what she just said, miss?"

"She meant something else, sir," Aiden began.

"Whose names are written in this book?" Mr. Gbomoh demanded.

"You must believe us if we tell you," Kimberley added. No need lying now.

"Oga, those names fit be people we go kidnap later," a militant suggested.

"Not true," Kimberley said. "My niece is right. You must hand us that book, Mr. Gbomoh, if you and your men want to survive the calamity about to befall this place."

"Tie them up and put them back on the boats," the MEND spokesman ordered the man he called Kpakol. "We have to move them out of here now."

"What for?" Aiden wondered aloud.

"Keep quiet," the rebel spokesman snapped, handing over the white book to Kpakol. "We will investigate this wet book later, but now I think we should be moving the hostages. I don't think this area is secure any longer."

"You cannot run away from this enemy, Mr. Gbomoh," Kimberley told the man. "You must give us the book and let us go."

"Oga, allow me to slap this girl right now," Godspower said. "Be like say she dey craze. Make I reset her brain one time."

Kimberley felt the surrounding temperature drop and heard Rachel screaming. She grabbed the white book from Kpakol as the militant lost his balance. Everything slowed down. Mr. Gbomoh looked amazed as demonic shapes sliced through his body in midair. His frozen men and bewildered hostages had surprise pasted on their faces as the devilish storm caught them unawares, each person dealing with his or her own terror.

The book's magical dome protected the three time-travelers as well as two other hostages who'd been sitting close to Kimberley when the Gray Ones appeared. These unearthly apparitions continued their onslaught in droves, pummeling the dome from all sides and pushing their long hands into it. They started reaching out for the book as they howled horribly.

"What is happening?" one of the hostages in the dome demanded, staring at the long hands jutting into the bluish structure now protecting her. "This is not Ikwerre magic o!"

"What's happening to everyone out there?" her male colleague asked and she looked outside with foreboding. She screamed as another demon threw up another hostage and went through the terrified fellow with ease.

"They are so many!" Rachel cried, holding up the book with Kimberley. "This doesn't look good."

"It had never looked good," Aiden said, cowering below Kimberley's arms. "Looks like it's getting worse instead."

As the dreadful Booklords froze away, fresh ones replaced the ash fluttering into nothingness. The two hostages in the white book's dome started shouting.

"Take my place," Kimberley told Aiden, nodding at his silent question. The boy held up the book and she moved her numb hands away from the cold emanating from the ancient relic. No need to delay their ultimate weapon any longer.

"It's not working," Aiden said as soon as he locked hands with Rachel. The book's icy filaments felt as cold as ever, but this time there was no reassuring boom to cap their effort. "Why is it not working?"

"I feel tired," Rachel confessed. "Maybe that's why."

"Or maybe Mariah was right about the boom," Kimberley said, and frowned at something she just saw in the distance. "We have a new problem," she pointed out, nodding towards the human materializing at the edge of the forest clearing.

On seeing the weird man forming out of nothing before her very eyes, the perturbed woman taking refuge in the dome with Kimberley and the others screamed terribly, shutting her eyes and hugging herself beneath everyone.

Carl Bain moved swiftly. His repeated strikes shook the white book's spherical protector until his fists became bloodied. Still he hammered on.

"We have got to get out of here now," Kimberley said. "He's going to break the dome very soon."

"But we haven't met the man Mariah told us about," Rachel said. She saw the shapeless demons push Mr. Gbomoh's body into one of the boats on the creek near the clearing.

"If only we could create the boom," Aiden exclaimed, trying to open the mysterious book suspended by icy filaments in the middle of everything. "It's frozen solid." He sounded frustrated as he watched another long hand stretch out towards the book.

Carl Bain's fists fell on the magical dome again and a crack appeared on the unearthly structure. "The beginning of the end, my friends!" the human minion bellowed with glee. "The beginning of the end."

"Yeow," Rachel shouted when a Booklord's scrawny arm seared her skin before its owner froze away. Surprisingly, she was calm this time.

Carl Bain landed another blow on the dome and the two hostages sheltering in it with the time-travelers screamed.

"I wish we had a cross or an ankh," Kimberley said, looking around.

"Or a pen," Rachel said.

"I have a marker," the female hostage trembling below said in a shaky voice as the mysterious human outside slammed his fists on the dome an umpteenth time. Another crack appeared on the protective hemisphere.

"Okay, give it to me," Kimberley said. Another demonic hand pulverized when it grabbed the white book near her. The sharpie exchanged hands and the Portwood police sergeant drew a bold ankh on her palm.

She brandished the symbol and the Booklords vanished with their human minion. The mysterious dome also disappeared.

"What just happened?" the female hostage who'd been saved by the dome wondered. She stared incredulously at Aiden. "Who are you people?"

"You won't believe me if I tell you," the boy replied, looking around. "It's a long story."

The male hostage who'd also sheltered in the mysterious hemisphere stood up and walked around the clearing like a zombie. Apart from the few people the book's dome had protected, no living thing was in the vicinity. Even the grass had all withered away. "Oh God," the man exclaimed when he saw Mr. Bruno Gbomoh's body in one of the flying boats on the creek near the edge of the clearing. "Witchcraft everywhere."

"What do we do now, Kim?" Rachel wondered aloud. "The man we're looking for could be among the dead."

"Mariah said he'll find us," Kimberley said. "We just need to prepare for another attack now." She drew an ankh on Rachel's right palm.

"Can I have my marker back?" the female hostage survivor asked Kimberley.

"Not before this," Kimberley told her, drawing an ankh on the woman's palm with the marker. "This will protect you from those demons," she explained to the Nigerian.

"Please protect me as well," the male hostage survivor urged the Portwood cop. "I don't know what you people are or where you came from, but I need the protection as well," he said.

Kimberley drew an ankh on the man's palm.

"*Aru*," the fellow said in Igbo.

"What did you say?" Kimberley demanded.

"Bad thing," the man said. "It means 'bad thing' in Igbo."

Kimberley rolled her eyes. Of course, Nigeria had so many tribes. The Igbo tribe was one of the three biggest ethnic groups in the country. "Where is Aiden?" she asked Rachel. "I need to draw an ankh on his palm."

"Over here," Aiden called out from a hut near the clearing. The only structure in the area. The lonely environment had started creeping him out.

"What are you doing there?" Kimberley demanded, turning towards the hut. "Aiden, you know you're not safe there. We should always be together."

"You need to see this, Kim," the boy replied from the hut. "I think I've found our man."

*   *   *

Carl Bain twisted and turned in the whirlwind he'd suddenly found himself in. The ghostly forms shrieking all around him meant only one thing. There'd been another defeat in the hands of those three meddlers. The whirlwind was the aftermath of that defeat.

The American hustler tried to stop his tumbling motion with his magic, but realized he had none. He wondered how the symbols had gradually come to affect him and his masters even when they were just drawings. He could remember back in Germany when the female cop had engraved a cross on his gloves and it could only irritate him and his masters. What changed?

Presently he stopped spinning and crashed to the ground on his back. His infernal masters appeared all around him, their high-pitched deliberations an annoying experience for him.

"What the hell?" he yelled at some point, blocking his ears with his hands. What were they arguing about? His fate? A new plan? Whatever.

Their leader shimmered before him.

"Manipulate the female cop," it conveyed. "She is not a Bookbearer."

"And she is confused," another demon pronounced behind the American.

"As you wish, my masters," the human thug said. Even if the policewoman was not a Bookbearer and this plan could fail, he might be able to retrieve his own package instead.

"Retrieve the manuscript first," the demon leader warned him.

He'd forgotten they could read his mind.

*   *   *

Kimberley looked down at the man whose fellow militants called Kpakol. "He must have passed out," she figured. "I don't think he's dead."

"Why do you say so?" Aiden wondered.

"He is still breathing," Kimberley said, pointing at the Nigerian's chest.

"Okay," Aiden said. "Guess you're right."

The Portwood sergeant knelt beside the militant and took his semiautomatic rifle before shaking him vigorously. "Time to wake him up," she said.

Kpakol started, screaming like a deranged fellow. His AK47 pointed at him silenced him. "Wetin you dey do, you this woman?" he demanded in Nigerian pidgin.

"Get up," Kimberley ordered him, the semiautomatic unwavering. "We need to go on a journey with you now."

The man obeyed and raised his hands in surrender.

"Any need for that, Kim?" Aiden asked.

"Whatever," Kimberley said. "Now, move out of the hut," she told Kpakol.

Rachel watched this party step out of the hut with incredulity. She studied the rebel whose hands were up in the air. "Is that him?"

"You tell me," Aiden quipped. "He's not dead, is he?"

"And so?"

"He could be our guy if he's not dead," Kimberley said. "Look around you."

"Whose guy?" Kpakol began. "Are you people the police or army? Which one una be?"

"What's going on here?" the surviving Nigerian female hostage demanded. She sat down near the hut. "Are you arresting him?"

"You should leave now," Kimberley advised her. "The army will soon be here so leave before they come. I hear they don't joke around."

"Answer her question joor," the surviving Nigerian male hostage began and Kimberley glared at him. The Nigerian female hostage started walking away and the Nigerian male hostage reluctantly stood up to follow her. "*Aru ebe n'ile*," he grumbled in Igbo. "Bad thing everywhere," he told a frowning Aiden when he walked past the boy.

"Now move," Kimberley ordered Kpakol, prodding him with the AK47.

The four individuals followed a pathway cutting through a dense forest now bordered by dead trees alongside the clearing.

"Why did you tell that woman that soldiers were coming?" Rachel asked Kimberley.

"Just to make them leave us," Kimberley replied. "I'm hoping some locals will find them and take them to the city."

"What of us?" Aiden wondered aloud.

"We'll stop here and do it," Kimberley said, halting abruptly.

"Do what?" Rachel asked, bumping into Aiden, who had also stopped quickly.

"Find out if he's the one," Kimberley said.

"Okay." Rachel clenched and unclenched her fists. "Let's do this."

"Please don't kill me," Kpakol urged his captors. "Na money make me enter MEND."

"We'll do no such thing," Kimberley said. "Rachel, touch him."

The little girl nodded and stepped forward. She held the militant's right hand and the man froze like a statue. Kimberley noticed his pupils disappear and lowered the semiautomatic rifle. It wasn't needed anymore.

The MEND militant blinked all of a sudden and looked around him.

"So, what's your name now?" Aiden wondered.

"Kpakol," the man said. "My name is Kpakol."

"And you're a militant?" Kimberley demanded, raising the AK47 again. She feared the worst.

"No," Kpakol objected.

"Your name shouldn't be Kpakol," Rachel said. "I just touched you."

The man turned to the little girl. "My name is Kpakol Abdul," he told her. "I fled the Mine when the Romans came for your father."

Chapter 22
KPAKOL

RACHEL'S heart skipped. "So, you were there that day?" she asked the man whose revelation had jolted her.

"Yes, I was," Kpakol said. "A day before this incident, I had come across the Roman soldiers plotting their operation in the city. I was a slave spy for the Sicarii Kabbalah and relayed what I had seen to your father's cult that same day."

Kimberley drew nearer. "And?"

Kpakol's face fell. He turned to Rachel. "Your father did not heed my warning like the other members of the cult. He gave his colleagues pieces of the white book to escape with, but decided to remain behind with you, his daughter."

"Yes, I know that already," Rachel said. "The Booklords killed my father before the Romans found the Mine. Father made me escape with the book when these demons came the first time. I met his dead body when I returned, and then the Roman soldiers arrived and I had to leave again. I have been traveling forward in time ever since, the Booklords tormenting me and killing everyone I come across, except these two good friends of mine." She smiled at Kimberley and Aiden.

"Actually we've been moving forward in time ever since we met Rachel," Kimberley added.

"And backward as well," Aiden reminded her. "How come you haven't changed your name all these years?" he asked Kpakol.

"I realized that I couldn't do so the first time I used the white book," Kpakol said. "Only my surname changes. Kpakol has stuck with me ever since."

"We need to find the other book," Rachel told the Nigerian. "Mariah said you'll help us."

"You met Mariah?" Kpakol asked the little girl.

"She's okay," Aiden allayed.

"She is bad news," the slave spy said. "I'll advice you not to listen to her."

Kimberley frowned. The so-called Sicarii Kabbalah Masada must have had a fair share of internal wrangling. Who was telling the truth? "We'll still need your help, Kpakol," she said to the militant-turned-slave.

"But I was just a slave spy," Kpakol pointed out.

"But Mariah said you knew members of the Inner Circle," Aiden aired.

"Do not trust that woman," the Nigerian emphasized. "She was trouble then. I know she could still be trouble now."

"Why shouldn't we trust her?" Kimberley finally asked.

"She had a lover back then," Kpakol said, turning to Rachel. "A member of the Inner Circle and a very close friend to your father, Rachel."

"Do you have a name?" Aiden demanded.

"I have forgotten his name, but he was a very powerful member of the Sicarii Kabbalah Masada," Kpakol replied.

Kimberley frowned thoughtfully. "Okay, she said. "How come you've survived the Gray Ones all these years?"

"Various ailments," Kpakol replied, looking himself over. "I'm diabetic this time."

"Yeah, sure," Aiden said. "The Booklords can't touch a sick person."

"You know me, but I have never seen you before," Rachel began. "Why didn't I meet you back at the Mine?"

"Of course, I know you," Kpakol said, scratching his head. "Since I was a spy at the Mine, I always hid my identity." He looked at Aiden. "And I think I've met you before," he told the boy.

"What of me?" Kimberley asked the African.

"I don't know you."

"Oh."

"Concerning the black book," Aiden resumed. "The Bookmakers must have passed over some tricks to you?"

Kpakol grinned. "I'll help you look for the other book, though I must warn you to return the book in your possession."

Aiden smiled and Kimberley rolled her eyes. "Here we go again," she said.

"Mariah will never tell you to return the book to the Gray Ones," Kpakol noted. "This is the only safe option."

"Why do you say that?" Rachel demanded.

"Your father would have wanted that," Kpakol said.

"Not true," the little girl said. "Father would have never wanted me to return the book to those demons."

Kpakol started saying something and stopped himself. "Okay," he rather said. "I promised your father that I will help you, Rachel. He was a good man and I will do everything in my power to help now that you've found me."

Kimberley wondered if she'd been wrong about the Gray Ones. Kpakol's assertions were not helping her state of mind. "Is it true that Shurabi cannot save anybody killed by the Gray Ones?" she asked.

Kpakol sighed. "Mariah told you that?"

Kimberley nodded.

"That is true, but I think it's also possible that the Gray Ones could save their victims as they claim without the help of Shurabi." The Nigerian turned to Rachel. "Your father told me this, though I never witnessed this miraculous occurrence back at the Mine."

"Is it also true that the black book will find us if we did not look for it?" Aiden asked. "Mariah said so."

"The Gray Ones will never wait for that to happen before they retrieve the white book, boy," Kpakol replied. "So that approach will not help you in the long run."

"What will help us?" Rachel demanded.

"Any Bookmaker seeking help must discover and read out the hidden Hebrew writing on the book's pages," Kpakol said. "Then and only then will the black book's position in time and space, as well as a means of getting to this reality, be revealed to that Bookmaker."

"But why can't the Bookmakers read the hidden Hebrew writing on the book's pages even though Mariah said it was visible to them back at the Mine?" Aiden wondered.

"Remember it is only some of the Hebrew words that were visible to the Bookmakers through Shurabi," Rachel told him. "Mariah also said that." She gave Aiden the book. "Can you see any of the writings? I could only see the names I wrote."

Aiden turned blue. "Not now, Rachel," he stammered. "Besides, I can't see with this light. It will soon be dark."

The setting Sun caught everyone's attention. The chirping insects became louder.

"It's getting late," Rachel said. "We must be going, Kim."

"Now I remember there's a house somewhere around here," Kpakol said. "Our leaders use it whenever they're in the vicinity." He looked down at the rough pathway, deep in thought.

"You say you've met me before," Aiden began. "I don't think I've ever left Portwood in my life."

"Yet I still think I've seen you before," Kpakol said.

"Maybe you saw my great grand father?" Aiden wondered aloud.

"Good," Kpakol said, ignoring him. "Here's the path to the house."

"Any one at home?" Rachel wanted to know.

"No need for that," the militant-turned-slave-spy said. "We only guard the house when people like Mr. Bruno Gbomoh decide to spend the night."

"Maybe Aiden would see the hidden writings on the book when we get to the house and some light," Rachel enthused.

"Maybe Rachel would see the hidden writings on the book when we get to the house and some light," Aiden enthused.

"Maybe you two should shut up now," Kimberley said.

"There's the house," Kpakol announced, pointing ahead at a gated wall surrounded by shrubs. The environment looked like a hastily done job and the wall protecting the bungalow had spaces in-between its bricks.

Pushing open the creaky gate, Kpakol ushered his new friends into a compound looking more like a junkyard.

"What's with the drums and black goo?" Aiden asked, threading carefully lest he misstepped and landed on the thick black oil all over the place.

"Illegal refinery," Kpakol said. "We make some money when we sell petroleum from here."

"You guys pollute your land as well?" a surprised Kimberley asked. "Is it not enough that you're fighting against oil pollution from foreign companies that don't care about your land?"

"Sorry about that," Kpakol said. "But remember we also have to survive in this jungle." He looked for the door keys behind a wooden stool and opened the front door.

Kimberley followed the slave spy into what appeared to be a living room. The cozy interior had electricity.

"Lights," Rachel said as she entered the room with Aiden. "We can check the book now."

Aiden moved to open the white book.

"I was wrong about the Gray Ones," Kimberley said.

"What do you mean?" Rachel asked her.

"We need to give them back the book, Rachel," Kimberley said.

Aiden could not believe his ears. He turned to Kpakol, who just stood there saying nothing.

"She's right," the Nigerian finally said. "That is the only way to end this."

"She's wrong," Rachel objected. "And we're not returning the book."

"No, we're doing no such thing, Kim," Aiden said rather sternly. "What's gotten into you?"

"Nothing," Kimberley replied. "I just realized we've been wrong all this time."

"How?" Rachel cried. "My father is dead and I've got to finish what he started."

"So is Jim and...and many others I don't even know their names," Kimberley said. "They never deserved any of this and...and I'm going to bring them back if ever there's such a chance."

"The Gray Ones cannot even bring back their dead," Aiden thought out loud. "How then are they going to bring back Jim and the other people they killed?"

Kpakol bent forward. "Who's Jim?"

"None of your business!" Kimberley snapped at him. She brandished his AK47 semiautomatic and he stepped away from her with the two kids. "Aiden, hand over the book."

"Aiden, don't," Rachel said. "I don't think she's herself. Something's controlling her."

"We should all calm down now," Kpakol tried. "We won't succeed if we don't work together."

"Watch me," Kimberley snapped. She pointed the gun at Aiden and he gave her the white book. Blunt cold shot up her arm and paralyzed her. The book's magic dome reappeared, engulfing her alone. "Holy!" she let out before her vocal muscles lost power.

"What is that?" Kpakol exclaimed, staring at the white book's cold protective hemisphere.

"You haven't seen that before?" Aiden asked him. "You haven't seen the dome before?"

"What's the dome?" the baffled Nigerian demanded.

"It's the structure you now see before you," Rachel explained. "It is formed by the Ice of Masada to protect the book."

Kpakol lost her. "The Ice of Masada?"

"You don't know about that?" Aiden asked the man. "What then do you know?"

"Yahweh gave us the Ice and Fire of Masada to protect the books, Kpakol," Rachel explained. "My father and his friends must have kept you in the dark about this."

"The Fire of Masada protects the black book?" Kpakol asked her. "No wonder."

"No wonder what?"

"Never mind," the African said. "I was just wondering," he added. "If the books have protection, that must mean only one thing."

"That we shouldn't give them back?" Aiden asked. "Obviously."

Rachel nodded and turned to look at the frozen Kimberley. "Pity you forgot that only a Bookbearer can hand over the book to the Booklords," she reminded the stone-cold woman. "Your plan has already failed due to this."

Kpakol frowned. "I thought you guys were friends?" he pointed out.

"Whoever wants to sieze the book from us becomes an enemy and the Ice of Masada will treat him or her as one, no matter who he or she is to the Bookbearer," Rachel explained.

"You've done your homework," Kpakol commended.

The little girl glared at him.

"What did I do?" he asked her.

Kimberley could not talk. The cold had frozen all her muscles and she just stood there like a statue, clenching her teeth in the intense chill that had engulfed her inside the book's protective hemisphere.

"She's suffering," Rachel realized all of a sudden. "How do we save her?"

A puzzled Kpakol turned to Aiden, who looked up, rolling his eyes.

"I think she's safer than us right now," the boy said.

"What do you mean by that?" Kpakol asked him.

"She's in the protective dome and we're not?" Aiden pointed out.

"And so what?"

"It's getting cold again," the boy explained to the slave spy.

"And?"

"That means the book is trying to warn us about unearthly interference," Rachel said.

Aiden looked at his arm and turned to the others in alarm. "The ankh Kim drew on my arm has faded!" he announced. "The sharpie's ink didn't last one minute!"

Rachel's face lost color. She looked at her arm and turned white. "They're coming back, and we don't have protection this time?"

"Who's coming back?" Kpakol asked her. "The Gray Ones?"

The magic dome surrounding Kimberley and the book glowed blue. The ceiling made squeaky sounds before the bungalow's roof blew off and a black-garbed Carl Bain made his entry with his infernal masters.

"Yes," Aiden cried. "The Gray Ones!"

"What is happening?" a freaked-out Kpakol demanded.

Carl Bain landed before the three individuals awestruck by the power he exuded as he floated in through the gapping hole once covered by the roof. "Finally, the end is here!" he snarled at them.

Aiden and Rachel stepped back in fear, pulling Kpakol with them.

The sudden presence of the man in black surrounded by howling forms had shocked the Nigerian into stupefied silence and for a moment, he appeared clueless as to what next to do.

Carl Bain laughed at the defensive action the three before him just took to protect themselves from him. The African with the children he had never seen before, but he knew exactly what to do to this man. "Your end is here!" he told Kpakol, his hands outstretched. Nothing happened and he appeared before the Nigerian to punch the man on the chest, pushing the fellow backward with the force.

Kpakol crashed into a cupboard that fell on him. He remained motionless.

Carl Bain could not understand the problem with this new character. Even his demon masters, who had planned to kill this man, now avoided the African at all cost, rather flocking to the dome and the one individual inside it.

Senselessly, the Gray Ones blocked off the blue glow emanating from the white book's hemispheric protection by stacking up on the dome. Repeated incursions into this structure and the subsequent punishment of freezing off as demonic ash ensued.

"Okay, he's sick," the American thug understood after his infernal masters conveyed this information to him. "I get it. I should ignore him."

The human minion turned to Aiden and Rachel cowering at a corner of the sitting room.

"No, please don't kill us," a terrified Aiden exclaimed, holding Rachel with both hands.

"You will not succeed," Rachel cried underneath the boy.

"You should be begging for your life like your friend, girl," Carl Bain snapped. He stretched out his hands and watched with satisfaction as a powerful force slammed into the two kids, pushing them high up to the edge of the wall, before allowing their bodies to crash to the floor, visibly dead.

"Oh well, forget it," he said and turned to the immobile woman holding up the white book in the bluish dome now the gregarious focus of his demonic masters ever since they arrived. "Well, well, well, what do we have here?"

Kimberley had tears in her eyes. She had placed Aiden and Rachel in harm's way by acting irrationally.

"Nothing to say for yourself, huh?" her nemesis growled outside the dome, rubbing his fists. "Not to worry, I'll help you open your mouth."

Carl Bain slammed his fists into the magical dome. Repeatedly, while ignoring the ongoing battle between the Booklords and the weakened Ice of Masada defending the revered book. He did this until his hands became bloody and he heard the expected crack.

Still, he pummeled on. A second crack encouraged him. A third crack strengthened his resolve to smash the infernal dome at all cost. A fourth crack could only mean the beginning of the end for all his enemies.

The white book's unearthly hemisphere smashed into smithereens, its pieces flying off in all directions. The Gray Ones swarmed into the space it previously occupied, engulfing its only occupant as they tortuously pierced her body from every angle. This infernal inundation left the Portwood sergeant gasping for air as soon as her paralyzed muscles found strength again. She let go of the white book and the demons seized the ancient artifact. They pulled the female officer's devastated body into the air, away from the house.

A satisfied Carl Bain looked around at his handiwork. The two kids still lay where they fell, obviously dead, but the Nigerian Sicarii Kabbalah slave spy no longer lay underneath the fallen cupboard. The man must have used unknown sorcery to disappear, the American hustler thought. "Oh well, who cares?" he concluded, heading for the front door like he owned the place.

Moments later, Kimberley found herself falling back to Earth after her tormentors left her body in droves. She crashed to the ground, stunned into silence by the excruciating pain.

Carl Bain appeared before her, the Booklords hovering above him at a reasonable distance. "Give me my package," he snapped.

Kimberley pulled out the small cube from her jacket's right pocket and handed it over. She had no more fight left in her.

"Now, for your punishment," the American thug said gleefully.

He broke her legs and dislocated her knee joints, and she screamed until she lost her voice.

"That's for Pripyat," Carl Bain snarled. "And this...this is for wasting my time all these days!"

The human minion stepped back and let out a thunderous bolt of lightening at the injured woman.

Kimberley crossed both arms over her face. She remained in this defensive position until curiosity made her peep through her crossed arms.

At the forest trees swaying in the night breeze before her. At the twinkling stars dangling from the clear night sky high above her head.

At the white book lying on the ground in front of her.

This time she cried without losing her voice.

Chapter 23
AIDEN

KPAKOL reappeared in the living room, confusion his best friend. What just happened? Where did those things come from? These were not the Gray Ones he'd been used to all these years. They were visibly more aggressive. More diabolical. He wondered whether he was wrong about returning the book to these demons. Perhaps he'd mistakenly identified them as the Gray Ones rather than the Black Ones. But, they looked and moved like the Gray Ones. They were just more vicious. More daring.

The African slave spy looked around at the chaos now the living room. Pools of ash littered everywhere, and a shattered glass-like material covered a considerable part of the sitting room's floor. Kpakol did not know where the pools of ash came from, nor could he figure out what the bluish glassy material scattered everywhere was. What happened to his new friends?

"Kpakol, you're alive!" Aiden whispered, rubbing his hands together as he emerged from the next room with Rachel. "We thought they took you away as well."

"The man in black, who is he?" Kpakol began. "And what were those things?"

"The Gray Ones," Rachel said. "I thought you knew."

"Yes, they looked like the ones attacking me all these years," Kpakol said, waving his hands around the room, "but I could be wrong after this."

"No need for anything now," Rachel said dejectedly. "They've taken the book and Kimberley with them."

"Be strong, Rachel," Aiden consoled her. "There's still hope."

"Which hope?" Rachel asked. "How do we save Kim and recover the book now?"

"At least, I have her cross, remember?" Aiden pointed out. "It shoos the demons away," he explained to Kpakol's inconvenient stare. "I think it fell from her pocket when they vanished with her."

"And how will the cross help us get back the book, and…and find Kimberley, Mr. Hope?" Rachel wanted to know.

"I-eh," Aiden stammered.

"Stop talking!" Rachel cried. "It's useless and you know it. We've lost. They have the book, and Kimberley might as well be dead right now."

"Not true, Rachel," Aiden said. "W-We still have the cross," he stammered. He did not know what else to say.

Kpakol took the religious symbol from the boy and caressed it between his fingers. "A cross chases them away?" he asked in surprise.

"Yes," Aiden said. "An ankh also does that."

"I see," Kpakol said, looking around while deep in thought. "So, where did the ash come from?" he asked Aiden.

"The Gray Ones leave their dead behind," Rachel replied.

"And that's the ash?"

The little girl nodded.

"What of…"

"The book's magical shield," Aiden cut in. "Protected Kimberley and the book. Looks like the man in black smashed it."

"Who is that man?" Kpakol wanted to know. "He tried to kill me."

"He does that every time we meet," Rachel said. "Try to kill us, I mean."

"He wasn't that different back at Portwood," Aiden reasoned. "Now he's more than a monster."

"The Booklords must be using this human," Kpakol said. "Interesting."

Rachel rolled her eyes. The slave spy fell short of her expectations when he opted to vanish in the heat of the Booklord's attack. "How did you even disappear?" she asked the African.

"I still have a piece of the black book with me," Kpakol said.

"The black book?" Rachel sounded confused. "You tore out a page of the black book? How?"

"Can't he do that?" Aiden asked.

"Only if he was authorized to do so back at the Mine," Rachel said. "Obviously, he wasn't."

"So what happened back at the Mine, Kpakol?" Aiden asked the former militant.

Kpakol seemed uncomfortable with the question. "I – eh…we…"

The kids waited for his answer.

"The slaves working for the Sicarii Kabbalah at the Mine decided to…to steal a page of the black book when it became obvious that…that the Romans or the Booklords might one day invade the Mine," Kpakol explained. "We tore the page into pieces and shared it amongst ourselves. That's how I escaped the Mine." He displayed a piece of an extraordinary-looking paper.

"Okay," Rachel said. "That explains a lot." Names scribbled on the piece of paper covered its two faces.

"Anyway this paper could help us find and retrieve the black book?" Aiden asked Kpakol.

"I don't think so," Kpakol said. "I know no such spell."

"What if we place it inside the white book and see what happens?" Aiden proposed. "When we find Kimberley and the white book, that is."

Rachel started. "Did you hear that?" she asked the others.

"Someone just screamed outside," Kpakol said, frowning.

"I know that voice anywhere," Aiden said. "Kim."

*   *   *

Kimberley stopped crying and tried to move. She could not do so since her legs were broken. She pulled herself up and stretched out a hand for the white book lying on the ground a few feet from her.

Black smoke exploded before her and cleared to reveal her tormentors. The man in black materialized amidst his unearthly allies.

Kimberley's right arm touched the white book before her nemesis stepped on this arm, laughing. "Lemme go," she pleaded, struggling to free her arm. "Please, let me go."

"And why should I do that?" Carl Bain wondered. "I am winning, you know." He pushed the Portwood sergeant to the ground with his other foot and allowed his infernal masters to pin her down while standing on both arms. "You know we made you demand that your friends return the book, right?"

Kimberley stared at the American thug. "H-How?" she wondered.

"My masters controlled your mind," Carl Bain said. "Brilliant, right?"

No response.

"You don't even know why we left you in a hurry before I could kill you."

"I-I don't understand," Kimberley said. The demons holding her scorched her arms. The scenario reminded her of their attack in Germany. "W-What are you saying?"

"You formed the symbol with your arms before I could kill you," Carl

Bain said with a smile, noting the woman's forlorn look. "Now, I must finish what I started."

The Booklords' human minion broke the Portwood officer's arms and relished her resulting anguish expressed as unending screaming. "Now, you die," he said, his eyes resting on his victim's chest as he stepped backward to bring his hands together.

He vanished a second time with his demonic masters as Aiden, brandishing Kimberley's cross, ran up to the female sergeant's battered form with Rachel and Kpakol.

Kimberley fainted.

"She's losing blood!" Aiden noted.

"Quick, hold hands," Rachel urged him, touching Kimberley's right hand.

Aiden took Kimberley's left hand and Kpakol's right hand; while Rachel flipped open the white book.

They all appeared in a blue hospital room, a peacefully sleeping Kimberley occupying the only bed in this room.

Kpakol looked at Aiden, and stared at the boy the next time he turned to look.

Aiden stared back. "What?"

"I've seen you before."

"You said that before," Aiden returned. "What's new?"

"Now I know where I saw your face," Kpakol said. "Back at the Mine, before the Romans invaded it."

"What are you saying?" a confused Aiden asked the man.

"You could be a reincarnation of one of the two unique Bookbearers the Sicarii Kabbalah thought would one day have the ability to read out the entire Hebrew words Shurabi hid in the two books," Kpakol said in one take, breathing in deeply afterwards.

Lost for words, Aiden turned to Rachel. This bombshell revelation only meant one thing. "Did you really just appear in Portland while running from the Gray Ones like you told us?" he asked her.

Rachel gulped. "I can explain."

*   *   *

Carl Bain relished what he had done to Kimberley. He hated the way his entertainment ended abruptly, but at least he retrieved his package and broke his archenemy's legs and arms. Whatever happened to the white book was not....

The American hustler decided to think of something else owing to very obvious reasons.

'All thoughts are porous,' he heard in his head. He knew what conveyed this message to him, but he dared not turn to look lest he died at the spot.

The Gray Ones appeared around him, their shapes visible miles from where he sat waiting for them.

'You've been a fool,' he heard behind him, but remained immobile. 'You could have killed her when you had the chance.'

"I guess it's okay to say that since I wanted to see her suffer first," Carl Bain snapped. "Why didn't you kill her with your enormous power then?"

His head ached. He knew the punishment would come.

'She was of no concern to us after helping us,' the lead demon conveyed to him. 'You want her dead, but we will allow this after we use her again.'

"This will not work next time," Carl Bain reasoned. "We can never convince her the way we did this last time, unless you can make her do what she did again. As for me, I will surely kill her next time we meet."

'We can manipulate her again, so be ready to kill her when the time comes,' the Booklord conveyed. 'We have failed to control or kill the boy and the girl, so you must physically kill them next time, without your powers. The boy you must kill first, because he is very dangerous.'

"And what of the sick man?"

'He is sick, but kill him too if you must live.'

"Yeah, I will do anything for you guys as long as I have retrieved my package," Carl Bain said, feeling for his small package in his black coat's inner pocket.

'You fool,' his senior master said. 'What you are looking for is no longer with you. It fell off when you turned to flee from the boy's symbol.'

Carl Bain couldn't find his beloved package in his coat's pocket.

His rage engulfed him.

*   *   *

The spotless blue room had many medical gadgets surrounding the only bed in it. Aiden turned to look at Kimberley as she slept on this bed. He wondered how he arrived at the fact that a doctor had earlier told him that she had suffered a mild concussion after a road traffic accident. Luckily for her, there were no broken bones.

The boy remembered something and rummaged through his pockets for it. He brought it out and peered at it for some time.

Rachel stared at the small box with him. "Is that?"

"Yeah, it is," Aiden said, tucking the package into Kimberley's pants' right pocket. "I found it on the ground near Kim before we got here."

"Found what?" Kpakol began.

"That man must have taken it before we reached Kim," Rachel pointed out, ignoring the slave spy. "Wonder how he lost it again."

"Lost what?" Kpakol asked her.

"Kimberley's property," Rachel replied without looking.

"He must have mistakenly dropped it when he fled my cross," Aiden reasoned. "I'm glad I found it."

"It only spells trouble for us," Rachel said. "You could have left it there."

"Not true. If I did that, we won't have it with us when he comes back, and he would think that we've hidden it."

"Yeah," Rachel agreed. "Guess you're right."

"Of course, I'm right."

Kpakol watched this drama with a smirk. He felt useless.

Aiden's attention came back to the little girl in the room. "Okay Rachel," he said. "I think you have some explaining to do."

"Aiden, I'm so sorry," Rachel began. "I just didn't want to draw attention to you when we met, so I ignored you."

"Draw attention to me?" Aiden asked her.

"I didn't want the Gray Ones to suspect you," Rachel said, "until you have stayed with me long enough for the white book to start protecting you."

Aiden stared at her. "And what of Kim?"

"She happened to be there at the right time," Rachel said, tears in her eyes. "Kim has been there for us, and we have failed her when she needed us the most."

It all made sense now, Aiden thought. How he was able to handle the white book and support Rachel. This also meant that the Gray Ones must have discovered his importance in all this and he shivered at the thought. He turned to Kimberley and she woke up.

"Where am I?" the Portwood sergeant wondered, looking around her. She frowned when she saw the other three in the room. "Where are we?"

"Y-Your fractures have healed, Kim," Rachel stammered. "It's a miracle."

"Fractures?" Kimberley frowned. "What are you saying?"

"You don't know?" Aiden asked her.

"It could be the white book," Kpakol said. "Maybe since she went through severe pain, she cannot remember what she underwent after her reincarnation."

"Whatever," Rachel said. "It saves us a lot of headache, though."

"But you have to tell her what you told me, Rachel," Aiden told the girl.

"Tell me what?" Kimberley started.

"We've to go now," Rachel rather reminded everyone. "The Gray Ones are not that far behind us, and we will be ahead of them if we keep moving forward."

"You can't be saying that now," Aiden began.

"But she's right," Kpakol said. "We can't wait for those things to get here."

"Okay." Aiden sighed. He picked up a pen on the table beside the hospital bed and gave it to Rachel without a word.

The little girl pulled out the intravenous line on Kimberley's left wrist.

"Yeow!" the female sergeant shouted, her hands trembling. "Why did you do that?"

"Don't worry," Aiden said, turning to Kpakol. "She'll forget the pain after the time travel, right?"

"How can I forget the pain from broken legs?" Kimberley asked. "That fool must pay for what he did to me."

"And she remembers," Aiden said. "Guess we just needed to touch her."

"We've left Nigeria, right?" Kimberley wanted to know.

"Yeah," Aiden said. "We left after you tried out a particular theory and it…it failed." Kpakol glared at him before holding his hand.

Rachel wrote her name in the book.

They all appeared in a forest wearing new attire. Kimberley had on a green shirt atop dark-green chinos pants and jungle boots. Aiden wore a brown khaki shirt on red chinos pants stuck into timberland boots, while Rachel had on a blue T-shirt atop black pants that cut off before black teenage boots shoed her feet. Kpakol's dark-red clothes had pockets all over its pants.

"We should have remained at the hospital," Aiden reasoned. "Let's move on from this creepy place."

"Let us rest here," Kpakol said, pointing at a tired-looking Rachel. "Our Bookbearer is weak because of the load she bears whenever she transports all of us at once. She needs to rest a while."

"No, I'm fine," Rachel began and sat down on a wooden stump. She gave Aiden the white book.

Her companions sat down on stumps strewn around the area. There were a lot of tree stumps in this forest.

"Maybe someone else should carry the load a bit?" Aiden suggested.

"Of course, this is possible," Kpakol said. "We will move faster, but we have to know those words hidden by Shurabi in order to move forward and you're very important in this process," he told Aiden.

"And how is that?" Kimberley wanted to know.

Rachel looked away and Aiden grinned. Kpakol faced the Portwood Police officer and sighed. "The boy is a reincarnation of a Bookbearer the Bookmakers thought would one day have the ability to read out the entire Hebrew words hidden in the two books."

Kimberley's jaw dropped. "Holy!" she let out. "I don't believe you."

"It's true, Kim," Aiden supported. "That's why I can do many crazy things with her." And he pointed at the strange little girl who'd started it all.

"How is this possible?" Kimberley demanded. She turned to Rachel, realization finally dawning on her. "You!" she snapped. "You've always lied to us! To me!"

"I was trying to protect him," Rachel defended, pointing in Aiden's direction. "I didn't want anything to happen to you guys."

"But I lost Jim due to this!" Kimberley exploded. "And every other person back at the station!"

"I am sorry, Kim," Rachel begged. "I am so sorry."

Chapter 24
BRAZIL

KIMBERLEY turned to Aiden. "This is all so confusing," she said, holding her head with both hands. "I – I don't know what to believe anymore." Who would have known back at Portwood that the juvenile had a bigger role to play in this crazy adventure?

"We can believe what we're doing now, which is to establish the third book through the ritual," Aiden said.

"We can do that after we find the black book," Rachel said. "We need to know where we are first."

"We're in a rainforest," Kimberley said.

"Isn't that obvious?" Kpakol asked dryly. "Question is, where, exactly, are we?"

"Whole place has been on fire for some months now," Kimberley explained instead. "People are saying that loggers, farmers and cattle ranchers are to blame for this, which will have an impact on the climate since this forest produces more than 20% of the world's oxygen."

"So sad," Rachel said.

Nobody questioned Kimberley's sudden expertise on climate change because nobody was surprised.

"Lemme guess, you're an environmentalist now," Aiden told the female cop.

"And we're in the outskirts of the Amazon Rainforest in Brazil," she dryly replied. "Waiting for our Bookbearer to regain some strength."

"Maybe if we have food?" Kpakol suggested.

"I just need to rest a while," Rachel said.

"At least we now know who the real enemies are," Aiden said, looking at Kimberley, who looked away. "Wonder if your theory is correct, Kpakol."

"Which theory?" the slave spy asked him.

"That the Gray Ones will help us if the book is returned?" Aiden specified. He nodded towards the environmentalist sitting on a tree stump. "Remember she had a near-death experience while testing this theory?"

"Also remember that things might have been different if Rachel, who is a Bookmaker, had given the Booklords the book and not Kimberley, who is not a Bookmaker," Kpakol said.

Aiden laughed. "Are you saying the Booklords were angry with the move so they reacted murderously with their human minion?"

"Well," the slave spy began. "I just think that you guys have done many things to piss off those demons. Hence, I have come to the conclusion that it will not be easy to do what I have initially told you guys."

Kimberley nodded in agreement. "You're right," she said, "though I wonder why the Booklords also attacked you."

"Yes," Kpakol said. "I was also surprised by their action since the Gray Ones have never shown any interest in killing me despite my ailment blocking their inability to do so all these years."

"If the Booklords had wanted to kill you all these years, they would have created a human minion from the population to do so," Aiden pointed out.

"Maybe they are trying to kill him because he now threatens their cause?" Rachel suggested.

"That makes sense," Kimberley said.

Aiden opened the book and thoughtlessly flipped through its pages.

"Is it cold?" Kimberley wanted to know, remembering her experience back in Nigeria when she rebelled without cause.

"Nope," Aiden replied. His eyes caught light on the book's center page and this light went out as soon as he saw it. Speechless, he looked around at the others, their blank faces a sign that nobody noticed what had just happened. Now he turned back to the open volume on his laps. English words appeared across the two pages facing him. These words turned into a foreign language and disappeared.

דרכימסקדושותתקדימהוהוואאחורה

"Sacred ways back and forth?" Aiden frowned. Could that be the Hebrew words hidden by Shurabi on the book? He saw through the book's interior. A young boy stood with two other people on what appeared to be a mighty wall with intermediate towers. This boy held an open book and kept staring at it. Did Aiden just see something significant? "Did you guys see that?"

"See what?" Kimberley sat upright.

Aiden's words tumbled out. "I think I just saw the black book…"

"Where?" Rachel stood up.

"I don't know…"

"We need to know what you saw, my boy, in order to figure out where this place is," Kpakol explained in earnest.

"I don't know," Aiden repeated. "Couldn't get more details before it…it all disappeared."

Rachel shook her fists in frustration and Kimberley looked away.

"Let's hope you'll see this vision again, my friend," Kpakol said.

"Is that fire?" Kimberley asked no one in particular, pointing out a distant burning area of the forest.

"That doesn't look natural," Kpakol said. The fire burned like a wall with no space between burning trees. No escape gap. "That doesn't look natural," he repeated.

The others started drawing back.

"We should leave right now?" Aiden warned, opening the strange book. "The Booklords might be causing this."

"Or it could just be a fire," Kimberley countered, holding her head. "I still think we should return the book to the Gray Ones."

Rachel started, looking around. Kpakol watched Kimberley closely.

"Are you okay, Kim?" Aiden wondered. For once, he thanked the white book for not giving the sergeant a gun this time around.

"What did I just say?" Kimberley asked herself.

"What almost killed you the last time?" a fuming Rachel snapped.

Kimberley almost responded, and then she changed her mind. "Aiden, you're right," she said. "We should leave right now."

Carl Bain's appearance threw everyone off guard. He grabbed the white book as it froze up and formed a dome around the humans.

The forest fire raced round the mysterious hemisphere and engulfed it as the Gray Ones materialized all around the book's icy protector, howling and screeching as their infernal flames burned down trees and shrubs meant to oxygenate life.

Kimberley's numb surprise did not stop her fear-stricken limbs from attacking the mad man who had broken her legs in Nigeria when she realized he could not move a muscle despite all his efforts. Her move encouraged the others to get out of their surprise mode and attack the human minion with their fists and legs, pummeling him from all sides as he just stood there holding up the white book.

Kpakol kicked the American hustler's right knee repeatedly, hoping to break it, but the evil minion remained standing, like a statue. He looked around the dome for a sharp object or knife. He found nothing.

"Touch the book! Touch the book!" Kimberley yelled at Aiden. "Touch the book!" she urged Rachel, who moved to obey.

Carl Bain felt deadly cold creep into his heart while eating into his soul. This supernatural phenomenon numbed the pain coming from the kicks and jabs his attackers presently landed on him. He knew why he could not move at the moment. Seizing the book was a mistake. He could have killed the boy first.

"It's too high, Kim!" Aiden cried, reaching out towards the white book on tiptoe. Kpakol lifted him up and Kimberley lifted Rachel up.

"No!" Carl Bain shouted, the enormity of what they wanted to do downing on him, but too late, the loud boom blew the dome and the Gray Ones away, smothering the fire since raging around the human figures now strewn around a cowering Carl Bain. Surprisingly, he still held up the white book.

But he no longer had his powers.

Kpakol got up and punched the strange man in the face.

Carl Bain blacked out.

"What did you do back there?" Kpakol demanded, turning to Kimberley. "I never saw anything like that, not even at the Mine."

"Good to know," the Portwood cop said. "The kids can push back our enemies when they touch the book together during an attack."

"So I was right about you two," the African slave spy told Rachel. "You two can help us end this."

"That is exactly what we're trying to do," Rachel said, glad that recent events had convinced the African of the deceitful nature of the Gray Ones.

Carl Bain lifted his head and Kpakol knocked him out again.

"We should kill him this time," Kimberley said.

"No," Rachel said, frowning at the last speaker. "No more killings...let's just go."

"He'll come after us again," Kimberley told Rachel. "You know he'll never stop until he gets what he wants and kills all of us." She remembered the tiny silver box and searched for it in her pockets.

"Is that what he wants?" Kpakol wanted to know, staring at the small metallic cube in Kimberley's right hand.

"That and the white book," Aiden said.

"What is it?" the slave spy wondered.

"We still don't know," Kimberley said, holding up the solid miniature box. "Could be high tech."

"Or could be just a small silver cube worth some money," Kpakol said. "Doesn't look high tech to me."

"If it's just silver, no need for him to come after us like he keeps doing," Kimberley reasoned.

"Sure of that?" Aiden wondered, picking up the white book and opening it. He didn't know what he was looking for. Maybe a reenactment of the vision he had witnessed a few minutes ago? He flipped through the book's pages.

"What are you looking for?" Rachel asked him.

"Nothing," he replied. "Anything helpful," he added. "Like I saw some words when I opened the book's middle pages a while back, but now I can't see anything."

They all turned to him.

"And which words did you see?" Kpakol asked.

Aiden frowned while trying to remember. "Sacred...ways back and...forth?" he said.

"Just that?" Rachel asked him.

"Yes," he said. "What do they mean?"

"You sound disappointed," Kimberley told Rachel.

"The words don't mean much," Kpakol said. "That is why I am also disappointed."

"Why do you say that?" Kimberley probed. The African picked up a stick and wrote on the charred soil:

דרכימקדושותקדימהוהואאחורה

"And what is that?" Kimberley demanded.

"That is what I saw," Aiden said. "Sacred ways back and forth."

"How come you could read that?" Kimberley frowned.

"Most Bookmakers and Bookbearers can read it," Kpakol said.

"In any language, though it usually appears in Hebrew," Rachel added.

"And that's Hebrew," Kimberley concluded. Was it that obvious? "So, what do these words mean?"

"Back at the Mine, we thought they were part of a sentence," Kpakol said.

"Like just a phrase?" the Portwood police officer asked him and he nodded.

"Sacred ways back refers to the other book, the black one," Rachel said.

"And sacred ways forth means the white book?" Aiden inferred and the little girl nodded.

"The Bookmakers felt the complete sentence, when revealed by gifted ones, would hasten the creation of the third book by merging the two books in our possession at the time," Kpakol said.

"Or cause the black book to appear before us right now and initiate the emergence of the third book," Rachel said.

"Whew," Aiden let out. "That's a lot to take in." Was he really a gifted one?

Firefighters appeared from the smoke still rising from the burnt wood all around the time-travelers.

"Surprise," Kpakol said, looking around at the dozen men. "Have you guys been waiting to come out after the fire went out?"

"We've been fighting another fire a few kilometers near that hill," one man said, pointing at a distant twirl of smoke.

"We heard the thunder clap," another man said. "We thought it was an explosion and we got here as soon as we could." He saw Carl Bain lying on the ground in the midst of the foreign tourists before him. "Is he okay?"

"Of course," Kimberley said quickly. "We saved him from the fire."

"What caused the blast?" another firefighter asked her, stepping forward with an oxygen apparatus. "Your friend must need air."

"No," Kimberley said before Kpakol nudged her. "Ok," she added, glancing at Carl Bain lying on the ground before them. "Reviving him is our number one priority now." She rolled her eyes.

The firefighter stepped forward with the oxygen apparatus and knelt beside Carl Bain. He placed the mask over the American hustler's mouth and fiddled with the oxygen apparatus.

"We don't need him awake," Rachel whispered. "He could get his powers back."

Aiden frowned. Of course, the little girl was right. Even the firefighters would be in danger if Carl Bain woke up with his powers intact.

"What can we do?" Kpakol whispered.

"We can leave now," Kimberley whispered.

Aiden spotted an indelible marker pegged into the other's shirt pocket. "I have an idea," he said, reaching out for the pen.

"What for?" Kimberley asked him as he took the marker.

"Watch me," Aiden said and knelt beside their human nemesis, opposite the fireman trying to revive this knocked-out minion of the Booklords.

"What are you doing?" the Brazilian asked him.

"A joke?" he pointed out, laughing. "My brother will know what I did when he wakes up, and boy, won't he be mad?"

The fireman smiled at this explanation and told his colleagues about it, in Spanish. Kimberley and her group gave Aiden's story support by nodding at whatever the firefighter was saying whenever his colleagues looked in their direction.

Aiden continued with what he was doing. He soon got up and handed back the sharpie to Kimberley.

"And what did you do?" Rachel asked him in a whisper.

"I bought us some time," Aiden mouthed.

"With a sharpie?" she asked him incredulously.

"Yeah?" he replied.

Carl Bain woke up and turned violent. Hitting the fireman who had revived him, he tore off the oxygen mask as the poor fellow he accosted crashed to the ground. The other firefighters rushed to contain him while Aiden and his colleagues quietly left the raucous scene.

"What exactly did you do?" Kimberley asked the boy as they made their way through the burnt forest.

Aiden laughed. "It will take some time before our friend realizes what I did," he giggled. "I drew little crosses and ankhs on his left hand and arm."

"Good idea," Kpakol said.

"I also got this, Kim," Aiden said, handing the Portwood sergeant a piece of paper.

"What is it?" Rachel wondered aloud.

"It's the piece of the white book our friend used to follow us from Portwood," Aiden giggled.

"To think it has been in his pocket all this time, even as he crossed many timelines," a surprised Kpakol said.

"Do we need it?" Rachel asked. "We have the book itself."

"Might be handy one day," Aiden told her.

"Sure," Kimberley said, taking the piece of paper.

Kpakol cleared his throat. "You must try to see those hidden Hebrew words again," he told Aiden. "I think that is the only way you could locate the other book."

Aiden opened the white book and stared at its blank pages as he flipped through the volume. "Nothing here," he quipped, frowning. "You think the Gray Ones will soon show up?"

"They won't be coming anytime soon," Kpakol said. "I think your defense of the book back there considerably weakened and confused them."

"Exactly why they would want to kill us both as soon as possible," Aiden said.

"Exactly why you should be focused on those words in the book right now," Kimberley told him.

"I'm trying to," Aiden replied, going back to the white book's middle pages. "I don't know why I'm not seeing anything."

"Relax, it will come," Rachel told him. "I know you'll see it again." She had never doubted him.

"We just need to move as far away from that crazy man as possible," Kpakol said. The young boy called Aiden looked at him. "Yes," he said. "Despite whatever you think you achieved with that marker."

"Okay," Aiden agreed, turning back to the open book he held in his hands. What he saw made him gasp.

"Have you seen something again?" Kpakol demanded and the boy nodded.

"I see the words again," Aiden said. "Sacred ways back and forth, greed and misery…."

"Greed and misery what?" Rachel urged him.

"I can't see the words anymore," he replied. "They have all disappeared."

"And you did not see the other book again?" Kpakol asked.

Aiden shook his head.

"Does it matter?" Kimberley asked.

"We're not getting anywhere," Rachel grumbled. "Some words are still missing."

"Okay," Kimberley said. "Now what?"

"Now we wait for those words to appear again," Kpakol said, stopping in his tracks. "We must avoid human populations around here in order not to put more people in danger if the Booklords regain their strength, so we must wait right here in the forest."

"Must we remain in the forest?" Aiden whined. "Another fire might break out."

"We still have the book," Rachel pointed out. "It will protect us if they come back." Her faith in the white book's ability to do this had been restored after the incident in the forest.

"And what if it doesn't do so this time?" Kimberley wondered aloud. "What if we can't fight back this time?"

Nobody replied her and she shrugged.

All the fight had left her.

Chapter 25
RETRIBUTION

CARL BAIN dropped the bloodied oxygen canister and sighed angrily. Twelve bodies lay around him as he stood there fuming at his stupidity. The boy and the female cop would have been dead by now if he had done what his masters had directed him to do. Of course, his anger blinded his thinking when he confronted the woman back in Africa. However, he could not understand what happened there in the forest a few minutes ago. He could have killed the boy before seizing the book. That way, the threat the kid earlier posed would have been eliminated going forward. But he did not do this. Instead, he had gone for the book, and now he had nothing to show for his efforts.

Not even his powers.

The American hustler looked down at his palms, wondering what had happened to him. The two kids must have repeated what they did back in Ukraine, when they caused his infernal masters to disappear while he lost his powers in the process. He turned his left hand around and stared at the tiny cross markings on its dorsal surface.

The reason he presently couldn't use his powers.

Carl Bain's left forearm also had these drawings etched on it. He tried to rub off some of the symbols to no avail. They must have been written with indelible ink, probably a sharpie or a pen of that nature. If only he could find some water. Maybe a small stream located in the area.

The human minion looked around at his surroundings. There were no streams in his location, but he found a water hose that snaked out of this vicinity.

The pipe led him to a fire truck stationed near the edge of the forest. Luckily, water gushed out of the first tap he opened, and he washed off the marks on his arms and forearms.

"Yes!" the thief exclaimed when he started feeling energy course through his muscles. This sensation fizzled out as soon as he noticed it and intense fear replaced the feeling.

Carl Bain looked around him. The wind came from nowhere. Of course, they would come. Sweat covered his brows. His hands started shaking. He didn't want to die yet. "Please, don't kill me!" he shouted into the howling wind. He could have left those symbols on his person. "Please, I made a mistake! I could have killed the boy first!"

The Booklords appeared in all their gory glory. Carl Bain made to run and they pulled him back. An external force compelled the American thug to fall on his knees when the Gray Ones holding him sank into the ground. "No!" the scared man screamed. "Help me, someone!"

The snakes came from nowhere. Venomous Coral snakes of the Amazon slithering out in droves with one clear objective. To kill the human minion.

The serpents approached the struggling man and surrounded him. They sank their poisonous fangs into his flesh from all sides.

"No! Please, no!" Carl Bain screamed with his eyes shut. "It's horrible!" The overwhelming pain paralyzed him, forcing him to fling his eyes wide open.

He realized there were no snakes.

No pain.

Only his fear.

'Your last warning,' rang out in his head. 'Kill Aryeh, Rachel and Kpakol before it is too late.'

Carl Bain knew Aryeh to be the boy, Aiden. "I will not fail this time," he said, picking up a machete left by one of his dead victims. He stood up and his masters pointed him in the right direction.

*   *   *

Kimberley looked around her as she played an imaginary drum with her right booted foot. She felt useless as they all waited for Aiden to visualize the hidden Hebrew words again. "We're just sitting ducks here," she finally said. "Our enemies are not resting like this."

"What can we do now?" Aiden began. "I still can't see those words." The white book lay open on his laps.

"Don't worry," Kpakol said. "You will soon see those hidden words by the grace of Yahweh."

"Yahweh is God, right?" Aiden asked and Kpakol nodded.

"Yahweh has been merciful to his people," the slave spy said. "He has protected us through many wars and now we stand ready to control our destiny."

"The modern state of Israel isn't doing badly last time I checked," Kimberley grumbled. "Must I always repeat that?"

Kpakol feigned annoyance. "I am talking of Jews all over the world, miss," he said. "We can do better than this modern state you talk so highly of."

"And what's wrong with that state?"

"Everything that could go wrong?" Rachel interrupted.

"Do you even know what we're talking about?" Kimberley chided, glaring at the little girl.

"Yes, I do, Kim," Rachel said. "Israel is a country governed by corrupt leaders now. We're always at loggerheads with our neighbors. This is an unnecessary distraction from our main purpose of being here. Of being alive. Yahweh would never have allowed that if we had followed his commandments and performed the ritual. Maybe the Messiah would have arrived by now and peace here on Earth made a reality."

"You know all this at your age?" Aiden was blown away.

"I make it my business to know during my travels," Rachel replied. "I visit libraries whenever I can."

"Whenever you can?" Aiden asked her. "Whenever you're not running from the Grey Ones? How's that even possible?"

"Impressive," Kpakol said thoughtfully. "Impressive."

"The Messiah?" Kimberley began. "Christians say he's here already."

"Not true," Kpakol intervened. "We're still waiting for the Messiah."

Kimberley responded no more. She caught Rachel staring at her as if warning her not to do anything foolish again. "Let's use the sharpie on ourselves like Aiden did on Carl Bain back there," she suggested all of a sudden. "We need to protect ourselves from those things now more than ever."

"The sharpie ink doesn't last, remember?" Aiden reminded her. "It fades after a few hours?"

"Brazil is not as corrupt as Nigeria where there are no checks on product quality," Kimberley assured him. "No need for your concern."

The sharpie exchanged hands and many ankhs were drawn.

A moderately chilly wind ensued.

*   *   *

The black-coated man appeared with his infernal masters near the enemy. "Good," he said. "We're out of sight." He saw the boy scribble something on the little girl's arm and smiled. "They're writing symbols on their arms. This will not save them this time."

The shrubs and trees around the Gray Ones started dying, their leaves a kaleidoscope of greens and browns. Carl Bain felt the atmospheric chill and turned to his masters. "We must act quickly before they notice us," he said, brandishing the machete. "Of course, I have a plan."

*　　*　　*

Aiden turned towards the trees to his left as soon as Rachel did the same thing. Their eyes met and they realized they dreaded the same situation. The boy cleared his throat and turned back to Kimberley, who had vaguely repeated a question in his direction. "What, Kim?" he wondered and the sergeant stared at him.

"Guess you're enjoying all this, right?" she let out.

"No, I'm..."

"Better this than juvenile jail time for you, right?"

An embarrassed Aiden looked down at his feet. "No need to bring that up now, Kim," he said. "I never asked for this."

"Says the boy who killed his mother by running away from home and ending up in a juvenile prison before running away again from a foster home to accidentally meet a little girl who takes him on an adventure ridiculing time and space."

"What are you saying?" Rachel thought she didn't hear what she just heard.

"Did you run away from home?" Kpakol asked Aiden.

"Yes, eh but not the way she just said it," Aiden stammered. He turned red. "It's...It's complicated."

"Then uncomplicate it," Kimberley interrupted. "Tell them why you left home and joined a gang of criminals."

"I didn't join any gang," Aiden countered.

"I believe you," Rachel said.

"Okay," Kimberley kept up. "If you didn't do that, how did you come across this?" She displayed the small box from her pocket. "How did this man now after us come to know you, Aiden? Please explain."

"Please stop doing what you're doing to him," Rachel said. "You're wrong."

"No, Rachel," Aiden said. "She's right." He was teary eyed. "I killed Mum by running away. I deserve to die."

"No, you don't," Rachel said, turning to Kimberley. "You're despicable."

"Is this helping us now?" Kpakol asked no one in particular.

"No, it's not," Kimberley said. "I just needed to get that off my chest."

"By making him cry?" Rachel exclaimed. "You know what we're going through, Kim, and you bring this up now?"

Kpakol cleared his throat. "Okay then, let's talk about this later? We need to leave if Aiden cannot see the writings. No need hanging around here."

"Yes," Kimberley said. "You…You're right."

"Odd that you bring up Aiden's issue at this dangerous time, miss," Kpakol said. "Are you acting with outside influence?"

"Of course, not," Kimberley said. "Do you think I am?" Kpakol stared at her and she looked away. "You suggested we talk about this later, remember?"

"Yes, I remember," the slave spy said. "We'll talk later, when we're safe."

"Have you seen anything?" Rachel asked Aiden, stepping up to him.

"No," Aiden replied. "Nothing yet."

Kpakol cried out and crashed to the ground. Carl Bain swung the bloody machete at Kimberley, missing her by inches as she avoided the blade and brushed his legs off the ground. She kicked away the machete before he could use the weapon again and slammed her right heel on his chest. He rolled away as she brought down her heel again. He grabbed Rachel who proceeded to bite his arm and elbow his stomach.

"Yeow," Carl Bain shouted, releasing the girl, who ran to Aiden. The boy watched from afar.

"Lost your powers?" Kimberley began as she watched her enemy's every step. "I don't even know your name."

"Carl Bain to you, ma'am," the man announced with a smile. "And who am I fighting?"

"Sergeant Kimberley Reyna of the Portwood Police Department to you, mister," Kimberley replied. "I see you don't have your powers."

"He's been affected by the ankhs we drew on our arms, Kim," Rachel shouted. "He can't use his powers here."

Carl Bain eyed the girl. "My demon lords stripped me of my powers as soon as I appeared in your midst," he told her. "This eliminated the effect of those worthless symbols on me."

"They're not worthless," Aiden stammered, handing the white book to Rachel.

Carl Bain glared at him. "I will kill you after I kill your friends, boy," he snapped. "After all, you got me into this mess."

"Is this about your package?" Kimberley jeered, pulling the small box out of her pocket. "Come and get it again, boy."

"Okay," Carl Bain said, looking around for his machete. Not seeing the weapon, he picked up a tree branch and broke it into two. "Now, you die."

Repeatedly thrusting the jagged end of the stick at his opponent, Carl Bain moved into her space. The sergeant avoided the thrusts as best as she could, going backward before kicking away the stick with a high right foot swing. She swung back her right leg, intending to hit Carl Bain's neck with the deadly kickbox, but the American hustler held her leg and threw her off-balance by pushing the leg he held.

Kimberley fell and quickly got up before her opponent got to her unstable figure. His right fist smashed into her jaw and she fell backward in a daze.

The human minion straddled his enemy and broke her nose with his right fist before Aiden smashed him into oblivion by swinging a heavy tree branch at his head. This action prevented another affront on Kimberley's nose.

"Kpakol," Rachel screamed, running towards the slave spy's immobile figure.

"He's dead," Aiden said dejectedly. "Nobody can survive that cut."

"Yes," Kimberley agreed, picking herself up. She looked for Carl Bain's machete and found it in the tall grass. "Look away," she told the children, going over to pick up the weapon.

"What do you want to do with it?" Aiden asked her.

"Something I should have done a long time ago," the Portwood sergeant said.

"No, Kim, don't do it," Rachel pleaded.

"You can't do that, Kim," Aiden began.

"Yes, I can," Kimberley said. "Now, look away." She cut off Carl Bain's head in one fell swoop. The long grass hid this bloody deed from the wide-eyed kids. "Let's get out of here."

Chapter 26
GREENLAND

KIMBERLEY and the kids appeared on a snowy landscape wearing Eskimo-styled clothing.

"The symbols are no longer on our arms," Aiden realized. "Where's the sharpie, Kim?" he requested.

"I no longer have it," Kimberley said.

"Must it be a sharpie?" Rachel asked.

"Right," Aiden agreed. "Anything that writes will do."

Kimberley looked around her at the disappointing snow. "Nothing to see here," she said. "Just snow."

"There's a building," Rachel pointed out with her right index finger.

"Looks tiny from here," Aiden observed.

"It's far," Kimberley said. "Let's get closer." There appeared no other choice.

The time-travelers started running towards the structure.

An explosion threw them apart, spewing the Gray Ones through the ice sheet they'd been running on.

Aiden dropped the white book as the eruption flung him far out like the others. The book formed the magical dome around itself, freezing away the demonic entities near it.

A shrieking Booklord pinned Rachel to the ground. She turned her head and realized that the others were also going through this gruesome experience.

Kimberley looked away as the infernal creature holding her screamed into her face. She felt tired and stared at Aiden as he struggled with his own aggressor. She felt like something repulsive was trying to enter her. Something more powerful. More assertive. Something trying to pass through her so as to control her being.

The Portwood sergeant saw Rachel get up as if in a trance. The little girl walked over to the mysterious book and picked it up despite the mysterious freezing protection around the volume. Kimberley tried to say something, but nothing came out of her mouth. "Rachel, no!" she finally screamed, before realizing that the little girl could not hear her.

Rachel raised the white book up and the most hideous Gray One Kimberley had ever seen withdrew from the horde and faced the little girl, who moved to give this spiritual creature the book.

Carl Bain appeared before Aiden and stabbed the boy on the chest. Rachel screamed at this shocking violence while a stunned Kimberley could only stare as the American gangster stabbed the boy again.

"You thought I have died?!" the human minion growled. "Not when I have my demon lords on my side, boy!"

The screaming Rachel started struggling for the white book with the Gray One facing her.

The bullets hit Carl Bain before he could stab Aiden a third time. The Booklords left their human minion behind as they fled. They faded away as the American thug died a second time.

A new character ran over to Aiden and disappeared with the boy.

"Where did they go?" a stupefied Kimberley wondered, looking around her.

"I-I don't know," Rachel replied, shaken by the events of the last few seconds. Heaps of mysterious ash littered an area surrounding the white book on the ground before her and she cringed at the thought of the unearthly creatures rising up from these grave sites to torment her again. "Aiden...someone t-took him away."

"I saw that," Kimberley said.

"Maybe we'll get some answers from the house?" Rachel nodded towards the structure.

Kimberley stood up beside the little girl and faced the two-floor wooden house. She looked at Rachel, who stared at Carl Bain's body. "He didn't die, even though I beheaded him," the Portwood Police sergeant told the little girl. "You know what that means."

Rachel nodded. "They can bring back the dead," she said and picked up the white book.

"Is that why you wanted to give them the book?" Kimberley asked her. "Or is there any other reason for that?"

"I-I wasn't thinking straight," the Bookbearer confessed. "Something was influencing me."

"I wasn't thinking straight back in Nigeria as well," Kimberley said. "Something was also influencing me, which means only one thing."

"Like Uncle Ezra said, they can control anyone they want to control."

"Exactly, though it looks like it's easier for them to control non-Bookbearers," Kimberley reasoned.

"But they must have controlled me now."

"Yes, maybe they can easily control Bookbearers as well." Kimberley held her head.

Rachel looked at Carl Bain's body. "Is he still alive right now?"

"I doubt he's dead," Kimberley said. "Though I still hope he's gone for good."

"Over here!" someone called out to them from the house in the distance. "Your friend is okay."

"Who is that?" Kimberley began.

"I don't know," Rachel said. "We should find out."

A man stood at the distant building's entrance. He wore attire similar to what Kimberley and Rachel had on. Both time-travelers walked up to this fellow, who had penetrating blue eyes and a deep brow. His handsome smile lit up his chiseled face, which exuded confidence. This tall man literally stooped to avoid the door's lintel.

"Hi, my name's David Hoyte and I'm a glaciologist here in Greenland," the man introduced in a British accent. "I saw what those things did to you and I decided to help since I knew how to."

"Yes, I knew you could help, sir. I wrote your name in the book and it brought us to you, remember?" Rachel frowned. What was she saying? "Where is our friend?"

"He's okay now, and safe."

The little girl walked past the tall man into the house. "Aiden," she called out. "Where are you?"

"Over here, Rachel," Aiden replied. "Just come upstairs."

"What did you do to save him?" Kimberley asked Mr. Hoyte, glad to hear the boy's voice again.

"Well, I shot the guy attacking your friend and ferried your friend's wounded body into the future with a piece of the white book I had with me," Mr. Hoyte said. "I now brought back the healed body afterwards. Please call me Dave."

"Sergeant Kimberley Reyna of the Portwood Police Department," Kimberley introduced. "You can call me Kim." She walked past Dave and climbed the stairs to meet Aiden.

Mr. Hoyte followed her.

Aiden and Rachel were sitting on the only bed in the room. Kimberley hugged the boy. "Good to see you, old friend," she said. "Glad you made it."

"Glad to see you too, Kim," Aiden said less enthusiastically. He hadn't forgotten Kimberley's outburst back at Brazil. "That killer stabbed me twice and I can't even see a single wound now."

"Because Mr. Hoyte here took you into the future and back, like you guys did for me back in Brazil," Kimberley pointed out.

"Thank you, Mr. Hoyte," Aiden said.

"Call me Dave."

"You saved my life, Mr. Hoyte," Aiden said. "I am grateful."

"Well then, you're welcome," Dave said. "I guess you guys are...hungry? I'll go make us some breakfast downstairs."

"Jeremiah Mizrahi, were you a Bookmaker back at the Mine?" Rachel asked him.

Mr. Hoyte froze. "When I discovered that as my name, I did not like it, so I stuck to Dave," he said to no one in particular. "I'm a Sicarii Kabbalah Masada or Sikama for short, Rachel, and like you know, Sikama members are Bookmakers, most of who can bear the two powerful books they made. Some slaves also joined the Sicarii Kabbalah Masada back then."

"So, you knew me then?" Rachel wanted to know.

"Of course," Dave said. "Who didn't know the commander's daughter then?"

"She came from the Mine," Kimberley said dryly, rolling her eyes.

"She's the reason those things are after us," Aiden supported the police officer with.

"I see," Mr. Hoyte said. "I believe your father gave you this?" He pointed at the mysterious book lying on the bed.

"Yes, he did," Rachel said, picking up the book. "We need your help. That's why we came looking for you."

"How did you know my name?"

"Well," the little girl began. "I knew you back at the Mine, though we kept a distance. Your name just popped up when we needed to run into the future again."

"I see," Mr. Hoyte repeated. "When I saw the attack of the Gray Ones from my house, I knew what to do with an ankh I've always had with me. You know an ankh or a cross symbol drives them away?"

"Or a 'T' sign," Aiden added.

"Okay," Kimberley said. "The weather here is cold, so guess we never realized that the white book was freezing up as we ran towards your house."

"Yeah," Aiden agreed. "No wonder those things ambushed us."

"Excuse me," Mr. Hoyte said and left to get breakfast.

"Wonder why no one is talking of hunger anymore," Aiden said, looking himself over.

Rachel hugged him again. "How can we be talking of that when Kpakol was killed and you almost died, Aiden?"

"Kpakol?" Dave asked at the door. He dropped a tray of sandwiches and hot tea on the bed's side table. "You met Kpakol?"

"Yes," Kimberley said. "The guy you shot killed him."

"Kpakol was trying to help us retrieve the other book," Rachel said. "He even knew members of the Inner Circle."

"How?" Dave seemed confused. "I mean, how can Kpakol know so much? He was just a slave at the Mine."

"Here we go again," Kimberley said, holding her head with both hands. "Why would Kpakol lie to us?"

"Did he?" Rachel began.

"Kpakol lied to you," Dave said. "The other book is no longer with Man. I've seen that through Shurabi."

"Wait a minute," Kimberley said. "Are you saying Mariah also lied to us?"

Mr. Hoyte laughed. "You met Mariah? No wonder."

"No wonder what?" Rachel asked him.

"No wonder you believed Kpakol. He repeated what Mariah told you."

Kimberley frowned. Who to believe? Something fishy was definitely going on. "Kpakol told us not to trust Mariah," she said.

"And then he tells you to look for the black book?" Dave asked her.

"Well, actually, he told us the black book might have left this world," Rachel said. "He said that we might be too late."

"Okay, he's right about that."

"Can you just explain like everybody else?" Aiden told the tall man. "Starting from Shurabi?"

"First we need a sharpie, Mr. Hoyte," Kimberley interrupted. "We have to protect ourselves first with ankhs on our arms."

Dave Hoyte nodded, left and returned with her request. "Shurabi is a hard one to explain," he began as his guests drew ankhs on their arms. "It is a spell the Booklords imparted into the two books we presented to them. Shurabi infused invisible Hebrew words into these books. Words that practitioners of Kabbalah Ma'asit who studied Shurabi could see and read if they're worthy."

"We know that, Mr. Hoyte," Rachel said. "We need you to tell us something we don't know."

"Shurabi told me a long time ago that the other book's Bookbearer had voluntarily handed over this book to the Black Ones," Mr. Hoyte said.

"How?" Kimberley asked.

"Any Bookmaker can see all the hidden Hebrew words when the other book is still in the hands of a human being," Dave Hoyte said.

"Really?" Kimberley began. "Mariah said that…"

"She obviously lied, Kim," Aiden cut in.

"Or he's lying," Rachel said, nodding towards their new host.

"Whoever told you that even half of the hidden Hebrew words appearing in one of the books mean the presence of the two books in our world lied to you," Mr. Hoyte said.

"And why should we believe you're telling us the truth?" Kimberley asked him. "Why should we assume you're not lying to us?"

"How do we know you're telling us the truth?" Aiden wondered.

"Who amongst you have tried to see the hidden words on the book?" Dave asked.

"I tried to do that," Rachel said.

"Me, too," Aiden said. "I could only see part of a complete sentence."

"And who are you?" Mr. Hoyte asked the boy. "How come you can see the hidden Hebrew words?"

"He's a boy from my town," Kimberley said. "Kpakol said he resembles a remarkably gifted Bookmaker back at the Mine."

"Yeah, been thinking about that," Dave said. "He looks like someone back then, and he can see some of the hidden words."

"What does it all mean?" Rachel wondered.

"It means Kpakol could be right," Kimberley said, eyeing Mr. Hoyte. "And that our friend here is not telling us the truth, or most of it."

"I've told you what I do, and where you are right now," Dave began. "I've talked about the Sicarii Kabbalah Masada, and…"

"No, you haven't," Rachel said. "What do you really know about the Sicarii Kabbalah Masada?"

"I know little about the Sikama, since I was never a member of the Inner Circle," Mr. Hoyte said.

"How many people made up this Inner Circle?" Rachel asked.

"They were more than twelve men and women, I think," Dave Hoyte replied with a frown. "These were the Elders, as we called them then, who solicited on our behalf in the Inner Circle, and represented Jews the world over whenever the Angels of the Most High came down to Earth for discussions concerning our emancipation from Emperor Constantine."

"Emperor Constantine?" Kimberley frowned. "Where did that come from?"

"Okay, I could have told you guys earlier," Rachel said. "The Sicarii Kabbalah Masada initially wanted to depose of Emperor Constantine before something happened that caused them to take up a different objective."

"They wanted to use the books to remove the Emperor?" Kimberley asked her.

"Initially," Mr. Hoyte began, "the Sicarii Kabbalah Masada was a Jewish endeavor to assassinate the Emperor before Yahweh gave this cult the books and her members decided to do a greater good for the Jewish race with these gifts. That was when I joined the sect."

"Awesome," Aiden joked. "That's a joke," he added.

"You joined the sect as a Bookmaker?" Rachel asked the tall man.

"Yes. I was a parchment specialist in Rome before I heard about the sect through a friend who also recruited me for the sect."

"So, what was your job?" Kimberley asked.

"Eh, the Bookmakers needed to make more books they could keep in reserve should any of the two great books go missing. These reserve books needed to be made with the right material, and that's where I came in," Mr. Hoyte explained. "I worked with the specific direction of Jehoash because he was also a parchment specialist and discovered the right material for the two great books. I went around the country looking for this material and conveying it to Rome anyway I could."

"Were any of these reserve books ever made?" Kimberley asked.

"No," Dave Hoyte said. "Unfortunately, the material I collected was seized by the Romans before it got to Rome. I don't know what became of it, because we fled the Mine when we got word that the Romans and the Booklords were coming."

"How did you flee?" Rachel asked.

"We escaped with pieces of the white book," Dave Hoyte said. "A page from the book was torn to pieces and shared amongst us."

"Do you still have this piece of paper?" Kimberley asked him.

"Of course," the glaciologist said, bringing out the paper. "I told you I used it to save your friend."

"Did you ever think of destroying this piece of paper?" Kimberley asked.

Mr. Hoyte hesitated. "I couldn't burn it so I kept it in a safe with the intention of throwing it away whenever I'm out at sea."

"Glad you didn't do that," Aiden said.

"Aren't we all?" Dave Hoyte smiled.

"Was my father in the Inner Circle?" Rachel asked.

"Yes, he was."

"Back then did you know anyone who was a member of this circle?" Kimberley demanded.

"I knew many people," the man replied. "Ben Haddad, Ezra, Jehoash, Ezekiel Raib; need I continue?"

"So you can help us get to one of these people?" Rachel asked.

"Of course, my dear," Dave Hoyte replied. "If it will help your course."

"Anyone but Uncle Ben Haddad," the little girl said.

"And why do you say that?" Kimberley demanded.

"Father said he was a bad man."

"What if your father was wrong?" Aiden pointed out. "What if this man was the leader of the Sicarii Kabbalah Masada?"

"He wasn't the leader," Rachel responded.

"So who was their leader?" Aiden asked her.

The little girl looked away. "I-I don't know," she confessed.

"Who led this Inner Circle, Mr. Hoyte?" Kimberley asked.

Dave Hoyte turned to Rachel. "Your father, Rachel. Jehoash led the Inner Circle with Ben Haddad."

Chapter 27
MELTING ICE

THE bullet holes on his body disappeared and he sat up, looking around at the emptiness created by the vast expanse of snow. He looked at his hands and the bloodied knife lying beside him, now sunk halfway into the snow.

Carl Bain smiled and looked up. He knew who'd brought him back to life again. "Now, they'll know!" he whispered, the smile still playing on his lips. "I'll keep coming until they return what is mine. What belongs to my masters. I'll keep coming until they all perish. I'll never die!"

The American thug stood up and felt all over the front of his coat. No sign of a tear. He didn't even feel the pain anymore. Good.

He picked up the knife and looked it over. He wished he had a gun. The knife became a Glock G34. Good. His masters heard his wish.

He wondered why they remained invisible.

Carl Bain saw the lonely house and appeared before it. He couldn't vanish again. He knocked on the main door.

*   *   *

"He's the one, Kim," Rachel reported, peeping through the bedroom window.

"Looks like he has a gun," Aiden whispered beside her. "Where did he get a gun?"

"His demon friends must have granted him one," Kimberley said. "This guy is now a certified pain in the ass. Can't imagine he's alive after I cut off his head."

"No problem," Dave Hoyte said, cocking his firearm. "I will keep killing him until he leaves you guys alone."

The man outside knocked on the main door a third time.

"So, Dave, what's the plan?" Aiden asked.

"Simple. We gun him down."

"Remember he has a gun," Kimberley pointed out. "I hope you're good with yours."

"You don't need to worry, dear," the man replied. "I got this." He walked to the door. "You all should stay here."

"I'm coming with you," Kimberley told him, moving towards the door. She saw a shovel and picked it on her way out of the room.

The man outside knocked on the main door a fourth time as Kimberley quietly descended the stairs behind Mr. Hoyte.

A short corridor led to the main entrance and the Portwood sergeant took up position behind a door leading into this passage while Dave Hoyte hid behind a low cupboard placed beside the lobby's entryway.

Carl Bain kicked open the main door and dove into the lobby shooting like a mad man. A shot missed his right shoulder and he let off some bullets at a low cupboard directly ahead of him, hearing a man cry out before scampering away from this furniture while shooting in the fellow's direction. He couldn't see his attacker owing to the darkness surrounding him, but he could hear the noise the man made in haste.

The American minion got up and ran after his target, never expecting the sudden facial slam that blacked him out.

"Quick," Kimberley shouted. "Let's get out of here before he wakes up!" She dropped the shovel and picked up Carl Bain's Glock. David Hoyte appeared at the door as Aiden came down the stairs with Rachel.

"His powers are ineffective here," Rachel observed.

"We drew the ankhs," Aiden reminded her.

"He almost got me," Dave said, feeling the scratch wound on his right arm. "Go outside," he told the kids. "I don't want you to see this."

"See what?" Aiden began.

"Go, Aiden," Kimberley ordered the boy.

Aiden nodded and pulled Rachel into the small lobby. They went out through the main door.

Mr. Hoyte shot Carl Bain in the chest and forehead. "For good measure," he began, "let's throw him into the sea."

Kimberley shot the dead man twice, in the chest and forehead. "How do we do that?" she asked.

"I have a work chopper behind the house," Mr. Hoyte said. "I often fly out to the northernmost part of this island for environmental studies and monitoring."

"Okay, let's hope drowning will end him," Kimberley said. "He'll just rise up and follow us if we can only delay him."

"He'll drown in the water," the Bookmaker-turned-glaciologist said. "That will stop him."

"I hope you're right," Kimberley murmured with a frown. "So, you can't help us?" she asked the Bookmaker.

"Not as much as I would have loved to," he said. "We could have tested a theory I proposed if you had a piece of the black book with you, maybe the piece with Kpakol?"

Kimberley started. "And how did you know about that?"

"Right, I knew the slaves got hold of a page from that book and shared it amongst themselves to escape with," Dave said. "I sensed at the time that Jehoash knew about this and didn't want to say anything concerning the matter."

"Okay, so what's the theory you wanted to test out?"

"Actually, I have two theories," Mr. Hoyte began. "The first one is that I think something might happen if we bring materials from the two books together. Like a piece of the books? Maybe we'll create the third book."

"And what's the second theory?" Kimberley asked him.

"I discovered I could read all the hidden Hebrew words on my piece of paper whenever I'm flying towards the northern part of this snowy island," the Bookmaker said.

"So, what does that mean?"

"It means that the North Pole could be an aperture to the spirit realm, and that if I had the white book with me when I went up towards the North Pole, I might be able to read the complete hidden Hebrew sentence written on the book."

"And what would that accomplish for us?" Kimberley demanded. "Sorry, I'm still lost here."

"This is just a theory, dear, but I think we would be able to retrieve the other book from the spirit realm if we can read the complete hidden Hebrew sentence on the white book's pages."

Kimberley's lower jaw dropped. "Interesting," she said. "So, what are we waiting for? Let's fly out right now."

"Okay," Dave said. "But we'll need to tie our friend here to the chopper first." He went into the adjoining room and came back with a dining cloth. Kimberley helped him wrap Carl Bain's body with the material. She also helped him to move the human minion's body to the backyard, where an Airbus H125 obliviously sat on its helipad.

Mr. Hoyte inspected the chopper before tying a heavy stone to Carl Bain's trunk using strong climbing rope he got from the helicopter's cabin. He also tied the dead man's legs to the left landing skid directly underneath the chopper's front passenger seat and gave Kimberley a penknife. "Open your door and cut the ropes when we get to the ocean," he told her.

The Portwood officer nodded and took the knife. She went back into the house, walked over to the main entrance and opened the door. Aiden and Rachel were hugging each other while sitting on the front steps. "You can come in now," she told them.

"Gosh," Aiden exclaimed. "It's so cold out here." He helped Rachel up the stairs and into the house.

"We're leaving now," Kimberley said, ushering the kids across the passage and out the door leading to the backyard.

"With the book?" Rachel asked.

"With a chopper stationed over there," the Portwood police woman replied, pointing at the H125 single engine helicopter. "We dump our friend's body in the ocean, and then we fly towards the North Pole."

"What for?" Aiden sounded perplexed.

"Um...so that we can try and retrieve the black book?" Kimberley said.

"How?"

"Jeremiah, a.k.a. Mr. Dave Hoyte here, says he has a theory that the North Pole is a gate to the spirit realm, because he could read all the hidden Hebrew words on his piece of paper whenever he is flying towards the pole."

"Then we should go to the North Pole," Aiden began.

"Uh, no need for that," Mr. Hoyte said. "I think we could do what we need to do by simply flying towards the pole."

"And how did you know that?" Rachel asked the tall glaciologist.

"I'm a scientist, remember?" David pointed out. "I hope we won't be disappointed, though." He entered the chopper. "All aboard now. Please put on your safety belts, as well as the headsets for communication."

The traveling trio obeyed him. They also helped him close the chopper's air-tight doors.

The Airbus H125 started up and lifted high into the air, the sound of its twirling rotors muffled inside its cabin. The aircraft started forward, its main rotors doing the heavy job. It was soon speeding over a vast wasteland of snow.

Kimberley looked down in awe at the white landscape spread as far as the eyes could see all around her. She saw slush coming down a slope and became curious. "What's happening over there?" she asked the aircraft's pilot, pointing down at the event.

"That's melting snow," David Hoyte replied, banking the vehicle for a better view.

"Okay, right." Kimberley cared less.

"You know an ice sheet two miles thick covers most of this island?"

"Okay. Go on."

"Well, we now know that due to global warming, the ice forming this sheet is melting at a rate we've never before witnessed," the scientist continued. "Water from this melting ice drains into a large aquifer underneath the ice sheet."

"I see," a confused Kimberley said.

"Greenland's ice sheet is shrinking owing to this melt, and it's losing mass several times faster than it was just a few decades ago," David continued. "Every year, the ice sheet loses some weight as ice flows from its middle through glaciers at its edges to spill into the ocean."

Kimberley's interest had peaked. "Go on," she urged.

"Under the Greenland ice sheet lies what we call the bedrock," Mr. Hoyte resumed. "A year ago, we used radar to image the hills, mountains, valleys and depressions on this bedrock that the ice floats over. We got to see channels the size of the Grand Canyon hidden under the ice sheet through this method, and we later discovered that these channels funnel ice and water off of Greenland and into the ocean. We also learnt that water can get to these channels through crevasses that open up from cracks on the surface of the ice sheet. These crevasses are expanded by water from the aquifer beneath the ice sheet till they get to the channels draining into the Arctic Ocean."

"And how does all that science help our current predicament?" Rachel demanded. Aiden glared at her and she frowned. "What?"

"Nothing bad in getting to know Mr. Hoyte's work, Rachel," her traveling companion said. "He's been good to us."

"Aiden, I don't trust him," Rachel whispered.

"You forget you have a headset, Rachel," Kimberley interrupted. "We can all hear you."

"No need to worry, Rachel," Dave Hoyte said. "I'll leave you guys if this experiment fails, so you can trust me." The chopper flew over a clear blue lake.

"And what about the science you've been talking about?" the little girl asked him. "How is that relevant to our unique situation here?"

"It's not important to you," Mr. Hoyte said. "I'm just passing time by telling you what I do. We still have like an hour of flying, so in that context, telling you about my work becomes relevant."

Rachel said nothing.

"And if you haven't noticed, Rachel, the book has been showing us a pattern in the places we've been to," Kimberley pointed out. "Man-made environmental disasters, wars and impending nuclear doom. What Mr.

Hoyte has been telling us is a man-made environmental disaster."

"That pattern you talk of is a coincidence," Rachel said. "I think."

"Then that's a mysterious coincidence," Aiden exclaimed. "We just can't ignore the coincidence. The book is trying to tell us something by laying out this pattern."

"Whatever," Rachel dismissed.

"You see that lake down below?" Mr. Hoyte resumed. "It was formed as a result of warm air melting the surface of the ice sheet. Its presence, though, is causing more ice to melt since it absorbs most of the warmth from the Sun, unlike the ice sheet, which reflects most of this warmth from its white surface."

"You said the ice sheet is shrinking," Kimberley began. "Is the surface melt the only action causing this reduction in size?"

"In this part of the ocean, water at the surface tends to be chilly and fresh. However, if you dove down a few hundred feet, you could hit part of the Gulf Stream current, which is a warm, salty layer coming straight from the tropics with the warmth of the equatorial sun in its watery bonds," Mr. Hoyte said. "This means that the Ocean is also contributing to the shrinking of the ice sheet from underneath it."

"What good will this scientific knowledge do for the world, Mr. Hoyte?" Aiden asked.

"Well, the ocean soaks up the excess heat already trapped in the atmosphere by human-caused climate change," Dave said, banking again. "Over time, there will likely be more and more warm water available to melt ice. And you must know that right now, melt from this island's ice sheet is the single largest contributor to sea level rise worldwide."

"Sea level rise," Kimberley noted. "That means coastal towns and cities across the world are in danger of flooding and submersion, right?"

"Exactly, dear. Unless we stop the human activities that assist global warming and climate change, our coastal cities and facilities will always be in danger of this disastrous consequence decades from now. It can only get worse if we don't act."

"And blah blah blah," Rachel said.

"Someone is very rude today," Kimberley noted.

"Whatever," Rachel said. "Let's focus on our mission?"

"Could you loosen up already?" Aiden began.

"How did you come to know about the Booklords fearing the ankh?" Rachel asked the pilot, ignoring the last speaker.

"At the Mine, dear. We knew about the symbols at the Mine, but we couldn't wait for the Romans to come so we planned our escape as soon as we could."

"There," Kimberley cut in, pointing. "We're at the coast."

"Just open the door when we get to the ocean," Dave said. "I'll do the rest."

Kimberley turned on her seat and made sure that Aiden and Rachel were adequately buckled to their seats. She opened her door and went to work on the rope holding Carl Bain's dining-cloth-wrapped body to the chopper's left landing skid.

The human minion's body fell and splashed into the ocean moments later.

"Done," Kimberley told the pilot, who nodded and banked sharply to the right as he turned back to land.

The helicopter touched down in no time.

"Okay, people, time to test out my theory," Mr. Hoyte said, shutting down the chopper. "Give me the book, Rachel."

"No way," Rachel said. "I can test your theory from here."

Dave Hoyte brought out his gun and Kimberley remembered she had one as well. She couldn't find it on her person.

"Don't bother looking for it, dear," Mr. Hoyte said. "I made sure you didn't come along with it." He aimed the firearm at her chest.

"You son of a..."

"You were right not to trust me, Rachel," Mr. Hoyte chuckled, ignoring the Portwood police officer. "I had always wanted to lay my hands on any of the two great books and this opportunity will never come again in a million years! Or, shall we say, a million lifetimes?"

"So, your theory was all made up?" Aiden asked him. "There's no chance of finding the black book here?"

"Everything I told you was made up, except the hidden Hebrew words being completely visible only when the two books were in the hands of men."

"C-Can't we work something out?" Kimberley tried. "Can't we agree on a way forward we can all benefit from?"

"Really, you sound pathetic," Mr. Hoyte said. "But not to worry." He turned to Rachel. "I simply want to continue the good work you guys started."

"And what's that?" the little girl asked, tightly hugging the white book.

"I'll look for the black book and initiate the ritual while you guys die here since, frankly speaking, you don't have anywhere to go from here."

"And what will you gain by doing just that?" Aiden demanded.

"Power, my dear," Jeremiah, a.k.a. Mr. Hoyte, replied. "The power to choose my destiny."

Rachel's hug tightened around the mysterious volume. "Not gonna happen," she said. "You'll have to kill us first."

"Very well then." Mr. Hoyte cocked his gun and pressed it into Kimberley's navel.

"No, please don't," Rachel surrendered, handing over the book.

Kimberley was touched.

"Good," Mr. Hoyte said. "I knew you would come round. Now open the doors and get out."

Nobody obeyed him.

The glaciologist chuckled again. "God, I wish you guys could look at your faces in a mirror right now."

Kimberley pushed away the Bookmaker's gun with her right hand and his shot shattered the helicopter's windscreen. She held up his right hand with both hands as he struggled to bring back his firearm and he dropped the white book before punching her repeatedly with his freed left hand.

Rachel grabbed the book.

David Hoyte let out another shot that smashed the window beside the police sergeant.

"Now, Rachel!" Kimberley shouted, struggling to immobilize the glaciologist's right hand. She put her shoulder on his face to obstruct his view and make it harder for him to punch her. He grabbed her hair and pulled her head backward. "Now, Rachel!"

"I don't know where to touch you, Kim!" Aiden cried as he held Rachel's left hand.

"Not her gloves!" Kimberley pointed out. "You're both wearing gloves!"

"Oh," Rachel realized, flipping open the book. Aiden hastily pulled off her left glove.

Dave Hoyte tried to bang Kimberley's head on the chopper's dashboard. She resisted the push. "Touch my waist!" she shouted at Aiden, who pulled off his second glove and pushed away her shirt to touch her right flank.

David Hoyte found himself alone in the Airbus H125 and angrily fired several rounds at its shattered windscreen.

*   *   *

Deep inside the Arctic Ocean, human hands tore out of a dining cloth wrapped around their male owner's body as it sank. These appendages untied the heavy stone dragging this man to the bottom of the ocean and the fellow freed himself from the dining cloth before swimming back up to the ocean's surface.

Four bullets fell off his body as he swam. Two from his chest and two from his forehead. The deep wounds located on these parts of his body healed and fresh skin closed them up.

He barely noticed, because vengeance ruled his heart.

Chapter 28
INDIA

KIMBERLEY appeared in a train coach without the kids. She coughed twice and took in a deep breath. So it worked? They'd all been in the chopper before she found herself in that closed coach. What must have caused her separation from the children? Perhaps Aiden's touch had almost disengaged prior to the space-time travel. Perhaps not.

She coughed again.

"Ticket, please," a staunch railway worker said at the compartment's door.

"I...." Kimberley fumbled around as if she knew where she kept her ticket. "I-I can't find it," she confessed. "It must have fallen off somewhere or something."

"Then you must fall off the train with it," the man returned, glaring at her. "Who are you and where are you going?"

"Well...um...my name is Everly," Kimberley said. "I'm on tour for a New Delhi picture book I'm working on." Somehow, she knew she was telling the truth. She realized she had on a nice red pantsuit.

"Can I see your passport, please?" the cold man demanded.

Kimberley coughed again. "Of course," she said, reaching out for a handbag lying on the seat opposite her. She coughed again.

"You have been coughing?" the ticket man asked her and she nodded.

"It's dry. Started yesterday, and I think it's this dusty place."

"No wonder," the Indian said in Hindi, hastily pulling out a face mask from his right trouser pocket and putting it on.

"No wonder what?" Kimberley asked him as she handed over her passport and ticket.

"No wonder you're alone in this carriage," the man said in the same language, gingerly taking the woman's passport and ticket. "You can speak my language?"

"Is that a problem?" Kimberley asked him.

"No, miss," the railway officer said. "Your coughing is the problem."

"How?"

"Your fellow travelers abandoned the coach because you were coughing, miss," the man explained. "They think you have the virus."

*   *   *

Carl Bain got to the top of the coastal mountain and stared at the helicopter perched there. The man railing inside the chopper made him curious. He appeared near the aircraft.

David Hoyte scampered out of the Airbus H125, trying to make sense of what he just saw. Of course, the Booklords were now on to him, no thanks to his little escapade with the three Bookbearers who just outwitted him. The man now in the chopper should be lying at the bottom of the Arctic Ocean right that minute. No scientific breakthrough could explain the unbelievable appearance of this man in that helicopter.

He pulled his pistol and heard a disheartening click when he tried to shoot. He'd expended all his bullets in his rage.

"What a shame they finally left you," someone said near him, and he spun round to see the man who appeared in the helicopter's cabin standing behind him with an expressionless face. "Those three cannot be trusted, you know."

"W-Who are you?" Mr. Hoyte demanded, slowly drawing backward.

"Y-You can't be serious, right?" Carl Bain mocked the petrified man. "You killed me a few hours ago and you can't even remember me?"

David Hoyte searched through his pockets for something

"You left it back at the house," Carl Bain said. "If you were with it, my powers won't work."

The glaciologist sprawled on the ground before the human minion. "Spare my life, please. Don't kill me, Master."

Carl Bain's demon lords appeared around him and the prostrating Bookmaker.

"Please, don't kill me," the pleading man cried as he looked around him.

"My masters say they left you alone on this remote island after you agreed not to interfere in this matter anymore," Carl Bain said. "You just broke that agreement."

"Those kids caused all this," Dave complained. "They made me dream of the outside world again!"

Carl Bain smiled. "Actions have consequences," he said. "Now, you'll pay the price with your life."

The human minion disappeared with his demonic superiors, leaving behind a dead glaciologist.

On to the matter at hand.

*   *   *

Kimberley couldn't stop staring at the man. "Which virus?" she finally asked him.

"You don't know about it?"

"Oh, no – no," Kimberley realized. "I only have common cold. The dry cough is just that...dry cough...no other symptoms."

"We will drop you off at the next station, Miss Everly," the Indian officer told her while returning her passport and ticket. "You can look for a test center from there."

"But..."

"No need to argue about this, Miss Everly. I believe this decision is in your best interest."

Kimberley nodded hesitantly. She stood up as the railway ticket officer's footsteps receded from her compartment's door. Of course, she could start planning her next move after leaving the train. Having the virus could also help her evade Carl Bain and his demonic masters in the long run.

Kimberley could recall she was in India if her alternate memory served her correctly. Central Delhi, to be precise. Odd that the book had transported her to India. She wondered why the mystic volume had deemed it necessary to bring only her to the ancient city. What was happening to Aiden and Rachel at that very moment? What would happen to her in India's capital? She couldn't wait to leave the train.

Mariah had said she knew that humans were still in custody of the black book because the Bookmakers could still see some hidden Hebrew words on the white book. Mr. David Hoyte had said he knew that the black book had left Man's world because the Bookmakers could not see some of the hidden Hebrew writing on the white book. Both Bookmakers deferred in their interpretation of what to see on any of the two books before either book could be assumed present or absent on Earth. Which Bookmaker was right?

The next station was the New Delhi Train Station. Kimberley checked her belongings and turned towards the door. The many faces staring at her startled her.

"What's going on?" she demanded.

"We heard you have the virus," a rough-looking fellow explained as he pulled down his face mask.

"So we've come to throw you out," another said.

Kimberley was lost for words. She knew that even though these people looked fearful, unkempt and ignorant, nothing would stop them from carrying out their threat. And she had no option here. They were too many.

"Okay, as you can see, I'm about leaving," she began. "But the train is yet to stop."

"No problem," a grumpy old man said. "We can throw you out of the window."

Kimberley noticed the cabin's open window. "Oh," she said. "Never knew that was an option."

"Go back to your couches," the railway ticket officer who had met her before ordered the onlookers, pushing the grumpy old man aside.

"But she's in our cabin," the old man protested.

"Yeah," another fellow said. "Where do we go?"

"She'll soon drop off," the railway worker said. "Then you can come back here. You won't have to worry about her after she has gone."

Kimberley scrambled. The window beckoned her. She slid through it and kicked the fellow grappling for her legs. A quick heave and she found herself on the carriage roof.

She could have reacted faster when she noticed something odd about the ticket man's appearance. Yes, he wasn't wearing a face covering this second time he entered her coach. A peculiar situation for him, knowing that he had hastily worn this piece of protection when he first assumed she had the virus.

Now, even if she had left the train at the next stop, the coach she'd occupied would have been sealed off, pending a thorough decontamination process by the relevant authority. No serious worker would allow passengers to reoccupy that cabin, and no reasonable passenger would agree to that request.

How stupid of her not to have realized all this early enough.

The bullet whizzed past her and she glanced backward as she ran, effortlessly hopping over carriage junctions. The three men had followed her, guns blazing. Typically what Carl Bain would do if he discovered she had the virus. His powers would be ineffective against her due to the disease, so he'd come for her without the help of his demonic masters. And since he alone was no match for her, he would naturally activate many goons to join him in the fight.

Another bullet swished past the Portwood officer. What an erratic aim.

A second train traveling in the opposite direction passed by and Kimberley jumped over to its roof. She grabbed a side pole and slid down on the train's other side, hanging from the pole as the vehicle passed her assailants standing on the other train's roof.

The men spewing death failed to hit their target. They jumped over the wide gap between the trains and moved to see the side of the second train. The woman had already entered a carriage through an open window. They knew this because someone kept coughing in a cabin near the pole. One by one, they stooped to grab the side pole and slid down on the train's side. The old man with them lost his grip and fell off as the train increased its speed.

"Excuse me," Kimberley told the cabin's occupants, feeling guilty for spreading the virus as she made her way to the door. She left as her pursuers swung into the cabin, Carl Bain leading the way.

"Police business," the human minion announced before heading for the cabin's door. His cohorts followed him.

The bullet scraped Kimberley's shoulder before she realized that a good marksman had joined her enemies.

Carl Bain.

She pushed open the door leading into the dining carriage and stumbled into a waiter carrying food and drinks. As the surprised man reacted to the accident, Kimberley raced across the carriage, avoiding diners whenever she could. Her pursuers shot at her when they rushed into this dining carriage, hitting some diners and stumbling into many waiters.

Kimberley fled into another carriage and locked the door behind her. This carriage had coaches and a long corridor. She felt the train slowing down, but kept going. Her assailants smashed the locked door's window and she rushed into an open coach before they let off some shots. The occupants of the coach – a boy and two girls – stared at her as she walked over to the cabin's only window and threw it open.

A scorched terrain greeted her eyes when she looked outside. This wasteland had no hiding place and she regretted her last move. She would be shot if she jumped out of the window. She could only stand her ground in that coach.

If only she had a gun.

The kids drew back when the door flew open and the ticket officer rushed into the cabin. Kimberley pounced on the man from behind the door as he ran to the window. They fell backward, crashing to the floor as the second man ran into the cabin and hastily put two bullets into his colleague's chest. Kimberley shot this second hitman with the gun she wrestled from the dead ticket officer's hand and trained the weapon at the open door, pushing away the dead man lying atop her.

The three children were crying.

No sign of Carl Bain.

"Quiet, please," Kimberley told the kids and drew back to the open window.

Presently, the train slowed down at a station and stopped. Kimberley heard police whistles and quickly climbed out of the cabin through the window. She landed in a dark tunnel and tucked the gun into her belt before stepping out into the light all around the station. She strode into the crowd gathering around the train, hoping to lose whoever was looking for her.

"There she is!" someone shouted and she pulled out her gun. The shot threw the crowd into confusion.

Kimberley ran.

"Police! Freeze!" Carl Bain shouted before shooting into the air.

"We must protect the civilians, sir," his deputy reminded him and he nodded grudgingly. The people running helter skelter didn't help matters. He kept his eyes on the target as he meandered through the cacophony all around him.

"We must not lose her," he told his deputy. "Put up road blocks outside the station."

"Yes, sir."

"And better still…" Carl Bain paused. "Never mind." A diabolic plan just materialized in his head.

Kimberley ran out of the station like so many other people. She headed for a cloth store situated near the railway station. The owner had fled in the present confusion, so she easily stepped into the shop and threw on casual wear that made for a sleek disguise. She added a hat and glasses after some thought.

Luckily, the female cop found a car its owner left running and sped off; confident she would never be tracked in her disguise.

"Stop!" a police officer shouted when she got to the railway station's gate, but she didn't obey him, crashing through the barrier and speeding into the highway. How did they identify her despite her disguise?

As she drove down the highway, several cars made u-turns after passing her and joined a long line chasing her. Kimberley gaped at this spectacle through her rear-view mirror. She knew who was responsible.

Carl Bain.

No doubt about that.

Since the Booklords could not attack her directly, their human minion had galvanized a huge crowd of drivers to pursue her, thereby keeping her tagged. Now the police did not need to comb around for her. She had a lineup following her car!

The Portwood police officer swerved into another road and her pursuers followed her. She turned left some minutes later and all the cars behind her did the same thing.

Blaring sirens.

Kimberley spotted three police cars in the mix-up behind her. She thought hard about what to do and a brilliant idea hit her. One that needed a sharpie or a pen. Rummaging through the car's pigeon hole, she found a pen. She hoped her theory would work.

Kimberley drove with her right hand while drawing ankhs on her right arm with her left hand. She now drove with her left hand and drew ankhs on her left arm with her right hand.

The crowd behind her petered out. Moments later, only the three Indian police cars kept up their pursuit. Her plan had worked.

Obviously, Carl Bain had no other tricks up his...

The lightning came from nowhere, catapulting the car into the air and away from the highway. The vehicle crashed a mile from the attack, glass shattering all around its only occupant.

Kimberley took off her safety belt and crawled out of the wreckage before falling on the ground, breathing hard. Badly bruised, she felt she'd broken some ribs when she coughed out blood and felt severe pain on her right flank.

Even though her aggressor could not face her with his infernal powers, he could still attack her car with said power, which was exactly what he just did. She should have known better.

Two squad cars stopped behind the third vehicle, which sped up to stop some distance from her battered figure. A familiar character stepped out of this last car.

"I admire your fighting spirit," Carl Bain said, stopping a few feet from his headache. "You know, other people would have given up by now."

"Hate to tell you this, but I'm not other people," Kimberley returned.

"We'll make a good team, you know," the American thug chided her. "You being my sidekick and all."

"Go to hell," Kimberley whispered between labored breaths.

"Not before you give me my stuff," Carl Bain said. "The little box you can't figure out?"

"Don't have it."

"We know that's a lie, dear," her enemy said.

"What's with the cops in their cars?" Kimberley digressed. "Using magic on them as well?"

"Why not?" Carl Bain wondered. "They don't need to know about my little box."

"Why? What are you hiding?"

"Just hand it over and I'll tell you."

"Come and get it then."

Carl Bain boiled. "You sniveling little…"

The blast killed him instantly, flinging him backward. He lay still as blood dripped from a gaping hole on his forehead.

Kimberley trained the gun on the first squad car. She wanted to eliminate that threat before the other police men could get out of their vehicles and run up to her position, but what she saw made her stop. One by one, the Indian officers were coming out of their cars and raising their hands in surrender. What changed? Did Carl Bain's magic lose its potency as soon as he died? What of his infernal masters?

"You're safe now," someone said beside her.

"From the Booklords as well," another individual said.

Kimberley turned to see seven locals wearing gas masks and carrying guns. Very unique guns.

Chapter 29
RUBBISH MOUNTAIN

THE squad cars zoomed off and Kimberley breathed a sigh of relief. Her heart had been in her mouth ever since she shot the crazy man now lying before her.

She looked around at her rescuers and counted them. Seven individuals wearing jeans and T-shirts while showcasing sophisticated gadgetry. Of particular interest were the strange-looking semiautomatics hanging from their shoulders. These weapons had ankhs engraved all over them.

"You are badly bruised," the Indian beside her said, stretching out his right hand. "Can you get up?"

Kimberley grabbed the man's hand and gingerly stood up. Her ribs were on fire. She perceived the stench in the air for the first time. "What's that smell?" she demanded.

"Rubbish Mountain over there," one of her rescuers pointed out. "She'll need a breather," he told a colleague, who nodded and stepped forward with a gas mask. "It will also protect us from the virus in her system."

Kimberley felt instant relief when she put on the equipment. "Who're you guys?" she asked her first contact.

"My name's Khan," the fellow said. "These are my comrades: Avi, Dev, Raghav, Rudra, Ikshita and Diya. Raghav is Rudra's twin." As he spoke, Kimberley nodded at each new face.

Khan's bold face and stoic neck fitted his muscular built. A bald head gave him that irresistible stamp of leadership he presently exuded.

Avi had bright penetrating eyes that looked deeply into one's soul whenever he encountered anyone. His long hair beautified his handsome face as it cascaded down his shoulders, and ankh tattoos covered his arms.

Dev looked like an Indian movie star who loved designer brands. His cropped hair and dark glasses gave him an artificial air of confidence he never failed to showcase. Hence, he came across as a selfishly pompous adventurer whose wild arm tattoos of nude girls underlined the fact that he didn't care about the Booklords and the two books so much as he cared about the health risks the Ghazipur landfill posed to local residents of the current vicinity.

The twins, Raghav and Rudra, had so much in common that Kimberley could only differentiate them from the way they carried their weapons. Same T-shirt and jeans. Same tattoos and hairstyle. Same earrings and piercings. Same weapons and gadgetry. Same face and physique. Same everything, except that they carried their guns differently. Raghav preferred hanging his weapon from his left shoulder while Rudra hung his from his right shoulder.

And then the remaining two individuals could have never been more different in everything. Ikshita's lean nature contrasted sharply with Diya's obesity. While Ikshita had tattoos, the other woman's skin had never gone under lazer. Diya carried a modified AR-15 semiautomatic, but Ikshita held a strange-looking handgun. And so on.

Kimberley stopped to study Ikshita's ominous face.

The slender Indian woman glared at the American. "Is there a problem?" she demanded.

"No, your face reminds me of someone, that's all," Kimberley admitted, looking away. "Thanks for saving me," she told Khan. "I'm grateful for you and your group. My name's Kimberley. Kim for short."

"We're Bookmakers, Kim," Khan said. "But then, you must have known this by now."

"No, but I believe you," Kimberley said.

"We also keep the Booklords at bay," Dev revealed with a smile. "How do we do that, though?"

"Our guns are designed to project ankhs on their transparent bodies all the time," Rudra said.

"So, the ankhs are projections?" Kimberley asked him, closely studying the graphics.

"Sure thing."

"Why not drawings? Is that not better?"

"We have rifles with ankhs drawn on them, but those are not so effective against the Booklords," Rudra replied.

"And how's that?"

"We waste money on ink redrawing those ankhs when they fade,"

Diya replied. "It's that simple."

"And the cops?" Kimberley began. "Why did they leave?"

"They've heard of us," Raghav said. "But they don't know we stay here."

"So when they saw us here, I think they got frightened," Ikshita said. "Now, they'll have to stay clear of the Rubbish Mountain."

"And what about this 'Rubbish Mountain'?" Kimberley wondered out loud, turning towards the huge landmark atop which hovered many vultures.

"What better place to hide our headquarters than a refuse dump higher than the Taj Mahal?" Khan began.

"Why did you choose this place for that?" Kimberley asked him.

"Can't you see?" the woman, Diya, said. "Nobody would want to visit a rubbish dump like Ghazipur."

"Landfill already takes up more than 50 football pitches of land," Khan chuckled. "That, right there, is why New Delhi is called the world's most polluted capital."

"Noted," Kimberley said dryly. "Can we go now?"

"No problem," Khan said. "After you tell us why you killed your friend?"

Kimberley remembered the dead man lying at her feet. "Oh, him?" she began. "He's a servant of the Booklords."

"Interesting," Rudra said.

"We need to take his body with us," Kimberley added and Khan frowned.

"And why is that?" he wanted to know.

"He's not dead," the Portwood sergeant said. "Once we leave him here, his masters will revive him and put him back on our trail without his powers."

Khan nodded at Raghav, who came forward and effortlessly flung Carl Bain's body over his right shoulder.

The group's leader followed a trail his colleagues joined. Kimberley walked up to him.

"We've been trying to retrieve the white book for many years now," he narrated, swinging his rifle to and fro. "This after we came to the conclusion that I was a Bookmaker."

"And how did you find that out?"

"For years, I had a piece of the white book in my possession, and one day I discovered by accident what it could do."

"So, you're the only true Bookmaker in your group?"

"Yes, Kim," the Indian confessed. "The others learned Shurabi and Kabbalah Ma'asit online."

"You don't say," Kimberley exclaimed, eyeing the arrogant Ikshita.

"We also studied the history of both codices before setting out to attempt their retrieval from a particular era using Albert Einstein's theory of Relativity."

"Let me guess, you're yet to succeed," Kimberley concluded. No need prolonging the lecture.

"Not yet," Diya said. "Your appearance showed us errors in our calculations and we just have to recalculate those miscalculations using improved formula we must derive from the data we've obtained from your time and space projections."

"I really don't get all that," Kimberley confessed.

"She just said we need your help to retrieve the books," Dev said.

"Oh," Kimberley let out.

"We're here," Khan announced. "Welcome to Rubbish Mountain or what is officially known as the Ghazipur Landfill."

Kimberley could only see a dirt road wounding up a man-made mountain of refuse approximately 70 meters high. Stray dogs, rats, scavenging birds of prey and thousands of human waste-pickers combed through this putrid landmark as dump trucks maneuvered its simple network of dirt roads. "Wow," she exclaimed.

"See the red lights at the top?" Khan pointed out as they went round the dump site. "They warn aircraft."

"Place was opened in 1894, reached capacity in 2002 and has been growing ever since," Diya said. "Our cities generate 180 million tons of waste each year, so this rapid growth will continue."

"The continuous dumping has severely polluted the air and ground water around here," Rudra contributed. "Local residents know that living here is extremely dangerous."

"Fires that can last for days regularly break out here due to methane gas coming from the dump," Avi took up. "People living nearby say the air is so toxic they can hardly breathe and many have complained of acute respiratory and stomach problems."

"Gross," Kimberley exclaimed. "What's your government doing about all these issues?"

Ikshita chuckled. "Nothing?"

"They think it's all due to plastics," Diya said. "I think it has to do with more than that."

Ikshita glared at the last speaker. Kimberley noticed.

"Our air pollution levels have surpassed emergency levels, Kim, and although many other activities contribute to this, we just need to recycle more waste products," Khan said as they went round another twisting bend. "Concentration of poisonous particulates in the air is now 20 times higher than the US recommended level."

"How do you live here?" Kimberley wondered.

"Yeah, about that," Khan began. He stopped before a door-like construction hugging the dump wall at the base of the humongous landfill and pressed a button on his person. Gears swiftly engaged somewhere inside the rubbish mountain and a slow whine came from the door before him. The wooden barriers disappeared into the sides of the frame lapping the refuse dump. This revealed metal doors that also slid open, cool air blasting out immediately from the gaping void leading into the Rubbish Mountain.

"Cool," Kimberley said. "So cool."

"We built a sophisticated lab and buried it under Ghazipur," Ikshita said excitedly. "The design came from yours truly."

"Ikshita is our technical geek, while Diya is our science brain," Khan explained as they all trooped into the waiting elevator inside the cool corridor.

Lights came on and Kimberley noticed ankh and cross symbols painted into the wall design all over the place, including the elevator's interior.

The decent lasted approximately 20 seconds.

The elevator doors opened to reveal more ankh and cross symbols in a hall brimming with sophisticated equipment and super computers.

"Wow," Kimberley repeated. "Do you guys really need all this?"

"We will see when we find out more from you," Diya replied.

"I've been doing well without scientific computations," Kimberley pointed out. "Well, with my friends, that is."

"We'll find out more after your treatment and refreshment," Khan told her, pointing to a door.

"Wait, treatment?" Kimberley asked him.

"We need to remove the virus from your body, first," Raghav explained, laying his human burden on the floor. He turned to Khan.

"Put him in the freezer," his leader told him. "He won't disturb us at all if he freezes over."

Avi assisted the tired Raghav to carry Carl Bain's body into another room.

"I have two questions," Kimberley began. "First, where's the freezer? And...and how will the virus be removed from my body? I hope it won't be painful."

"We have a cold room we call the Freezer," Ikshita said. "And the..."

"The virus will be removed through devirulation," Diya interrupted, ignoring Ikshita's visible annoyance. "You know it's painless, right?"

"I guess so," Kimberley said, not sure of her answer. She should know, but she couldn't trust her alternate memory's knowledge of the process. Unless something sparked off an update... "What's today's date?"

"X01.04.05," Avi said from a computer console. "Why do you ask?"

"Is that meant to be a joke?" Kimberley wondered. "I mean, that's not a date format, right?"

"Interesting," Diya observed. "You seem to be forgetting bits of your present life as a result of your transmigration."

"And what does that mean?"

"Let's nourish and clean your system first, Miss Kim, then we can continue," Khan said. "Obviously, there's so much you can teach us, and learn from us."

Rudra took Kimberley's hands. "Come Kim; let me take you to your room."

"Shouldn't you be afraid of catching the virus from me?" Kimberley asked him and he laughed.

"This place sterilizes itself, Kim," Ikshita explained. "The decontamination process started as soon as we stepped into the elevator above."

"Ikshita and I worked on that. The system rids any surface, including your skin's, of the virus," Diya revealed with pride and Kimberley rolled her eyes. Good to know.

She followed Rudra into a white room with a single bed. "Now what?"

"You have to take a bath first," Rudra told her. "Then you lie on the bed and wait for my return. Throw all your clothes into that washing machine. New clothes are in the wardrobe."

"Okay," Kimberley said. Rudra left and she undressed, making sure to remove Carl Bain's cube from her right pants pocket before throwing all her clothes into the washing machine. The white bathroom had no shower, but when she stepped in warm water soaked her from its walls as soon as she closed its door behind her. The shower stopped when she picked up the soap to lather herself and started again when she dropped the soap. "Okay, not bad," she commended. "Nice one, Ikshita." Of course, she remembered that Ikshita was the technology geek. The Indian resembled someone the Portwood officer had met before, but she still couldn't place the woman's face.

But then she just couldn't understand this group. How could these 'Bookmakers' be working to retrieve the two books with only scientific computations? Surely, the history of the codices should have told them that mysterious manifestations were involved here, not science. Unless science could finally explain how a time machine worked.

Kimberley finished in the bathroom and wrapped herself with a white towel. She stepped into the room and took out a blue T-shirt and gray jeans from the wardrobe. Now dressed, she picked up Carl Bain's package from the bed and studied it. Nothing new to see. No opening. Just a small solid cube.

Kimberley put the small item in her jeans pocket and lay on the bed to wait for Rudra's return.

"Done," he said at her door, smiling.

"What?"

"Done," the Indian repeated, entering the room. "You've been officially devirulated."

"H-How?"

"Once you lie on the bed, your body is scanned for the Mars-Cov-6 virus and any trace destroyed. The bed is the Devirulator."

"Where you watching me all this time?"

"Of course, not," Rudra said. "The process informs me when it's finished with a beep on my wrist." He brandished a wrist band on his right wrist.

Kimberley got up. "So, what are we waiting for? I'm ready for the interview, then."

"Right. This way, please."

Rudra walked ahead and Kimberley followed him. Back to the hall with all its consoles and gizmos. All her rescuers were waiting here.

"Okay," Diya said, getting up from her seat. "First thing we do is get answers to some questions."

"I have some questions for you guys first," Kimberley began.

"No problem," Khan said. "Let's hear them."

"How do I trust you guys are the real deal?" Kimberley asked him. "How do I know that you guys really want to help your people?"

"Remember I told you I'm a Bookmaker," Khan said. "You have nothing to fear. If you would like to know our Jewish names as an assurance of our devotion to Israel, no problem."

"Wrong answer. I trusted a Bookmaker once and he flipped on me and my friends."

"You're not traveling alone?" Avi asked the Portwood sergeant.

"Thought I said that before," Kimberley replied. "Two kids have been traveling with me. A boy from my town and a girl who says she is the daughter of a Bookmaker at the Mine. She started all this."

"Rachel," Khan said.

"Yeah, you would know her," Kimberley noted.

"She's the daughter of Jehoash, one of our leaders at the time. Her father gave her the white book before he was captured or killed by the

Booklords, I'm still not sure which is it."

"She used the book to escape capture," Diya continued. "If she was with you, Kim, that means only one thing."

Kimberley nodded. "Rachel had the white book with her when the three of us were together in a chopper, before we tried to escape the Bookmaker who betrayed us and...and I got separated from the kids after Rachel used the white book to transport us out of danger. Just don't know why I appeared here in India in the year X01 without them."

"Truly baffling," Dev said. "So, the guy in the freezer was after you?"

"Yes, right before my eyes, the Booklords contracted Carl Bain to terrorize, defeat and capture us. He is very useful whenever their powers cannot touch us."

"And when is that?" Ikshita asked.

"Whenever we got infected by a disease or drew ankh and cross symbols on our bodies," Kimberley replied. "This guy came after me now because I had the virus and his infernal masters could not touch me."

"Okay," Diya said. "That means we could also get information from him if we can wake him up, right?"

"Don't even think of doing that," Kimberley warned. "Only his masters can wake him up from death, and we should be happy we can't do that."

Khan frowned. "And why's that?" he asked. "We can restrain him and...voila, problem solved."

"If we can wake him up, that is," Kimberley pointed out. "It's beyond technology." She stopped short of saying that waking up the human minion was a very dangerous thing to attempt.

"Noted," Avi said. "Anything yet, Diya?"

"No," Diya replied, her fingers gliding effortlessly over her keyboard and her eyes fixed on her monitor. "Obviously, recalculating these miscalculations will take time."

"Where did you get your data for the calculations to begin with?" Kimberley wondered.

"From you, of course," the Indian scientist replied. "Since you came in here, we've been collecting data about your aura and using it to recalculate where your reincarnations have been to on Earth, back 400 years."

"Wow," Kimberley whispered. "Are you guys really scientists?"

"That's understandable," Khan said. "You don't believe us, but you have to know that scientists and spiritualists now see their separate fields as pursuing a single goal."

"Which is?"

"Knowing the origin of the universe."

"I don't believe that," Kimberley said, "but I should be dead by now if I'd lived my life the normal way, so I'm in no position to argue with you."

"Yes, you are," Dev said. "You have recent memory…"

"I call it current memory," Kimberley interrupted.

"So, you must know what is happening around you now."

"In this current life, I'm an author, not a scientist," Kimberley pointed out.

Diya cleared her throat. "Okay then, as I was saying, we've been collecting data about your aura and using it to recalculate where…"

"And what would those recalculations actually show you?" Kimberley wondered.

Diya turned to Khan, who nodded. "We think our assessment will show us two things. First of all, it will show us the best point in your travels where you and your friends could have easily retrieved the black book from space and time, so that we can contact the girl, Rachel, and go back to that time with the white book."

"You can do that?" Kimberley asked her. "I mean, find the best point in our travels where we could have easily retrieved the book?"

"Yes, Diya can make the system do that," Rudra said. "She is the best in the country."

"Secondly, we're also trying to use our supercomputers to find the hidden Hebrew words completing the sentence on the books' pages," Diya said.

"Will that work?" Kimberley asked her.

"If anyone could complete the hidden part of the Hebrew sentence, then the black book would reappear in Man's world," Ikshita said.

"Heard that before," Kimberley noted.

"We want it to appear in our headquarters," Avi aired. "That will be swell."

"So far, we've been able to narrow things down to fifty-thousand-word combinations that could complete the sentence," Ikshita revealed.

"Two Bookmakers told us about the hidden Hebrew words on the books," Kimberley said. "Their Jewish names were Mariah and…"

"And who?" Khan asked her.

"Mr. David Hoyte."

"That's not a Jewish name," Raghav said.

"I know, I must have forgotten his name," Kimberley apologized, looking at Ikshita. She now knew where she had seen that face before.

Mariah.

Ikshita was Mariah, no doubt about that. Same mannerisms. Same voice. Same face, but a different name and personality. This particular reincarnation of her old friend always seemed bitter about something. Like she was seeking revenge for something someone did to her.

Something she couldn't control.

"Kim?" Rudra repeated.

"Huh?"

"I was saying we would love to hear what those Bookmakers told you about the hidden Hebrew words?"

"Well, Mariah told us she knew that the black book was still with a human being, because the Bookmakers could still see some hidden Hebrew words on the white book," Kimberley remembered. "Mr. David Hoyte said he knew that the black book had left Earth, because the Bookmakers could not see some of the hidden Hebrew writing on the white book."

"Wow, look at that," Ikshita said.

"They both disagree on the theory that the two books could be assumed present on Earth if the Sicarii Kabbalah Masada could decipher the complete hidden Hebrew writing on either book," Kimberley added.

"They base their arguments on the meaning of the remaining visible Hebrew on the two books," Diya stated.

"Yes," Kimberley said, trying to act normal despite what she now thought she knew about Ikshita. "What do you guys think about what you just heard?"

"Since these Bookmakers only had issues with what to see on the books before either book could be assumed present or absent on Earth," Raghav began, "I think these arguments will complicate the matter."

"And why is that, Raghav?" Rudra asked his twin.

"Can't you see? Both sides disagree on the assumption that the Hebrew sentence visible to the Sicarii Kabbalah Masada has to be complete before the black book could reappear in Man's world, so it doesn't matter whether the black book is here on Earth or not."

"Can you explain further?" Khan asked his colleague.

"If Mariah is right, then the book will find us, and if the other Sikama is right, then we need to unveil the remaining hidden Hebrew before the book finds us," Raghav said. "All in all, the book will eventually find us. We only need to work on Mr. David Hoyte's theory, because Mariah's theory is already acting out if it's true."

"You're saying we only need to bother ourselves with discovering the hidden Hebrew words left?" Diya asked him.

"Exactly."

"Good point," Kimberley said. "Since that's the only thing left to do after Mariah told us her theory has always been the truth."

"So, this Mariah told you the other book will find you?" Khan asked her.

"Been thinking of that," Kimberley said, "though I still wonder if the book will literally appear like she said."

"It should if this Bookmaker you encountered is correct," Dev said. "Remember we're dealing with mystical books here."

"Yeah, another good point," Kimberley said. Right now, she could believe anything. "Can I see the word combinations your computations have brought up?" she asked Khan, who turned to Rudra.

Raghav's twin brought up the combinations on a screen.

"We would need to get to Rachel and the white book in order to see if these word combinations can help any Bookmaker or Bookbearer to discover the hidden word combination making up the Hebrew sentence on the white book," Khan told Kimberley. "I suggest we rest and do the work tomorrow since it's already late."

"And I second that," Diya began.

"Does it matter if we rest or not?" Kimberley asked. "If we find Rachel in another place and time, our being tired or hungry won't be an issue. Trust me, I know."

"I have to pack my gear before we leave," Dev pointed out.

"No need for that," Kimberley told him. "The book decides who you'll be wherever we're going, so, no need for any gear, you'll also get new equipment in the deal."

"Not true," Khan said. "I have travelled with equipment before. This becomes a more sophisticated gear if you're heading into the future, so I have to pack my gear now."

"Same here," Avi said.

"Same here," Raghav said.

"Same here," Diya said.

"Same here," Rudra said.

"Same here," Ikshita said.

"Okay, I get it," Kimberley whined. "How come I'm yet to experience changing gear during my travels?" An idea popped into her head and she turned to Ikshita. "I'll help you pack your things, dear. I need some good gear, myself."

"No problem," Ikshita said. "I'm beginning to like you."

Chapter 30
JAPAN

RACHEL blinked twice and opened her eyes. At first, she couldn't place her environment, and then she remembered the helicopter, as well as what happened inside it.

Her eyes focused on her present space and she marveled at her surroundings, which looked like a large mall with massive supporting pillars jutting up to form a gigantic roof of many arches above her tiny figure. Many people thronged the mall, laughing and talking as they carried on with their lively interactions while ignoring the little girl lying on the floor in the middle of the vast hall.

Rachel got up and noticed the white book lying on the floor near her right foot. She picked it up and looked around again.

"Looking for me?"

"Aiden! What happened to you?"

"I should be asking you the same question. Took me time to find you. Where are we?"

"I really don't know," Rachel confessed. "Place looks like a mall or something."

"We can only find out if we ask somebody," Aiden said. "C'mon."

"Is that a coat?"

"What?"

"What are you wearing?" Rachel asked him.

Aiden couldn't appreciate what he had on. "I need a mirror," he said, searching the hall for one.

Rachel brought out a smartphone from her pocket and turned on the front camera. Her friend gaped at his figure.

Aiden wore a black jacket unlike any he'd ever seen, with buttons lining up the sides. An insignia he couldn't place graced the right side of his chest. One for a boating club or some similar venture. "Well, what matters if I'm wearing a nice jacket?" he wondered. "That doesn't help us know where we are, does it?"

"We'll remember soon enough," Rachel said, studying the hall. "Where's Kim?"

"Haven't seen her," Aiden said. "I wonder what happened to her. What do we do now?"

"I don't know," Rachel said. "We might as well continue without her."

"Or we find her by writing her name in the book?" Aiden proposed.

"We'll do that if we don't find her here," Rachel said. "Right now, we have to focus on finding the Bookmaker I brought here before the Booklords arrive here. I know Samuel will help us."

"Okay." Aiden felt ashamed of the fact that he had a little satisfaction in the news that Kimberley had lost her way in the course of their timely travel. Probably due to the way he held her hand during Rachel's mysterious transportation across time and space. Did he intentionally do that? After all, he could never forget how she tortured him by blaming him for his mother's death back in Brazil. Of course, Rachel was worried about the sergeant's whereabouts. It showed on her face and shaking hands. "We'll find her," Aiden assured.

"Did you feel that?"Rachel asked her traveling partner.

"Feel what?"

"It moved," the Jewish girl said. "The hall just moved under my feet."

"Are you saying we're on a spaceship?" Aiden's confusion knew no bounds.

"Nope," Rachel said. "More like a boat?"

"Does that explain why a boat symbol is on my jacket?" Aiden asked her.

"Maybe…" Rachel's voice faltered. Maybe not.

"Hey, Greg, keep up the good work!"

The man's voice shattered their thoughts and they stared as this fellow walked up to them and shook Aiden's left shoulder. He looked Asian and wore a jacket with the same insignia on Aiden's jacket.

"But now, we need you close to the east end, Greg," he said. "Clients are confused over there."

"Sure thing," Aiden said as the man walked away.

"Touch someone."

"What?"

"Touch someone," Rachel repeated. "That way, you'll know who you are in this time and place."

Aiden helped a little boy pick up a fallen toy and instantly realized himself when he touched the boy's hand while handing over the retrieved toy. "We're in a shopping mall on FC9," he told Rachel.

"I know," Rachel said, leaving the girl whose right hand she held moments ago. "FC9 means Floating City 9."

"A floating city. The ninth one. Wonder what Kimberley would think when she sees this. A floating city."

"Aiden, I'm the mayor's daughter," Rachel said. "You brought me here to show me something."

"Eh…right. I am employed at the mall as a mall boy, but…." Aiden turned to the receding figure of his senior colleague. He frowned.

"But what?" Rachel urged.

"Something's not right here, Rachel," Aiden said. "That guy wants me out of the way when…"

"When what?" Rachel demanded.

"When…uh…" Aiden tried to remember, frowning in the process.

"Does that have to do with me lying on the floor?" Rachel proposed.

"No. You were just watching the mall's ceiling."

"Oh."

"Yes!" Aiden exclaimed. "They're going to blow up FC9, Rachel!"

"Really?" a skeptic Rachel asked him. "And remind me how you got to know about this?"

"I heard them reciting their plans in the staff lounge when I went looking for Sam."

"Who?"

"Sam…. He's my best friend here. I went looking for him and hid when these guys came in."

"These guys? Sam? Aiden, Sam could be the person we're looking for."

"No time to explain or find out, Rachel," Aiden said, pulling his fellow traveler along. "I'll do that later, but first, we have to stop them."

"What if we find Samuel and get out of here?"

"What if the place blows up before we find Samuel?"

Reluctantly, Rachel followed him past the crowd at the Café Center and down a flight of busy stairs leading to a lower deck. The breathtaking beauty of the floating city became obvious when they stepped out onto a terrace looking out at the ocean and saw the other floating cities dotted across the place.

"Wow, cool," Aiden exclaimed. "Never seen anything like this."

The buoyant super structures had three to four massive buildings jutting out from a behemoth floating base shaped like a cylindrical iceberg. Transparent tube-like bridges traversed the curvy housing structures of each floating city at various levels and Aiden could see peculiar transport vehicles moving back and forth within these tubes.

"We're in Japan," Rachel began.

"Yes," Aiden said. "That guy back there was speaking Japanese."

"We're speaking Japanese now."

"Okay?" Aiden looked around him at the busy terrace and saw few Asian faces amidst a sea of tourists. He didn't blame them. Who wouldn't want to see the beautiful scenery out there over and over again? "What's today's date?"

"X26.04.02?" Rachel said, looking at her smartphone. "Weird."

"That's crazy," Aiden said. "A different format. This must be the future."

"Of course," Rachel said. "The world has been using a new calendar dating system for like twenty years now. I now remember this from History class in school...I think."

"Thought I told you to stay at the east end, Greg?" a man standing behind them asked in Japanese.

Aiden turned to see the mall staff who earlier commended his work inside the mall. "Yeah, I...uh," the boy stumbled in the same language.

"Well, what are you waiting for? Go there already," the man snapped and stumped off, going down a flight of spiraling stairs devoid of human traffic.

Aiden followed him, pulling Rachel along.

"Aiden, what if he has a gun?" Rachel whispered.

"He won't see us."

The steps descended into a dark corridor. Aiden stopped at the edge of the lowest step in confusion.

"Why are you following me, Greg?" his target asked in the darkness, putting on a rechargeable lamp. "Thought I told you to..."

"I wanted to show Miss Dewy what the other floating cities looked like from the lower terrace here, Hiroki," Aiden lied, pulling Rachel past the man. "We won't waste time."

"Okay then," Hiroki said. "Be quick about that."

Aiden hoped he was right about a lower terrace. The sound of waves crashing on the floating city's hull and the dim evening light basking the edge of the dark passage ahead encouraged him.

The children went round a corner and another terrace rewarded their blind effort. This lonely platform lay closer to the water surface and the view from here was breathtaking.

Hiroki joined the two kids here. "What a beautiful sight," he said.

"Are you trying to blow up FC9?" Rachel asked him.

"And why would you ask him that?" Aiden blurted out.

"And why won't we damage it?" Hiroki stunned the kids with.

"Why should you?" Aiden demanded.

"Because these floating cities pollute the planet, boy," another man said as he emerged from a corridor leading to the terrace. "Making one inoperable will show the world how dangerous these badly designed super structures are for all of us."

"You guys won't succeed," Aiden said in English. "You'll all be caught and locked up."

"No, we won't, Greg," a third younger man said, stepping out from the same corridor. "Our organization has been doing this for some years now and nobody has caught any of our agents yet, and as long as we think the floating cities are bad for the planet, we'll continue doing this."

"That's Sam," Aiden told Rachel. "I never knew he was amongst the plotters."

"And I never knew you heard our plans, or part of it, Greg," Sam said. His manga hairdo and young Asian face indicated a zest for daring risk most young men of his age would gladly avoid. The youngest of the three Japanese men sounded like a born leader.

"I work here, Sam," Greg pointed out. "Gotta protect the place, since it's hard to get a job right now, you know."

"Then I suggest you find a new job," Sam said. "We're not backing out from this, because the world needs to see our resolve to save this planet."

Aiden scuffed. "Do you really think you're saving the planet by doing this? The floating cities are one of the wonders of the modern world, you know, but I can see that you guys are not happy about that."

"Last time I checked, we have conquered almost all our problems through science and green technology, Greg," his new friend said. "This is the century of sustainable development, man. Why can't we do the same thing for our oceans by using green technology to design more sustainable floating cities? Those that don't cause more harm to the planet like the ancient architects predicted years ago? Whatever happened to those green designs of the past? How did we get it all wrong?"

"Yeah, how did we end up with these gas emitters and drainpipes instead?" Hiroki asked, drawing nearer.

"What are you going to do with us now, Sam?" Rachel asked with a nervous smile, looking around for an escape route.

"I don't know, Miss Dewy," Sam said. "If only your boyfriend here had stayed out of our business in the first place.... And you can only jump into the ocean from here. Your fate is sealed now. Please, hand over your possessions, including your smartphones and that...that storybook."

*   *   *

Ikshita led the way down a flight of stairs and across a passage leading to her room. "So, what's your story?" she asked her companion, breaking the awkward silence impeding their newfound friendship ever since they left the others.

"Well, I…eh…" Kimberley could only blurt out. How could she forget how to form a sentence when it mattered the most?

"I understand," Ikshita said. "You still can't get your head around it all. That happened to…"

"I am a cop back at my town," Kimberley said. "I found Rachel on a snowy road and ended up on this journey with her after I lost my boyfriend."

"Sad to hear," Ikshita consoled, unlocking her room's door. "I know a friend who's gone through that mess and he says it's never a good feeling."

"What about you?"

"Me?"

"Yeah, how come you don't know your history?"

"About what?" Ikshita's voice had changed as she entered her room.

Kimberley hesitated. "Is it true that Khan is the only Bookmaker amongst you? Ever tried to remember your past or make something spark off some kind of memory from your 'alternate life?'"

"Alternate life?" Ikshita appeared puzzled.

"Previous life?" Kimberley prodded, following her new friend into the room.

"Never had a previous life," Ikshita said, squatting to drag out a black bag from underneath her bed. "I'm Indian by birth," she explained. "Khan's theories fascinated me, and still do, that's why I'm here."

"Really?" Kimberley wondered whether she had made a mistake about the Indian's real identity. After all, people could resemble other people. She touched Ikshita without giving this a second thought, and nothing happened.

Ikshita remained squatting, holding on to her black duffel bag.

Kimberley leaned forward to stare into the Indian's eyes and realized that the woman's pupils had disappeared, leaving a lost and confused expression on a beautiful face.

Kimberley got up and turned towards the room's door. "That settles that then," she concluded.

"Settles what?" a familiar voice asked her.

"That you're not Ikshita. Welcome back, Mariah."

"Oh, thanks," Ikshita, a.k.a. Mariah, a.k.a. Oxana, said. "I feel alternate memory flooding my brain." She got up and pressed a button on the wall to slide open a hidden aperture. Guns filled this large cupboard.

"What do you need that for?" Kimberley wondered out loud.

"Watch and see. Please don't try to stop me."

"I'll do that if you try to kill people."

"Then I have no choice, Kim, old friend," Mariah said, turning a pistol on Kimberley as she slung a classic AR-15 over her right shoulder. "I have to lock you up here for awhile."

Kimberley knocked off the pistol and Mariah spun round to floor her with a vicious right-leg kick.

"Sorry, dear. It's just for awhile."

* * *

"We can lock them up until after we damage the city, Sam," Hiroki proposed.

"Yes, that's a good idea, Hiroki," Sam said. He turned to Rachel and pointed at the book she still held in her right hand. "Hand that over as well, Miss Dewy."

"I already gave you my phone," Rachel pleaded. "Is that not enough?"

"Why do they call you Sam?" Aiden put in. "You're Japanese, right?"

"And what does that have to do with anything?" Hiroki wondered, coming to stand behind Aiden.

"You don't know why I'm called Sam, Greg?" Sam asked his friend. "Is this a joke?"

"Well, remind me again?" Aiden pleaded in a small voice.

Rachel hid the white book behind her. It felt a bit…cold?

"Not so fast," Sam told her. "Give me that storybook of yours."

"It's just a storybook," Aiden said. "You said it yourself, Sam."

"There could be a listening device in that book, Sam," the other man in the group said.

"Yes, Yoshito," Sam agreed, glaring at Rachel. "Hand over the storybook, Miss Dewy, else we'll take it by force." Yoshito stopped behind the girl. He grabbed the book.

"No, don't!" Rachel exclaimed, but the deed had already been done. The man's immobile figure stood behind her, his eyes boring a hole into the back of her head. The fellow must have touched her hand while taking the book. This means that he could have had a previous life under Shurabi! Wow. "Greg, the book is getting cold," she told Aiden.

"What?" Aiden cried. "And we have no ankh!"

"What are you too on about?" Sam snapped. He glanced at Yoshito, who stood behind Miss Dewy. "Yoshito," he said, frowning at the girl standing before this co-conspirator of his. "What have you done to him?" he asked her.

Rachel avoided the frown. "Well, eh…he…"

"What's happened to Yoshito?" Hiroki asked before deciding to step away from Aiden towards the corridor and take something near the passage entrance.

Rachel sighed and said nothing.

"What's going on?" Yoshito demanded all of a sudden. "Where am I?" Obviously, something had happened to him.

Rachel grabbed the white book when she noticed the man's uncertainty as well as the dropping temperature. She pushed Aiden away. Sam lurched towards her. The book's protective dome reappeared before the infernal windswept in from the sea and into the building's corridor. It splattered black demons on the mystical dome as it swished past. It also went through Hiroki and he cried out before crashing to the floor, his retrieved gun skidding off from his open right hand. The wind swooshed up the spiral stairs and disappeared onto the deck above.

"What's going on?" Yoshito asked again, squatting inside the dome beside the girl. He could see Samuel and another boy in the bluish transparent structure. "Samuel?"

"Glad you know his name is not Sam," Rachel said underneath the immobile Samuel. "He just became someone else."

"Just like you, Yoshito," Aiden said, trying to reach out a hand towards Rachel.

"What?"

Hellish hands penetrated the bluish glow protecting them, reaching out for the book before freezing off as mysterious ash. The icy strands from the white book held up. Rachel maintained her stance despite the freezing cold.

Aiden succeeded and a resounding blast cleared the blackness all around them, the evening sky a blessing to behold once again.

The dome disappeared.

It all happened in seconds.

"Where am I?" Samuel wondered, getting up to look around him. "What happened here?"

"The Booklords attacked, Samuel," Rachel said.

"Rachel, is that you?" Samuel turned towards the little girl's voice and saw Hiroki's body lying on the ground. "Ahab!" he exclaimed and ran to the body. "Can someone tell me what's going on?!" he cried.

Yoshito came to stand beside his kneeling figure.

"Someone brought us all here with one of the books, Samuel," Yoshito said. "You and I. And Ahab."

"Rachel did that, Azriel," Samuel said. "Now, she'll tell us why."

"True," Aiden said. "I'm so sorry it turned out this way."

"And who are you?" Yoshito, a.k.a. Azriel, asked him.

"We need to help those inside," Rachel cut in, standing up with the book close to her bosom.

"Hope we find survivors," Aiden said.

"There won't be any," Samuel said. "Those demons kill like crazy."

"We'll still go," Aiden said, pulling Rachel along with him. Azriel joined him and Samuel stood up.

The former mall worker looked back at Ahab's body before joining the others. "Those creatures will come back," he said as they walked through the passage. "I hope we have a plan?"

Rachel cleared her throat. "We need to draw ankhs on…"

"Ankhs? That's a good idea," Samuel said. The staircase leading up to the mall was lifeless. So was the mall. "I told you there won't be any living soul."

"Let's protect ourselves, first," Rachel said, brandishing a golden pen. "Found this near those bodies," she sniffed, drawing ankhs on everybody's arms. "Now, we're safe from the Gray Ones."

"They killed all these people?" Azriel exclaimed, looking around. "What are we going to do?" He had tears in his eyes.

"Azriel, hold yourself together," Samuel reminded his friend. "You've seen this before. You know this is what happens when the demons show up. Be strong."

"I have forgotten how to, my friend," Azriel said. "Never wanted to go through this again." He frowned at the two kids whose escapades had finally brought this calamity back into his life. His eyes finally rested on Jehoash's daughter. "What do you want from us, Rachel?"

A forlorn Rachel looked at her shoes. "We need your help to…to…"

"Help us end this," Aiden said. "We have the book and no one to help us."

"But you have power, boy," Azriel said. "What you two did back there have never been witnessed by the Sicarii Kabbalah Masada ever since the Romans destroyed the Mine."

"What of before that?" Rachel wanted to know. "Has such a thing been witnessed before the Romans destroyed the Mine?"

"Yes," Samuel said. He sat down on a chair close to gaming consoles. "I know someone who can help."

"And what's his name?" Aiden asked.

"Ben Haddad."

"Oh," Rachel said. Trembling, she turned to Aiden, who frowned at her.

"Okay, let's go look for this guy out there," Aiden urged.

"Let's – Let's see if there're survivors first," Rachel began.

"But..." Aiden began.

"Fine by me," Samuel said, getting up. "It will be fruitless, though."

The four survivors searched the large hall for signs of life. They saw nothing but whole families hugging one another while lying on the ground, or scattered around a father or a mother, or a particular sibling.

"Nobody deserved this," Rachel cried. She had tears in her eyes.

"If only FC9 wasn't this huge," Aiden said. He hated it all. "We'll use the elevators to check the rooms on every floor of this building."

"Waste of time," Samuel said. "We know there're no survivors. We need to leave now. The police will be here very soon. We shouldn't be waiting around when they show up."

"Suite yourself," Aiden said before Rachel tugged at his jacket. "What?"

"We mustn't forget the bigger picture, Aiden," she whispered. "Let's continue on our journey. These people are already dead."

Aiden had big eyes. "But you said we must..."

"Listen to your friend, dude," Samuel said. "Glad that you have the white book with you. We've been trying to find one of the books for years now before we lost our identity here in Japan. What you did here saved the Cause. Ben Haddad will definitely know how to stop the demons and initiate the ritual, so we must go to him now."

"Who's this Ben Haddad?" Aiden asked. "The one we've heard about?"

"And what's your name again?"

"Aiden," Rachel said. "Without his help, we'll all be dead by now."

"Good to hear," Azriel said. "Now we have to go look for old Ben using the book."

"I think I need to get something from my room before we leave," Samuel began. "A page of the white book was shared amongst us at the Mine, and that has been our means of travel ever since my friends destroyed theirs," he explained to Rachel.

"And how did they do that?" Aiden asked.

"By shredding it. It's paper, remember?"

"Oh."

"We had to destroy the pieces so that we won't think of using it again. This helped us evade the Booklords," Azriel explained.

"We decided to save my piece of paper in case we needed it in the future no matter the risk," Samuel said. "So far, the Gray Ones haven't bothered our time travels, though."

"Until you guys showed up now," Azriel pointed out.

"So sorry about that," Aiden stammered.

The group left the hall. Rachel slowed down beside Aiden.

"What's going on?" he whispered to her. "Why did you change your mind on looking for survivors all of a sudden?"

Rachel swallowed hard. "Aiden, Uncle Ben Haddad was a bad man back at the Mine."

"Okay," Aiden whispered. "How did you know that?"

"Father told me."

"But he can still help us, right?"

"He wanted the books for himself back at the Mine," Rachel whispered. "He will help only himself if we go along with this. What do we do now?"

"We must escape then. And find Kimberley."

Sirens blared outside.

"The cops," Samuel said. "Forget my paper, we have to leave now."

The survivors of FC9 went round a corner. They walked into a group of military-styled folks garbed in covert black with weapons at the ready.

"Not so fast, friend," one of the operatives said. "Just raise your hands nice and easy."

"Identify yourselves," an older fellow ordered.

"Question is, who're you guys?" Samuel began. "You don't look like Japanese police to me."

"We're not Japanese police," the first man said. "We're Sikama. Hey, where are you going?"

"What?" Samuel turned to see Jehoash's daughter scampering away with her friend. "They're with the white book!" he yelled at his new colleagues before going after the kids with Azriel.

"What? Stop them!" the commanding officer shouted, and his men surged forward. "Get them before we leave! Get them before the cops break into the city!"

Aiden took the spiraling staircase two at a time, Rachel directly behind him. They entered a side room and quietly closed its door before footsteps came trudging down the staircase outside.

"Got the pen?"

"Yes," Rachel whispered. She opened the white book and scribbled Kimberley's name. "I hope we're doing the right thing."

"They're many now, Rachel," Aiden whispered. "You know we can't risk being with that group. Sooner or later, someone's gonna want the book for himself and that will not help us."

"You're right. Hold my hand."

Outside, Samuel saw a bright blue glow underneath a door and rushed to open this closed aperture before the light went out.

The room had no occupant.

Chapter 31
SIGN OF THE TIMES

"YOU killed them."

"I had to."

"Why?"

"I have my reasons."

"I hate you." Kimberley had tears in her eyes as she sat on the floor. Khan, Avi, Dev, Raghav, Rudra and Diya. All dead. Gone. Like the wind. Killed by their own trusted friend. "Why did you kill them? You lived with them for years. You had an alternate memory, which you enjoyed with them."

Mariah said nothing as she knelt beside her old friend, the AR-15 at arm's reach. "Those guys were a separate faction of Sikama that wanted the book for themselves and…"

"How did you know that?" Kimberley demanded.

"The ankh symbols everywhere, Kim," Mariah replied. "This faction I talk of uses the ankh symbol to defend themselves against the Booklords, unlike the true Sikama, whose members use the sign of the cross. This group's idea about how to carry out the ritual is a selfish one designed to grant powers from the third book only to their members. I noticed the ankh all over the walls here, and I–I had to do what I did."

"I still don't believe you," Kimberley said. "You might as well kill me, too."

"How can you say that, Kim? You're my friend, remember?" Mariah placed her right hand on the other woman's left shoulder. "We've gone through a lot together. I was just trying to protect you."

"By killing them?" Kimberley wore her anger on her face. "Who are you right now, Mariah?" She shrugged off the other woman's hand.

"Hey, I'm still the Oxana you knew back at Chornobyl, Kim. I haven't changed."

"Make me believe you," Kimberley challenged.

"Okay." Mariah coughed and stood up, hands outstretched towards her old friend. "Let me help you up. There's something you need to see."

A curious Kimberley reached out and got up with Mariah's help. "What is it?" she demanded. What would make her change her view of the Bookmaker standing before her?

"Follow me."

Mariah picked up the AR-15 and opened Ikshita's door. She stepped out into a quiet passage made more poignant by the events she partook of an hour ago.

Kimberley stepped out as well and followed the Sicarii Kabbalah Masada through the spotless white passage.

They went back to the underground station's main hall. Mariah led Kimberley to an open laptop and brought up a recorded video from one of the hall's security cameras.

The Portwood sergeant refused to look at the body lying in a pool of blood on the floor beside the desk on which sat the laptop. The only body in the hall. Somehow, she knew it was Diya's.

"I have two things to show you," Mariah began, playing the recording. "This video shows they never trusted you."

"How did you know where to look?" Kimberley wondered.

"My alternate memory, dear. I had to put it to good use."

Another part of the station lit up on the laptop's screen. Five distinct individuals were arguing about something, ignoring the robotic camera recording silently in the background.

"How do we know she's not an imposter?" Raghav asked the others. "How do we know she's saying the truth?"

"Good point," Khan admitted. "What can we do to prove her sincerity?"

"But we've been tracking her journey," Diya began. "The system doesn't lie."

"No system is perfect," Avi said. "She might as well be a spy for the government."

Kimberley hissed and looked away. "This proves nothing," she said. "It's okay to doubt my identity in this situation. This only means that…"

"They also agreed with the Second Theory," Mariah cut in.

"What?"

"The Second Theory? None of the books are on Earth if no one can see the hidden Hebrew on the books' pages?" Mariah explained. "Only one book is present on Earth if one can only see half of the hidden

Hebrew on the available book's pages?"

"Aunt Shira and Mr. Hoyte said that as well."

"That those two said it doesn't mean they believed it and intended working with that theory. This faction of the Sikama Order does exactly that."

"But that's not true," Kimberley refuted. "We concluded that irrespective of the theories, first or second..."

"We?" Mariah hissed. "You really thought they were carrying you along, right?"

"Well, they..."

"Deceived you, dear. They made you feel at home in their midst."

"What are you saying?"

Mariah brought up another video from the laptop. In it, Diya and Khan were discussing.

"You don't believe the First Theory about the books, right?" Diya asked.

"No, I don't," Khan replied.

"I don't believe it, too."

"It is foolish to think that half of the missing Hebrew words visible on the white book's page means that the black book is still on Earth. Only the dumbest person would agree with that notion."

"So, what should I take away from this video?" Kimberley asked her guide.

"Don't you see?" Mariah sounded frustrated. "The Sikama faction I told you about also thinks the First Theory is wrong."

"And why do you think they're wrong about the First Theory?"

"Simple. The Second Theory assumes that one of the books has left our world if only half of the hidden Hebrew words on the other book can be deciphered by the Bookmakers and Bookbearers of the Order. It doesn't explain the fact that even if all the hidden Hebrew words were not visible, any one book must still be in the hands of a human to physically see that all the hidden Hebrew words were not visible."

Kimberley nodded. "You could be right."

"Of course, I am," Mariah stressed. "This is why they will never succeed."

"If you think they'll never succeed, why then did you kill them?"

"They do get in the way all the time, Kim," Mariah replied. "They would have killed me if they knew who I was before I became myself again. Thanks to you, that never happened."

Kimberley's eyes had fresh tears. She was complicit in their deaths. "So, what do you think we should do now?"

"We must forge ahead. Find the other book and perform the Ritual. I know someone who can help us."

"And who is this guy?"

"His name is Benjamin Haddad," Mariah revealed. "He will help us find the black book, perform the ritual and defeat the Gray Ones." She unruffled a piece of paper.

"How come you never directed us to this wonderful fellow back in Pripyat?"

The Bookmaker cleared her throat. "Well, I was still trying to find out what you and the kids stood for back then," she replied. "I needed to know whether you guys were affiliated with the Sikama or not, as well as which faction I could be dealing with at the time, so I diverted you to Kpakol in order to delay you and give me time to access the situation."

"I see," Kimberley whispered. "That diversion almost got us killed. No need to ask after Kpakol's whereabouts."

"I'm sorry for what happened, Kim," Mariah apologized. "His death will not be in vain."

"What's the paper for?" Kimberley wondered out loud.

"Oh, it's a piece of the white book I pried from Khan's dead hand," Mariah said. "We'll use it to find the kids and the white book. Then we can look for Ben Haddad."

"And what happens to this place?"

"Already set explosives around here."

"You what?" Kimberley stared at the other woman. "Mariah, that's inhuman!"

"Nothing is fair on Earth, Kim. You of all people should know that," Mariah retorted. "Besides, blowing up this place will eliminate your little headache as well. Now, what's his name?"

"Carl Bain?"

"Exactly." Mariah picked up a pen lying on the dead Diya's desk and prepared to scribble a name on the mystical piece of paper she had earlier brought out. "Now, hold my hand and..."

"Mariah, something's happening," Kimberley observed, looking around. At the shifting images of the hall's walls and equipment. At the unstable floor dizzying her out. "What's happening?"

"Someone must have written your name in one of the books," Mariah said, grabbing Kimberley's right hand. "It gets bumpy when that happens to me."

"I can't see you!" Kimberley shouted before oblivion embraced her.

*   *   *

Carl Bain opened his eyes to sunlight streaming in from above. He looked down to see his battered body slowly fleshing out in a disturbingly horrible manner. Muscle fibers blackened by an unknown disaster were changing color, merging together and attaching back to brittle bone becoming white porcelain-like masterpieces right before his very eyes. Blood vessels and nerve threads ran down this biological transformation in various directions as they pierced origins and insertions in the course of this mysterious physiological exercise.

The human minion moved his left upper limb and felt intense pain at his joints. He welcomed the appearance of new skin wrapping up this transformation since this major tissue eliminated the pain as it covered his entire body.

Looking around for the first time, Carl Bain noted the devastation caused by the explosion he did not witness. This bomb had caused a gaping hole at the top of the structure through which sunlight spilled down to his supine body from above. He sat up and thanked his infernal masters for bringing him back to life.

"Someone's down here!" a voice called out from above him. "And he's alive!"

Carl Bain looked up and saw several police and fire service men looking down through the aperture above him.

"Hey, mister, what happened here?" an officer called down to him.

"I-I don't know," the American hustler replied.

"Hang on down there," the policeman said. "We'll help you out. Hey! What's happening?!"

An officer screamed terribly and careened off the edge of the crater formed by the bomb blast, landing with a thud beside Mr. Bain. One by one, the dead bodies fell into the damaged structure underneath Rubbish Mountain, crashing to the floor all around the surprised naked thug, until no officer stood atop the gaping hole, or anywhere near the Sikama's secret headquarters.

The Gray Ones appeared all around the huge hole, their blank faces evoking a sense of apprehension in their human minion down below.

"Thank you," Carl Bain said, standing up with gratitude. He nodded at the demonic leader materializing in the hole with him. "Yes, I'll do whatever you want me to do. I won't fail you again."

*   *   *

Again, there were prophecies and rumor mongering by proponents of war. In X35.08.30, the nuclear arms race boasted a total of 500 countries, while only four nations had the most advanced explosive weaponry. Up to this date, science and technology had enjoyed a dizzying period of mind-boggling discoveries and inventions that had changed the world for the better, causing the addition of economics, climate and environmental activism to the list of job descriptions detailed at the World Museum of Redundant Occupations.

The best brains in mega companies had kept up the so-called techno-scientific revolution by filling the world with inventions of such brilliance that even better energy sources were deemed necessary for the good of all.

A need eventually fulfilled by the discovery of commercial quantities of Compound V, which finally banished nuclear energy to the doomsday list of destructive matter and gave rise to better vehicles with which Mankind could visit other planets and go beyond charted galaxies. The discovery of this cheap and efficient energy source also evolved communication gadgetry so much as to usher in the age of *TelepathyG*, rendering *XiG* obsolete, and making mind control communication a possibility.

Of course, the smartphone, the generic car module, and the jet engine lost their relevance after this milestone, becoming ancient relics fit for only collectors, artistic playboys and the halls and corridors of the world's most renowned museums.

In the field of Planetology, the Earth headquartered the Federation of Earth-like Planets or FEP. This body coordinated the various Earth-like discoveries Mankind had made over the years, making the advances in science and technology available to the many companies investigating new planets with habitable promise. However, despite the marathon breakthroughs supporting world development and galactic frontiers, these Earth-like planets struggled with enormous challenges in their terraforming processes and were yet to be the viable vehicles of human migration their billionaire founders envisaged. Hence, primary Earth's population could only be controlled until techno-science could make these potentially habitable planets habitable. The science of population control became the golden egg and companies looking into population control sprouted all over the globe.

Technology for Population Control or TPC had research facilities in almost all the capitals of the world.

Kimberley woke up in such a research facility.

"What's this place?" the Portwood sergeant demanded, looking at the woman standing before her and holding her hand. "Mariah? Is-Is that you?"

"Yes, Kim," Mariah replied. "In this establishment, I am an enhanced biologist and you're my personal body guard."

"Personal guard? H-How did we get here?"

"One of your friends must have written your name in the book, dragging you forward in time to this future. I was lucky to have correctly identified what was happening and grab your hand back in India when you started seeing double."

Kimberley marveled at the sci-fi environment all around her. The elevating platform with no cables attached. The transparent wall panels adequately equipped for *TelepathyG* communication. The revolving security doors opening at the wave of a hand. The mini no-wheels platform transporting individuals and groups of individuals around the large hallway. She also marveled at the fact that she knew the principles behind these technologies. "Why do I think that today is X35.08.30?"

"Because, you're right," Mariah said. "Look, it took me some time to figure out who I am and how I got here, but we don't have time to lose. Rachel and the boy will be looking for you right now and we don't want to keep them waiting."

Kimberley followed her. "Where're we going?"

"To my office. We'll be safe in there."

"From the Gray Ones? They're demons, remember?"

"Yes, I do. I was talking about their human servant."

"The ankh can defend us against..."

"The cross, you mean..."

"Whatever," Kimberley let out. "We just need a sharpie or some indelible ink."

"I have some markers in my office," Mariah said before the footsteps behind her stopped. "What now?" she asked her body guard, turning to see why the other woman had stopped.

Kimberley heard a freezing sound to her left. She stared as the rotating doors swung round and vomited two men into the lobby. They were dressed like her. "Something's going on here apart from population research, right?"

"You're a security personnel here. You should know," Mariah said, turning away.

"Yeah, I knew what they were doing before you touched me," Kimberley said, moving forward. "I'm just knowing again after you touched me." Technology for Population Control might as well be The Plutonium Company.

Mariah's cozy office had a small lab attached to it. "There is talk of war, Kim," she said, looking for a sharpie in her drawers. "That's why TPC is now producing weapons grade Plutonium-239."

"The primary fissile material for nuclear weapons in the '90s. Why are they still using it?"

"Cause it still works," Mariah said, drawing a cross on her arms and handing over the marker.

Kimberley drew ankhs on her arms. "What next?"

"We look for the kids."

"Okay." Kimberley saw the futuristic weapon hanging on the wall near Mariah's window and took it down.

"Yeah, it's yours," Mariah replied to her inquisitive look. "You left it there before you went out this afternoon."

"And you followed me outside, intending to change me when I wasn't armed."

"The proper precaution," Mariah murmured.

"Okay, you have a point there." Kimberley looked the weapon over and 'rewarmed' it. She marveled at the word. "Lazer?"

"Yes," Mariah said. "High grade lazer. It kills instantly." She picked her lab's coded keys from her desk and closed her blinds by waving her hands. "Let's go."

"Where are we, exactly?"

"K9235.88."

"Is that supposed to be the name of a city or what?"

"Cities have no names now. They ditched that a long time ago."

"Yes, I know," Kimberley said, scratching her head. "We should be in…"

"C'mon, girl," her mistress urged her. "We have no time to waste."

Outside, the streamlined boxes floating on the major roads and gliding past at breakneck speeds baffled Kimberley. "What's the tech behind that?" she wondered.

"Elevator V," Mariah replied, stopping before what should be a car park. Only more of the streamlined boxes lined the space from end to end. Mariah pressed a button on her key and one of the boxes beeped. "There's my system."

"You mean your car, right?"

"Vehicle is a better word."

"Wow."

Silent motors swung open the system's doors and Mariah entered first. Kimberley noted the four stands jutting out of the vehicle's four edges to keep it above ground before she joined her friend inside. Mariah's lean figure sat on one of the opposing long sofas stretching across the system's sparsely lit interior. "No controls?" Kimberley asked as she sat down. "So what do we do now?"

"I want to use the system's UTS1 to track down your friends."

"Aiden and Rachel? Have you noticed there are so many boys and girls on the streets outside right now? Holding hands?"

"UTS1 is a Universal Tracking System," the Sikama explained, typing orders into a *TelepathyG* screen she materialized on her right arm. "It also measures human vital signs so we won't miss any heightened heart rates or blood pressure levels coming from any boy and girl duo on the streets."

Kimberley gaped at the virtual *TelepathyG* screen. How did Mariah do that?

"Found them!" the other woman said. "They're heading over to Street K9235.80 right now."

The streamlined vehicle came to life and left the ground. Kimberley heard humming as the cube system retracted its four legs and left the park. "Sure it's the kids?"

"Nope, but it's worth checking out."

"No driver?"

Mariah frowned at Kimberley.

"Of course, I knew that." A nervous giggle followed.

The streamlined box swooped out of the area and joined other Elevator Vs on the main road. Mariah charted a route on her *TelepathyG* screen and the mysterious technology disappeared into her wrist band.

The Elevator V arrived at what looked like a school district. "We're here," Mariah said. "Keep your eyes open for your friends. A boy and a girl wearing brown and green cardigans respectively. They will…"

"Aiden! Rachel!" Kimberley moved to open the vehicle's magic doors and they peeled back automatically. "Good to see you guys again."

"Kim!" Rachel shouted, running towards the police officer. "I thought we've lost you."

Kimberley hugged the little girl. "It's okay, dear. I'm still here. A lot has happened since we parted ways after Greenland." Aiden didn't look too glad to see her again.

"Hi," he said timidly.

"Hi," she replied with a smile. Awkward.

"Mariah!" Rachel shouted, jolting Aiden. She hugged the Bookmaker and turned to Aiden. "Remember Mariah?"

"Why not?" Aiden blurted out, hands in pocket. "Who wouldn't?" He thought of his mother.

"What's wrong with him?" Mariah asked Rachel. "What has happened since I last met you guys?"

"A lot," Kimberley and Rachel chorused.

"We brought Kim here with the book," Aiden explained. "Then we came to her."

"And I tagged along," Mariah said. "I hope it will be worth it."

"The world is…preparing for war?" Rachel asked herself. "Read that from someone's *TelepathyG* screen right now."

"Yeah, there are war rumblings. Two countries want to go to war," Mariah said. "They've been showcasing their various weapons, both nuclear and conventional."

"And how did you know that?" Aiden asked.

"I'm an enhanced biologist," the Sikama said, "and my company is now building nuclear weapons."

"Wow," Aiden said. "We can leave this place right now?"

"I'm a guard in the research facility where Mariah works," Kimberley added. Nobody laughed. "What now? Where do we go from here?"

Mariah cleared her throat. "We have to..."

"I wonder whether Aunt Shira and Uncle Ezra were right about the other book," Rachel cut in. "Is it still here with us on Earth or has the Booklords taken it?"

"But I told you, dear," Mariah began. "Shurabi and Aiden's visions of the black book point us to the truth."

"Your version of the truth," Kimberley corrected.

"The truth, Kim," Mariah emphasized. "David Hoyte and Aunt Shira lied to you."

Kimberley frowned. "You killed those people in cold blood, Mariah."

"Killed which people?" Rachel began.

"All in the past," Mariah said. "I did it to help us in a tight spot in India, Kim."

Kimberley's frown deepened. "It's not..."

"You were in India?" Rachel asked her, eyeing Mariah. The little girl no longer trusted the Bookmaker.

Kimberley sighed. "Uh, yes, we..."

Rachel disappeared.

"Where did she go now?" Aiden wondered, looking around.

"And she has the book!" Kimberley cried.

"No, she doesn't." Aiden raised the volume for her to see.

"Is that..."

"The book?" Aiden helped. "Turned into this gadget when we arrived here."

"The books can evolve," Mariah explained. "They change with the times."

"So what just happened to Rachel?" Aiden asked her.

"Someone with paper from the book just wrote her name on it," Kimberley reasoned. "We have to go to her through her name on the book."

Aiden frowned. "Which one?"

"Anyone," Kimberley said. She took the book from the boy and flipped it on. "Hold hands, everyone."

"Remember your gun," Mariah told her, going into the Elevator V and coming out with the weapon.

"Really? Do we need it?" Aiden asked.

"The weapon could become another weapon," Mariah said. "It has happened to me."

Kimberley slung the futuristic weapon over her right shoulder and opened the white book again. She searched for Rachel's name and scrolled down to it. The name had a bluish glow and she marveled at this phenomenon. "Hold hands," she repeated and pressed the glowing name with her right thumb once she knew the others had obeyed her directive.

As usual, flashing scenes sped past and a crazy wind sucked the three individuals into a vortex. Darkness finally swallowed everything.

Chapter 32
TWO FACTIONS OF THE SIKAMA COIN

BRIGHT light enveloped the three time-travelers and they realized a different environment surrounded them when their eyes adjusted to the light. It all looked like the hold of a cargo plane.

"Rachel!" Aiden called out.

"Aiden, let's know where we are and the dangers we face before you announce our presence," Mariah whispered.

"Sorry."

Kimberley turned to Aiden. He wore a brown ensemble with so many zips and futuristic gadgetry, and held a kind of spongy sophisticated tool she had never seen before. "What's with the overall?" she asked him.

"What's with the military uniform?" he asked her, nodding towards Mariah.

Kimberley noticed that the other woman wore a white version of the tight-fitting blue garb she had on.

This uniform had a speaker *TelepathyGi* unit held in place by Mariah's right ear. A high collar attached to a broad band wrapped around Mariah's neck, while stiff shoulder protectors held in place by visible bands underneath the Bookmaker's armpits covered both shoulders.

Mariah's uniform tapered down to her waist and broadened beneath a black belt lined with small bags and a pistol's holster. The leotard-like attire extended down to her legs and ended inside tough-looking boots.

"Looks like we're in a plane," Kimberley whispered.

"We'll be in one if we had gone back in time," Mariah pointed out.

"We're in a spaceship," Aiden said, looking around him. "A very big one."

"And you have a very big gun, Kim," Mariah said.

"Oh." Kimberley realized she held an enormous black futuristic gun with a cube-shaped muzzle emanating a bluish glow. Display buttons letting off blue light lined the sides of this super equipment, making squeaky computerized sounds as they brightened and dimmed. "Wonder how to use this thing," Kimberley said. "It has no trigger."

"Check out the black button on the side," Mariah said.

The blue flash whizzed out from the weapon's muzzle and disintegrated the equipment sitting before them as well as the table on which sat this equipment. Kimberley's mouth remained open.

"Hey, we have intruders in Cargo Bay 2!" the speaker above their heads cranked out before falling silent again.

Aiden frowned. "Intruders?"

"I think that means us," Mariah said, looking around. "We need to get out of here." She drew her pistol and admired it. "Hmmmmmm."

"There's the door," Kimberley pointed out, moving towards a square outline on the white wall. "No handle, how do we open it?"

The door slid open and the three time-travelers froze in their tracks. Those outside the bay also paused in motion.

"That's how," Aiden said.

"She has a Q-gun!" one of the men on the other side of the door realized. "Open fire!"

Kimberley pushed Aiden away from a lazer blast, diving in the opposite direction. She fell behind cargo as she saw Mariah shooting at the newcomers while dodging lazer fire. Raising the Q-gun, the Portwood sergeant swung it out around the wooden crate protecting her and saw her opponents scatter like flies. She had not even opened fire!

"Run for your lives! Abandon ship!" the speaker above crackled.

"Abandon ship?" Aiden looked at Kimberley across the bay behind some cargo. "They fear your gun, Kim."

"Yes, they do," Mariah chuckled.

"Why am I wearing the same uniform with these people?" Aiden wondered.

"We'll find out soon enough," Kimberley allayed.

"There they go, running like rabbits," Mariah said, looking out through the many round windows surrounding a part of the storage compartment. Escape pods were flipping out of the space vessel in droves.

"Rachel!" Aiden shouted again.

"That may not be her name here," Mariah told him.

"Why did they call us intruders?" Kimberley wondered, picking herself up.

"That's the question we need to ask," Mariah said, looking at the wall near the door. Her attention had been drawn to a symbol on this part of the wall. "Look at that," she told the others.

"Look at what?" Kimberley asked.

"It's an ankh symbol," Aiden said.

"It's a relief on the white wall," Mariah said.

"So?" Kimberley looked at the white wall.

"Keener eyes would have missed it."

"And?"

"It's an ankh, Kim. My Sikama faction goes with the cross symbol, remember?"

"Yeah, I remember," Kimberley said.

"And why is that important?" Aiden asked.

"There are two factions of the Sicarii Kabbalah Masada with two conflicting theories about the meaning of the hidden Hebrew words in the two books," Kimberley explained. "Mariah's faction protects themselves from the Booklords using the cross symbol instead of the ankh."

"I see," Aiden said.

"So, we're members of the Cross Sikama in this time, right?" Kimberley asked Mariah.

"Yes, we are."

"No, I'm not," Kimberley said. "It means nothing to me."

"You have no choice," Mariah said. "Let's get to the control room and secure it."

The three adventurers left the cargo bay and moved down a white passage.

"Obviously, this is a cargo ship," Mariah said.

"Why do you think so?" Kimberley wondered.

"This is the length of the ship. Those doors along this passage lead to cargo holds like the one we just left," the Bookmaker replied. "The ship's cockpit lies ahead of us."

"Mariah, how come you know so much about this ship?" Aiden asked.

"We reviewed Class B Wellington XC Cargo ships built by Wellington Constructions from X10.02.40 to X31.02.40 before embarking on this mission," the Sikama said.

"Mission?" Kimberley frowned. "So, we're really intruders?"

"Yes, we are."

A small elevator took the three time-travelers up to the control room, which was a spacious hall with all sorts of humming consoles and flashing lights. Obviously, Mariah knew her way around.

"There's nobody here," Aiden said.

"They all left," Kimberley aired. "This Q-gun must be huge." She caressed the weapon.

"Done," Mariah announced, shutting down a computer system. "We're on autopilot now, heading to our Earth's moon."

"And what were we on before?" Aiden wondered.

Mariah laughed. "They set the ship to switch off ten seconds from now and limp into space. We couldn't have restarted it, and we would have all died in here when our oxygen ran out."

"Or we would have left the ship with the white book after finding Rachel," Kimberley pointed out.

"What if Rachel has left the ship and we're the only ones in it right now?" Aiden reasoned.

"We won't find out if we don't start looking for her right now," Mariah said.

"And how do we go about doing that?" Kimberley demanded.

"My *TelepathyGi* system has mapped out the ship's design and tracked life forms within its shell."

Aiden was all ears. "And?"

"And I spotted life forms in Cargo Bays 3, 4, 22 and 45," Mariah continued. "We gotta check out Cargo Bay 22. The life form in there is feminine."

"Feminine and human?" Aiden began.

"Yes, but we can only know for sure by going there," Mariah said. "Let's go."

"We'll check all the cargo bays you mentioned," Kimberley said, brandishing her big gun. "I don't trust that *TelepathyGi* system."

"As you wish," Mariah said. "Not because of your Q-gun, remember that."

Cargo Bays 3, 4 and 45 harbored strange animals.

"Remains 22," Kimberley said, approaching the cargo bay. The door slid open and revealed a young girl sitting on the farthest end of the compartment's floor.

"Rachel!" Aiden shouted, running up to her. "Seeing you have never felt so good."

"They took the book!" the little girl exclaimed. "They said they will do with it as they pleased."

"Then we need to look at the ship's captain's log and know what's happening here," Mariah said. "They must have a secret base on the Moon." She hurried out of the cargo bay. "I'm going back to the control room to find the log."

"Did they torture you?" Kimberley asked Rachel.

"No, but they weren't nice, either." Rachel wore a futuristic contraption of pink sleeves and brown leggings complete with a brown corset wound round her waist atop a flared purple skirt. "What do you think they will do with the book?"

"I don't know," Kimberley said. "Maybe they'll look for someone who can do something."

"Maybe look for Ben Haddad?" Aiden quipped.

Kimberley turned to him. "That name just keeps popping up, doesn't it?"

"The men back at FC9 said they will help us by taking the book to him."

"What's FC9?" Kimberley wondered out loud.

"Floating City 9," Aiden replied. "We stayed on it back in Japan, before we brought you forward and then Rachel disappeared."

"Did these men have a piece of the white book?"

"Yes, Samuel had a piece of the book." Aiden frowned. "Come to think of it, he could have followed us here."

"That makes sense," Rachel said. "They will come after us if they have the means."

"Mariah, anything on the captain's log?" Kimberley asked the Bookmaker in the cockpit through *TelepathyGi.*

"Yes," Mariah said. "In their haste, they forgot to take the white book with them. It's in Cargo Bay 4."

"A creepy thing is in there," Aiden reminded everyone.

"Let's hope the Q-gun can scare the creature into inaction," Kimberley said.

Cargo Bay 4 opened to reveal a swollen animal snorting like a pig despite powerful jaws that harbored huge fangs.

"Mariah, are you sure the book is in here?" Kimberley asked the Sikama. "No sign of any book here."

"You have to go round the big guy," Mariah told her. "Find a way to…"

The Q-gun's whiz scared the hybrid daring the three time-travelers and it drew back to a corner of the compartment. The white book lay on a pedestal at the farthest end of the bay. A black pistol lay beside it.

"Wow," Rachel said, looking at the behemoth animal grunting a few feet from the pedestal. "No wonder they didn't bother to get the book before running away."

"It's now a normal book again?" Aiden frowned in his confusion.

"How do we get the book, Kim?" Rachel asked, looking at the frightening creature grumbling at a corner of the bay.

Kimberley brandished her weapon. "Stay behind me."

The creature guarding the book backed into its sleeping quarters as the humans moved into its lair. Its massive snout hid half of its face and its fangs looked dreadful up close.

"Got it," Rachel said, stepping away from the pedestal with the ancient volume. She backed Kimberley. "I took the gun, just in case."

"Good, let's get out of here," the Portwood sergeant said. "That thing has been dreaming of eating us ever since we came in here." She fired off another shot from the heavy gun and the animal cringed when a part of its sleeping quarters disintegrated.

The humans got to the bay's massive doors and closed it behind them. The creature within growled and honked in anger, thumping around in frustration.

"Phew," Kimberley let out. "Let's go to the control room."

"Expecting you guys," Mariah quipped through her *TelepathyGi* communicator.

The trio had left Cargo Bay 4 open. Aiden peered into this compartment as he passed it. "Kimberley, look," he exclaimed.

"What's wrong now?" Kimberley stopped to follow the boy into the bay.

Aiden pointed at one of the cargo bay's round windows. Rachel looked and drew back in alarm.

"Wonder how long they've been there," Kimberley whispered.

"What is it?" Mariah demanded from the cockpit.

"The Gray Ones are outside the ship," Kimberley told her. "That means Carl Bain could be with them."

"They can't come in," Aiden said. "The ankhs will keep them out."

"And Carl Bain can't force his way in, because he won't have his powers to do so."

"Just be careful," Mariah said. "Be on the lookout for that guy. He's crazy."

"As long as there are ankhs in the ship, they can't come in," Kimberley said. She felt one of the demons' hollow faces roaming over her body, its slender fingers sliding silently across the heavy glass controlling the ship's interior environment. "Hate these things," she grumbled.

"Someone's here, Kim." Mariah's voice trembled.

"Who?"

"The ship's captain."

*　　*　　*

"Let me have the book and, and I'll be on my way," the man said, holding Mariah from behind while pointing a weapon at her chin. "I see you have a Q-gun."

"Scared of a Q-gun?"

"Don't try me, woman."

"You ought to give up now, captain," Kimberley kept the weapon pointed at the man.

"We will let you go, if you simply let our friend go right now, sir," Rachel said, her weapon unwavering. "Why do you think you can succeed with four of us against you?"

"You'll know when it's too late," the captain said. "Now, hand over the book."

"Not on my life," Kimberley said. "When this is over, I'm gonna arrest you."

The captain laughed. "It will be over for you guys alright, very soon."

"Aiden, now!"

Aiden slapped the spongy material he'd had with him all this while on the back of the captain's neck and the fellow froze before him. "Glad to be of service," he murmured.

Mariah wriggled out of her captor's arms and pulled the X54 pistol from his right hand. "What's that thing you used on him?"

"It's a paralyzer," Aiden said. "I think it paralyzes any animal."

"I can remember now," Kimberley aired. "Aiden, my alternate memory tells me you work on this ship as an Animal Pacifier, whatever that means."

Rachel giggled and Aiden frowned at her.

"No wonder you had on their uniform," Mariah said with a laugh. She looked at the human statue once her captor and smiled. "Too bad. He just failed his mission."

Kimberley stopped before the group and raised an old-fashioned sharpie. "We need to protect ourselves with ankhs."

"And crosses," Mariah added.

"Suit yourself." Kimberley used the permanent pen on her arm.

The others took turns with the sharpie.

"Where did you get it?" Rachel wondered aloud.

"In one of the cargo bays," Kimberley replied.

"They use it to mark the animals being transported," Aiden said, feeling pleased with himself.

"Is that the Moon?" Rachel wondered, staring at the cargo ship's main monitor.

"Yes, that's the Moon, and we just arrived." Mariah sat down on the pilot's seat. "I'm shutting down auto pilot."

Rachel was amazed. "You know how to work this thing?"

"She trained for it," Kimberley said, beginning to appreciate the situation. "We are meant to save Rachel from this ship. Thing is, who organized it?"

"The Cross Sikama," Mariah said. "You should know that by now."

"Not that," Kimberley said. "I mean, who is their leader?"

"Better still," Aiden cut in, "are we supposed to land on the Moon?"

"No need for that," Mariah said. "Once we land, we leave with the book."

"Leave for where?"

"To see someone who can help us end this," Mariah said.

"And who is that?" Kimberley asked.

"Are we supposed to land on the Moon?" Aiden repeated.

"No," Mariah told him, "but landing on the Moon is not a bad idea."

"Who will help us end all this, Mariah?" Kimberley repeated. "Ben Haddad?"

"He's a bad man," Rachel warned. "Father told me that."

"He worked with your father, Rachel," Mariah said. "If there's anyone who could help us now, it's him."

"I guess he's worth a shot," Aiden said and Kimberley frowned at him. "Samuel wanted us to go see this guy, Kim," he defended.

"Look, guys, we have no other options," Mariah argued. "Our enemies want to take the book to him, so why shouldn't we do so as well?"

"If they want to take the book to this fellow, why do you call them our enemies, Mariah?" Rachel asked the Sicarii Kabbalah Masada.

"Maybe they'll kidnap him or something," Mariah added. "We shouldn't wait to find out, should we?" Nobody continued the argument. "I guess that's a 'no.' Now, let's end this."

"What about him?" Aiden asked, pointing at the ship's captain's living statue. "Should we leave him on the ship?"

"As long as nobody revives him by slapping his neck with that paralyzing agent, he's fine right where he is now," Mariah said, guiding the Class B vessel to its landing port. The ship's descent was uneventful, and it soon landed on the port. "There," she finally said. "Time to get out of here."

"Wellington XCX12, you are surrounded," the *TelepathyGi* communicator crackled. "Power down and exit the ship if you want to live. This is Samuel, by the way."

"Samuel?" Rachel's mouth remained open.

"The guy you met on FC9?" Kimberley asked her.

"Yes," Aiden said. "This means they chased us here."

Kimberley crossed her arms. "Go on."

"Samuel and his friends wanted to take us to Ben Haddad when they realized Rachel's real identity."

"That was the right thing to do," Mariah said.

"The right thing?" Kimberley frowned as she turned to the last speaker. "How come you still see them as enemies, then?"

"That they wanted to do the right thing doesn't mean they were the good guys, Kim," Mariah explained. "It simply means they knew the right thing to do. Whatever they use this knowledge to do will be up to them."

"You really know how to win an argument," Kimberley grumbled.

"Landing on the Moon was a bad choice," Rachel began.

"Makes no difference," Kimberley said. "We're leaving right now, eh, Mariah?"

"Exactly."

"Not really," someone said behind them and they all looked up. The ship's captain seized Rachel from behind and the little girl flung away the white book before her assailant snatched her weapon and pointed it at her chin. "Don't move!" the man warned Kimberley when she made to step forward. "Just hand over the book."

"I thought you guys said he will be paralyzed until we revive him?" Kimberley asked Mariah.

The weapon went off, startling everyone except the shooter, who brought the gun's hot muzzle closer to his victim's face. "Give me what I want right now or I'll destroy her face right here right now!"

Kimberley nodded at Aiden and the boy kicked the book back to the captain since he was very close to the ancient volume.

The man forced Rachel to bend down and pick up the mystical volume. He backed out of the control room still holding the little girl as cover. "Nobody moves or she dies," he snapped, getting to the double exit doors and punching the buttons that opened it. He soon slipped out with Rachel and punched buttons outside the room.

Rachel stamped her foot on her captor's boot, distracting the man enough to jump away from his grasp. Kimberley swung her weapon up and the blue whiz slammed the closing door, blowing away the double structure and flinging the Ankh Sikama behind the doors out into the long passage stretching all the way down the ship's length.

The time-travelers rushed into the passage as the fallen captain picked himself up and grabbed the white book before scampering down the passage. Kimberley shot at him again.

The man anticipated the shot and crashed to the ground before it got to him. The destructive blue wave swept over his prone body and he got up and disappeared round a corner.

318

"He's heading for the escape pods!" Kimberley shouted. "Quick, we must not let him leave the ship. You know what that means for the book."

"Yes," Aiden cried. "Carl Bain and his friends are still outside!"

Rachel joined her friends as they raced down the long passage to the junction where a perpendicular corridor crossed the longer passage. The fleeing captain slammed the door of an escape hatch. Kimberley fired at the hatch's door, blowing it open.

"He's gone!" Mariah cried, stopping before the smoldering door. She heard the escape pod crash to the ground outside. "They will swarm in here now."

"This is all your fault," Kimberley snapped. "We could have left a long time ago."

"Better still, we could be in luck if they actually kidnapped Ben Haddad," Mariah said.

"And why would they actually do that?" Rachel began.

"Because they're a different faction?" Mariah replied. "The Ankh Sikama will…"

"Oh, stop that bullshit," Kimberley snapped. "Tired of hearing that."

Mariah looked hurt. "But it's the truth, Kim."

Shouting and lazer fire echoed outside.

"What're they shooting at?" Aiden wondered.

Kimberley checked her Q-gun. "We need to get out there and get back the book. It will be very dangerous, so the kids will stay back."

"But I want to go…," Aiden began. "We can do some good, you know."

"Or die trying," Kimberley added. "You have a *TelepathyGi*. We'll call you when we need you."

Mariah brandished her weapon and drew nearer Kimberley.

"We jump out through this escape hatch and find cover," Kimberley said. "We'll know what next to do when we get there." She switched her weapon's action to 'daze.'

Mariah nodded. Her hands trembled.

Kimberley faced the open escape hatch, beyond which she could see nothing. "Now!"

Both women hurried down the length of the hatch and jumped out. The glaring lights and blaring noise from many lazer firearms stunned them at first, but they fell back into darkness and the flashing lights vanished.

"We're underneath the ship," Kimberley whispered, peering out of the cargo boxes blocking the lights. The spaceport had few buildings in the middle of a desert-like rocky terrain the Moon boasted as its surface.

A firefight between the humans and their infernal visitors had ensued. Nobody had the upper hand at the moment.

"They're shooting at the Booklords," Mariah whispered.

"And the book's dome is already in place!" Kimberley observed. "Our captain friend is freezing in there."

She spun round at the presence behind her and let off a shot from her huge weapon. It smashed into Carl Bain and pushed him into some cargo boxes behind the hiding female duo.

"He doesn't have his power," Kimberley said.

"They're shooting lazer ankhs at the demons," Mariah pointed out. "That must be affecting him."

Kimberley shot the human minion again and he collapsed before both women.

"He's no threat to us. Let's get the book," Mariah urged, stepping around the huge cargo boxes before her and putting her gun into use. "C'mon, Kim," she persuaded her friend. "The Booklords are distracting them."

Kimberley followed her. "What do we do?"

"We kill as many as we can!"

Kimberley looked surprised. "What if we just stun them? No need to kill them, right?" Her colleague had already sped into the battle, shooting anyone in her way. "Right." Kimberley looked at Carl Bain's body for the last time before stepping out into the light and noise of those killing and being killed.

Her huge Q-gun stunned those who got in her way. The strange weapons displaying ankhs instead of spewing lazer marveled her and she slung two of these over her right shoulder as she headed for the white book's freezing protective dome.

Kimberley scattered the demons surrounding the mystical hemisphere with one of the new weapons in her arsenal and the dome disappeared. "Get up and raise your hands!" she ordered the cargo ship's captain cowering on the ground before her.

The man obeyed her and she pulled the white book from his right hand. "Now, you must…"

Mariah came up beside Kimberley and shot the man twice.

"What did you do that for?!" Kimberley boiled.

"I had to, Kim," Mariah said. "He would have done the same thing to us if he had the chance."

"Kim, can we come out now?" Aiden's clear voice came through on the *TelepathyGi*.

"We're coming back, Aiden," Kimberley replied, glaring at her Sikama friend. "Still think this Ben Haddad was brought here after being kidnapped?"

"No," Rachel relayed through her communicator. "I still think he's bad news, Kim."

"No need to find out if he's here," Mariah said, ignoring the little girl. "I think we should leave now if we're to avoid future situations we may not be able to control." Her head directed the other woman's eyes to look out over the Moon's rocky landscape. A space vehicle quickly approached the spaceport from the east.

"More men," Kimberley noted.

The female duo raced back to the ship.

"How do we get back into the ship?" Kimberley asked.

"No worries," Aiden said from within the spacecraft. "We're back in the control room and we just figured out how to open the main exit."

"Just go to the right of the long shaft, Kim," Rachel directed the two women outside.

An opening exit door awaited them on this side of the cargo vehicle. Getting back in became a piece of cake.

"These men were a different faction of the Sikama," Mariah repeated after she had safely entered the spaceship's cockpit with Kimberley. "They never meant well for anyone."

"We cannot go to Ben Haddad, Mariah," Rachel repeated. "He will only help himself."

"I don't think your friends are with you on this, Rachel," the Bookmaker said.

Aiden looked away and Kimberley turned to Rachel. "We could see what happens, dear," she said. "This Haddad guy could have some answers we need."

"He's dangerous, Kim, you don't know him."

"Do you?" Kimberley asked the young Bookbearer.

"What if there had been some falling out between your father and Mr. Haddad, and your father now became opposed to Ben's views?" Mariah began.

"Okay, you know that's not helping, Miss Cross Sikama," Kimberley berated Mariah.

The Bookmaker rolled her eyes. "Just trying to help," she pointed out. "You're welcome."

"Thank you."

"I'll go with this if we have a Plan B," Rachel said and Mariah brightened.

"Of course, there's a Plan B," she enthused. "I'll tell you about it when we get there. It's all in my head."

Nobody said a word.

Mariah took their silence as a final approval of her plan, and picked up the sharpie they earlier used from a table. She stretched out her right hand towards Rachel. "Let me do the honors, dear, since I personally know him." The little girl gave her the white book and she wrote down a name on one of its page. "Hold hands, everyone."

Outside the Wellington XCX12 Cargo Transporter, Carl Bain hated the fact that he couldn't face his enemies with his powers. His infernal masters appeared all around him and he thought they would end his life there and then, but the instruction came through clear enough.

"Follow them!"

Chapter 33
THE UNDERGROUND CITY

NATIONS of the world ended the Red War in X40.05.02. No victor emerged from this momentous upheaval, though every partaker had wounds to lick. As a result of the war, multiple mega cities were incinerated and the planet lost 75% of its vegetation, leading to millions falling into poverty.

After the Red War, fallout dust covered the Earth's surface. This remarkably dense red dust originated from the weaponized particle in the most destructive weapon used in the calamitous war: *Endren X37*. A nuclear weapon named after the date the deadly compound came into existence.

Owing to the fallout, the Earth became a red globe when viewed from outer space, with temperatures going as low as 50°Q and as high as 200°Q around the equator on a daily basis. The stark challenge facing the planet could never be experienced at a more definitive place than the Amazon Rainforest, now more of a wood forest than anything else. The remaining animals surviving in this dead zone always went hungry for months before finding something edible, especially if they were herbivores like the iconic Scarlet Macaw.

Flapping over the scorched trees in search of food, a member of this predominantly red bird with stripes of blue and yellow across its feathers chirped and groaned as it flew over dry tree after dry tree. Almost all the greenery in the world had vanished the day the greatest red bomb detonated, because a large percentage of the Sun's photosynthesizing rays could not penetrate the dense red dust the exploding bomb spewed into the atmosphere on that day.

This dust could be seen for miles on end from where our time-travelers finally appeared. Of course, they all wore protective hazard suits and artificial respirators.

"Where the hell are we?" Kimberley demanded, looking around her. She could see several surface shelters down a valley to her right, and a steep slope leading up to a group of caves on her left.

"Good that we're together," Mariah observed. "Would have hated it if we had to start by looking for one or two of us."

"First, we need to protect ourselves from the Booklords," Rachel said, bringing out a sharpie.

"You brought that along?" Aiden asked her.

"Yes," the little girl replied. "It's not the one I took from the spaceship, but it will do." She drew ankhs on everyone's hazard suit, except Mariah's. The Sikama preferred a cross.

"We still need to know what happened here," Aiden pointed out. "Is it a bomb?"

"The bomb, knucklehead, the bomb." Mariah appeared on edge. She frowned. "It caused the red dust everywhere. Radiation levels are way too high here."

"How did you know that?" Kimberley demanded.

"A meter is working with my helmet screen. Could be new *TelepathyG* tech."

"*TelepathyG7*," Kimberley said, surprising herself. "My alternate memory also tells me we're hostiles here."

"And what does that mean?" Rachel began.

"That we should run?" Aiden suggested. "Those guys don't look happy to see us as far as I can tell."

The small speck in the distance grew rapidly.

"Who are they?" Rachel wondered.

"Doesn't matter, that vehicle is not slowing down," Kimberley noted.

The hovering vehicle bearing down on the small group had a reckless driver. Obviously, the fellow had one objective.

"I think we need to go now," Kimberley said, pulling Aiden and Rachel along. She saw flashes from the approaching unit. "They're shooting at us! Quick, to the valley!"

"No!" a new voice opposed from her left. A young black man stood above them halfway to the caves. "If you go into the valley, they will hunt you down and kill you. Just follow me."

Lazer bolts shot past, missing their targets as Mariah followed the new guy and Kimberley urged the kids to scale the slope. Up the steep slope they ran, putting all their strength into this effort now a matter of life and death. They kept up their speed for some time, until Kimberley turned to check on their pursuers, and noticed that the floating craft had stopped at the foot of the slope. Four figures stood around the vehicle, one person pointing up towards the fleeing group, while the remaining three kept up their lazer barrage.

"They will come up on foot."

"Why?" Kimberley asked their new guide.

"Their vehicle works with the red dust and there's not much of that on the slope," the young man explained. "By the time they trudge up to the caves, we would have been long gone."

The shooting stopped when the four individuals below started climbing up the slope.

"So, where are we going?" Aiden asked.

"Somewhere safe," their new friend replied. "The name's Jeremy, by the way."

"Thank you, Jeremy," Mariah said. "I'm Mariah and these are my friends, Kimberley, Aiden and Rachel."

"Good to see you guys," Jeremy said. "Now, to safety."

The cave inlets dotting the top of the hill varied in size. Jeremy led his new friends into one and switched on the torch on his hazard suit. A flight of stairs descended into the cave.

"Where does that lead us?" Mariah wondered.

"To the Main Corridor," Jeremy said. "You'll see."

Sure enough, the Bookmaker and her friends got to the bottom of the rocky stairs with their guide and exited this particular cave into a huge corridor the likes of which they had never seen. Rows of cave mouths lined up the opposing walls of this corridor.

"Those men will stop their pursuit here, because for them it will be futile to continue," Jeremy said.

"And why is that?" Kimberley wondered.

"All the cave inlets outside lead to this corridor and the caves we see on the opposite wall lead to more corridors and more caves."

"So, where do we go from here?" Rachel began.

Jeremy entered one of the caves lining the opposite wall and his new friends followed him. Emerging from this cave into another passage lined with opposing natural caves, he crossed five entrances before entering another cave. Coming out of this particular cave, he stepped up between two caves before the others. "Come, join me," he told his small audience and they soon crowded around him. "The entrance is a lift," he said before the ground gave way and a vertical tube took them all down to the city underneath. Jeremy liked the surprise on the faces of his guests. "Welcome to the city we call Resilience," he introduced. "The shelter we all cherish."

*   *   *

Carl Bain lifted the dying man up into the air with his right arm and released the fellow, who crashed to the ground. He looked around at his handiwork and smirked. His feeling of satisfaction at the moment could never compare to the gratification he would receive when he succeeded in retrieving his package and the white book. He knew exactly where his primary targets were currently residing in the vicinity. Their use of the caused symbols had drastically affected his plans and he hated the fact that he had hit this brick wall.

The human minion knew his masters were barely keeping him alive out of mercy. He also knew he only had one final chance to prove himself worthy of their trust. He didn't know how to effectively utilize this chance.

The four men lying around him never knew what hit them as they investigated the cavernous corridor he now stood in. Of course, he knew the ground had a hidden lift mechanism somewhere to his right. He just didn't care, because appearing in the city underneath was a piece of cake, and as long as his targets forgot to draw the caused symbols on their arms after removing their hazard suits, he could appear close enough to retrieve his package and the white book down below.

A new plan filled his head. He now knew what to do should his targets draw the caused symbols on their arms after removing their hazard suits. Of course, many would die. The more the merrier.

*   *   *

Rachel drew the symbols on their arms as soon as they removed their hazard suits. The decontamination room had little equipment save for a tube into which went all the discarded hazard suits.

Mariah saw a radiation device on the wall. "Good. This place is airtight."

"This way, please," Jeremy directed them, walking past an ultraviolet sanitizer. "This underground city was built before the war," he said, watching the others get sanitized. "It lies inside a thick underground concrete barrier equipped with systems that purify the reddish dusty air outside."

"Okay, good to know," Kimberley noted, stepping out of the sanitizer system.

Jeremy led them through an exit that brought them to the middle of a street scene within a very high arching white roof. Blocks of shelter units spread out as far as their eyes could see alongside straight roads.

Dazzling light lit the streets and many mobile units zoomed about the paved roads.

"Welcome to the city of Resilience," the young black man said. "Here, the rich tend to have good shelters while the poor suffer from rundown shelters."

"And where is your shelter?" Aiden asked.

"Down the street," Jeremy pointed out. "You'll also meet my family."

Kimberley looked at Mariah. Time was running out. "Eh, Jeremy, is there any place of learning in Resilience? We need to find someone who can help us."

"Yes, about that," Jeremy began, walking down the sidewalk. "You guys don't look like you're from this vicinity. Where are you guys from and where are you headed?"

Kimberley sighed. "We...We.... You..."

"You guys are safe here no matter where you came from, where you are headed, or why you had to put your lives in danger by exposing yourselves to the Kannibals."

"The Kannibals?" Aiden walked alongside Jeremy. "Who are they?"

"The flesh eaters, and that's 'Kannibal' with a 'K,'" Jeremy replied. "Plant food got scarce after the red bomb exploded, so outside the cities, cannibalistic communities have sprung up. You guys don't know about this?"

"That's terrible," Rachel exclaimed. "That's horrible."

"You said 'cities,'" Kimberley began, turning to Jeremy. "How many cities are there?"

"There are five other cities like Resilience in this area," Jeremy said. "Others are sited in other areas like Area 12.6 and Area 55.7. All these cities are linked together through underground tunnels. Ah, here we are." He stepped off the sidewalk and stopped before a shelter covered with graffiti. "My family love art, so they have this huge canvas they live in."

"Nice," Aiden said. "Who is the better artist, your wife or your kids?"

Jeremy laughed. "I live with my two sisters, boy. They're family."

Rachel brightened. "Would love to meet your sisters, Jeremy."

"You will, dear. Soon." The shelter's door opened and two young faces beamed at the visitors. "Guys, meet my younger siblings, Ginia and Tilia."

Ginia had black hair running down her neck and shoulders to shape a beautiful face. Her eyes were as wild and as innocent as Tilia's, both pointing towards a fine nose and a refined mouth. She couldn't have been more than twenty. "Welcome strangers," she joked. "We're happy to have you in our house."

Tilia nodded, but said nothing. The visitors came into their living room with her brother. "I'll warm a meal," she finally said and walked away.

"You don't need to do that," Kimberley began, but realized she was too late. She admired the living room and sat on a long sofa opposite the one Jeremy had taken. Aiden and Rachel sat beside her, but Mariah remained standing. Ginia left to help her sister and Rachel stood up and gave Aiden the white book before following the girl.

The shelter had a small cozy living room exuding warmth. Abstract art frames hung everywhere and the diffuse lighting suggested class, and taste. The two sofas in the room faced each other across a low, flat coffee table. Awkward silence hung over the parties sitting across this solid piece of furniture.

"First of all," Kimberley began, "how did the world change to this, Jeremy?"

Jeremy sat up. "You're serious you don't know?"

Mariah coughed for attention. "You're right, Jeremy, we're not from these parts. We…"

"We do know a little about the red bomb," Aiden interrupted her. "What we don't know is how the world became a dead red zone."

"The red bomb caused it," Ginia called out from the kitchen. "The Sun helps plants to grow only when it can cause photosynthesis to take place in leaves."

Jeremy cleared his throat. "The red dust prevents most of the Sun's rays from getting to the plants, thereby hindering this process."

"Artificial light can grow plants but not enough on a commercial scale," Tilia added from the kitchen.

"We use artificial light to grow the food we consume here," Jeremy said, "but this is expensive and can never last us all year round, even with the abundance of the energy source we thought would be cheap."

Kimberley noted the annoyance in the young man's voice. "You were talking about Compound V?"

"Yes," Jeremy said. "The big companies have made it so expensive right now. It's meant to be very cheap. It used to be."

A long silent pause followed.

"Do you have an army defending you in here?" Kimberley began.

"No," Jeremy replied. "Almost all the soldiers went to the war. We civilians occupied the underground cities when we got news of the red bomb."

"I thought there were established colonies on other planets," Mariah began. "What happened to those colonies? Did refugees reach out to them from Earth?"

Jeremy looked away. "The Red War started in the colonies," he said.

"Nations of the world destroyed one another's colonies before bringing the war down to Earth."

"I see," Mariah said.

Another long silent pause followed.

"What were you doing out there all by yourself, Jeremy?" Kimberley began. "Glad that you helped us, but how come you braved the dust and radiation just to do that?"

"I am a Volunteer Watch," Jeremy replied. "I save people who seek refuge from the Slums."

"The Slums?" Kimberley got confused.

"Yes. That valley outside leads to human settlement farms we call the Slums. In these farms, the Kannibals raise mammals for food."

"For food?" Aiden gulped hard. "Gross," he blurted out.

"Like, you mean people there are raised as livestock?" Kimberley was stunned. What had the world turned into?

Rachel couldn't believe her ears as she came in from the kitchen with some plates and spoons. "That's gross."

"Yes," Jeremy agreed. "People often escape from these prisons and the Kannibals hunt them down at the valley if these men, women and children fail to reach safety in time. That's where I come in, and the nearest settlement farm is where I think you guys escaped from, right?" Jeremy turned to Mariah for confirmation.

Kimberley coughed for attention. "No, we…"

"It's the Ankh Sikama, Kim," Mariah cut in.

"What?" Kimberley looked up and noticed Jeremy's surprise stare.

"You know about the Sikama?" Jeremy began.

"What about the Sikama?" Kimberley asked him.

"They run the Slums and we escaped from them," Mariah said. "We need to find the Cross Sikama right now."

Jeremy frowned. "There's nothing like…"

"An X2 mobile unit we could use to get to the other cities?" Mariah interrupted him. "We needed to find an intellectual amongst your people, Jeremy. We need to do that right now."

Kimberley sighed. "Jeremy, there's…there's something you really need to know."

The young man looked up. Ginia came into the living room with a pot of freshly cooked potato porridge. Tilia followed her sister with a jug of water. "And what is that?"

Rachel prepared the table in the middle of the group for a meal. "That we're not from these parts?" she quipped.

"But you've said that before," Jeremy pointed out. His sisters sat down beside him and dished out the meal.

"W-We're not really from anywhere near here, Jeremy," Kimberley said, receiving a plate of porridge from Tilia.

"Not even the Slums," Aiden added, scooping a spoonful of porridge from his plate.

"We're from the past, Jeremy," Mariah said. "We're here to stop evil before it destroys us."

"I see," Jeremy said in confusion. "The Sikama?"

"Yes," Mariah said.

Jeremy frowned as he ate. "You tell me you're from the past? How do I believe that? I need proof of your being from the past."

Kimberley shook her head in frustration.

"Look, Jeremy, we're good Sikama sent by Yahweh to stop the bad Sikama now causing mayhem in your world," Mariah said.

"The Sikama lead the Kannibals. How are you gonna stop them?"

"We have a magic book to help us stop them," Kimberley explained. "We only need to find someone who can help us use this book...properly."

Aiden displayed the white book for the hosts to see.

"That's the proof I wanted right there," Jeremy said. "An ancient book."

Aiden blinked twice. "Wait, you mean you guys don't use books anymore?"

"No, we don't," Jeremy said. "Seen any since you came in here?"

Aiden frowned. "Well.... What about the paintings?"

"We use *TelepathyG7* for everything now," Jeremy pointed out. "The artwork is later printed on the wall using Modu Print technology. There's no raw material for paper now."

"Ok, that explains that." Kimberley sat up. "Jeremy, we know you've been kind to us by giving us food when you know how scarce this food is, and we're very grateful for that, but right now, Jeremy, we need you to help us on this."

"We don't have magicians who use ancient tomes," Ginia chuckled. "Those guys died off a long time ago, even before the Red War."

"We only have scientists now," Tilia supplied.

"Yes," Kimberley whispered in relief.

"Like old Professor Goldenberg at the Bravery Plant Research Institute," Jeremy added.

Mariah brightened. "Exactly the kind of guy we need."

"Plant food is very expensive and only greedy companies have monopolized farming in the massive green house shelters they have constructed over the years," Ginia explained. "Because of this, the professor has been working on improving genetic farming for Earth's population after the Red War."

"He's a very busy man," Tilia said.

"Doesn't matter," Kimberley waived. "How do we get to this Plant Research Institute?"

"Bravery is the next city," Jeremy replied. "Follow Route 21 from here and you won't miss it."

"Okay, thanks," Kimberley got up. About time, she thought. "So grateful, Jeremy," she said. "We won't forget this."

"And you won't regret this," Aiden added, jumping up.

"I know you didn't tell me everything," Jeremy directed at Kimberley. "But I know you'll do so when you think the time is right to do so."

This moved the Portwood sergeant. She thought better of saying something and turned away. "Thanks for that," she murmured.

"I'll take you guys to Bravery on our X5," the young man surprised her with. "That way, I'll also see more proof of the story you just told me when it unfolds before me."

Kimberley rolled her eyes. "Okay, that's not a bad deal."

"Good." Jeremy stood up as well. "No time to waste, then."

Aiden turned to Jeremy. "So, where's the X5?"

"It's parked near the Canvass."

"The Canvass?" Rachel smiled.

"That's our shelter's name," Ginia said. "Tilia named it."

"So, who's the best artist amongst you guys?" Mariah quipped.

"Tilia," Ginia chuckled. "She's quite remarkable…"

"Are you getting this message on your feed?" Jeremy cut in, swiping out his virtual *TelepathyG7* screen from the gadget on his wrist. "There are…multiple reports of unknown deaths in the Resilience B23.551 area?"

Aiden realized he wore a wrist gadget as well. Everyone had wrist gadgets. How come he never noticed? Jeremy's screen appeared on the wall and he gaped at the violent footage coming from Resilience B23.551. People launching themselves into the air and crashing to the ground without cause, remaining visibly immobile afterwards as their *TelepathyG7* vital signs data pronounced them dead.

"What is killing them?" Jeremy wondered with a shaking voice.

Kimberley boiled. "Carl Bain."

"We can only help them if we go now," Mariah urged.

"How do we tell them to put this symbol on their shelters and rooms?" Rachel asked Jeremy, virtually sending him a message containing an ankh symbol.

"Good idea," Kimberley said. "Why didn't I think of that?"

"You don't have a cross?" Mariah asked Rachel.

"Oh, for the love of God!" Kimberley wailed.

"And what is that?" Jeremy demanded.

"That's an ankh, Jeremy," Mariah said. "The demons now killing your people avoid anyone who has an ankh or a cross near his or her person. If you can share that on your feed, many lives will be saved around here."

"Good idea," Kimberley agreed. "Now, on to Bravery."

Rachel smiled and Aiden frowned at her. "What?"

"I'm still getting used to this tech," she told him. "And I'm loving it!"

*   *   *

Carl Bain watched in dismay as the caused symbol appeared on every shelter in the five underground cities and beyond. He realized he could no longer use his powers and stepped out into the street. The huge virtual screens all over the place highlighted the current news that the spontaneous deaths had stopped. This meant that his infernal masters had ended their assault on the cities' occupants once the caused symbol showed up everywhere.

The American hustler turned away, deep in thought. No time to grieve this unfortunate turn of events. He needed a plan he could execute as a human being.

The voice came through loud and clear. The next city it is, then. He hailed an X5 unit.

"Where to?" the unit's operator asked him.

"Bravery," he said. "I have some friends I'm dying to meet over there."

And finally deal with.

Chapter 34
BENJAMIN HADDAD

BRAVERY'S city emblem consisted of a shield protecting a shovel and farm fork. Its major source of income included the many greenhouses constructed with custom armor glass and occupying acres of choice land in the underground farming city. These structures jutted out above ground level in order to enable the greenery they housed make use of the little remaining sunlight available to Mankind. Heavy security defended the glass openings against Kannibal attacks.

Whenever the red dust blurted out precious solar rays by settling on the greenhouses, the city's farmers used artificial lighting instead. Expensive artificial lighting from NGVTech, the energy company that had successfully monopolized Compound V.

Genetix wanted to change this narrative. The institute strived to improve genetic farming for Earth's population. This meant that crops being developed by this research facility could one day exceed expectations in the red environment the world's remaining greenery must now survive in.

The X5 unit swerved into the black gates of the research institute and stopped before a grand portico with a wide staircase taking visitors up to the main entrance. Its occupants exited before it powered down. They scaled the steps leading to the high-tech doors of the complex.

"Amazing," Aiden said, turning around.

"We need to see Mr. Goldenberg," Jeremy told a security personnel who stepped out to receive them.

"It's a matter of the utmost importance," a smiling Mariah said.

The unsmiling fellow nodded. "This way please."

Kimberley wondered why Mariah had a smile on her lips as they walked down a long crowded passage. Most of the passersby carried a particular plant probably on transfer from a nursery or some place with the right conditions for growth.

The guard stopped before a bold door atop which a LABORATORY sign glowed blue. He waved his right hand across the door and the aperture opened automatically.

An elderly man sitting on a traditional lab stool looked up from a crowded transparent laboratory table at the farthest end of the room as Kimberley walked over to his position with her friends. He had braided black beard properly continuous with thinning hair that shaped out the facial positions of deep brows and calculating eyes. An ignoble nose and a resolute mouth completed the fearless expression on his face, while the penetrating nature of his eyes accentuated this blank countenance. The man's pristine black suit looked out of place in the cluttered laboratory.

"What is it, Rewder? I thought I told you not to disturb my work?"

"Yes, you did, sir, but your visitors checked out and they said they have an important message for you."

"How did we check out?" Kimberley asked the guard.

"He ran a background check while we were coming here," Jeremy explained.

"They escaped from the human farm, sir," Rewder continued and his principal looked up from his work on the lab table.

Kimberley noticed the man's piqued attention.

"Now, did they?" he began. "And who's their leader?"

"Me." Mariah stepped forward, hands outstretched.

"What's the meaning of this, woman?" Mr. Goldenberg demanded, standing up from his laboratory stool without taking the Sikama's outstretched hand. "Who are you people?"

"We-We escaped from the Kannibals," Mariah said, withdrawing her hand. "We have relevant information for you, sir."

"Then let's hear it," Mr. Goldenberg bellowed. "Stop wasting my time."

"The Kannibals plan to attack your city," Aiden said. "What did I just say?"

Kimberley knew what just happened. Alternate memory. So, they actually had important information to share? Wow.

"Are you sure of this?" Rewder asked the boy.

"Yes, sir," Aiden affirmed.

"They dare not," Mr. Goldenberg said. "We have guards and an elaborate security system."

"They've found a way to go round your security, sir," Mariah said. "If only you'll allow me to show you."

Mr. Goldenberg sat down again. "I need to know your background story," he began. "Introduce yourselves."

"I am Sergeant Kimberley Reyna of the Portwood Police Department in Portwood, Oregon," Kimberley said. "I believe you must know Oregon, sir?"

Professor Goldenberg scoffed.

"The United States ceased to exist a long time ago, Sergeant Reyna," Rewder said. "I believe you should know that."

"It still existed in our time," Aiden said.

Mr. Goldenberg sat up. He thought he didn't hear the boy correctly. "Rewder, leave us."

"Yes, sir," the guard said, turning. He left the laboratory.

"Going with what you think you now know, sir, you must touch one of us," Mariah said, stretching out her right hand again.

The elderly scientist hesitated before taking the hand. His transformation wasted no time. The blank pupils preceded closure of both eyelids, then a frown and a reopening of both eyes. A reawakening and a response. "Mariah, my dear. So glad to see you again!"

Kimberley rolled her eyes. No bother. Both individuals were Bookmakers and must have known each other back at the Mine, although something really bothered her about Mariah's present countenance. Something she could not lay her finger on.

"It's a pleasure to finally meet you again, Ben," Mariah enthused.

Ben Haddad smiled and embraced his former protégé. "The pleasure's all mine, Mariah. The pleasure's all mine." He kept her at arm's length and admired her. "Just look at you. No scratch."

"We came with the book, Ben," Mariah said, pointing at Rachel. "We also came with her."

"No way." Ben Haddad peered at Rachel as if she wasn't there at all. He turned to Mariah. "Is she?"

"Yes, she is, Ben," Mariah chuckled. "She is his flesh and blood."

*   *   *

Carl Bain alighted from the X4 unit and walked up to the gates of the Genetix complex. His infernal masters had already smothered everyone in the compound except his protected enemies and those in their midst.

Despite the earlier warning his primary targets had sent out to residents of the city of Resilience and beyond, no lifeless occupant of the research institute had any protective symbol on their dead body and no cursed symbol projected anywhere on the premises. A possible *TelepathyG7* Exclusion Error T2 that had worked to the human minion's advantage, judging from the lifeless nature of the many halls and corridors inside the complex he was about to enter.

The American hustler simply walked through the black gates of the institute, ignoring the dead bodies littered all around him. He knew his enemies knew he had arrived, so he squatted beside a cold security personnel and retrieved a Colt XF9.0 RapidFire from the dead man's holster. He would need the weapon if he found himself in a situation where he couldn't use his powers.

More dead bodies as he walked across the empty passage and headed towards the laboratory door. How to open it? A wave of his right hand? He did just that and the door slid open to reveal a gratifying sight. His enemies supported by security personnel stood at the farthest end of the laboratory. "Well, well, well, what do we have here?" he began as he stepped into the brightly lit hall. "Is this a trap?"

"Not at all," Kimberley stammered, looking away. "We've decided to end this."

"Really?" Carl Bain could not believe his ears, but remained alert. "I know you don't believe the lie you just told me," he growled. "So, I'll ask you this just once. When will you reveal the trick?"

"There's no trick, my friend," Ben Haddad told the human minion. "You're just one person, and my men can deal with you right now, but they will not do that."

"Hmmmmmm," the human minion scoffed, looking around. "I'm not that helpless, am I?"

"You must have realized that you don't have your powers anymore?" Ben Haddad smiled. "Now, why is that?"

Carl Bain frowned and tried to start fire with his right hand. He could not. "I knew you drew cursed symbols on your arms," he said. "I knew that before I came here, old man. Now, hand over the book and my package." He raised his lazer gun.

"Wait, we have decided to give you the book and your package," Kimberley said. "No need for violence here."

"And we'll clean off our symbols so that you can leave this time and place without harm, if you promise not to harm us as well when we do so," Mariah added, looking at the laboratory floor.

"Really?" The American thug lowered his weapon. "Okay, I take my stuff and go my way, you go your way. No hard feelings."

"No hard feelings," Aiden repeated, looking lost.

"I feel your pain, boy," Carl Bain told him. "You win some and you lose some."

"Let's do this and get over with it," Rachel cried, blinking back tears.

Carl Bain smiled. If their Bookbearer had been crying, then

something must have gone terribly wrong for his enemies. Maybe the savior they thought they would find in the old man standing before him hadn't materialized? This sudden outcome must have destroyed their resolve to succeed, hence the present event playing out before him.

"*TelepathyG7* will project symbols all over the place as soon as you break our truce," Jeremy told the mysterious man confronting them.

"There won't be any need for that," Carl Bain said. "I'm a man of my word."

Jeremy nodded. He still found it hard to believe the revelations his visitors had earlier told Mr. Goldenberg, but he couldn't disprove the fact that he thought this mysterious fellow standing before them a rebellious murderer of some sought. For proof, he just needed to look at the man's appearance.

"Well then," Ben Haddad said. "What are we waiting for?"

"Where's the book, and my box?" Carl Bain asked him.

"Here's the book," Rachel said, handing over the ancient volume.

"And here's the package," Kimberley added, pulling out the miniature cube from a pocket.

The human minion smiled and collected the items with open arms. His enemies used a handkerchief to wipe away the sharpie marks on their arms and immediately, his demonic masters appeared behind him. He felt their mysterious presence boost his mystical energy and turned to his now-helpless enemies. "Good to know that you erased your cursed symbols," he told them. "Now, to end this."

"But you promised," Jeremy snapped and raised his right hand, meaning to swipe out the screen on his left wrist with it.

His hand froze in midair.

"You will do no such thing, my friend," Carl Bain said. "Too late for that." Fire burst out from his right hand and an explosive shield suddenly engulfed everyone.

The otherworldly force from this shield pulverized the American thug and all the demons empowering him, turning them into brown ash.

The small silver package clattered to the ground and the white book fell beside it.

*　　*　　*

Professor Baruch Goldenberg, now also known as Benjamin Haddad, let out the breath he'd been holding all this while. It worked. His plan had worked. The one he'd been working on all these years across space and time. The one he just had a few minutes to physically put together after years in alternate oblivion.

"Whew!" Jeremy let out. "It actually worked." He gingerly pushed aside some ash from the lonely heap lying directly before them with his right leg. "This guy would never believe this just happened wherever he finds himself right now," he chuckled.

"Of course, he never knew what hit him," Mariah emphasized. "He should still be dreaming wherever he is right now."

"I hope you're right," Kimberley said. She turned to Professor Baruch Goldenberg, or Benjamin Haddad, in disbelief. How did the old fellow do it?

The institute personnel amongst her friends stepped out and waited for their professor to speak. Of course, Mr. Haddad had alternate memory. "We'll need vacuumizers," he told them. "First thing's first; we clean up this place and burn the bodies outside. Now, go."

"Is-Is it really over?" Rachel stammered, standing up with the white book as the guards and institute staff trooped out. She surveyed the heaps of brown ash littered all over the laboratory.

"Won't they come back, Kim?" Aiden asked the female sergeant, his right fingers still interlocked with Rachel's left fingers. "Did we just win?"

Rachel blinked twice and gaped at the ash everywhere. "Is it really over?"

"It's over, my dear," Ben Haddad told her, placing his right hand on her left shoulder. "Your father and I studied Kabbalah Ma'asit together in order to discover how to destroy the demons, but he died before we could find a way to practically arrive at the conclusion we just witnessed." The elderly Bookmaker looked away and his voice softened. "I did this today for your father, my child. I did this for a friend who had always wanted to see the hills and valleys around Jerusalem again. One whose memory I will forever hold dear."

"Are the Gray Ones gone for good, Mr. Haddad?" Kimberley demanded.

"Call me Ben, my dear," the elderly Sikama said. "And I think the answer to your question is 'yes.'"

"But, how? How did you do it?" Mariah wondered.

"A simple theory I practicalized," Ben Haddad said. "The Ice of Masada had always needed a boost." He turned to Rachel. "You had all the ingredients for that boost right here with you all this time, but you never knew you did, my dear. For some years, I never knew about that as well, until I realized it all had to do with something Jehoash and I had always tried to figure out back at the Mine; why we couldn't draw the ankh in the pages of the books."

"We tried to draw the ankh in the book, Mr. Ben," Aiden said. "But we also failed to do so."

"Did we?" Kimberley wondered. "Never remembered us doing so."

"Mariah told us on the way to Pripyat that it was impossible to draw the sign in the book," Rachel said. "We never tried to do so afterwards."

"I see," Baruch Goldenberg said. The professor watched his men return with vacuumizers to begin the onerous task of removing the heaps of ash lying all over the place. "The two books are weapons the Booklords sought to retrieve and return to Yahweh," he said. "A task these former angels decided to undertake after Yahweh cursed them for conniving with Lucifer in producing the books. I hope you know the story?"

"The story?" Jeremy began.

"You remember, Kim?" Rachel said. "I told you about the books, remember?"

"Yeah, that story," Kimberley whispered. "Never knew we were fighting former angels, though." Of course, it all sounded so otherworldly. "So, why can't anyone draw the ankh in the pages of the books?"

"Your Bookbearer is a child," Ben said. "A Bookbearer must be strong-willed and mature enough to withstand and eventually destroy the forces after the book, and you usually don't find these qualities in a child, especially one who had just lost her father." He stopped before the laboratory table and sat down on his tall stool. "I must confess that, just like Rachel, not many Sikama are strong-minded enough to boost the book's defense and eventually destroy the demons trying to retrieve it. We couldn't do that all the time we were in the Mine. That's where we could have used the ankh symbol, but we didn't know about that. And poor Jehoash. He gave his daughter a task even he could not achieve at the time." The elderly Sicarii Kabbalah Masada paused. "The ankh symbol I placed in the book was a touch of genius," he said.

"And shaping it out from a stem was also ingenious," Mariah commended. She could hug the old man at that point.

A weary Kimberley nodded in agreement.

"You could have ended this a long time ago if only you had gone round the inability to draw an ankh in the book by putting something shaped like an ankh inside the book," Ben Haddad told her.

"Okay," Aiden said, wondering at the number of risky situations they would have avoided if they had done so. "We never knew it would work, so we never tried it."

"You haven't answered my question, Ben," Kimberley began, picking up Carl Bain's small silver box. "Why couldn't we draw an ankh in the book?"

"Mariah once talked of the books coming from the devil, Kim," Rachel remembered.

"I need to hear another part of that story from our hero, Rachel," Kimberley said.

"That, I'm afraid, is a mystery only Yahweh and Lucifer can unravel for you, my dear." Ben Haddad's chiseled face almost softened. "Of course, Lucifer had a part to play in all this, but just know that no one individual could draw the X or T signs in the books, until today."

Mariah frowned. "And what do you mean by that, Ben?"

The elder Sikama's countenance changed as he turned to her. "Up till today, Mariah, I never thought I would live to see the day a human being can draw the ankh symbol on the pages of the books, but behold this very individual is with us right now as we speak."

"And who is this person?" Kimberley wanted to know.

Benjamin Haddad, also known as Professor Baruch Goldenberg, nodded towards Aiden.

"Me?" Aiden sounded perplexed.

Rachel looked puzzled. "It's not..."

"What we witnessed today would never have happened if we did not have this young friend of yours with us today, Rachel," Ben Haddad said. "Putting the ankh sign in the book was just a part of the work we needed to do."

"I don't understand, Master," Mariah said.

"We also needed to create the boom," Rachel realized. She still held Aiden's right hand. "We did that without knowing it."

"And I must thank you two for trying unknowingly, my child." Ben Haddad beamed. "The force your friend helped you generate in addition to that created by the ankh symbol in the book boosted the Ice of Masada to a level that could only destroy our enemies when it confronted them."

"Wow," Kimberley let out. "Just wow."

"And I must confess that ever since I saw your young friend, Rachel, I've noticed his stark resemblance to someone I knew in the past," Ben Haddad continued. "A boy I think I came across back at the Mine."

Rachel turned blue. "The boy's name was Avigdor, Uncle Ben. Aiden is Avigdor's reincarnation, and I'm so sorry to be saying this now."

Kimberley looked at Aiden. She couldn't make out his present state of mind.

"I wrote his name in the book and came looking for him in his town, where the sergeant saved me from the Gray Ones," Rachel murmured, looking at the floor. "We all became friends after our perilous journey through space and time together."

Aiden wondered why he never became aware of his alternate self from the moment he met the strange girl who'd upended his life back in Portwood, just like everyone else. Or did he do that without knowing it? That was a puzzle he needed to unravel with Rachel's help.

"So, let's see you draw an ankh in the book," Kimberley told Aiden.

Rachel gave Aiden the white book and her sharpie and he drew an ankh on the book's first page.

"Draw in the middle," Ben Haddad told the boy.

Aiden did so.

Rachel looked at his work. "This means you're a stronger Bookbearer than me, Aiden. You will become a Bookmaker sooner than later."

"But why did the Ice of Masada protect us from the Gray Ones when we willingly gave their servant the book?" Kimberley asked the professor.

"We willingly gave him the book, Kim, but did the Bookbearer willingly do so?" Aiden wondered.

"Right," Kimberley said, nodding.

Baruch Goldenberg, or Ben Haddad, smiled at Rachel. "Did you know you drew the Gray Ones to the Bookbinders when you caused the spiritual entities of these men and women to move through space and time by writing their names in the book?" he asked the little girl.

Aiden smirked. "Aren't they called Bookmakers anymore?"

"I prefer Bookbinders," Ben said. "It sounds more noble."

"But I could not get to the Bookmakers if I didn't write their names in the book," Rachel protested. "There were no names in the white book when Father gave it to me."

"Yes," Ben agreed. "Your action, despite being an unfortunate one, was very necessary for you and your objective. Sadly, you appear to have gleaned little from my dead colleagues as regarded your quest during said quest."

"Can you read my mind?" Rachel wondered aloud. "I was just thinking the exact same thing..."

"You can help us, Mr. Haddad, by telling us what really happened at the Mine," Kimberley cut in, seizing the opportunity.

The professor cleared his throat and paused. "Initially," he began, "we, the Sicarii Kabbalah Masada, wanted to remove Emperor Constantine from power on behalf of my people, the Jews."

"So, why did your people want this Constantine guy out?" Aiden wondered.

"Flavius Valerius Constantinus fought for 18 years to become the only emperor of the Roman Empire after the death of his father," Mariah narrated. "As emperor, he legally banned the persecution of Christians and willingly legalized the divisions between Jews and Christians by

341

favoring the latter and condemning the Jews for having killed Yeshua, whom Christianity also knew as Jesus, their so-called Son of God. This led to the persecution of our people by overzealous Roman citizens."

"Interesting," Jeremy said.

"Go on," Kimberley urged. "The Emperor rightly condemned the Jews for killing Jesus Christ, or wasn't that what happened?"

Benjamin Haddad shook his head. "Contrary to Christian beliefs, it was not Yeshua or the first Jewish apostles who started a new religion called Christianity," he said. "Yeshua often told his followers while he was alive that he came, would die, and would rise from the grave in fulfillment of Jewish laws and Jewish prophets."

"Early Greek and Roman leaders caused the rift between Judaism and the new sect called Christianity," Mariah pointed out. "The faith of the Jewish and Gentile followers of Yeshua was originally called 'The Way,' and for the first 300 years of Christianity the Gentile followers of Yeshua kept the Passover. There was no celebration of Easter or Christmas."

"However, not long after John, Yeshua's last apostle, died around AD 99," Benjamin Haddad continued, "a known Christian leader at the time told his followers that it was foolish to profess Yeshua the Messiah and to Judaize at the same time."

"Judaize," Kimberley began. "What does that mean?"

"It means to practice Jewish laws and customs," the professor explained.

"One wonders how Yeshua, who practiced the laws and customs in the Jewish Torah, was even allowed into this new religion called Christianity," Mariah said. "But that's a question to ponder another day," she quickly added after Benjamin Haddad glared at her. "Yeshua became the Messiah and Christ was added to the Greek transliteration of his name."

Kimberley did not miss the said interaction between Benjamin Haddad and his female protégé.

"By the time the apologist and theologian, Justin Martyr, arrived on the scene, the Greek and Roman Christians have accused the Jewish people of Deicide — the killing of a Divine being, Yeshua," Benjamin Haddad resumed. "Afterwards, many emerging Greek-minded Gentile leaders taught against keeping the Lord's Biblical holy days described in Leviticus 23.

"They disinherited the Jewish people from the land of Israel by saying God has now given it to Christians; and they continued to speak derogatorily about Yeshua's brethren, the Jewish People," Mariah added.

"Then Constantine stepped in and legalized these opinions?" Kimberley concluded.

"Exactly," the professor said. "From the Council of Nicaea, the new emperor changed Yahweh's holy days and introduced Easter as the period Yeshua resurrected. This day would be distinct from the Biblical dates of Passover and First Fruits, which were the dates when Yeshua actually died and purportedly rose from the grave."

"We still don't believe Yeshua rose from the dead," Mariah pointed out.

"Nobody believes that story anymore," Jeremy quipped.

"Good to hear," Mariah murmured, looking away.

"The Sikama became relevant when the Jewish community in Rome decided to eliminate Emperor Constantine in any way possible, in order to better the Jewish way of life in Rome," Ben Haddad said. "Many of my kinsmen believed this goal was possible and joined the sect at the Mine in A.D. 316, months after the Emperors Constantine and Licinius had declared the edict of Milan."

"The Mine was an old abandoned Roman quarry near the Empire's capital city," Mariah chipped in. She smiled when the professor approved with a nod.

"And what is this edict of Milan?" Kimberley wanted to know.

"It's a proclamation issued by the Emperors to elevate Christianity in the Empire," Mariah said. "This made the public to start seeing the Jews as murderers of the elevated Christ, thereby initiating the public persecution of our people."

"We, the members of the sect, went about preparing for our mission by studying Kabbalah Ma'asit," Mr. Haddad said. "After several missteps, we were able to communicate with a group of Yahweh's angels led by Rau, the Guardian of His Western Regions and Beyond."

The professor paused. He liked the rapt attention his small audience displayed. "You know the spells in the books came from the devil?"

"So we heard," Kimberley said. "But you could be joking, right?"

Benjamin Haddad chuckled. "No, I'm not," he said. "These heavenly servants went into an unholy alliance with Lucifer just to help us…"

Kimberley frowned again. "Lucifer, the devil?"

"Yes, Lucifer." Mariah meant every word. "Rau promised us Shurabi, a fiendish spell of many evil powers, which Satan, the devil, had agreed to provide under one single condition."

"And what condition was that?" Kimberley asked.

"That Rau and his colleagues must win over Yahweh's heavenly servants for Lucifer within a given time after he had done his part," Benjamin Haddad said.

The small audience remained speechlessly amazed that the books had such a dark history.

"Our new masters showed us how to mysteriously make books using a procedure hitherto unknown to established civilizations and Roman codex makers of those days," the professor continued, "and this was how we came to be known as Bookmakers or Bookbinders by those trusted Jewish leaders intimated of our existence, objectives and supreme goal."

"So how did you come about the books?" Aiden asked, now fully engrossed by this interesting tale.

"It took us roughly ten years to get it right," Mariah continued. "Within this time, most of the books we produced were later discarded, because they could not carry the spell Satan wanted to bestow on them."

Benjamin Haddad turned to Rachel. "Your father succeeded where we all failed, my dear."

"Jehoash came up with a peculiar material he processed from papyrus to make the pages of the first book," Mariah said. "This material easily received the spell without much trouble."

"And with Lucifer's help, the angels imparted the spell of Shurabi into invisible Hebrew words they inscribed on the pages of this strong book, thereby transferring the spell to the book," Professor Goldenberg said.

"How did you come about the second book?" Aiden demanded.

"After the first book was made, the Sikama's Inner Circle realized that Constantine was not our main problem, because the Romans knew how to kill off their emperors." Professor Goldenberg paused for effect. "And even if we removed this emperor, who knew the kind of person the next emperor would be? This meant that our people might never be set free from the tyranny of Rome."

"And even if we were finally free of Rome, who knew the kind of barbaric kingdom that would rise up to subdue us again?" Mariah continued.

"Hence the thirteen original Bookbinders who formed the Cult or Inner Circle of the Sikama decided to ask the Booklords for something that would guarantee a better Jewish future as well," Benjamin Haddad said. "The angels had to turn again to Satan for help and this supreme demon leader imparted a second hellish spell of Shurabi, which could show the future, on a second book."

"The devil told the Sicarii Kabbalah Masada that both books could be merged after a third and final ritual. He also said that the wielder of the third book would be able to control his or her destiny," Mariah narrated.

"This made us forget Emperor Constantine as we mobilized all our resources towards obtaining the third book within a given time frame," Ben Haddad murmured. "Unfortunately, our angelic helpers fell from heaven after Yahweh discovered their betrayal around this time. They decided to get back the books from us and return it to God.

"But Satan, seeing that the Booklords could no longer help him destroy heaven, decided to prevent these former co-conspirators of his from getting the book by unleashing the Wind of Hell, which we all know as the Fire and Ice of Masada, on the ancient scrolls in order to protect them until we could conclude the ritual for the third book."

"In a way, Satan was helping your people?" Aiden wanted to know.

"So it seemed," Mariah agreed. "However, before we could organize the third ritual, the Booklords increased the frequency of their attacks on the Mine."

"Twelve of the Bookbinders except Jehoash and I decided to flee into the future after fearing for their lives," Ben Haddad continued from where his junior colleague had stopped. "Jehoash agreed not to reveal the twelve's whereabouts to the Sikama if the twelve agreed not to take the white book into the future with them. He had a hard time convincing the Sikama that the Romans were to blame for the disappearance of the twelve."

"So how did they escape then?" Jeremy wondered.

"They divided a leaf from the white book amongst themselves," Mariah replied. "You met some of them during your journey up to this point," she told Rachel.

Rachel felt sad. "I-I guess so."

"I tried to convince Jehoash to destroy the books owing to the danger surrounding us during this time, but he refused," Benjamin Haddad said. "If only he had listened to me."

"I don't believe you, Uncle Ben," Rachel snapped, chin up.

"He's saying the truth, dear." Mariah put her hands on the little girl's shoulders. "We would never lie to you."

Benjamin Haddad smiled at Rachel. "Of course, I would never do that to you, my dear." His smile became a frown. "Satan was about to reveal more steps for the ritual to your father when the Booklords attacked the Mine the same time that Emperor Constantine's army broke into the old quarry, my dear. Your father just had time to send you, his only child, into the future with the white book before the Gray Ones killed him and the Romans captured his wife and the remaining Sikama members along with the black book."

"So, leaving Emperor Constantine out of the picture was a grave mistake," Kimberley concluded and the old scientist nodded.

"He proved to be our undoing."

"What we should do next is a puzzling question that remains?" Aiden pointed out.

"Like I told you guys, the other book is still here on Earth," Mariah said, glancing at her fellow Bookbinder. "Now, we have someone who knows how to retrieve it for the sake of our cause."

"You're talking of the two theories concerning the hidden Hebrew words in the white book?" Kimberley began.

"Well...eh, not exactly," Mariah stammered.

"The black book is still on Earth," Mr. Haddad said. "Whoever told you otherwise lied to you."

"So, you believe the Second Theory is wrong, Uncle Ben?" Rachel asked him.

Benjamin Haddad nodded. "Yes," he said. "We just need to rest now and make history tomorrow."

"Sadly, not for us," Kimberley let out.

"What do you mean by that?" Mariah asked her.

The Portwood sergeant looked away. "We've risked our lives enough for this cause of yours, Mariah. I think we should be leaving the scene at this point, no matter which theory is correct."

Aiden looked up. "Are we going home, Kim?"

"Yes," Kimberley told him, taking his hand. "I think we're done here."

"And what of Rachel?" Aiden began.

"She will stay with us," Ben Haddad said. "So should you two...for a short time?"

"Not happening," Kimberley said. "We've done our part, Rachel. Now, you need to let us go back to Portwood."

"Come, my friends," Jeremy began. "No need for that now. We've won, remember? Stay as our guest for just two days, okay?"

Kimberley rolled her eyes. "Rachel?"

"I-I think I should stay," the little girl said, staring at the people cleaning the lab. "Father would want me to remain, because it's the right thing to do."

Aiden looked lost. "I-I don't know if I should stay," he said. "I do want to go home, but I don't have anywhere to go to."

"You'll stay with me," Kimberley told him. "That's settled already."

"We still need you, buddy," Mariah told Aiden. "Remember we still have to find the black book and perform the ritual. Who knows what other surprises you could spring for us?"

"Yes, Avigdor," Ben Haddad agreed. "We cannot afford to lose you now."

Kimberley noticed Aiden looking at Rachel. She knew what that meant. "We'll stay not more than a week under one condition," she said.

Aiden brightened. "Thank you, Kim. Oh, thanks."

Ben Haddad grinned. "And what's the condition, if I may ask?"

Kimberley smiled. "That we spend time with Rachel?"

"No problem," the old man said. "I will make arrangements for your quarters immediately."

"We'll be staying with Jeremy," Kimberley told Mariah. "So, no need to make space for us. We'll pay you guys a visit tomorrow."

"I'll miss you, Kim," Rachel said. "I feel it already."

"I'm still here," Kimberley chuckled, hugging the strange little girl whose presence on a lonely icy road one snowy day had started everything.

"I'm still sorry about Jim," Rachel told her. "I-I still feel all those deaths were my fault."

"Don't be," Kimberley soothed. "Yes, I lost Jim hours after finding you that fateful day, but I must admit that I've been grieving well for some time now. This spooky adventure finally coming to an end in the best of ways have helped me to remove my thoughts from my personal tragedy. More so, I'll soon be back home rebuilding my life with those friends of mine still alive and that is more than any average person could ask for." She turned to Aiden and took his hands.

"Kim, c'mon," Aiden protested. "Please, don't cry."

"Aiden, I must ask for your forgiveness," Kimberley whispered between tearful sighs. "Please forgive me, I beg you. I-I didn't know what came over me back in Brazil. I was a fool to have said all those horrible things I told you."

Aiden felt overwhelmed. He hugged the sergeant before his tears choked him. "Kim, I-I don't have a better friend," he stumbled over. "You've always been my family since…since Mum died."

This brought fresh tears to Kimberley's eyes. Professor Goldenberg handed her a blue handkerchief and she murmured her thanks.

Jeremy stopped beside her. "Look, Kim, I know you guys have been through a lot, but we need to go now. Got some things I need to do before sleep time."

Kimberley nodded and took Mariah's hands. "Take good care of Rachel, Mariah. We'll come visit. Promise."

"Yeah, sure Kim, old friend," the female Sikama assured. "And thanks for your help. You know I won't be here if not for your help."

"Time to go," Kimberley told Aiden and left the lab. She noticed the institute's remaining workforce commencing the removal of the bodies in the passage. Ben Haddad, also known as Baruch Goldenberg, shook her hand on her way out with Jeremy and the boy.

Rachel continued to stare at the laboratory entrance long after her friends had gone.

*   *   *

Benjamin Haddad turned to the little girl still staring at the entrance to his laboratory and cleared his throat. "Your room is being prepared, my dear," he said. "Tomorrow we get down to business after you must have rested well enough."

"It's all happening so fast," Rachel murmured.

"Come, my dear," Mariah said. "I'll spend the night with you."

Security Officer Rewder Hurt approached the trio.

The professor turned to him. "Yes, Rewder, what is it?"

"Concerning the news we received today, sir, about the Kannibals planning to attack Bravery, we've strengthened the number of night sentries around the city."

"Good, though there's nothing to fear," Ben Haddad said. "They can't win a fight with us, if they can even find a way to get in first."

A female staff stopped before him. "We're ready, sir."

"About time," a smiling Mariah quipped.

"Good." The professor turned to Rachel.

"What do you do here, Uncle Ben?"

The elderly Sikama never anticipated that question, but he had a ready reply. "The Red War affected our way of life, my dear, especially the natural process that helps us to make the bulk of our food."

"Photosynthesis," Rewder helped.

"Photosynthesis is very important in maintaining life on Earth, my dear," Ben Haddad continued. "After the Red War, the dust reduced this process, causing the amount of food available for animals, as well as other organic matter on Earth to drastically reduce. Most animals vanished after this, and the oxygen in the Earth's atmosphere fell to very low levels."

"Consequently, carbon dioxide removed from our atmosphere to make carbohydrates during photosynthesis millions of years ago is now returning faster than ever," Rewder pointed out.

"This phenomenon is already having a major implication on our climate," Mariah chipped in.

Rachel appeared attentive. "So, how do you help the situation?"

"No need for that," Mariah began. "We will leave this place and time very soon."

Professor Goldenberg glared at her and turned back to Rachel. "We're simply trying to genetically modify our common crops so that they can photosynthesize in a very limited amount of light, my dear. Now, you need to go and rest. Tomorrow, we'll begin."

"I can help you keep the book if it's a burden," Mariah suggested.

"Don't worry, Aunt Mariah," Rachel said. "There's no pressure on me now that the Gray Ones have been destroyed for good. I can handle it."

The little girl left with the female staff and Rewder went back to handling the institute's present problem of dead bodies.

Benjamin Haddad looked at his female protégé and frowned.

Mariah sighed. "What?"

"That didn't go well," her master said. "You have to be careful from now on. We cannot afford to lose her trust right now. You can't continue to make such mistakes. It will destroy everything we've worked for all these years."

Mariah nodded. "I erred. Please forgive me. I won't do that next time."

Chapter 35
KIDNAPPING A KANNIBAL

JEREMY glanced at his fellow X5 occupants and shook his head in disbelief. What a day it had been for all of them, most especially for him. Who knew that angels and demons actually existed in real life? That unearthly powers and spiritualism really existed in Man's world? People believed these things back in ancient times, but the major religions had disappeared a long time ago, leaving philosophers and psychologists to take their place.

The Resilience resident looked at the boy and female sergeant in the unit with him and wondered aloud, "I guess our mission was a success?"

"Kind of," the woman said. "Though I thought a lot of things were way off today."

"Like what?" the boy wondered.

"Well, like the fact that Mariah never hesitated when we met Benjamin Haddad."

"I don't get that?" Jeremy confessed.

Kimberley shook her head. The good fellow in the X5 with them would understandably be confused. "Aiden, I don't know if I'm taking things too far here, but I think Mariah is keeping some things from us."

"And why would she do that, Kim?" Aiden asked.

"I don't know," Kimberley let out. "This talk of Sikama factions fighting each other for the book, I just don't get it."

"The Kannibals running the Slums never talked of Ankh and Cross Sikama factions when I was there as their prisoner," Jeremy said.

"You were their prisoner?" Aiden blinked twice.

Kimberley had her eyes fixed on Jeremy. "Wait, you had this piece of information all this time and you kept it from us?" She clenched and unclenched her fists.

"Your friend interrupted me when I wanted to tell you at my shelter," the Resilience resident defended.

"And which friend of mine is that?"

"Mariah."

"Has Rachel been telling us the truth, as well, Kim?" Aiden whispered. "Everything she said about me could be a lie?"

"I know," Kimberley said. "Especially the reincarnation bit. Why don't you have alternate memory if you're this Avigdor guy?"

Aiden frowned. "Kim, do you think Rachel lied about me to protect me?"

Kimberley stared at the boy. "Protect you from what? Is she protecting you by saying you're someone from the Mine?"

"I don't know," Aiden stammered. "I'm just…"

"Can't understand you guys," Jeremy cut in. "I can only contribute to this conversation if I can follow you guys?"

Kimberley turned to him. "You're following us, aren't you?"

"What of the Boom, Kim?" Aiden asked her. "How did we achieve it when we were in the professor's laboratory?"

"I heard no boom back there," Kimberley countered. "Did you?"

Aiden paused. "I don't think I did," he said. "So, why would the professor and Rachel lie about that?"

"Well, I think if Rachel smells something fishy, she would want to make things happen by proclaiming she knows something or someone formidable so that the suspects will come out of their shadows."

"Okay, that makes sense," Jeremy commended.

"But she's putting herself in danger by doing so," Aiden pointed out.

"Rachel can communicate with us through *TelepathyG7* if she finds herself in certain situations, and I advised her to play along until she does so," Kimberley said. "I also told her to come to a conclusion about her new hosts before thinking of handing over the white book to that professor."

"So, you both planned this?" Aiden wondered aloud.

"No, this was Rachel's plan. I just helped her along," Kimberley said.

"Still lost here," Jeremy announced.

"We even put up a tear-filled show back there to convince our friends of our blissful ignorance should they finally turn out to be frauds," Kimberley said. Aiden coughed and she turned to him. "Are you okay, sweetheart?"

"I think so," the boy lied. "Did you mean what you told me back at the lab, Kim?"

"Yes, I did," Kimberley said without looking at him. "I am so sorry, dear."

"Are you?" He teared up.

Kimberley turned to him. "Yes, I am," she told him in a shaky voice. "That wasn't a script. I meant every word with all my heart and soul. I just need your forgiveness and will continue begging for it until you do so."

Jeremy shook his head. "Still lost here," he repeated.

Kimberley smiled at him, trying to regain her composure. "Our next mission is to kidnap a Kannibal," she announced.

"You out of your mind?" Jeremy began.

"Good, you understand that," the Portwood cop chuckled. "And no, I'm not out of my mind. We need to know what's really going on in the Slums with the Sicarii Kabbalah Masada."

Jeremy appeared confused. "And who are they?"

"The Sikama," Aiden whispered.

"Okay, never knew it was an acronym," Jeremy confessed. "Why would we want to kidnap a Kannibal when you guys have actually been held at a human farm?" he wondered. "You can't just forget everything that happened there, you know?"

"The Kannibal will help us remember since we've been there before," Kimberley said. "Remember the bigger picture, Jeremy."

"Which is?"

"We're from the past?" Aiden pointed out.

"And Mariah kept talking about good Sikama and bad Sikama," Jeremy tried again, ignoring him. "How am I supposed to differentiate between the two groups?"

"Very simple," Kimberley told him. "Good Sikama don't eat humans."

*   *   *

They met that night in Professor Goldenberg's study, a large room lined with floor-to-ceiling bookshelves holding volumes of all shapes and sizes. The man now also known as Benjamin Haddad relaxed on a big swiveling chair behind a huge mahogany desk on which sat an advanced *TelepathyG7* monitor, a traditional keyboard and several case files and hardbacks. Mariah, on the other hand, paced around the room, visibly anxious and annoyed.

"We need to seize that book as soon as possible," she said, walking to and fro with her hands on her hips. "Her friends might be coming back for her right now."

"They're not," Ben Haddad said. "You don't have *TelepathyG7*? It shows you what happens around this complex. Who goes in and who comes out."

"Really? We could also hasten up and leave this forsaken place."

"Patience," the professor said. "We must carry the girl along at this point. We must not destroy our good fortune out of carelessness."

Mariah looked like she would explode. "We can forget the plan if we don't act now," she said.

"Of course, we'll act soon," her superior said. "Rachel just needs convincing first, because without that book, the plan is as good as dead."

"And I hope we haven't altered the plan?"

"We will alter the plan if I say so!" the professor snapped, standing up. "Remember your place, woman."

"Forgive me, Master."

"Just shut up," her livid senior said and sat down again. "For your information, I'm not going anywhere anymore. We're living and dying here."

Mariah became alarmed. "But you said…"

"Forget what I said," Benjamin exploded. "I am one of the richest men in the world right now and I am not going to throw away all that wealth because of some ancient fable peddled by a forgotten tribe."

"But you know what the books can do, Master. Will you discard all that you now know about the white book?"

"I am not throwing away my knowledge, far from that," Benjamin said. "We will use what we know to achieve what we want to achieve, and that is to increase my wealth first. Initiating the ritual comes later."

Mariah could not believe her ears, but she had no choice. "Yes, Master."

The professor stood up and met his protégé halfway across the room. He placed his right hand on her right shoulder. "The white book must help us increase that wealth, Mariah," he said. "That is my original plan, my dear. That is our soul objective for now."

"That's a good plan, Master," Mariah said. "I like it."

"I have done well for myself, Mariah," Benjamin Haddad said. "With time you'll know the full extent of my wealth, then you wouldn't want to leave this time and place, not even for the good of a tribe that is no longer relevant in the present system."

"But the Sikama, Master."

"We'll get the white book and do our thing, then we'll see how we get the black book and initiate the ritual."

"For the Jews?"

"For the Sikama, Mariah. The red bomb detonated over our ancestral land and wiped off more than half of our population from the face of the

Earth."

"W-What are you saying?" Mariah's hands shook as they involuntarily went to her mouth.

"The Jews are no longer relevant, my dear," Benjamin Haddad said. "We, the ones still alive, must now use the books for our wellbeing if we intend to survive and eventually determine our destiny."

The duo heard receding footsteps outside the study.

"Did you hear that?" Mariah pressed.

"Yes, I did," the professor said. "Someone had been listening to our conversation."

"A child, judging from the sound of those steps."

*   *   *

Rachel walked into her room determined to evade spy technology in her current state. She locked the door and switched on her *TelepathyG7* wrist bracelet before she remembered that she could not use it in the research institute. Uncle Ben and Mariah would know whoever she calls as soon as she makes the call. Turning off the communicator, she went to one of the room's windows and stopped to think of what next to do.

She could go back in time with the book and start afresh, but then this action could erase memories that she'd acquired in the course of the present journey. Memories like how to destroy the Gray Ones and their human servants.

The Gray Ones.

The little girl cringed at the thought of undoing what had been achieved so far with the white scroll. Obviously, the Gray Ones would come back into existence if she went back in time at this critical juncture in her journey.

Rachel couldn't say what she'd do differently if she went back. Mariah's lies meant that Kpakol and Mr. Hoyte could have been saying the truth after all. Even Uncle Ezra. This got her thinking again. To what extent was she prepared to go in changing the story she'd already lived? If it came down to handing over the white book to the Gray Ones, would she willingly do that? Of course, she would if she was convinced that she had no other choice. Wasn't there any other choice? What would her father do in the current situation? He…would leave first before tackling the problem somewhere else?

Exactly.

Her mind made up, Rachel turned to the only bed in the room, on which she had earlier left the ancient artifact before leaving.

Nothing lay on the bed.

Someone had taken the ancient volume.

She had left the room's door unlocked when she left.

The knock on the door jolted her, but she regained her composure before unlocking the door with her bracelet. Mariah's smile did not help her mood in any way.

"Hello, Rachel," the Bookmaker said. "I hope you like this place?"

"Well, yes," Rachel quipped. "I was about going to sleep when you knocked. Anything the matter?"

"We returned your book, Rachel." Professor Goldenberg appeared behind his protégé. "Rewder said you left it on the bed when you went out. He thought it best to bring it to me. Of course, he meant no harm."

"Thanks, Uncle Ben," the little girl said. "I-I went out to look around. Felt bored."

"Oh, no bother, dear," Mariah said. "Next time, though, don't leave it about, even though here is safe."

"Okay," Rachel said, taking back the book from the professor. "What now, Mariah?"

"That's why we're here, my dear," Benjamin Haddad said with a wry smile. "Believe me; you'll love what comes next."

*   *   *

The three individuals faced the red dust and grueling cold when the camouflaged lift brought them to the surface. It got worse as they stepped out of the last cave facing the slope leading down to the valley, the blistering weather contrasting sharply with the peacefully warm atmosphere they'd experienced within the underground city.

"The temperature is...30° Qahrenheit?" Aiden peered at his helmet's screen in order to make sure of this. "It is 30° Qahrenheit," he repeated.

"Good that we have warm hazard suits," Jeremy said.

"Radiation levels are also through the roof," Kimberley said, watching a RadiaMeter.

"We need to get down to the surface shelters beyond the valley," Jeremy began, pointing this out with his right index finger.

"You warned us not to run to those surface shelters when we met you," Kimberley noted. "What changed?"

"That is the right place to spring a trap if you want to kidnap a Kannibal," Jeremy said. "I still don't know why I'm helping you guys on this."

Kimberley rolled her eyes. "Yeah, we know that this is madness. Thanks for the help."

"You're welcome." Jeremy looked down the valley. "Let's go now.

My time as a Volunteer Watch runs till Z9.65 HM."

"And what does that even mean?" Kimberley demanded. "Is that even a time format?" Jeremy stared at her. "Never mind, let's go."

"Aiden can wait for us in the Corridor of Caves," Jeremy said. "He'll be safe there."

Aiden nodded and drew back while the adults started down the arid slope that swept into the valley below.

The freezing temperature mocked the ineffectual heat radiating from the solar shape visible now and then through the intense red haze clinging to the atmosphere with ferocious tenacity.

"We save around two to three escapees from the Slum every week," Jeremy said as he climbed down the slope. "We could be lucky and run into a rogue party today."

"What's a rogue party?" Kimberley wondered.

Jeremy got to the valley first. "The Kannibals sent out to look for runaways from the human farm," he replied, surveying the rough road meandering through the valley. Kimberley joined him. "We'll hide somewhere down there," he pointed out with his right index finger.

"Those surface shelters look old and creepy," Kimberley said, but Jeremy ignored her, walking across the dearth road. "Okay."

"Back then, the surface shelters were the first set of solid structures the government claimed would save lives if nuclear war ever broke out," Jeremy narrated. "Their problem stemmed from the fact that they were surface facilities that took the brunt of the red bomb's explosion during the war. This rendered them useless after eliminating the many lives that had innocently sought refuge in these 'death' shelters, as they came to be called after the war."

The duo got to the crumbling structures lined up in rows on a very large land expanse. They sneaked in between two of these buildings and Jeremy turned to Kimberley.

"We wait here," he said. "Hopefully, we won't wait for long."

"I hope you're right," Kimberley said, squatting beside him. She heard screaming. "That was fast," she noted.

"That's a woman's voice," Jeremy said. "It came from the road."

"So, what do we do?"

"We'll cause a distraction when we see her pursuers."

"And then what?"

"And then we hide…and surprise whoever comes after us with this stunner." He brandished a pair of unique guns and gave the Portwood sergeant one. "Don't kill them, just stun them."

Kimberley wasn't convinced. "And what if they kill their fleeing prisoner before we see them?"

Jeremy said nothing.

Kimberley hissed and stepped out of hiding. "Over here!" she called out to the running woman, showing herself by waving her arms about. The female escapee turned towards her and scurried over to the ramshackle spread out all around her. "Hurry!"

"Did they follow you?" Jeremy asked the petrified female.

"Yes," the middle-aged woman cried, squatting behind the duo. "Here they come!"

Kimberley had little time to take in the woman's sunken cheeks, gaunt face and bony arms before turning back to the road to see a familiar vehicle emerge from the red haze drastically restricting all-round visibility. She clutched her weapon with both hands and showed herself.

"What are you doing?" Jeremy snapped.

"Speeding things up," she said, waving at the Kannibals. "Hey, over here!"

The unit swerved towards her and Jeremy pulled her into the jungle of derelict structures behind the female escapee.

"Now they know we're here!" he cried. "You've blown this! Are you insane?"

"They still don't know our number."

"Are you nuts? They have *TelepathyG7* just like us."

"Do I look dumb to you?" Kimberley demanded. "*TelepathyG7* only picks out people if your environment is red-dust-free. The red dust prevents the system's zaplites from doing a better job."

"Okay, sorry I forgot you claim to have alternate memory or whatever," Jeremy sounded furious. "Even if this is true, what is your plan, Sergeant Reyna?"

Kimberley halted her run. "We draw them in here and pick them off one by one until we can kidnap the last one."

"You're crazy, right?" Jeremy could not believe his ears as he stopped with the rescued prisoner. "They are seasoned soldiers. They'll simply kill us."

"Let's do this," Kimberley sounded exasperated. "Trust me. I have been a soldier more than once in this crazy journey."

"So, what do we do?" Jeremy asked her.

Kimberley turned to the woman they hoped to save at the end of the day. "We'll spread out and hide."

"If you say so, sergeant," Jeremy said, giving a mock salute before turning serious again. "Okay, here they come!"

"You go left and I'll take right," Kimberley whispered and sneaked off.

Jeremy wandered off in the opposite direction with the escapee. He pushed back the broken seal door of a surface shelter and stepped into the creepy structure with his new friend. Now he stopped to peer at the approaching mobile system through a splintered glass window, his weapon at the ready. All around him, the red haze moved like fog in and around the old shelters, poor visibility a result of this atmospheric catastrophe.

The B6 unit emerged from this man-made phenomenon and stopped before the surface shelters. Three armed men wearing black hazard suits stepped out of it and fanned out.

Jeremy knew that a rogue party usually had four members; hence the system's driver must have remained inside the unit, obviously with a drawn weapon. He turned to the woman and placed a finger on his lips before pushing open the shelter's door and slipping out into the haze outside.

Both men stared at each other as soon as they came face to face.

Jeremy stunned the Kannibal before the fellow let off a shot that missed him by inches. Holding his fallen opponent by a leg, he pulled the guy's body into an open shelter, took the man's lazer gun and stepped out once again, his vigilance now heightened by the abrupt event. The stun usually lasted a day, so they would be long gone before the poor dude regained consciousness.

Farther in-between the decommissioned shelters he went, looking for the next black hazard suit. Jeremy hated the fact that, despite his visibility enhancer, he could not see single objects until he was close enough. This technological failure could be blamed on the use of obsolete equipment after the Red War. The lack of innovative ideas and system manufacturers post-belligerency immensely contributed to the absence of new technology in the present era. He just hoped this monumental mistake caused by Mankind wasn't about to cause him his life.

The stun shot sounded ahead of him and he moved faster. He wasn't surprised to see Kimberley dragging a Kannibal by a leg into one of the shelters. "Remember to get his gun," he said, moving forward. "Remains one person."

The sudden shot went through Jeremy's right arm and he dropped his weapon in pain. Expecting the next shot to end his life, he turned to see the remaining Kannibal fall before Kimberley, her lazer gun whining as it reset to 'stun.'

"That was close," Kimberley said, putting away her gun and grabbing the fallen Kannibal by the legs.

"I thought they fanned out," Jeremy said, clutching his wound. "Damn this hurts!"

"I need to get you to safety."

"No, I can manage," Jeremy snapped. "Let's finish this."

*   *   *

Akron heard the shots and got out of the B6. He pointed his lazer gun into the red haze masking everything and looked around despite the poor visibility.

How did Mrs. Tully escape? Whoever helped her do so was in big trouble, because Grubb would never accept that kind of behavior from an employee.

He went round the B6, but saw nothing out of place. Those shots he heard were not VG lazer guns. Who shot his comrades? He didn't want to venture out to investigate since the commander had ordered him to stay put. If only he could...

The noise made him swing his head and weapon towards the rear end of his vehicle. "Who is there?" he bellowed. "Show yourself!"

The head blow knocked him out.

*   *   *

The Kannibal came round, holding his head. He realized many individuals surrounded him and tried to reach for his nonexistent weapon with shackled hands.

"About time," Kimberley said, glaring at the fellow.

"W-Where am I?" the man demanded.

"No need to know, Akron," Jeremy replied, his shoulder freshly treated and bandaged. "Don't worry. You'll be knocked out and sent back out there again after this interrogation."

"How did you know my name?" Akron demanded.

"It's written on your shirt."

The man feigned a smile and looked around. "I'm in one of your underground cities. A prisoner, obviously. I wonder whatever happened to our truce."

"Your people have been violating the peace accord, my friend," an elderly man said, stepping out of a dark corner of the room. "Good evening, Akron. My name is Kevin Smith, chairman of the Resilience City Board."

"We don't violate the peace accord, man," Akron said. "We only try to round up prisoners who escaped."

"That violates the accord if any prisoner runs to the caves for cover," Jeremy noted. "The underground cities agreed with the Kannibals about

359

that."

"They did?" Kimberley began. Who agrees with flesh eaters on anything?

"Some do get here and regain their freedom," the kidnapped Kannibal said.

"That's not true," Kimberley countered. "Cases of your comrades recapturing escapees in the caves abound. I know because I was a prisoner."

Akron looked her over. "I remember you. Grubb would love to see you again."

"And who is Grubb?" Jeremy demanded.

"One of our leaders. Please, get me out of here as soon as possible. He won't be happy with me if he hears I was caught."

"Not happening," Kimberley said.

"We want you to take back a message for us to your leaders, including this Grubb, Akron," Kevin Smith, the Resilience City chairman, said. "Tell them the underground cities can defend themselves against any attack the Kannibals launch at us."

"Remember they have to find the door first," someone joked and the gathered laughed heartily.

"Throw him out with a hazard suit," Mr. Smith told the city's Chief Volunteer Watch and left with his fellow administrators.

"Okay, Jeremy," the superior officer said as he left. "You heard the man."

"Where's my hazard suit?" Akron demanded soon after. "Just let me go, okay?"

Kimberley and Jeremy exchanged glances. They were the only ones remaining in the decontamination compartment with the Kannibal. "One more question, Akron," she began. "What do you know about the Sikama in the Slums?"

"Is that a joke?" Akron wondered with a frown. "You had Sikama friends in there, Kimora. You even escaped with one and two kids."

"Your point being what exactly?"

"That you know more about them than I'll ever do? Actually, your Sikama friend had a falling out with Grubb, that's why they say you fled with her and the two kids."

Kimberley nodded. She hated the fact that she'd found it so hard to use her alternate memory ever since she appeared in this time and place. Did she taste human flesh in there?

"So, your name was Kimora in there?" Jeremy asked her.

"What bothers me most is the nature of Mariah's quarrel with this...this Grubb," she said. "I wonder what caused it."

"Akron, ever heard of Ankh Sikama?" Jeremy asked the Kannibal, setting his gun to 'stun.'

"Ankh Sikama? Is that even a thing? Wait, what are you doing?"

Chapter 36
GRUBB

"SHE lied to us," Kimberley whined.

"Did Akron say that?" Aiden asked her.

"We're not sure of that yet," Jeremy said.

"He implied that," Kimberley said.

"I doubt Akron had a good source for that information," Jeremy said. "Remember he said you know more about the Sikama than he will ever do, Kim."

"Did he say that?" Aiden asked his fellow time-traveler.

"Yes, he did." Kimberley rolled her eyes. "Can't this thing go any faster? So much for our trust in technology."

"We'll get there soon enough," Jeremy said.

"Or tomorrow," Kimberley grumbled. "Christ, how did I miss Mariah's lies?"

"We all missed her lies," Aiden pointed out.

"And why can't I remember anything from the Slum?"

"I still can't do that," Aiden pointed out. "I just hope Rachel has a different story to tell."

"I hope she's alive and well," Kimberley said. "If anything happens to her, that will be on me."

"Here we are," Jeremy announced.

The X5 hovered into the Genetix complex and stopped before the research institute's expansive flight of entrance steps.

"Holly!" Aiden remarked. "You guys seeing what I'm seeing?"

"They were expecting us," Jeremy said. "They just jammed our *TelepathyG7*."

Guard lines stretched out from both sides of the major doorway down to the foot of the institute's front staircase. Professor Goldenberg, Mariah and Rachel stood before the establishment's massive entrance atop the flight of stairs on which these guards had formed the parallel lines. The men brandished lazer rifles.

"We can't go out there with our weapons," Jeremy noted.

"What do we do now, Kim?" Aiden wondered aloud.

"We'll confront them with what we know," Kimberley said, preparing to open the X5's only door.

"They won't let us walk away with the book just like that, Kim," Jeremy said. "You should know that by now."

"And I'm not gonna let Rachel suffer this alone," Kimberley returned. "I've let her down so many times before and I'm not gonna do that anymore. Are you guys coming or not?"

"Coming," the other two chorused, grudgingly getting up from their comfortable seats.

"Well, well, well," Mariah began on seeing the trio emerging from the X5. "Welcome back, Kim. I hope I can persuade you to stay this time."

"You lied to us, Oxana."

"What?"

"You lied to us," Kimberley repeated, taking the steps two at a time.

"No, I heard that the first time," Mariah said. "You called me Oxana? Where did that come from?"

"Forget it," Kimberley said.

"We met in Chornobyl, remember?" Aiden tried.

"No, I don't," Mariah said, her face contorting in anger.

"How dare you lie about that as well?" Kimberley asked her. "You told us about the First Theory in Pripyat and you led us to Kpakol as well. What are you now saying?" She turned to Rachel. "Mariah has been lying to us, Rachel. Kpakol was right about the black book."

Rachel seemed confused. "Kpakol was right?"

"Kpakol was wrong, my dear," Mariah countered. "The other book is still here with Man, and Ben will find it if it doesn't find us."

"Exactly," the professor supported, turning to Rachel. "Like I told you, my dear, they'll try to confuse you and take the book. Of course, they won't succeed, because they came late to this party."

"You old twisted man," Jeremy whispered in anger. "You..." Kimberley stopped his forward steps with her right elbow and turned to Rachel. "What have you done, Rachel? Did they try to convince you to hand over the book?"

"That's the only way to help my people achieve their destiny, Kim," Rachel said. "Father would understand."

"Your father will understand nothing, Rachel, if you do that,"

Kimberley snapped. "What did they tell you? How did they convince you?"

The little girl bowed her head. "I-I heard Aunt Mariah and Uncle Ben discussing our people's future in Uncle Ben's library. I left in anger because I thought that…that their plan was a selfish one. I now know the…the truth, Kim. They made me realize there was no other way."

"No other way to do what, Rachel?" Aiden demanded.

"N-No other way to…to achieve our destiny," Rachel stuttered.

"And did they mention the ankh and cross factions of the Sikama in this story they told you, Rachel?" Jeremy asked.

"That both sides started the Red War and destroyed Israel with the red bomb?" Rachel rapped out.

Jeremy shook his head. "Wow," he said. "And you believed them?"

The little girl frowned. "No, I…"

"Hearing that Mariah lied to us and that Mr. Hoyte was right, do you still believe them?" Kimberley asked.

"No, I…"

"And we were hoping you would remember any incident at the Slum," Kimberley regretted.

"No, I did not," Rachel replied. "Look, Kim, they were planning to…"

"You see, Sergeant Reyna," Professor Goldenberg, a.k.a. Benjamin Haddad, cut in; "your little Bookbearer here has done us a favor by believing in us and doing something we never thought she would ever do."

Kimberley's heart skipped. "Is this…"

"Okay, okay," Mariah began. "I lied to you guys about everything. Kpakol and Dave were right. The black book is no longer with Man."

"What?" Rachel began.

"Oh, no," Aiden let out.

"Thought as much," Kimberley said, raising both hands to the sky as she looked away.

"Aunt Mariah, what're you saying?" Rachel exclaimed.

"What difference does it make now?" Mariah chuckled. "I also lied about there being a Cross Sikama and an Ankh Sikama. I just didn't want any other Sikama to return the white book to my master, so I killed every competition."

Kimberley wanted to cry. "So, I was right about the Indians, Mariah?"

Mariah looked away. "It's a competition amongst us Sikama, Kim. The first to get to the finish line wins."

"And where is the finish line, Aunt Mariah?" Aiden asked her.

The female Bookmaker lit up. "I just did one more thing to help me get closer to that line, Aiden dear," she told him.

"And what did you do?" the boy returned.

"Just persuaded Rachel to voluntarily give the white book to Benjamin Haddad. That makes her lose her control of the Ice of Masada, if you must know," Mariah replied.

"And has she done that?" Kimberley demanded. "I doubt she has done that. Let's say you're still trying to persuade her to do that."

Professor Goldenberg joined Mariah in the laughter that ensued.

"If you can persuade her, Aunt Mariah, what will that do for you?" Aiden asked without confidence. "Just saying if you can persuade her, though I think you've already done..."

"Having done exactly that, something has been pointed out to me," Mariah interrupted, frowning.

"And what is that?" Rachel wondered aloud. She hated the way Kimberley and Aiden kept staring at her.

"That I don't need you guys anymore?" Mariah said.

"Well, even though that really hurts," Kimberley began, "I think you've gone mad."

"Okay, that's enough," Mariah snapped.

"Take them away," the professor ordered his personnel. "We don't want to cause a scene in front of the complex, do we?"

The guards drew near. They seized Kimberley and her two companions.

"What are you doing?" Rachel demanded, running down the steps to the Portwood sergeant as the professor's employees seized the latter.

"Seize the girl as well," Benjamin Haddad said and the guards held Rachel.

"You have no right, professor," Jeremy said, pushing back the men trying to obey their employer.

"I do, my dear," Uncle Ben said, drawing close to the black man as his men pushed the bound fellow past the institute's entrance. "Once the Kannibals invade the underground cities tonight, you'll sing a different tune," he whispered.

Jeremy whistled. "Okay, now we're in trouble."

"So, you know about that?" Kimberley cried.

"I know about a lot of things, my dear," the professor claimed.

"Uncle Ben, you lied to me. How could you?" Rachel shouted as two guards shackled her hands like the others. "Give me back my book, you vile old man!"

"Not happening, my dear," Mariah said. "Besides, we technically never lied to you if you claim you never believed said lie."

Aiden stared at the Sikama. "Are you serious right now?"

"You've always sounded funny in difficult situations, Mariah," Kimberley told the female Bookmaker as guards tied her up. "Even when you were killing people."

"Thanks, Kim dear. I'll take that as a compliment."

"Take that as a warning," the female cop said before her captors marched her away with her friends.

"Nothing here to see," Mariah told some gawking institute workers. "They're Kannibal spies and we will hand them over to the authorities."

"The Kannibals are coming for your lives!" Jeremy shouted. "You must flee now to the mountains and…"

"Hey, keep quiet, okay?" Rewder snapped behind him.

Mariah turned to the workers and shrugged her shoulders. "See what I mean?"

"Take them to my lab," Benjamin Haddad said as he walked behind the captives. "We all need to talk in private."

Rewder nodded. "Right away, sir."

"Rachel, do something," Aiden urged the little girl. "You can still control the Ice of Masada, right?"

"This situation means she is no longer protected by the Ice of Masada," the professor said. "And that means she cannot control it anymore, because she gave me control of that powerful protection once she willingly handed me the book."

"I did not willingly give you the book, Uncle Ben," Rachel negated. "You forced my hand."

"Does that matter anymore?" Mariah whined. "As long as you gave him the book, you cannot control your precious dome anymore, darling."

Rachel boiled. "Watch me!" She shut her eyes and held them in this position for awhile. Nothing happened and she opened them in dismay.

Mariah shrugged her shoulders and smiled. "See what I mean?"

The guards brought the captives into the professor's laboratory with its long tables and tall stools.

"Yes, they can sit down," Professor Goldenberg announced, walking over to a glass panel on the wall. He pressed some buttons and a platform on which lay the white book slid out from the wall. The elderly Sikama took the mysterious volume and turned to his little audience. "I tried to convince Jehoash to destroy the books, but he refused."

"Not true, Uncle Ben," Rachel said.

"You still don't believe that?" Mariah asked.

"But I know it's not true," Rachel said. "Before he died, Father told me he wanted to destroy the books, but you convinced him not to do so since you wanted to use the books for your selfish goals."

Kimberley started. "Wow," she whispered.

"Did he say that, my dear?" The professor smiled at Rachel. His smile became a frown. "I'm not surprised he told you that," he said, sitting down on a stool across the little girl's position. "Your father was delusional. He had ideas of grandeur and couldn't control his greed. He sabotaged our efforts by leading the Romans to the Mine and..."

"That's not true!" Rachel exploded.

"You don't know that, Rachel, because you were not there," Mariah said. "You just can't face the fact that your father lied to you."

"Is this really true?" Kimberley wondered.

"No, it's not true," Rachel cried. "They're just trying to tarnish my father's image."

"You forget your father was dear to me, Rachel, and I cannot lie against him," Professor Goldenberg said. "However, I had to spill this now because you think your father never did anything wrong as a Sicarii Kabbalah Masada. Wrong, my dear. Turns out he was actually the one who led the Romans to us back at the Mine."

"Satan was about to reveal more steps for the ritual to us when the Booklords attacked the Mine the same time that Emperor Constantine's army broke into the old quarry, my dear," Mariah continued. "Your father made us believe that he just had time to send you, his only child, into the future with the white book, while the Romans captured him and his wife and the remaining Sikama members along with the black book."

"So, how did you find out the truth about this?" Kimberley asked her. "What gave him away?"

Mariah smiled. "Jeremiah Mizrahi."

"Mr. David Hoyte?" Aiden began. "Knew I've heard that name before."

"And what about him?" Jeremy wondered.

"Mizrahi was a parchment specialist who discovered a page had been torn off from the black book and suspected that Jehoash had done this in order to save the servants of the Sikama from the impending Roman onslaught," Benjamin Haddad said. "You see, my friend, Jehoash, hated slavery and maltreatment, hence he wanted to save the servants from the military doom he had set into motion for his comrades."

"We know he secretly approved of the Emperor's edicts proclaiming that Jews should never own Christian slaves before this incident," Mariah quipped. "So, he hated the fact that there were slaves in the Mine."

"And is that a bad thing?" Jeremy asked. "No one should be allowed to own slaves, right?"

"Sure," Aiden agreed and Benjamin Haddad glared at him.

"As I was saying," the elderly Sikama continued, turning to Rachel,

"Jeremiah discovered this torn off page and brought the matter to the Inner Circle, where Jehoash, your father, was implicated."

"This forced Jehoash to reveal the Roman plot to invade the Mine," Mariah added. "The traitor could not explain why he just wanted the slaves to escape and finally decided to help the twelve Bookmakers who wanted to do so as well with a page from the white book."

"Father was not a traitor," Rachel cried.

"Of course, he was!" Ben Haddad said. "He destroyed our plans and caused so many deaths."

"You're not so different."

"What did you say?"

"You're not so different," Aiden repeated. "I mean, you've tied us up, taken the white book for selfish reasons, and plan on inviting a bunch of cannibals into the cities protecting your people. That definitely looks like what a traitor would do."

"My intentions are good, even if you think they are selfish as well," Goldenberg chuckled. "I tied you up so that you'll not meddle with my plans, took the white book so that I can put it into better use. More so, underground cities are running out of food all over the world, and my research has failed to improve our crop yield in this toxic atmosphere we live in, so commercializing the most abundant form of meat on Earth at the moment is a smart thing to do."

"You're mad," Kimberley said.

"What do you want to do with the white book?" Aiden asked the professor. "Leave this time and place with all its misery, right?"

"Don't worry, I'm not going anywhere with it," the man replied with a smile. "I am a leader here. I have wealth surpassing any other person in the cities, and I intend removing every leader in all the underground cities using the white book. This action will make me the only leader there is without firing a single shot, okay?"

"That's sick," Jeremy said. "You're a psycho!"

"I will turn some of the cities I conquer into human settlement farms," Benjamin Haddad continued, ignoring the Resilience citizen.

"You'll do this at a time when the world's population is dwindling?" Kimberley wondered.

"That's why the white book will become a transportation tool for the animals I'll bring in from other times and places," Benjamin Haddad said.

"Real animals?" Aiden asked.

"We're all animals, aren't we?"

"Wow," Jeremy said. "Deranged doesn't even come close."

"Young man, I feel like cutting off your tongue right now," Benjamin

Haddad snapped.

"He's not worth it, Master," Mariah said.

"Master?" Kimberley began. "And when did that happen?"

The professor chuckled. "Come, sergeant, you know she was my protégé back at the Mine."

"So I heard," Kimberley said. "Was she also more than that?"

Mariah slapped the other woman hard across the face. "Don't take that personal, Kim," she giggled.

"As long as I got to you," Kimberley said with a smile. "No hard feelings."

"Okay with the drama," Benjamin Haddad said. "We'll leave you meddlers here until the Kannibals invade. Your punishment will then come. Until then, bye for now."

"You forget the boy from the past, Master," Mariah reminded him as she glared at Aiden.

"Ah, yes," the professor said. "We'll separate him when we return."

"And Rachel?" Kimberley asked.

The professor-turned-elderly-Sikama's eyes lit up. "She's as useful as her dead father," he said. "Come, Mariah, we've got to prepare a welcome party for our invading guests."

"Good luck handling Grubb, Mr. Haddad," Jeremy quipped. "Let's hope he's as accommodating as you are in his dealings with enemies who become allies overnight."

Benjamin Haddad grinned. "I am Grubb."

*　　*　　*

Jeremy looked around at the little girl on his left, the boy opposite him across the lab table, and the resolute woman on his right, who'd shown him what courage looked like in the last few days. "Unbelievable," he whispered. "Who would have known?"

Grubb's party had left the four captives sitting on long stools in the research laboratory, their hands tied behind their backs. Only the humming sound of plant machinery resonated throughout the long hall.

Rachel didn't look up. "He fooled all of us."

"Imagine he'd worked at Genetix since the war's end. Who knows when he switched?" Jeremy continued.

"Switched to being a Kannibal?" Kimberley asked.

"Switched to eating human flesh," Jeremy put more bluntly.

"Yuk!" Aiden said.

"Guess he has a human barbecue around here," Jeremy joked.

"Not funny," Aiden said.

"Who knows how many city residents he had killed since he switched?" Kimberley asked. She frowned. "Since he switched?"

Jeremy felt concern for the sergeant. "What's wrong?" he demanded and she turned to him.

"Jeremy, I am beginning to remember."

"Remember what, Kim?" Aiden asked.

"What happened at the Slum?"

"And what do you mean, Kim?" Rachel demanded.

"I think Professor Baruch Goldenberg maintained a presence at the Slums and the underground cities by switching between two personalities from time to time," Kimberley stated.

"You're saying he changed personalities?" Jeremy blinked.

"Yes, I can now remember him being absent from the Slums for long periods and then reappearing all of a sudden. He must have been switching between roles then, shuttling between the Slums and the underground cities whenever he wanted to."

"Meaning he had inside help in the underground cities?" Aiden asked.

Jeremy frowned. "Doesn't surprise me."

"Back at the settlement, Grubb always wore a large hat that hid his face," Kimberley continued. "Now, we all know why he kept that up."

"And what of Mariah?" Rachel wondered.

"Well, she quarreled with Grubb at the Slum, that I remember," Kimberley said. "But just like you and Aiden, I can't remember any other thing."

Aiden looked away. "Right," he murmured. "But it's not our fault that we..."

"Wrong," Mariah cut in from outside. The laboratory doors slid open and a line of armed men dressed in black military garb trooped into the room. Professor Baruch Goldenberg, also known as Benjamin Haddad, also known as Grubb, accompanied his protégé at the tail end of this line of Kannibal troops. "I knew all along where we were, Kim," Mariah said with a smile. "I simply deceived all of you into thinking I didn't know a thing by showing that I didn't know a thing."

"The idea was to bring the Bookbearer and her friends to me in the long run," the professor continued, smiling at his longtime assistant. "Glad I played a small part in this little plan."

"Brilliant," Aiden said dryly.

"And what of the quarrel between you two at the Slum?" Kimberley asked Mariah. "Don't lie to me, because I know that happened."

"Oh, that," Mariah began. "That was an incident I keep wishing you never accidentally witnessed."

"We had issues about the way forward and we mistakenly argued about it at the settlement," Ben Haddad said.

"That's a good explanation," Kimberley said, looking away.

"What now?" Rachel wondered.

"You have new companions," Professor Goldenberg said, waving at a Kannibal trooper at the door. "You'll be surprised by how quickly this invasion concluded."

"And we can see that you've now dressed the part," Kimberley said, looking the man over. Grubb's attire consisted of a neat lime-colored shirt tucked into dark-green pants and showing through a long black overcoat with an upturned collar. A pair of leather boots completed this attire. "What of your hat?" the Portwood sergeant asked her captor.

"I don't need it anymore."

"Don't you think you're a bit...overdressed?" Aiden wondered.

"Silence!" the professor bellowed, turning to the soldier at the door. "Drego, bring them in."

The foot soldier nodded and turned towards the lab door. He ushered in well-dressed ladies and gentlemen who had their hands tied behind their backs.

"Unbelievable," Jeremy muttered.

"The cities' council members and chairman," Kimberley let out. "What will you do with them?"

Grubb smiled and grabbed the nearest man in the new group of prisoners. He pulled a shaken Kevin Smith, chairman of the Resilience City Council, to the front of his little audience. "I and my black troopers will hunt you all down at the shelters any moment from now."

"Except Rachel and Aiden," Mariah added. "If they agree to help with the book."

"You have the book already," Rachel said. "You don't need any help."

"Okay then," Mariah said. "If they agree to join us."

"I'm not eating human flesh," Aiden grumbled.

"You'll join us, boy," Grubb said. "Whether you want to or not. The girl can go. We don't need her."

"So, you need the boy, eh?" Kimberley began. "What for?"

"He's Avigdor in the flesh," Mariah said. "Haven't you been paying attention?"

"You think we've been lying about him?" Grubb asked Kimberley. "Why not ask your little friend here about that?"

Rachel looked away when Kimberley turned to her. "No need for that," the Portwood officer said.

"And why is that?" Mariah wondered.

"We-We knew about that, but we never believed it," Aiden said.

"Right, Rachel?"

No response.

"Very well," Mariah enthused. "This will be an exhilarating hunt!"

"Cannibals," Mr. Kevin Smith spat out. "Disgusting, all of you!"

"Yep, that's what we are," Mariah agreed. "We don't have a choice."

"You do have a choice," Kimberley started, glaring at her former friend. "You can move away from all this with your friend using the white book. Who knows what the world would look like in the near future?"

"No, thanks," Professor Goldenberg chuckled. "I don't think an opportunity to make money like this would ever come my way, and besides, I have come to love human meat."

Mariah looked away and Kimberley noticed. "And you love human meat as well, eh Mariah?"

"I will, very soon," the female Sikama snapped.

"Enough," Grubb said. "Rewder, take them to the shelters with the other prisoners. Let the hunt begin."

"Right away, sir." Rewder waved at his men and they forced up the captives from their long stools. Except Aiden.

A distraught Rachel turned to the boy as she fell in line with the other prisoners. "Aiden!"

"Hey, I'm not staying back," Aiden whined.

"You have no choice," Mariah told him.

"Enjoy it while it lasts, boy," Grubb said. "While we still think we have need of you."

"We'll come back for you, Aiden," Kimberley said as a soldier pulled her up from her stool. "That I promise you."

"Where are they taking us, Kim?" Rachel wondered out loud.

"Move!" a trooper shouted behind her.

"The shelters above Resilience," Jeremy told her. "I hope we'll get hazard suits; we won't survive out there without those."

"Of course, you'll be suited up," a familiar voice said beside him. "No need to poison our food with the red dust, right?"

"Akron?"

"So you remember me?" the Kannibal smiled. "How does it feel to be on the receiving end for a change, scum?"

"It's not over yet," Jeremy pointed out.

"It soon will be for all of you," Akron snapped. "I'll personally make sure of it for you and your girlfriend over there." He nodded towards Kimberley's direction.

"No, you won't," Jeremy murmured. "Keep dreaming."

Outside the laboratory, Grubb's dystopian dictatorship had

established itself. Men and women in the bizarre black uniform had overrun the place. These were the core Kannibals, whose love for cannibalism knew no bounds. Some of these characters were busy at a construction site comprising many buildings outside the complex and the prisoners gaped at the massive project as they filed into X9 units.

"I know you're wondering what they're doing," Akron said to the approval of his comrades. "They're building a human settlement farm for the employees of Genetix, he he he."

"One of the many to be sited in Bravery," a female Kannibal added.

"And here we go," Jeremy said. "The fools have taken over."

Akron laughed. "You're the fool, my friend. You should worry about your two sisters now languishing somewhere in Resilience waiting to be cooked."

Jeremy started. "Ginia! Tilia! Gosh, I forgot about them. No!"

Raucous laughter accompanied this dire revelation.

"Don't worry," Akron told Jeremy. "I will link them to you when we get to Resilience. Finally, I'm not all that bad, eh?" His comrades mumbled their agreement all around him.

Jeremy said nothing as he ducked into an X9 unit with Kimberley and the little girl. "I guess so," he finally muttered under his breath.

The mobile units moved out of Genetix, Grubb's A2 leading the lineup. More detailed infantry patrolled the streets of Bravery. Here and there, these human eaters herded more civilians in groups like cattle.

Rachel stared at this bizarre scenario through the X9's glass aperture nearest to her seat. She only had Aiden on her mind. "What do we do now?" she wailed.

"We could cause a revolt," Kimberley began. "Or we could have decided not to hand over a certain mystical book to our enemies."

The little girl looked away. "They forced me to hand over the book, Kim. They did so by threatening to kill you and Aiden."

"Did they now?" Kimberley boiled.

"Well, newsflash, everyone," Jeremy proclaimed. "They still want us dead."

"If we let them," Kimberley said, looking around at the human cargo in the mobile unit's voluminous interior. "They all appear weak...docile..."

Jeremy nodded in agreement, looking around. "You're right, now that I think of it; they all look inebriated."

Rachel frowned. "And what does that..."

"It means 'drunk,'" Kimberley cleared. "Wonder why we're not affected by whatever affects them."

"Is it installed in this unit?" Jeremy began. "Some sought of gas expeller?"

"Why are we not affected?" Kimberley asked again.

"Can the book still be protecting us?" Rachel wondered, staring at Jeremy. "Has the book ever protected him?"

"Good question," Jeremy said.

"And why is that?" Kimberley frowned as she went through her pockets. Carl Bain's tiny silver box was no surprise. The piece of paper, however, brought back cold memories.

Jeremy blinked twice. "What's that?"

"Is that a piece of the book?" Rachel demanded.

"I-I think so," Kimberley stammered.

The X9 stopped and its doors swished open. Kimberley tucked Carl Bain's unremarkable item and the piece of paper into her pocket just before the Kannibals appeared on the open unit doors.

"Get out, all of you!" a troop leader barked at the prisoners.

"Act drunk!" Kimberley whispered before getting up from her seat and tailing the last individual to leave the unit.

Rachel and Jeremy followed her lead and stepped out of the mobile unit behaving like the other prisoners.

Grubb's A2 slid open and the chief Kannibal jumped out of the vehicle wearing a dark-green hazard suit and carrying a VG lazer gun. Mariah and Rewder joined him from another unit dressed in hazard suits. "Good, the drug is working from the look of things," the professor observed.

"That will make it easier to pick them off during the hunt, Master," Mariah said. "Though for some reason, our new acquaintances have refused to be affected by the poisonomial gas." She stared at Kimberley, who was trying to appear drowsy like the other prisoners.

"Hey, don't blame us," the Portwood police officer defended. "Maybe your gas is ineffective owing to our time-traveling adventures?"

Mariah's eyes turned to slits. "It will still be my pleasure and honor to hunt you down and kill you, my dear."

"Move along now," Grubb exclaimed. "No time to waste now. We still have three other cities to invade after the hunt."

"And what makes you so sure that they aren't preparing to attack you right now, wise guy?" Jeremy asked the chief Kannibal.

"Because they're cowards just like you and your friends right here," the cannibal chuckled. "The fools have forgotten how to wage war and must be barricading their precious cities right now while shaking in their skins."

"Exactly what they're doing, sir," Rewder said behind his master. "Our spies report this."

"Wow, he has spies," Jeremy muttered. "What else is new?"

"My men inside those three cities will help me seize them from within after the hunt," Grubb said.

"And what of the rest of the world, huh?" Rachel snapped. "Will they just stand by and watch you devour them?"

"They have no choice," Grubb replied with a smile. "I have the white book now, remember?"

"Trust me, you won't get far with that," Kimberley said.

"Says our new Bookbearer," Mariah mocked. "May I suggest you focus on staying alive and leave the thinking to wiser folks?"

"To use the book on many people, you must have met them in person first, or know their full names," Rachel pointed out.

"I was the chief scientist at Genetix for years, little girl," Grubb said. "Trust me when I say I've met so many world leaders during my scientific tours and conferences. Now, enough of this. Enjoy your lives while it lasts." He left the forlorn group to inspect his men.

"That was a waste of our time," Kimberley noted.

"Where are we?" Rachel began.

"Resilience," Jeremy said, looking around. "I must find my sisters."

Guarded by the black-clad invaders, the city's poorest residents had lined up before their living quarters. Heaps of dead bodies lay at road junctions in-between the blood-splattered walls of various residencies. Jeremy stared at the incredulous imagery with a hopeless expression on his face. The dead must have opposed the cannibalistic invaders in exchange for their lives.

"Grubb will start with the poor and downtrodden," Rachel said. "That's just not right."

"They will be herded into the human farms," Jeremy whispered beside her. "Despicable."

"Obviously, his soldiers will celebrate their victory by cooking the people they just killed," Kimberley said. "Gross."

"We have to use the paper, Kim," Rachel urged.

Kimberley nodded. "When we're alone."

"That opportunity might never come," Jeremy said, pointing with his head. "They're bringing hazard suits for us."

A large B4 unit stopped before the civilians emerging from the X9 units and its doors swished open to reveal hazard suits lined up in rows inside the vehicle. A Kannibal trooper handed out the safety wears as the prisoners filed past.

"If you want to do something, do it now," Jeremy whispered behind Kimberley.

"No, they might kill you if we disappear," Kimberley said.

"Just stop Grubb," Jeremy insisted. "I can face death without fear."

"Then who's gonna save your sisters?" Kimberley shot back.

Jeremy stopped in his tracks and the drowsy fellow behind him pushed him forward. "My sisters," he began. "I just forgot to figure them into all this." He spotted Akron talking to some prisoners in the line and spat out. "The cannibal lied to me."

"Did he?" Rachel asked.

"Ginia! Tilia!" Jeremy spotted his sisters sitting on the ground beside Akron. "If they join us I have a fighting chance of saving them."

"I think so, too," Kimberley said, staring at the two girls as she got to the B4 unit's door and received a hazard suit. Akron had called up both girls. Kimberley wondered what the Kannibal wanted to tell them.

"He's pointing at us," Jeremy said. "They're coming this way."

"Here are your sisters for what it's worth," Akron yelled at him. "They've decided to join you outside."

Jeremy embraced his two siblings. "Thank you," he told the Kannibal. "I'll never forget this."

"Don't bother," Akron chuckled. "You'll all still die out there."

"That was mean," Ginia muttered after the man had moved on.

"But he's right," Kimberley pointed out.

"For now," Jeremy said, receiving his hazard suit and making way for his sisters to get theirs. "We'll make our move once we leave Resilience."

The Kannibal troopers herded the small crowd of prisoners from the X9s into a huge cave harboring an atmospheric filtration unit ten times the size of the one Jeremy led the time-travelers through some days back. Heavy doors slid open and a gargantuan cube revealed itself. Another set of doors opposite the first set probably led one out of the underground cities. Grubb's men pushed the drowsy prisoners into the voluminous compartment.

Rachel freaked out. "Okay, where are we?"

"We use this place for transporting mobile units to the surface above whenever we need to do something out there," Jeremy explained. "This is the exit that can accommodate all of us at once."

"Attention, everyone!" Rewder yelled from a central spot. "Our soul director will now speak."

"Soul director?" Kimberley gaped in utter bewilderment. "This dude must be smoking something."

Benjamin Haddad came to stand near his chief Kannibal with Mariah and two flamboyantly dressed men. "Now, listen up," he began. "This is your last chance to live before you become meat for our tables." The professor pointed at the decompressor's next set of doors. "The moment those doors open, we'll give you a minute to run and hide before we start hunting you." Murmuring broke out amongst the prisoners. More people in fancy hazard suits touting lazer guns came to stand near the professor.

Kimberley turned to Jeremy. "And who are those?"

"The hunters, I guess," the black man said. "Obviously these are the rich folks from Resilience and beyond who think that cannibalism should be a sport."

"And have paid heavily to be participants today," Tilia added.

"From what I see here, not all rich folks approve of this," Kimberley said, looking at the Resilience City chairman, whose spotless white suit had turned dirty brown.

Jeremy followed her eyes and scoffed. "Mr. Kevin Smith? Guy's got principles, but he's no hero for the poor and downtrodden."

"He's so corrupt," Ginia added.

"And inept," Tilia said.

"Okay, I get it." Kimberley robbed her eyes.

"So, what's our plan?" Ginia asked her.

"Those doors will open after I count five and you must find your way to the surface and hide," Grubb continued. "Good luck."

"What the hell?" Kimberley wondered. "What has luck got to do with this?"

"He's just laughing at us," Jeremy said. "It's all an irony to him."

"Still, we must all stay together," Rachel reminded the adults.

"Until we find a good shelter," Kimberley agreed.

"Five!" Grubb shouted, and the huge doors disappeared. The prisoners scampered up a long wide inclination leading up to these heavy mechanized barricades. As she pushed forward, Kimberley noticed Chairman Smith climbing over his fallen citizens in his bid to quickly get as far away as his human legs could carry him.

She did not blame him. The goal was to stay alive.

The first set of prisoners got to the open doors at the top of the wide passageway and scampered out into the red dust now covering the Earth's surface.

Chapter 37
A NEW RECKONING

THEY all started down the slope leading to the valley below. Many misstepped and tumbled in the course of trying to regain balance amidst the momentum pushing them downwards. Many yelled out after serious injury to their person.

Kimberley sped down the slope with her friends on either side of her position. To her right, Tilia and Ginia huffed and puffed as they exerted the energy needed to outrun those bearing down on their backs while maintaining their balance going down the slope. On her left, Jeremy held on to Rachel as he ran, making sure she did not misstep.

"Hang on!" he shouted. "We're almost there."

The valley below loomed. Many jumped into it several inches from its dry base. Many broke bones doing so. The fortunate ones veered right and hurried off to the 'death' shelters.

Kimberley got to the valley's base.

Lazer fire!

"They've started shooting!" Jeremy yelled.

"What do we do now?" Tilia asked as she landed on the valley's base and turned right, Jeremy and Rachel right behind her.

Kimberley turned right and looked up the slope she'd come from as she ran. "We need to find a good shelter, where we can use the paper undisturbed!" she shouted, looking at the lonesome structures spread out before her in a haze of red dust. "There!" she pointed out, making a beeline for the chosen structure. Jeremy and the others followed her.

"Murderers!" Jeremy croaked, looking up the slope now on their right. "Those they've killed are tumbling down!"

"Jeremy, focus!" Kimberley told him as she ran. "We have to get to safety first and get out of here!"

As the other prisoners scurried past, Kimberley got to the worn-out shelter and worked the door. She couldn't dwell on how she knew the door sequence at the moment.

The bomb-proof doors slid open to reveal a long brightly lit room covered in red dust. Presumably, the dust had settled on furniture and equipment in the room owing to a lack of circulating air to keep it suspended in colloidal motion. Kimberley entered the long narrow cubicle and the others slipped in behind her, as well as three odd prisoners who saw the entrance open.

"You just made a mistake," Jeremy told the two men and one woman. "You'll be trapped..."

"They can come with us," Rachel said.

Jeremy frowned. "What do you mean? We're not..."

"They can come with us, Jeremy," Kimberley said, closing the doors. She couldn't initiate the lock sequence for both doors.

"What if we fail?" Jeremy asked her. "What if we fail to disappear? What if we're not..."

"Going anywhere?" Ginia put in. "Then why did we run into this trap?"

"It's not a trap," Rachel said. "We'll leave this place in no time."

"I still need to see what this magic paper can do," Jeremy said.

"You still doubt what we told you," Kimberley noted. "Prepare to be mesmerized." She punched the buttons on the door panel again. "I can't lock us in."

"The Kannibals hacked into the area's computer system and reprogrammed it a long time ago so that nobody can lock these shelters from within," one of the two men said.

"There's electricity here. Everything's working here, except the air filtration and those door locks," the woman with the men said.

Sustained lazer fire and death yells from outside broke the silence.

"Let's get out of here," Kimberley said, reaching into her pocket. "Gather away from the door." She handed the piece of paper, as well as a red-dust-covered pen she picked up from the only desk in the room, to Rachel. "Let's hope it writes."

"It doesn't need to," Rachel said. "How do we hold hands?"

"Undo your hazard gloves," Kimberley ordered everyone, reaching out to initiate that procedure for her gloves.

"What?" one of the two men began. "You don't mean that, do you?"

"You don't mean that," Tilia repeated.

"And why should we do that?" Ginia began.

"Do as she says, girls," Jeremy said, beginning the process of doing so for his suit.

They all hesitated except Rachel.

Kimberley glared at everyone. "Unless you want to remain here?"

The protective gloves started coming off.

"What of the radiation?" the female prisoner with the men asked.

"It has no effect on us where we're going," Kimberley allayed.

Rachel picked up her paper and pen from where she'd dropped them when she removed her gloves and looked up. "We're going back in time."

"What for?" Jeremy wanted to know.

The lazer fire outside sounded nearer and nearer as if descending down the slope.

"We need to retrace our steps and know where we made a mistake," Kimberley explained. "Hold hands." She stared at her hands. Her exposed skin had turned reddish in color.

"The red dust will eventually tear off your skin if you don't leave the area soonest," Jeremy explained. "Let's hope you're right about the piece of paper."

The Portwood sergeant ignored him. "Hold hands," she repeated.

Moments later, the bomb-proof doors slid open and Akron stared at the gloves lying on the floor at the farthest end of the long room. "Odd," he said. "Thought I heard voices in here."

*　　*　　*

Kimberley looked around and blinked twice. The scene had changed. Original old-fashioned cars occupied the roads once again, and the buildings were classic skyscrapers. The Portwood cop wore ordinary clothes, just like Rachel sitting in the Lamborghini Urus beside her. She felt rich.

Jeremy and his two sisters came out from a street shop and walked towards Kimberley. The Portwood sergeant could not find the three individuals who'd joined them in the journey back at the shelter, though she found it comforting that she could remember that future incident.

"There they are," Rachel said, pointing out three individuals entering a Jeep on the opposite sidewalk. Two men and a woman.

"Guess they have a different life now," Kimberley said. She couldn't blame them. Leaving the crazy future they'd experienced behind as they embraced a new life for themselves was the best they could hope for and she would never disrupt that serenity by walking across the road and touching one of them. At least, she remembered that future. "Sometimes, I wish we…"

Rachel turned sharply. "Never met?"

Kimberley looked away. "That came out wrong," she said. "I'm sorry."

"I'm sorry, too, Kim," the little girl said. "For putting you through all this."

Kimberley smiled and ruffled Rachel's hair. "Helping you was hard at first, then it slowly became worth it."

Rachel nodded. "We could just leave things as they are, Kim," she said. "But remember Grubb would be with the white book and...and who knows what else he would do with it?"

"And he has Aiden," Kimberley muttered. "Our job is not yet done."

A younger Jeremy stopped before her with his two sisters, grinning as he stood up straight. "Glad you could make it, Miss Sweeney," he chuckled. "The art pieces are in the car. Philia will go get them for you."

"No need for that, Jeremy," Kimberley said, taking the African-American's right hand. "We're just visitors here and we don't have time."

Jeremy's face turned expressionless and his pupils disappeared. His two sisters noticed this.

"What have you done to him?" Ginia, a.k.a. Philia, demanded as she reached out to disengage the locked hands. Miss Sweeney touched her hand, and even reached out to grab her sister's hand.

"Where are we?" Jeremy began, breathing hard. He stared at his motionless sisters. "Have we?"

"About time," Kimberley said. "And yes, it worked."

"Unbelievable," Jeremy muttered. "Where are we now? Place is ancient."

"San Francisco in 2016 A.D. It says so on that billboard," Rachel pointed out.

Jeremy held his sisters who'd just come out of their stupor.

"Are we alive?" Ginia began.

"Did it work?" Tilia asked.

"We're safe now," Jeremy told them.

"For now," Kimberley stressed, turning to Rachel.

"And what's our plan?" Jeremy asked.

"We find a quiet alley and wait for the Booklords...and Carl Bain," Rachel said.

Kimberley scoffed. "And how does that work, my dear?" she wondered. "Those creatures and their servant are no more, remember?"

"We went back in time, Kim," Rachel said. "Hopefully this action will reestablish their existence at this time."

"Yeah, right." Kimberley rolled her eyes. "Meaning they could decide to haunt us from the past forever?"

"Not really," Jeremy began. "I think your little friend is saying that this means we cause those demons to be whenever we go back with any piece of paper from the book to a time in the past when they existed on Earth, right, Rachel?"

"Right," Rachel agreed. "Maybe," she added.

"You're not sure of this?" Kimberley noted.

"You kinda lost me there, little one," Jeremy said. "I want to see how this works."

"And should we be afraid of these…these demons?" Tilia sounded petrified. "Because a hooded horror is staring at us from the shop across the street."

Kimberley started, mouth agape. "They're back already?"

"Yes," Rachel said. "They're here already, and I hope they realize they've been beaten once before."

"They're many," Jeremy said, looking around the parked Urus. The ominous figures had appeared all over the place, just standing and watching. From barbing salons, grocery stores and restaurants.

"No one's noticing this?" Ginia wondered out loud. "They're all just going about like nothing's wrong."

"Maybe they don't…see what we're seeing?" Jeremy suggested. "Maybe these demons are invisible to them?"

"Everyone, get in the car," Kimberley ordered, opening the driver's door. She zoomed off once they were all seated.

"What's the plan, Kim?" Rachel asked her.

"They'll have to play by our own rules this time," she replied. "Time to find that alley."

"There's one right there," Tilia pointed out and Kimberley took the right turn.

"Thanks," she said. "Almost missed it."

The heavy Urus stopped halfway into the dark alley between two buildings. Her occupants disembarked and stood around the Lamborghini.

"This place gives me the creeps," Ginia confessed. "I hope those things don't attack us."

"They won't," Rachel assured, picking up a piece of wire she spotted on the ground. "I'm hoping they know we know how to destroy them now."

The Gray Ones had materialized at the ends of the alley and on the roofs of the two buildings forming the dimly lit passage.

Jeremy's sisters jumped back into the Urus. "What next?" he wondered.

"We summon our old friend," Kimberley said, reaching into her pants' right pocket.

"Ok, that makes sense," a familiar voice said behind her and she smiled.

"Carl Bain," she introduced, turning to face her old friend, who wore a cowboy-styled ensemble of brownish hues and grays complimented by dark leather straps and Durango Rebel boots. His mean facial expression remained partially hidden underneath a cowboy hat slightly angled over his head. "You couldn't wait for your summons, cowboy."

"I didn't choose to come back," Mr. Bain snapped. "For some crazy reason we're yet to find out, you guys decided to do something that eventually revived the essence of my masters. They decided on their part to bring me back to life."

Silently, the Gray Ones surrounded the Urus and their human minion. Kimberley looked around the crowded alley and finally fixed her gaze on the American hustler. She felt a slight shiver go up her spine. "Who would have thought that we will eventually meet in such a bizarre situation after trying so hard to kill each other, huh?"

The American criminal smiled. "You must be in dire need of our help to have undone the one event you wanted so badly," he said.

Rachel glared at Carl Bain. "Yes, we need your help, Mr. Bain," she said, "but don't think that we'll ever forget what you did on behalf of your demonic masters."

The largest amongst the Gray Ones shimmered in the little girl's face and she did not even flinch.

Kimberley found herself facing an unremarkable Carl Bain before she could appreciate this remarkable moment. "Hold it steady now," she warned him. "Remember we can now snuff out your life just like that," and she snapped her fingers to drive home the message.

"Oh, please," her adversary said. "You don't even have the book."

"We have a piece of it," Rachel began.

"Very well, then." Carl Bain cleared his throat. "My masters would like to know what you want." Three of these infernal abominations drifted out to take positions beside him. "Speak now or…or…"

Kimberley frowned. "Or what?"

"Or we destroy this city."

"Not after I've shown you the ankh I just constructed, Mr. Bain," Rachel warned, hiding the object behind her back. "Remember we can destroy your masters along with you by just snapping our fingers."

Carl Bain looked around furtively. "That's not true," he said without conviction. "If only I can remember…"

"From what I've heard so far, you have no memories, dude," Jeremy reminded him. "Like you were just brought back from nothing."

"Your masters interacted with the Sikama in the past," Kimberley began, staring at the largest unearthly horror floating near the American hustler. "What can they tell us about Benjamin Haddad?"

"He wanted to lead the Sikama back at the Mine and lost out to Jehoash, Rachel's father," Carl Bain revealed.

"And how did you know that?" Kimberley demanded.

"My masters just told me."

"I already knew that," Rachel said. "Tell us what we don't know."

"He had a lover at the Mine. One of his fellow Sikamas."

"Mariah?" Kimberley wanted to confirm her suspicion.

"Yes," Carl Bain said. "Her name was Mariah."

"Okay, that's new," Rachel admitted.

"I guess I've known for some time," Kimberley said.

"The two lovers had plans for the two volumes and the ritual," the human minion continued. "Plans that ran contrary to what the Sikama stood for, so they couldn't help Jehoash carry out the Sikama's original plans, and the cult entered a tumultuous period from then on."

"A period they never recovered from," Kimberley said.

Carl Bain nodded. "Of course, Ben Haddad sabotaged the cult when he assisted the Romans in discovering the Mine after he thought that Jehoash wanted to keep the books for selfish reasons."

"But Father wanted to destroy the books," Rachel began.

"Your father feared the cult had been infiltrated and wanted to fish out the guilty party. He discovered the traitor was his best friend, Benjamin Haddad, and a confrontation ensued between both men. The aftermath of that fight was your father's death."

Rachel froze and Kimberley felt it, reaching out to hold the little girl with both hands.

"Wow," Jeremy said. "Do we need any more evidence of this guy's treachery?"

"Benjamin Haddad connived with Rome to destroy the Sicarii Kabbalah Masada in order to steal the books in the chaos that would ensue during this plan, but unfortunately for him, Jehoash ferried away the white book through his daughter now standing before us, while the Romans seized the black book and vowed to keep it under lock and key forever," Carl Bain continued. "In the end, this traitor could only save himself and his lover by fleeing into the future with a piece of divine paper from the white book, hoping to improve his understanding of Shurabi while waiting for another opportunity to retrieve the two books and find his true love, who lost her way during their escape."

"Uncle Ben killed my father?" Rachel asked the American hustler, who nodded solemnly. "It...It all makes sense now," she stammered. "He...He was just lying there after Uncle Ben came to visit..."

Kimberley boiled. "We will find him and...and do away with him."

"I like that!" Carl Bain lit up.

"Like what?" Kimberley frowned.

"Recent events must have turned you into a vicious killer," the human minion directed at the Portwood cop. "I like this new you."

"Not true," Kimberley murmured and looked away. She felt Jeremy's stare and turned sharply. "What?"

"Nothing," the Resilience resident said.

"My masters say your Bookbearer has given this...Benjamin Haddad, or Grubb, the white book, and that you escaped from his cannibalistic soldiers by going back in time, without the boy, who this chief cannibal has imprisoned."

"That's correct?" Jeremy looked around when none of his new friends voiced their agreement. "The dude plans to sow chaos with that spell book in my time."

"We need you to help us destroy him now before he leaves this time and space," Rachel said. "That way, he won't lay his hands on any of the books in the future."

"You say you're not with the book right now?" Carl Bain's eyes turned to slits. "Why would you lie to us?"

"But it's true," Rachel began, showing both hands. "We don't have the...white book?" She stared at the mysterious volume in her right hand. "But of course," she exclaimed. "We went back in time and, based on the laws of Shurabi, we still have it in our possession."

Carl Bain snickered. "And how do we believe you when you have just revealed to us that you cannot be trusted?"

"Are you guys helping us or not?" Kimberley asked the Gray Ones. She feared her frustration had spilled out into the open. "We can find Grubb without your help, but we think he is too powerful, even at this point in time, and we might need your help to defeat him."

"Kill him, you mean?" Carl Bain fixed his gaze on the Portwood-sergeant-turned-time-traveler. "My masters say you must give us back what belongs to us before we can help you."

Kimberley scoffed. "Very funny."

"Give us the book right now?" Carl Bain urged her.

"We have to save Aiden first before considering your request, Mr. Bain," she replied. "That's a joke. We'll never give your masters the book."

"And what stops us from taking it right now?" the human minion dared.

"That's impossible," Kimberley said. "We won't hesitate to destroy you guys again."

"Help us and we'll give you what you want," Rachel said.

Kimberley couldn't believe her ears. "What? No, Rachel. Your father never trusted them, remember?"

"My father is dead, Kim," the little girl said. "It's time to move on."

Kimberley could only stare. "I sacrificed Jim for this?"

"Let's trust them to bring him back, Kim, don't worry," Rachel persuaded her, and turned to the servant of her former adversaries.

"Of course," Carl Bain agreed. "It all depends on if you show commitment right now."

Kimberley reached into her left pants pocket and brought out the tiny silver box, which had been in her possession from the very beginning of the entire charade. She gave it to her arch rival without a word.

"My package," Carl Bain enthused. "At last."

"And what the hell is that?" Jeremy wondered aloud.

Carl Bain smiled. "It's a nuclear device," he said. "It turns a city's water system into a freaking hydrogen bomb her inventors called Red Bomb 1."

Kimberley gaped at the American thug. "You son of a..."

*   *   *

The Booklords hovered around the place, creating a gloomy kaleidoscope of shadows in the dark alley as the time-travelers faced their human minion down below.

"You mean that cube contains the material used in producing the first red bomb?" Jeremy stared at the cowboy who just came back from nothing.

"Unbelievable," Tilia said as she watched the unfolding drama with her sister from within the Urus.

"And what's with the first red bomb?" the mean-looking cowboy asked her brother.

"Its final successor will be used to destroy the world as we know it in the distant future," Kimberley said.

"I don't know what you're talking about," Mr. Bain said, pushing the tiny item into his pants' right pocket. "That cube you just saw is my passport to immense wealth."

Kimberley simmered. "Give it back, Carl."

"No, Kim, we had an agreement, remember?" Rachel interrupted.

"He'll sell it to people who will destroy the world, Rachel."

"What're you saying?" Rachel wondered. "The destruction of this world will happen, whether you like it or not. We've witnessed it in the future, remember?"

"I think you should listen to your friend, Miss Reyna," Carl Bain chuckled.

"We had an agreement," Jeremy said, "but in due course, I'll destroy that thing if it's the last thing I ever do."

"Good luck then," Carl Bain told him. "I'll kill you before you ever try that."

"I'll…"

"Hey!" Rachel shouted. "Can we try and focus on our current mission right now?"

"Of course," Kimberley said, glaring at Carl Bain. "We can settle scores later." She turned to the little girl with the other two in order to plot their next move.

"Baruch Goldenberg's first name is still on the book," Rachel began.

"And what do you mean by that?" Jeremy asked her.

"We wrote that name when we were looking for our man the first time," Kimberley said. "Glad it's still there, because that's all we need now."

"We just touch it and we go to his location," Rachel said.

Jeremy wanted to hear more. "And then what?"

"We snuff him out," Carl Bain said. "It will be a piece of cake."

"Remember he could destroy you and your masters, so be careful for your own good," Kimberley warned him.

"Okay, gather round me and let's do this," Rachel said.

Jeremy's sisters refused to come out from the Lamborghini and Kimberley handed them the car's keys as well as the piece of paper from the white book through a window. "Lock yourselves in, and if we don't come back for you, touch Rachel's name on that paper. That will bring you to us."

Now, the three friends held hands with Carl Bain and the Gray Ones encircled this new alliance of former adversaries. Rachel touched Benjamin Haddad's name, causing an instant disappearance of the former enemies.

Ginia breathed a sigh of relief when the Booklords also faded away.

*   *   *

Detective Steve Davis of the Harvard University Police Department, also known as Carl Bain in alternate Shurabi reality, sat down beside Xenia Tribe, also known as Kimberley Reyna by her late boyfriend, Jim Hawkins. "He's here," Carl Bain said and his audience nodded. "My masters say he has a big glass ankh in his office, though." Davis wore a suede suit and his accomplice had on dark shades and a black leather jacket.

"No problem with that," Evan Crawford said. Also known as Jeremy Irons by his two loving sisters, the English scientist wore a black suit and tie that created an official air around him. "I've requested an audience with our man as a foreign scientist interested in research collaboration. Once I get into his office, I know what to do."

"Once you smash the ankh, the Booklords can swoop in and whisk him away, Mr. Bain," Rachel said, dotting a backpack in which she had placed the white book.

Carl Bain nodded. "Right."

Kimberley stared ahead. "Remember not to kill him, Mr. Bain."

"Yes, I remember," Carl Bain said. "Though, I don't know why you want to do so. Better for you that he's gone as soon as possible."

"I agree with that assessment," Jeremy began. "We can't give our man time to figure out what to do. He might actually get away before we know it."

"We won't let him get away," Rachel said. "We'll tie him up once we get him out of this place."

"How come we didn't find him in 2016 San Francisco like you said we would?" Jeremy began, turning to Kimberley.

"That assumption was wrong," she replied. "The book took us to the actual date and place of his existence. Hence, the name, Elijah Cunningham, a biologist at Harvard in 2014."

"Thanks to the Booklords for identifying him when we got here," Rachel said. "Could have taken ages for us to do that without their help."

"My masters appreciate your gratitude," Carl Bain conveyed. "They hope you'll eventually reward their work by handing over the book."

Kimberley still found it strange that she could be planning a mission with someone who'd tried to kill her from the very beginning of this arduous adventure. She didn't trust the American hustler anymore than she trusted his demonic superiors.

"Dr. Cunningham is ready to see you now, sir." The secretary's fresh voice interrupted her thoughts and she readjusted her dark shades.

"About time," Jeremy said, standing up. Without another word, he went into the passage lined with office doors, walked up to the door marked Dr. ELIJAH CUNNINGHAM and knocked on it.

"Yes, come in."

Jeremy opened the door and walked in. His eyes scanned the room and missed nothing. The middle-aged man in long-sleeved shirt sitting behind a mahogany desk, the Indian tomahawk affixed to a platform on the coffee table to his left, the expensive artworks on the wall, as well as the large glazed ankh hanging on the wall to his right.

The black man seized the tomahawk and smashed the glass ankh into smithereens. Wind swept into the room through the open windows and disappeared almost as quickly.

"Not so fast, Mr. Crawford," Ben Haddad said, standing up from his seat with a pistol in his hand. "Wow, I almost missed that."

Jeremy froze, his heart beating fast and his thoughts racing ahead of him. Why didn't the demons play their part?

"Actually, they tried to," the biologist pointing a gun at him said. "You see, the breeze we just witnessed represented their futile attempt to kill me, my friend. Glad I always carry one more ankh on my person." He unbuttoned his shirt to display a gold ankh necklace hanging from his neck. "Now you die."

Jeremy dodged the shot and slid across the mahogany desk, spinning round in time to kick off the gun from Mr. Haddad's hand. He went for the man's throat and yanked away the golden ankh before falling off the table.

"No!" Ben Haddad screamed before the killer wind swept into his office again and slammed him into his wall of framed art. The shattered frames and broken glass flew all over the place as more unknown characters burst into his office. "Who the hell are you guys?"

"Your worst nightmare," Kimberley said.

Jeremy pushed over a chair and the Booklords forced their prisoner to seat down. "Who we are? You'll soon know."

Carl Bain appeared holding a knife and the incarcerated man cringed. "Good catch," the American hustler said.

"Remember we agreed to tie him up?" Jeremy aired.

"Of course," Rachel said as she entered the chaotic office.

Carl Bain frowned. "Let's do away with him now that we have him."

Rachel glared at him. "No."

"Why not?" Kimberley surprised herself with the question.

"He's under Shurabi, so killing him now will simply give him new life," Rachel explained.

"Not true, Rachel," Kimberley said. "Mariah…"

"Mariah has been lying to us, Kim," Rachel snapped. "She must have lied to us about the Gray Ones, reincarnation and Shurabi."

"Really?" Carl Bain stared blankly. "So how come I didn't find this 'new life' when I got snuffed out with my masters, huh?"

Rachel rolled her eyes. "Different story."

"I think you died a different kind of…of death, Carl, because you were a mortal servant to the Gray Ones," Kimberley tried to explain.

"You must have been snuffed out just like that, but I don't believe Mariah lied to us, Rachel."

"Okay," Jeremy began. "Can someone tell me what the argument is about?"

"He's not coming back to life through Shurabi if my masters kill him now and his dying body is not quickly transferred to another place and time through the book," Carl Bain said.

"And how did you know that?" Rachel began.

"My masters just told me."

"See, Rachel? Mariah was right," Kimberley muttered.

Benjamin Haddad hit his right shoe's heel on the wall and a small ankh sprouted from underneath the shoe's toe. Carl Bain and his demonic superiors vanished and their target pulled out a small pistol from his right pants pocket. "I should have known. You came back from the future to stop me from doing what I must do."

Kimberley and Rachel raised their hands in surrender.

"You will eat your fellow humans in that future, man," Jeremy said, raising both hands.

"You lie like a child," the Sikama said. "I will find the books and execute the ritual. That's why you came back to stop me with the Gray Ones."

"You're delusional if you think you carried out the ritual in the future," Kimberley said.

"You see? You never said I didn't get the books," the Sikama said. "And I think you have them here." He pointed the gun at Rachel. "What's in the bag, girl?"

The little girl's face went blank. "I – uh...I'm Rachel, Uncle Ben," she stonewalled. "I am Jehoash's daughter."

"You're what?"

Kimberley grabbed the Sikama's hand holding the pistol before a shot posted a hole on the office ceiling. Jeremy stooped and broke off the tiny ankh attached to the man's right shoe as the latter went for a sheet of paper on the desk.

Carl Bain and the Gray Ones reappeared. "Where is he?" the American hustler shouted, looking around in rage. "I will kill him with my bare hands!"

"He just vanished," Jeremy said in-between deep breaths.

"He what?" Rachel stared at the spot on which Ben Haddad previously stood. "You let him get away!" she accused everyone.

"No, my masters did not," Carl Bain said. "Your friend had so many ankhs with him."

"And a sheet of the white book," Kimberley added, pointing at the paper their target left behind on the desk.

"If only you guys had stuck to the plan instead of arguing over what I couldn't understand," Jeremy muttered. "Now, we just have to go look for him again."

Kimberley frowned. "If we go into the future and come across the Red War, we will eventually lose the white book to our man through a series of unfortunate events, right Rachel?

"Yes," Rachel said, looking at the boy opening the office door. "We will also lose Aiden to him, again."

Kimberley gaped at the individual standing in the doorway. "Aiden," she muttered. "Is that really you?"

"Who?" the boy at the door asked.

"Impossible," Jeremy said.

Rachel disagreed. "Shurabi will always align the events of space and time," she said. "That way there will always be continuity."

"Aiden who?" the boy at the door asked again.

Rachel stepped forward and touched his right hand. "That will help," she said, turning to Kimberley. "I don't know if we should bring him with us, Kim."

Kimberley frowned in thought. "You fear he'll eventually become Ben Haddad's prisoner again?"

"No." The little girl shook her head. "I'm afraid he'll just wind up in Uncle Ben's custody once we get to the year of the Red War."

"So be it, we're taking Aiden," Kimberley said. "We'll defeat Ben Haddad when we get there."

"What of my sisters?" Jeremy wondered out loud.

"They will do what we told them to do," Rachel said.

"Where am I?" Aiden wondered, shaking his head in a bid to clear his mind. "Kim, Rachel, Jeremy? What're you guys doing here?"

"Hold my hand," Kimberley told him instead. "We're getting out of here."

Chapter 38
INEVITABILITY

THE sudden change surprised no one. The red dust did.

"And Aiden is nowhere to be found!" Rachel cried, looking around through the head screen of her hazard suit.

"Luckily, we know who has him," Kimberley said.

"And the Booklords are still with us," Jeremy pointed out. "We are in one of the shelters outside Resilience," he added, operating the doors' computer system to slightly slide the noiseless barricades open and peep outside. He spotted two distant figures in the red haze.

"We're in the very same shelter we escaped from," Rachel said with a wry smile. "Wearing the very same hazard suits."

"How strange," Carl Bain said. "Unlike you guys, I can do without those weird suits."

"Stop bragging and tell us what is happening inside Resilience," Kimberley snapped at him.

"Kimberley! Is that you?" a familiar voice shouted outside.

"My sisters are here," Jeremy said, peeping out through the narrowly open doors.

Kimberley and the others joined him to watch the two small figures grow bigger. "They did what we told them."

"They sure did," Kimberley agreed. "Yes, Ginia, come right over and we'll open up for you!" she called out.

"My masters just snuffed out two Kannibals waiting near these doors," Carl Bain announced. "Grubb's men are everywhere."

"Can you take them all out?" Kimberley proposed.

The American thug smiled. "Done."

"Thanks," Jeremy said, operating the doors to open up wide. "Ginia!

Tilia!" he cried, walking over to embrace his sisters.

"We made it, Jeremy," Tilia said with joy.

"We're not yet out of the woods, sis," Jeremy pointed out.

"Place is a death zone," Kimberley exclaimed, stepping out of the dilapidated shelter into a gory war-like scenario of undeniable massacre. Bodies in black hazard suits littered the landscape amidst human entrails intentionally left behind. "They must have hunted down all these people and disemboweled them for food."

"Welcome to the future, Mr. Bain," Jeremy said. "This is the environment created by the offspring of your tiny box."

"The red bomb has destroyed the Earth, Mr. Bain," Rachel said. "Now you know what that little thing can do."

"And you think I care?" the human minion grumbled. "After all, this is not my alternate reality."

"Alternate what?" Kimberley had heard the phrase before.

"Alternate reality," Carl Bain repeated. "Remember my masters can bring back your dead if you want them to come back, just as the book brought them back into existence when you went back in time."

"Why can't the book bring back our dead as well?" Jeremy wondered.

"Under Shurabi, one could come back in the future as someone else if one died of natural or physical causes," Rachel replied. "So, in theory, yes, I would expect a reversal of this mythical process when we go back in time with the white book, or move forward in time with the black book, up to the specific date of birth of the said individual."

"But this is not the case when the Gray Ones do the killing," Kimberley said dryly.

"Exactly," Rachel agreed.

"I know where you're going with this," Kimberley told Jeremy.

"C-Can the effects of the red bomb be reversed?" Jeremy tottered.

"Reversing such a massive physical catastrophe would most likely drain the strength of the Bookbearer performing such a task, killing him or her in the process," Rachel explained.

"How did you know that?" Kimberley began.

"Experience, Kim," Rachel said.

"So, my masters tell me that Shurabi prevents this sought of reversal from happening," Carl Bain concluded for her.

"And Grubb was delusional in saying he could use the book to mass-populate the Earth again for his cannibalistic activities?" Kimberley wondered.

"I think so," the little girl said.

"Unless a very powerful Bookmaker wields the book?" Carl Bain added.

Kimberley found herself thinking of Aiden. "I know we can still do some good right here, right now," she urged everyone, heading towards the valley as the others followed her. "Can your masters take out all the Kannibals in the cities?" she asked Carl Bain.

"Already on it, but it will take some time."

Rachel turned to the human minion. "Did you take him out, Mr. Bain?"

"No. My masters failed to do so," Carl Bain said. "Grubb is with his lover and the boy in a secure room."

"And the book?" Rachel asked. "As you can see, we don't have it."

The American hustler nodded. "The book is in that vicinity."

They started up the slope, trying not to stare at the human remains oozing blood all over the place, as well as the dead bodies lying everywhere. Soon, the giant doors of the vehicle hatch through which Grubb sanctioned his hunting expedition loomed.

"How do we get in?" Ginia asked, rubbing her hands over the closed doors.

Carl Bain stared at her. "Why? Through those doors, of course."

"But, they're shut tight."

Eerie forms materialized all around the time-travelers. The Gray Ones ferried the humans through the massive metal doors and vanished into thin air once the job was done.

They did not remove their hazard suits.

"Grubb should be in his laboratory down at Bravery," Jeremy calculated.

"He's in Resilience City's Administrative Building, inside the chairman's office to be precise," Carl Bain said. "He knows we're coming, but he doesn't know what to do."

Kimberley nodded. "What of his victims?"

"Still in their prisons, but grateful for the turn of events."

"Of course," Kimberley agreed. "Dead Kannibals everywhere. Who wouldn't be grateful?"

"This fight just got a whole lot easier, thanks to our new allies," Jeremy said, turning to Carl Bain.

"And thanks to our enemies not having the time to draw ankhs and crosses," Rachel said.

Carl Bain nodded. "Sure thing."

Outside the huge atmospheric filtration unit, more dead bodies in black suits greeted the small group. Mobile units carrying dead occupiers as well as frightened prisoners dotted empty streets. Jeremy led the others in unchaining the civilians and helping them out of the idle vehicles.

"They were going to slaughter us!" one old man cried as he stepped down from an X9 unit. "And, can you believe it? They claimed they had to, because there was no food left."

"It's over now," Jeremy said, turning to help another person.

"This is slowing us down," Carl Bain complained. "We need to move quickly."

"We don't even know what we're going to confront," Kimberley pointed out.

"My sisters can help these people while we continue," Jeremy said to everyone's approval.

The Resilience City's Administrative Building sat in a compound close to the main road leading out of the city into Bravery. Dead Kannibal troopers lay on both sides of the road amidst abandoned mobile units facing different directions. Kimberley picked up three lazer guns and gave one to Rachel and Jeremy. "Just in case," she said.

Up the road they went, squatting as they paused at the gate to look around before sneaking in like real soldiers. The place was deserted; save for some ignoble fluffy group of rabbit-like animals that scampered away once the humans approached their position near the main building's entrance.

"No one in sight," Kimberley ascertained and lowered her weapon while looking around. "Guess we can just walk right in and confront Grubb."

"Notice the falling temperature, Kim?" Jeremy asked her. "It's never been this cold in Resilience."

"Or around your administrative building?" Rachel specified, staring at the structure's entrance. "It's the book, Kim. Look."

A lone figure stood at the top of the stairway in the building's main lobby. A boy to be precise. He had his hands behind his back.

"Aiden!" Kimberley called out, working the door computers to open the heavy transparent lazerproof doors. The cold blast from within shook as well as surprised her, literally pushing her back half an inch with her companions.

"That was why my masters couldn't get to your Grubb," Carl Bain told her. "The boy is protecting your enemies with the Breath of Lucifer."

Jeremy didn't hear well. "The Breath of who?"

Rachel appeared lost.

"The Breath of Lucifer, your so-called Ice and Fire of Masada," the human minion continued, staring at the boy standing on the stairs. "Satan's breath blows cold for the white book and erupts as fire for the black book. I no longer have my powers, because my masters have left this vicinity. They fear Satan's breath."

"Khabawsokar said that in Egypt, but I didn't understand what he meant at the time," Kimberley said.

"Who's Khabawsokar?" Jeremy asked her.

"Whatever," she said. "We have to save Aiden first."

"Don't come any closer!" Aiden warned her from atop the staircase. "Don't do so if you want to live."

"What did he do to you, Aiden?" Rachel shouted into the chilly wind emanating from within the building.

"Nothing," Aiden said. "He just showed me who I am."

"What's really going on?" Jeremy wondered.

"You're not a killer, Aiden," Kimberley began, noticing Mr. Bain taking some backward steps. "You are better than him."

Aiden boiled. "I didn't kill anyone!" The cold blast exploded from him, blasting his audience out of the doorway and sending them crashing to the ground a few feet away. "You could have protected me from those bullies when Mum passed away, Kim, but you didn't! Now, I can protect myself!"

"W-What are you talking about?" Kimberley stammered, wincing as she sat up from the ground.

"I'm talking about him," Aiden snapped, pointing out Carl Bain, who was crawling backward on his haunches away from the others. "Now is my time to deal with him."

"Aiden, he's with us now," Rachel said.

"Doesn't matter."

"You cannot do this, Aiden," Kimberley said. "This is not who you are."

"He cannot do what?" Jeremy began.

"Wrong, Kim," Aiden said. "You made me believe I killed my mother all these years, because...because I ran away from home when she needed me most on her sickbed. Now, I'm going to face my fears. I am not going to run away anymore."

Carl Bain froze. He could no longer move. "What have you done to me, boy?"

"Aiden, stop whatever you're doing right now," Kimberley cried.

"It's too late, Kim," Aiden said, stepping down the stairs. He revealed the ancient manuscript he held in his right hand and a bluish glow emanated from the book. This incandescent light immersed his right hand and changed to a lighter hue.

"Aiden, what did he do to you?" Kimberley wondered as she drew back on the ground with Jeremy and the others, apart from Carl Bain, who remained incapable of motion.

"Nothing," the boy repeated. "He just showed me who I am."

Jeremy stopped before Carl Bain as the boy got to the foot of the steps. "And who do you think you are right now?" he asked Aiden.

"Move out of the way or I'll hurt you as well," Aiden snapped at him.

"Do your worst," the Resilience citizen said.

"Jeremy, move out of the way," Kimberley warned.

"Aiden, don't do this," Rachel warned.

"Aiden, leave them for now," a new voice said behind the boy. Grubb stood at the top of the stairs with Mariah, Rewder, Akron and two other Kannibal troopers.

"You murderer!" Jeremy shouted, standing up and raising his weapon. Akron shot it out of his hand and he calmed down.

"What have you done to Aiden, Uncle Ben?" Rachel demanded.

"Surprised to see me still alive?" the professor asked. "You went back in time to stop me, but failed woefully."

"We're still on it, smart guy," Kimberley said, picking herself up.

"With who?" Grubb lit up. "With a revived fool, who can't even move, or his overrated demonic masters, who now owe you their existence? Nah, you have failed, and woefully, too."

Rachel couldn't hold back the tears anymore. "What did you do to Aiden?"

"Nothing, my dear," Grubb said, raising both hands as he came down the staircase, his lover closely following him. "I just showed him how powerful he could become if he chose to and he listened to me. Amazing, right?"

"Hi, Kim," Mariah quipped. "Enjoying yourself?"

Kimberley ignored the last speaker. "A-Are you saying Aiden is really Avigdor?" she asked the professor, turning to Rachel.

"Of course, he is," Grubb said. "And Avigdor has the power to find the black book."

"With that other volume, we can then perform the ritual," Mariah said.

"So, you see, Aiden," Grubb continued, "you can ignore these humans and their powerless demons for now, because we have bigger achievements ahead of us." He stretched out his right hand towards the boy. "Just give me the book."

"Not yet, Master," Aiden said. "Let me kill him first."

"Let him be, boy," Grubb urged. "He's not worth it, and we have better things to do."

"Yes, Master," Aiden surprised everyone with. The blue glow surrounding the book disappeared and Carl Bain scampered away from the group as soon as he could move.

Kimberley smiled when she noticed Mariah staring at her.

"What are you smiling at?" Mariah demanded.

"Isn't it obvious?" Jeremy asked, standing up in front of Carl Bain. "You guys don't control the boy."

"And you've been trying to convince him to hand over the book for some time now," Kimberley added. "This means you could have manipulated him, hoping to get something from him afterwards..."

"And that is not working out, even though he calls you 'master,'" Rachel said, stepping towards Aiden. "I don't even think that you have ransacked any other city apart from Bravery and Resilience, Uncle Ben."

"That's not true," Mariah said. "Aiden is protecting us from the Gray Ones as I speak. If not for your insolent intrusion, we would have commenced our master plan already. How about that?"

"With which army?" Kimberley asked. "Last time I checked, the Gray Ones have been smothering your cannibalistic force while you were hiding."

Grubb hid his surprise well enough, but his protégé did not. She swiped up the *ThelepathyG7* screen on her wrist.

"The ankh image will stop that nonsense if I send it to the troops, Master," she said as she worked. "Right, Kim?"

"Too late for that," Jeremy quipped. "I hope."

"Goodness, only ten soldiers are still alive?" Mariah gaped at her virtual screen.

"Good to hear," Jeremy said, smiling.

Grubb glared at his protégé and said nothing. He turned to Kimberley. "You're right about Aiden, but then you cannot convince him to give you the book, either. I have nothing to lose if he kills your man here, but I am not allowing that, am I?"

"So?" Jeremy demanded.

"What do you want?" Kimberley asked the professor.

"A truce. You go your way and I go mine."

"That will never happen," Jeremy said. "After all you did? After all you killed?"

Kimberley nodded in agreement. "You know that won't happen, right?" she asked Grubb.

"Well, then," Grubb said, "I guess that ends negotiations."

"And you just lost Aiden," Rachel quipped, holding up the book.

"You stupid girl!" Grubb exploded and reached out his right hand to grab the book, but the little girl dodged him.

"Where am I?" Aiden wondered.

Kimberley took out Rewder and Akron before both men could raise their guns, and Grubb, a.k.a. Benjamin Haddad, scampered up the stairs with Mariah.

"What just happened?" Jeremy demanded.

"Take Grubb out, Carl!" Kimberley barked into her *TelepathyG7* communicator.

"Still can't do that," the panting fellow said on the other end. "He has an ankh with him."

"Are you still running?" Kimberley wondered, scaling the lobby steps after Grubb.

A puzzled Aiden turned to Rachel. "What's going on?" he asked her.

"We still have work to do," Rachel said, grabbing his hand and going after Kimberley.

Jeremy hesitated before following the younger duo.

The Booklords were waiting for Kimberley at Chairman Smith's sealed office door. She blasted the computerized lock and the doors slid open.

Grubb fired several shots at her from the other end of a banquet hall, but she used the long table in the middle of the large room, as well as the ceramic dishes containing food on this table, to protect herself. Grubb's erratic shots broke some of the ceramic on the table, spilling their contents for all to see. Kimberley felt like vomiting after figuring out what she saw in these broken dishes. The others crouched beside her and Jeremy took aim with his weapon. "Hey, don't shoot!" she ordered him. "You might hit Mariah."

"Really?!" Jeremy snapped. "You'll protect her now?"

"I heard that, Kim," Mariah called out. "You still care for me, don't you, Kim?"

"Unfortunately, I don't," Grubb said, dramatically pointing the lazer gun at his lover's head and blasting a hole through it.

Mariah fell as her blood and brain matter spewed out in the process, crashing to the ground with a thump.

"No!" Kimberley screamed and set off her blaster on the male Sikama, who escaped by entering a lazerproof cubicle close by. "Die, you murderer!"

Jeremy fired some shots, but knew he was too late. "We had him!" he cried, and cursed away inaudibly.

"You know it's over, Ben," Kimberley said. "You don't have any route out of this."

"But I do," Grubb said, putting his right hand into his overcoat's right pocket. He stopped and looked out at the long table in the middle of the room. A piece of paper lay on that table.

"You cannot come out and pick it, Ben," Kimberley said, looking at Mariah's blood encircling the dead woman's head at the foot of the cubicle Grubb ran into. Perhaps Shurabi would give this now lifeless Sikama another shot at life? That is, if all that was true. "I'll kill you before you even step out of that box!"

"She betrayed you for a long time, my dear," Grubb said. "Why do you now feel bad for her?"

"Because you made her who she eventually became," Rachel answered for Kimberley.

"And we all saw you kill her," Aiden added.

"You fool," Grubb told the boy. "I showed you your future and you botched everything."

"Maybe he was never a fan of human meat?" Jeremy suggested, staring at the meal laid out on the long table in large dishes. He grimaced at the sight of human body parts in the stew spilling from the broken ceramic very close to his position. "Is that…"

"As the only surviving leader of the Inner Circle guiding the Sicarii Kabbalah Masada, I demand that you hand over the white book to me!" Grubb bellowed, shaking all over.

"Now you've gone crazy," Kimberley muttered.

"Crazy, you say? Bah!" The agitated professor walked to and fro in the small lazerproof cubicle, clenching and unclenching his left fist. "Even if you refuse to give me the book right now, it will surely happen in the future after I get away from here."

"You can only get away with paper from the book, Uncle Ben," Rachel reminded him.

"But I will get the book. You forget you willingly gave it to me. I claim Bookbearership!"

"I didn't willingly give it to you," the little girl corrected. "I reluctantly gave it to you."

Voices came from outside. Many voices.

"Perhaps, we do not need to deal with you, ourselves," Kimberley said. "The spirit of your victims have come back to haunt you."

"What the hell?" Grubb blurted out, trying to look out of the windows of the long hall.

The voices grew louder as their owners entered the administrative compound.

"And finally, we didn't even need the Gray Ones to give you the final punch," Kimberley said, signaling the others to sneak out of the banquet hall with her. She met Carl Bain outside the Chairman's office.

"This doesn't change our deal, Kim," the American thug said.

"Don't worry," Kimberley allayed. "We still have a deal."

"What about the piece of paper from the book, Kim?" Jeremy asked.

"Grubb will be torn to pieces before he can get to that paper,"

Kimberley pointed out.

"Now, why would that happen?" Aiden wondered.

"Poor boy," Kimberley said. "What did he brainwash you with?"

"How did you get him back, Rachel?" Jeremy asked the little girl, even though everything still seemed fantastically unreal to him.

"I couldn't change him until I touched him," Rachel replied. "That makes me wonder if…"

"Uncle Ben made Aiden believe he was Avigdor," Kimberley suggested. "That's the reason Aiden could fully control the book like he did. I doubt if he could do that anymore in his new state."

"But I could use the book before," Aiden began. "Remember the big bang?"

Rachel shook her head from side to side. "You have never controlled the book like this, Aiden, and I don't think you would be able to do so again. If only we..."

"Who's Avigdor?" Aiden began.

"Someone we should look into later," Kimberley replied as she came down the stairs with the others. She glanced at Rachel and thought it strange that even towards the end of all that had happened, the little girl still had some explaining to do.

The noisy crowd outside streamed into the lobby and migrated up the stairs in the opposite direction.

"He's in there," Jeremy told these angry citizens as they trudged up to the opulent banquet hall and office. The sound of lazerfire jerked his head around, but then how many could a single weapon take out before an angry mob exerted the ultimate revenge?

"This is the end for him," Kimberley said. "And if Shurabi should take him to another life and time after this, he won't have the book to plot evil with."

"A revenge Mariah would approve," Rachel added. "It's all over now."

*   *   *

Or was it? The time-travelers walked back to Jeremy's residence in silence, each person with his or her own thoughts.

Carl Bain broke this silence. "Time for your part of the deal, Kim."

"We don't have a deal until you destroy that device," Jeremy said. "You must…"

"Forget it, Jeremy, we do have a deal," Rachel interrupted.

"But he…"

Kimberley stared at the black man. "We'll cross that river when we get to it," she told him.

"No side deals," Carl Bain warned.

"Of course, not," Kimberley said, feigning offence. She stopped and turned to Rachel. "It all depends on you now, Rachel. Remember your decision will be final."

Rachel looked around her; at the underground city this weird journey had finally brought her to, and sighed. "Father would want me to be happy."

"You know my masters could bring back your father right after you give them the book?" Carl Bain began.

"Not true," Kimberley said. "Stop lying to us, Mr. Bain. Ben Haddad killed her father, so the Gray Ones cannot bring him back."

"But he could be living as someone else in this present time," Jeremy said. "That is, if I actually understood what you guys have been saying."

"Yes, according to Shurabi," Kimberley said, holding her head with both hands.

"I wouldn't even want him back into this chaotic world without the books," Rachel said. "I think he will understand this decision."

"According to Shurabi, that decision was never yours to make, Rachel," Kimberley told the Bookbearer. "If your father is alive right now, you can only look for him or who he has become."

"I-I don't know what to say," Rachel stammered excitedly. "Now that I know who killed him, we can find him if we want to!"

"According to Shurabi," Jeremy reminded everyone.

"Yes, according to Shurabi," Kimberley repeated.

"Okay," Carl Bain began. "Fulfill your promise and my masters will give you a leaf from the book to find your father with." Everyone stared at him. "Of course, I am joking!" he chuckled. "That was never part of the deal."

"You know we can keep fighting the Booklords right now, right Rachel?" Aiden asked and Carl Bain's face lost all color.

"For what?" Rachel demanded. "A future that can only cause more fighting? More wars? More deaths?"

"So that we can use the book to find your father," Aiden said. "Remember we now know how to destroy…"

"Father would want peace right now," Rachel told him. "I've decided to look for him some other day."

Kimberley sighed, though she couldn't tell whether the sigh was of relief or disappointment.

"I support your decision," Jeremy told Rachel, looking at his two sisters coming up the road beside an X9 transporter. "We must learn to make peace not war, and that involves destroying certain tools made for war." He frowned at the American hustler.

"Not gonna happen," Carl Bain said. "I know I could be on my way back to Portwood after this…this escapade, so that tiny device I just retrieved is coming with me 'cause it's my retirement you see right there."

"Hope you can defend that in court?" Kimberley asked the American hustler.

"And who's gonna sue me?" he chuckled. "No one, I assure you, my dear. No one."

Jeremy hugged his sisters when they arrived and entered the X9 to inspect it. Kimberley smiled as she watched the siblings make harmless banter in the big transporter. She noticed Rachel watching her.

"I want to live with you, Kim."

"Done." Kimberley brightened. "Aiden will also be moving in with me as well."

Rachel smiled. "Okay by me," she said.

"Okay, Rachel." Carl Bain sighed. "My masters are waiting for you."

The little girl sensed the gray forms emerging all around, their unearthly shapes shifting uncontrollably without reason. She'd finally lost her sense of fear, making two very good friends in the course of this wild adventure. She wasn't going to let them down anymore.

She gave the white book to the Gray One its colleagues called Brezennigger, or the Angel of Death.

"We'll need a leaf from the book," Kimberley began.

"No need for that," Carl Bain said, looking at Rachel.

"But we'll need it to look for Rachel's father and go back home," Aiden said, while Jeremy nodded in agreement. "We can't…"

"The Bookbearer understands what I mean," Carl Bain interrupted, and Rachel nodded.

"I understand," she said.

*   *   *

Kimberley woke up in a replica of her old office and blinked at the familiar fluorescent tubing basking the room from above with bright incandescent light. Marveling at the designer's attention to detail, she saw her favorite pen on her desk, the writing pad Officer Bates usually provided every morning from the supplies department, as well as an invite from Jim for dinner at Mercy's. The trash can beside the desk and the heavy rolls of elaborate city mapping by the window further convinced her that she sat in a similar office to her old one.

Or did she rearrange the room?

"We need to see her!" someone said in the main hall and Kimberley looked up to see the girl she'd tried to rescue that evening talking to Patrol Officer Lyndon Bates amidst...

Kimberley couldn't believe her eyes. Patrol Officer Bates in flesh and blood? She moved to her office door. Where did they find the girl? The familiar boy with her new friend was also trying to get a message across, but the girl was more persistent. "Please we need to see her! She's the only person who can help us!"

Kimberley couldn't believe her ears. Whatever happened to the little girl's talk of the book?

Lyndon was trying to herd the kids back to the reception hall as Kimberley stepped out of her office. "This is no place for kids," he said. "Get in there and I'll go get her for you."

"Wait!" the female sergeant called out to him and Rachel instantly recognized her when their eyes met.

"Where have you been?" Kimberley asked the little girl, moving towards the trio in the middle of the boisterous hall. "Who did you say was coming after you back in the car?"

"You won't believe me if I told you," the girl replied calmly.

"What are you two going on about?" a confused Lyndon wanted to know.

"Hi, Kim, is that the girl you were talking about on the radio?" Dispatch Officer Kate June asked her while crossing her office door.

"Eh, yes, Kate." Kimberley could only stare. Dispatch Officer June?

"What a lovely soul," the woman continued. "Thought you said she was hurt?"

"Well...I – eh..."

"Hi, dear," a lovingly familiar voice said beside her.

"Jim? But you..."

"Yeah, I wanted to prepare a special dinner for us," her boyfriend said. "But I later figured Mercy's will be an easier option, owing to our load of work here."

Kimberley hugged him. "Oh, Jim, I really thought I'd never see you again."

"I...missed you, too, dear," Jim replied, holding his girlfriend while wondering what they were really talking about.

"Is he the boyfriend you couldn't stop talking about, Kim?" a mischievous Rachel began.

"Excuse me, Jim." Kimberley grabbed the little girl and started towards her office, Aiden and Officer Bates closely behind. "Where did you find her, Aiden?" she asked the boy.

"I didn't find her," Aiden replied with a frown. "She found me."

"Okay, how did she do that? Sure you didn't find her?"

"Of course, not," Aiden said. "Why are you all focusing on her alone?"

"Not true, Aiden," Kimberley said. "I haven't forgotten you ran away from your foster home some days back, if that's what you mean. We'll discuss that later." She found it odd that the boy smiled at her.

"Nice desk," Rachel said on seeing Kimberley's table from her office door. She rushed over to the desk and sat down on one of two chairs facing Kimberley's chair opposite the desk.

"What's going on, Kim?" Lyndon asked his superior as he closed the door behind him. Kimberley looked at him and shrugged, shaking her head. Now she turned back to the strange girl.

"Okay, what am I not getting?" she wanted to know.

"A bad man is after us, Kim," Aiden said in the quiet room. "And he has a gun."

"And why is he after you?" Kimberley found this news to be of the highest importance. "What have you done this time?"

"He...He wants this...." Aiden revealed what he had in his hand. A package wrapped in polythene.

"And why are you bringing this up now?" Kimberley asked him absent-mindedly.

"Well, I thought this was the right moment to bring it up if I was ever going to get your attention, since none of you guys have taken any interest in me ever since I came in here with my little friend here. Maybe parking the squad car a few blocks away has been a mistake, since its shattered rear windshield would have done a better job of getting your attention."

Kimberley stared at the boy. "What?"

Rachel moved to get up and Kimberley stopped her by holding an arm.

"Lyndon?"

The patrol officer took the package from Aiden and untied it. He studied the white powder in it and looked at his senior colleague. "Coke?"

"We'll discuss that later," Kimberley surprised herself with. "Give me the package and take some armed officers with you to scout the vicinity for an armed man looking for the kids. Arrest him whenever you find him."

Officer Bates handed over the parcel and left.

"You know what happened," Aiden said with a smile. "Finally."

"Took me some time," Kimberley said, bringing out Carl Bain's tiny silver box from the white stuff. "We'll find a way to destroy this," she added.

"And what is that?" Rachel wondered.

Kimberley smiled. "You've forgotten already?"

"That," Aiden said, "is a tiny silver box."

Kimberley stared at him.

"What?" He shifted in his chair.

"This, right here," Kimberley said, "is the prototype of a nuclear device destined to be used in a future world war called the Red War."

Aiden frowned. "I knew that."

Kimberley laughed, tucking the tiny silver package into her right pants' pocket. "Of course, you did."

"He said he wants to share something with us, Kim," Rachel began.

Aiden hesitated. "Well, I...eh...it's about the book."

"And what about it?" Kimberley asked.

"I saw something on the book's pages when I was in that trance back...back at Resilience?"

Rachel waited for him to continue. "And?"

"And now I know what I saw," Aiden continued. "The complete Hebrew sentence written in the white book, in English."

"Can you remember the words?" Kimberley marveled at her calm demeanor.

"Sacred ways back and forth, greed and misery the third implies," Aiden said.

"Greed and misery the third implies?" Kimberley frowned. "Wow."

"Crazy, right?" Rachel said. "I think this means that the third book will bring misery to greedy people of the world."

"Let's hope you're right," Kimberley said. "No need to look for that one, I guess."

Rachel said nothing.

"Okay," Aiden began. "Now we have the complete Hebrew sentence, what next?"

"Do you know what that means?" Rachel asked him.

"What does it mean?" Kimberley wondered.

"The other book is again in the hands of a human being, just as David Hoyte predicted. We can..."

"Okay, wait now," Aiden interrupted the little girl. "Do we have to start all this again?"

"No," Rachel said. "But we could if we want to."

Kimberley laughed. "How?" she chuckled. "We don't have the white book, do we? Remember we couldn't even get the Booklords to give us a leaf from the book. Thank goodness for that."

Rachel looked away. "But.... But, we...do have...something..." She brought out a piece of familiarly strange paper. "I... I kinda took it from the dining table when...when no one was looking."

Kimberley could only gape at the girl. "No wonder you understood what Carl Bain meant."

Rachel gulped. "And remember I still have to find my father."

Aiden's mouth remained open.

THE END

THE BLACK BOOK

Part 1 of the BOOKLORD ADVENTURE SERIES
Excerpt

MAY 26, 1940...

Suddenly, the place became colder and darker.

"Matthew, Matthew," nine-year-old Stephanie whispered, shaking her twelve-year-old adopted brother. "Matthew, wake up. Wake up, Matthew."

He did, quickly sitting up to look around in confusion. He could only make out his younger sister's shadowy silhouette from the blackish-gray all around him. "Why is it so dark?" he asked her, blinking. "What happened to the light?"

"I don't know," Stephanie said. She was sitting beside her brother, hugging herself. "Matthew, something's wrong. I can feel it."

Matthew frowned as he used his eyes a second time. Only a blanketing gray hue stared back at him from all sides. Where were the familiar outlines of his desk, chair, and shelves? "Is this my room, Steph?" he asked.

"I don't know," Stephanie repeated, turning to her left, then to her right. "It's so cold out here."

"Out here?" Matthew shook his head. "We're not in my room? What happened, Steph? Who brought us out?"

"Nobody," Stephanie said. "Nothing happened before it–it happened." She could feel her brother's bewildered eyes on her. "I–I don't know what happened, Matt, but–but something's wrong. I know it."

Matthew sensed the fear in her voice. Whatever happened must have surprised her. "I must have fallen asleep," he said. He felt downwards with his hands for his bed sheet and mattress, which was hard. Very hard. No, he was actually on the floor. No doubt about that. Why was he on the floor? What happened to his bed?

"Matthew, I'm scared," Stephanie said, and her adopted brother stared at her dark figure. She wore a funny-looking jacket atop pants and had a scarf around her neck.

Wait.

"What happened to your sweater, Steph?" Matthew asked. He could remember what his sister had on before he slept off...now she wore something else. When did she replace her lovely sweater with that odd jacket? "You've changed your clothes, Steph," he said.

"So have you," Stephanie retorted. "When did you change them? And what's that on your head?"

"I don't know," Matthew confessed, reaching up to touch his head. He wore a cap. He also felt a scarf around his neck as he brought down his hand. "You're right," he said, rubbing both hands. "What happened to our clothes, Steph? When did we change them? And it's really cold out here..." Something was lying beside his left leg. It was the book. He picked it up and turned to his sister, meaning to ask her about it, but stopped short. He could now see her face, as well as their environment. "This is not my room," he said.

The floor formed a continuous wall on both sides of their present position, extending upwards to meet high above their heads. It then zoomed off towards an opening far away. "It's like we're in a tunnel," Matthew said. "Look...over there." He was pointing at the distant round aperture through which weak light spilled into the place. His younger sister followed his arm and stared at this opening, beyond which could lie the answer to their dilemma. "How did we get here?" Matthew asked.

"I just wanna go home," Stephanie whined.

Matthew stood up. Maintaining his balance on that sloping floor was easier than it looked. He raised his right hand but failed to touch the tunnel's ceiling. Now he turned to the clear-cut opening in the distance, which probably encircled dawn breaking outside the structure. He wanted to get to that edge but kept wondering whether that was the best thing to do.

"Matthew, what happened to us? How did we get here?"

Stephanie's voice sounded very cautious and distant in Matthew's head, which was filled with all kinds of confusing thoughts. He turned to her with a baffled look. He didn't have a ready reply. "We must get to that light, Steph," he finally managed. "It's the right thing to do."

He helped her up and took the lead as they started moving towards the opening. Curiosity urged them on, but on hearing men's voices coming from beyond the tunnel's mouth, they stopped to turn startled faces at each other.

"What if they're bad people?" Stephanie asked.

"I don't think so," Matthew said. "I know they'll help us." Still, he hesitated. Amidst the voices, he could also hear metal on metal as well as strange-sounding engines. Someone was shouting at the men. "They must be speaking a foreign language," he said. "Can't get a word."

"Then let's go back," Stephanie suggested.

"No," Matthew said. "We mustn't be scared, Steph."

"I'm not scared," Stephanie blurted out. "I'm just being...careful."

"Careful about what? Those men could be working near the mall, you know."

"Then how did we get to the mall, Matt? And–And these men are speaking funny...where're they from, Matt?"

Matthew frowned. What if they'd really walked out of the house in their sleep? He'd heard Mom and Dad discussing news about a boy who did just that in the neighborhood some days back. 'Sleepwalking,' they called it. Of course, that would answer all their questions if it was true, but how did they both sleepwalk at the same time? That could only deepen the mystery, and the only way to unravel it was to go outside through the tunnel's gaping mouth, where the noisy men spoke in a foreign language surrounded by their noisy engines. Matthew turned to his sister and took her hand.

"What?" she began.

"Trust me, Steph...," he said. "We need to go outside right now if we want to know what's really happening...you trust me, right?" She nodded. "Good, let's go."

The voices and chugging vehicular noise grew louder as the children approached the tunnel's entrance. More light spilled into the place, but they were yet to make out anything through the round aperture ahead of them.

Stephanie didn't hesitate to voice her concern. "Matthew, let's go back," she said. Her brother was acting deaf. "Let's go back, please?"

"Almost there, Steph," he murmured. "We can't go back now."

"Why not?"

Matthew took his time. "Because we–we need to know where we are. We can't do that if we turn back now."

His sister fell silent. They were a few feet from the tunnel's concrete edge. A dog barked in the distance, startling them both. Stephanie stopped to listen to the animal and Matthew had to slow down for her to catch up. He felt a bit relieved after this occurrence, though. It showed that people were living nearby. "Those men outside can only be construction workers, Steph," he told his sister as they walked towards the tunnel's entrance. "They're definitely driving tractors and bulldozers. The engines sound very familiar now."

But Stephanie still thought her brother had it all wrong. Something weird had happened to them, and they were yet to find out what it was.

They got to the tunnel's mouth and realized that they were in a cave. The illumination was artificial. Bright light bulbs shone through intense smoke, which was the reason for the drastic reduction in visibility. These fumes wafted into the tunnel as the children stood on its edge staring at their surroundings. They could hear the familiar sound of a train's engine chugging away to their left, but could see neither the train nor its *tracks owing to the smoke. More so, the voices and vehicular engine noise were now at their loudest. The workers were shouting at one another.*

"What if they're bad people?" Stephanie asked again.

"No, they won't be." Matthew sounded exasperated.

"And we can't see," Stephanie continued, but her brother ignored her. The structure's edge was wider than it looked from afar. He bent down and jumped over it out of the tunnel. His feet hit the ground almost immediately. He started coughing. Stephanie climbed out of the tunnel without jumping. It wasn't that high above ground. She began to cough as well. "What now?" she asked. "We still can't see. The smoke..."

"We must move away from it," Matthew said. He pulled his sister forward in a bid to do this, and they almost ran into a gray wall, which had suddenly loomed out from the smoke. Withdrawing behind a shield-like appendage attached to this imposing obstruction, they peeped out at the people working in the place, as well as the new structure blocking their way.

"What is it?" Stephanie wondered aloud. Her brother shook his head as his eyes swept across this behemoth metallic contraption. Then he noticed something. The many wheels attached to the wall? Weren't those things below the wheels train tracks?

"It's part of the train," Matthew exclaimed. "Look." His sister followed his pointing finger upwards and to the left of their position.

The high wall was one of a group of connected freight cars that swept out before them from the locomotive engine, which idled away fifteen or twenty freight cars behind their position but had been hidden by the smoke coming from its exhaust port. The children had stopped coughing once they stepped away from the smoke's direct path, but their eyes were beginning to water owing to the intensity of the exhaust fumes surrounding them.

"The smoke is too much," Stephanie complained.

"We're in a cave, Steph," Matthew said as if his sister was yet to appreciate this fact. He was studying their surroundings. "I can't see any windows, so no way out for the smoke. We must find a way outside as soon as possible."

"What of the tunnel?" Stephanie asked. "Is that not a way out for the smoke?"

Matthew blushed. Of course, the tunnel could be a large chimney for the trains stopping in this underground station. They had stopped coughing simply because the smoke was now going into the tunnel and would soon clear. The train was probably warming up to leave the station. How could he have missed that? "You're right, Steph," he agreed, nodding. "But we still need to get outside right now. We can't know where we are if we remain here."

"Do we have a cave at home?" Stephanie asked.

"Yes, but I don't know if it's this big." Matthew was studying the men, most of whom were driving tractors and bulldozers onto platforms in-between the train's freight cars. "They don't look like construction workers," he said. "They don't even look like townsfolk. They look more like officers...soldiers."

"Are they good people?"

"I don't know, but I think they are."

"Told you we shouldn't have come out," Stephanie began. "Now we can't go back without being seen."

"Stop whining like a baby," Matthew chided her, although the warning continued ringing in his head. She could be right. None of the men looked friendly in their gray jackets and face caps, and why were some of them carrying guns? What were they protecting the other workers from? Certainly not people from Sleepy Lake, who could never harm anyone. Were they guarding the train's cargo of vehicles, which all looked shiny and new? "Those tractors and bulldozers," he began.

"What about them?"

"They're painted dead green instead of yellow. That's very odd. Tractors and bulldozers are usually yellow, and what's with the cross on their sides?"

"Who's there?" a man demanded behind the children, and they turned to face him with beating hearts. Dressed in a gray overcoat unlike the other workers, this unsmiling fellow had a fierce-looking pistol, which he pointed at the two before him, even though he had seen that they were kids. Slowly, the children stepped backward, the tunnel's mouth their primary destination. "Halt," the man shouted, and they stopped in their tracks. At least, he spoke English.

"Excuse me, sir," Matthew began, "but we need to get back to our house? It seems we're lost."

"French Jews," the man exploded, visibly agitated. "How did you get here?" He drew nearer and the children moved further backward.

Matthew stared at the man's uniform and suddenly became alarmed as realization dawned on him. Why was a very small version of the cross painted on the tractors and bulldozers pinned to this fellow's great overcoat? Slowly, he pulled Stephanie further backward.

"Answer me," the man roared and quickly came at them.

"He's bad, Steph," Matthew shouted. "Back to the tunnel." He turned and scampered into the tunnel behind his sister.

The officer stopped and turned to some guards behind him. "They came through the tunnel," he yelled. "Follow me. We must catch them before they escape to French pigs and tell our secret. Quickly!" He clambered into the tunnel. Both kids were making progress down its dark belly. "Stop right there or I shoot," he called out. "Halt!" He went after them.

"Matthew, he has a torch!" Stephanie shouted with fright.

"Stop talking! Run."

The path was difficult at the pace they were going and smoke from the train now filled the structure, making them cough the more as they blinked back overwhelming tears. In addition, a new source of light basked their backs and this was not good.

"What if he shoots us?" Stephanie asked, ignoring her brother's order.

Matthew looked back at the figure bearing down on them and realized that the tunnel and smoke were also hampering the man. Due to this, they'd given the fellow a wide gap and that was good. "He can't try it here," the boy breathed. "It could hit him instead."

But their situation was about to get worse. The tunnel suddenly opened into a bigger one, and they tumbled out.

Matthew grabbed Stephanie. He wasted no time.

"Where are we going?" she asked him. They'd been running for a while, and she was beginning to tire.

"We mustn't stop now, Steph," Matthew urged her. He knew they couldn't stop then. They didn't have that luxury. "Gosh! It's a dead-end," he suddenly cried, and they almost crashed into the high wall cutting them off around the corner. Sunlight spilled in from a wide window high above them, and they realized it was still noon. "We can't get up there," Matthew said. For the first time in his life, he was scared stiff. Stephanie looked like she'd seen a ghost.

Their fear burst out from behind them, and they backed the wall. Matthew pushed Stephanie behind him and faced the new threat. "What do you want from us?" His voice lacked confidence.

"Jewish pigs," the man spat out. He wore weird-looking pants, which he tucked into black leather knee-length boots. "You belong to a concentration camp."

"We're not Jewish pigs," Stephanie said.

"Leave that for me to decide," the man growled, and the little girl zipped her mouth. The soldier glared at Matthew and put away his service pistol to take a step forward.

"My...sister's right, sir," the boy said boldly. "We're not French, and we're not Jewish. We're Americans, and we've lost our way."

"Americans?" This appeared to be significant because the man *stopped in his tracks. "Lost, you say?"*

Matthew realized that the fellow had never said a word of German.

"But it's true," the officer continued, covering the distance between them. "You don't speak like the French. You don't look like them. You're only dressed like them...and I can see that now."

Matthew sighed in relief.

"So where is it?"

"Where is what?"

"The book, you fool," the soldier snapped, fuming. "I know you must be with it. I've waited for a year now and will strangle you if you lie to me."

The boy realized he was still holding the book before he was brutishly grabbed by the neck, and it was desperately snatched from him.

Matthew's attacker could not contain his excitement and shook all over as he pushed the boy to the ground, and threatened a scared Stephanie further back. "Must escape! Must escape!" the man muttered repeatedly as he quickly flipped through the book's pages, and tried to use the light pouring in from above.

Suddenly, a deafening noise erupted in the enclosure as a staccato burst of machine gun fire poured in as well. The German officer was riddled with bullets before he could discern what was happening. His men faced the same fate when they appeared behind him. The whole place was like a blur. Stephanie was screaming.

"Quick," a new character snapped near the scared children. "We must get out of here! Rapide!" He pumped more bullets into the enemy.

Matthew grabbed the book and scampered through a secret door of rock behind Stephanie.

He could hear the bullets raining down behind him.

*   *   *

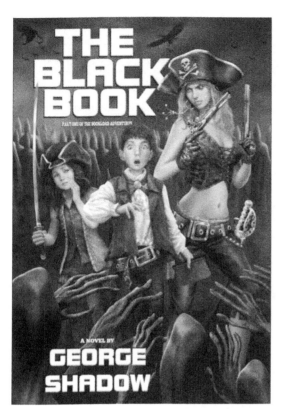

THE BLACK BOOK

whisks its characters away from their serene lives into an ancient dispute.

Hurry! Call 08080599540 or contact mailgeorgeshadow@yahoo.com **for orders.**

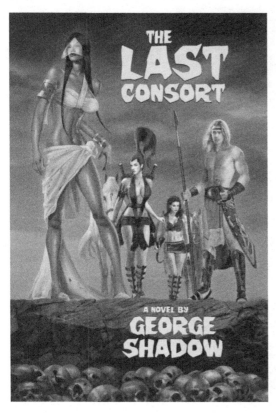

THE LAST CONSORT

In the beginning was the Mist, and the Mist was worthless...
Until a Being far greater than Man came and wielded it in Her arms...
Then the Mist became strong...
And dangerous...
And before Mortal Man's very eyes came to pass, the extinction of two kingdoms and a half...
For the Mist was in search of its consort...
And she was in the prime of flight...
Only her discovery can stop it...
Only Mortal Man can find her...

Hurry! Call 08080599540 or contact mailgeorgeshadow@yahoo.com **for orders.**

Ukachukwu Chidube George (aka George Shadow) has been writing for almost three years now. Creativity is his first love, and he has as his motivation for the BOOKLORD ADVENTURES, such titles as the HARRY POTTER Series by J. K. Rowling and THE LORD OF THE RINGS by J. R. R. Tolkien. Such wonderful works of literature are rarely repeated these days, and this was partly the reason for his embarking on the BOOKLORD ADVENTURES SERIES. He has completed a few other romance and fantasy novels and his stories usually take up magic and mystery as themes, with a large dose of history (both real and fantasized) thrown in. He also has some finished short war stories he intends publishing as a book of short battle stories in the future.... Titled THE WAR CHEST, this will be a collection of poignant battle tales from around the world.

THE BLACK BOOK is the first part of a fascinating series of six books he has tagged the Booklord Adventures and is a beautifully written novel filled with very funny scenes. It is suitable for children, teens, and even their parents! Thoroughly researched and passionately expressed, this book is a must-have for book collectors and fantasy lovers.

To order additional copies of this book, contact:

mailgeorgeshadow@yahoo.com

or call 08080599540 if you are in Nigeria.

www.georgeshadow.com